2BIRDS

A NOVEL

TOM FRANCISKOVICH

To reach the author, visit TomFranciskovich.com or email hello@TomFranciskovich.com

United City Press paperback edition March, 2020

United City Press and its logo are trademarks of United City Press, LLC

For information about special discounts for bulk purchases, please contact United City Press Special Sales by email at info@unitedcitypress.com

Library of Congress Cataloging-in-Publication Data:

Franciskovich, Tom, author.

2BIRDS / Tom Franciskovich.

New York, NY: United City Press, 2020.

LCCN 2020933619

ISBN 978-1-950548-07-1 (hardcover)

ISBN 978-1-950548-05-7 (paperback)

ISBN 978-1-950548-04-0 (ebook)

ISBN 978-1-950548-06-4 (audio)

LCSH Global warming—Fiction | Overpopulation—Fiction | Survival—Fiction. | Dystopias | BISAC FICTION / DystopianP

LCC PS3606.R373 T86 2020 | DDC 813.6--dc23

Manufactured in the United States of America

Cover artwork by Mattias Fridh

10 9 8 7 6 5 4 3 2 1

*For Sheryl, my best friend and co-conspirator
who told me to drop everything and write this book.*

1

As far as problems go, this one was obvious—there were simply too many people. Everyone it seemed, and particularly the Prags, described the situation with a metaphor: The planet was a worn-out old hound dog overrun with fleas, every day becoming more panicked and desperate to shake off those ravenous little bloodsucking parasites. It took a while, but it finally happened.

The rise of the Pragmatist Party surprised everyone, especially its leader. Formed twenty years earlier by a few earnest community college political science instructors intent on making lamb chop side-burns fashionable, the party was founded on a single premise: The never-ending battle over ideology was speeding the human race toward extinction. Liberals and conservatives could not agree on anything—not a single thing—even if doing that thing meant saving mankind. And it was only getting worse. The politicians were content to burn up in a ball of flames on an overheated planet, so long as the other side got the blame. The Pragmatists, or the Prags, as they called themselves, reasoned that by eliminating ideology, there remained a small but real shot at finding a solution. Survival.

For years, the Prags were nothing more than a curiosity. A freak show populated by a few dozen policy wonks—poli sci nerds—most of whom showed up for its one and only annual convention because the flyer advertised free coffee cake. Those who stuck around for the afternoon session were treated to a discussion which lured a handful of its attendees to sleep. From the outside looking in, it would have been impossible to know that this was not the fall semester of Statistics 101, but the birthplace of a modern political juggernaut.

A single item was ratified at their one and only convention: The party slogan, "Follow the truth wherever it leads." It should be noted that a very brief and polite debate broke out concerning the use of an exclamation mark at the end of the phrase. Exclaiming instead of stating, some argued, conveyed emotion and, therefore, the presence of ideology, which ran counter to their entire reason for existence. Those in favor of the exclamation mark lost in a landslide vote, twenty-eight to three. Ending up on the wrong end of lopsided elections would become familiar territory.

"Follow the truth wherever it leads," with or without an exclamation mark, as it turns out, makes for a slogan that is as inspiring as an empty box of cereal. And the bumper sticker whipped up by a first-year graphic design student gave it an amateurish, unserious feel. Set in white block letters which jumped out against the solid purple background—a symbolic blending of red and blue states—the words "Vote Prag" were centered above the slogan. The party never cracked one percent in any contest for any office ranging from city council to county commissioner. Outside of the founding members, no one had ever heard of the Prags. Politics without ideology failed to catch on with the voters—except for one. And one was all it needed.

———

Growing up in the years leading to Armageddon had its benefits. Since the world was ending soon, children were granted a wide berth. Incidents of mischief rose in lockstep with the temperature. The adults figured that it was only fair that the kids had a chance at some fun before their inevitable and much too early demise arrived.

A pack of neighborhood boys dubbed themselves the "Hilliard House Hooligans." All five of them appeared to move in concert up and down the hallways of the sprawling, five-story, concrete-gray apartment complex. The government used to call it "low-income housing" before they renamed it "workforce housing," which served as further insult because the robots had already taken most of the blue-collar jobs. Everyone living there instead referred to their collection of buildings as "the projects."

When boredom crept in, as it always did after a few rounds of the same tired old video games, the Hooligans would return to their favorite pastime: Torture. It always seemed to be getting close to dusk at the projects when the Hooligans would corral their favorite target. Jason Harper was a stick-figure kid and devoid of pigmentation, sheet white, which was convenient, since he, like the rest of mankind would soon become a ghost. Only in his case, he had a certain translucent quality. His skin lacked a basic opacity. When he took off his shirt to counteract the lack of air conditioning, his father would tell him he looked like a spring roll, just like the ones pictured on the flip side of the laminated menu at the Chinese restaurant he was caught robbing last year. From a distance, hair-thick blood vessels were visible on the ghost and his organs, too, at a closer vantage point.

But, what the Hilliard House Hooligans loved most about Jason Harper—the kid everyone called "Jace"—was his reaction to just about everything. If you did so much as graze a twig against the lower back of the scrawny little twerp, his response would have been no different had a commando knife been plunged into his spine. Yelping, spitting, gasping for air before the tears fell. It was always the same with Jace, and it never got old.

The reaction is what they were seeking, and the reaction is what they got. With most of the other kids, it required some legitimate damage. Not with Jace. If someone presented a pocket knife, he would first hyperventilate. If they pricked him with it, he would flail on the ground as if a fresh-hauled tuna flopping around inside the boat. Once, the oldest Hooligan held up his own hand in front of Jace and pricked himself, which produced a single drop of blood on his upright and outstretched middle finger. Same response. The mere sight of flowing crimson drove the little ghost to the brink of madness. He rolled around in the weed-filled flower bed, screaming and choking and gasping.

The Hooligans operated as a democracy. Majority rule. Two of them thought it went too far, but the three who voted "Yes" got their way. It was, therefore, decreed that young Jace would be tied up to the bottom of the bridge at the quiet end of the creek. The week before, one of the perpetrators went to a birthday party where the kids took turns smashing a *piñata*. It gave him the idea.

The veggie spring roll would not hold still. He kicked and screamed and cried and flopped. They ordered him to calm down, but nothing worked. Any touch was a blow torch sizzling the skin. One Hooligan lost his patience. His second punch landed with more much more force than the first. Both legs buckling in response, and Jace was out cold. Making a human *piñata* would be much easier now, they laughed, while binding the wrists and dangling the half-corpse from a stolen nylon rope.

Fanning out now, the crew scoured the immediate area for sticks. It did not take long. With each of them returning, and now forming a circle around the *piñata*, Jace regained consciousness.

Thwack! Whack! Swap!

The blows rained down in a furious barrage, one after another. Unending.

Jace convulsed. He vomited. Mucus spewed from his nose. His feet bicycled kicked eighteen inches above the dried and cracked creek bed. It was too much, far too much. Everything went dark before his eyes rolled back and his head dropped forward.

The beating continued.

It was one of the two Hooligans who had voted "No" to the beating, who called the ceasefire. "He's had enough!" was all it took to stop the others, each of them now winded and exhausted and secretly grateful for the rest. After reaching a consensus that the kid was, in fact, still alive they voted to cut him down. It was dark now, and he could spend the night in the creek. His parents would be stoned out of their minds by now and would not even realize their spring roll had been missing.

Through his half-opened left eye, Jace recognized the Hooligan. Now standing over the heap of skin and bones, he heard him say, "The little punk is fine—let's get out of here!" A chorus of laughter and exuberance and victory answered the declaration.

Jace scrambled to take inventory as he heard the footsteps fade away. When he was sure they were out of earshot, he summoned his remaining energy to call out in defiance, "I'm going to kill you! All of you! And you're going to thank me for it!"

The bats darted back-and-forth overhead in the enveloping dusk. There were no stars in the skies because there were never any stars. It had been many years since they spotted one through the pollution. Jace wondered if this was how it felt to die as he again lost consciousness.

———

As expected, both of his parents were high. They did not notice it when he walked in. They never did. The Hilliard House apartment complex was always noisy, with doors slamming and people yelling. His squeaky, muddy tennis shoes made no difference. Both of them, mother and father, were frozen in a familiar posture. Sitting straight on the couch, their eyes were closed, heads cocked back, mouths wide open, and arms flailed out as if preparing to flap their wings and fly away. Except they were already away. Already somewhere else. They were stoned. Jace understood this all too well.

He also understood where to find the gun.

Rifling through the milk crate, which doubled as an underwear drawer, it was there, just as it always was, in the cigar box. Grabbing the full clip and ten bullets, Jace then stuffed the pistol into his backpack between the laptop and the tablet. One his way out of the bedroom, he glimpsed himself in the mirror. It was rage that had boiled up from the lining of his guts and migrated to his face. He switched off the light.

As Jace opened the front door again and stepped out into yet another scorching and smoky and ashen day, he wheeled around and spat a sarcasm-dripped, "Bye, Mom; Bye, Dad—I love you." Neither one of them stirred.

There was no way he would make it into school with a handgun, loaded or not. And getting caught would guarantee another trip to juvenile hall. His off-campus stash spot would have to do. Adjacent to the playground, on the other side of the fence between two juniper bushes, when he was sure no one was looking, he retrieved the pistol and in one fluid motion placed it on the backside of the trunk between two low-hanging branches. He covered with twigs.

School that day dragged on even longer than normal. Everyone wanted to know what had happened. They asked why his face was so smashed in, one eye bloodshot and half-closed. Something about a hover board accident. That was all he would share.

It was lunch when he spotted them, The Hilliard House Hooligans. They were holding court in their usual spot, laughing and carrying on with one another. He winced with pain when his jaw tightened, but Jace knew what he had to do. There was no other choice.

As always, there was a gangly pack of kids migrating from the elementary school to the Hilliard House. In the middle of the amoeba, a loose orbit formed around the Hooligans. Before catching up to the group, Jace stopped by the juniper bushes to retrieve his stash. Scurrying undetected toward the mass of kids, his left hand wrapped around the warm pistol handle. It was concealed by his backpack, cradled as if it were an infant swaddled to his chest. With a massive jolt of anxious energy, he bounded three steps in front of the Hooligans, planted both feet and dropped the backpack to the ground.

At first lunging forward, the Hooligan in front froze as he realized the veggie spring roll had a gun trained on his forehead. It was not the gun that frightened him so much, but the madman brandishing it. The eyes, the bruised and bloodstained eyes. They revealed only emptiness. Whatever the opposite of a thing is—empty, void, space—that's what he saw. The Hooligan had heard his teacher say once during story time that the eyes are "windows to the soul." If that were true, Jace had no soul. Terror permeated.

The crowd parted and gasped at once.

Time stopped.

Jace adjusted his grip. The Hooligan whimpered. Then he stammered and begged and cried.

The weight of the gun was too much, so Jace propped it up with both hands and rested his elbows against a still-tender rib cage.

There were no words exchanged. Frantic, the Hooligan attempted to read Jace's intentions. He couldn't. The eyes continued to register nothingness.

An area around the crotch in the Hooligan's shorts darkened in moisture, as a stream of yellow cascaded down his bare leg. The entire collection of students exploded in laughter.

Jace finally addressed him. "Are you ready to die?"

"No, please, Jace, please, don't do it," whimpered the Hooligan. "We didn't mean to hurt you. We're sorry." His head bowed, his eyes shut, his arms outstretched in surrender.

Jace savored the moment before responding. "You have two options: I can put a bullet through your greasy face right now. Or, you can take off your pee-pee pants, put them on your head, crawl over here, bow down and kiss my feet and say, 'Jace is King.' It's your choice."

The Hooligan dropped his head further in humiliation, his shoulders heaved up and down with each tear. There was no choice.

Nervous chatter overcame the witnesses to history—each would retell this story many years later both on and off the record—as the Hooligan shimmied off his shorts revealing powder blue boxer shorts soaked all the way through. Then, sliding the shorts over his head, he kneeled down to his hands and knees. Inching his way toward the gun-wielding *piñata*, his tears marked his path forward toward the shoes. Craning his neck, he pressed his lips against the mud-caked shoe before gazing up toward the gun baring down on him.

"No, no, no," announced Jace with exaggerated flair. "Both feet!"

Again, blubbering tears which arose from a time-stopping combination of terror and humiliation streamed as the Hooligan then leaned over and also kissed the left foot.

"Now, say it! Say it, you worthless piece of crap!" shouted the gun-wielding six-grader with the vacant eyes. "Say it!"

"Jace is King!" the stripped-down Hooligan announced before collapsing, his entire body heaving and sobbing. The humiliation and defeat were both total and absolute.

The crowd roared by reflex, celebrating the peaceful transfer of power.

Jace lifted his right leg and placed his foot in triumph on the back of the vanquished Hooligan. Thrusting his unarmed fist skyward, he dipped into the dramatic bow of an experienced showman.

Everyone then collapsed around him. He grimaced with each embrace. A few of the jubilant classmates then hoisted him to their shoulders. A chant sprang to life: "King Jace! King Jace! King Jace!"

2

It always puzzled Jace, just how focused reporters would be on this period of his life. Compared to everything else, it was uneventful. The beginning of the three-year span he would later call his "personal renaissance" was marked not by something that happened, but by something that did not.

The night his father stopped showing up was an oddity more than anything else, and not much different from an ally cat failing to appear at the front doorstep begging for table scraps after dinner. It was not unusual for him to disappear for a few days at a time, but when those few days turned into a few weeks, Jace felt his heart swell with hope. His father only ever cared about what he could take from someone else. Except for a smattering of odd jobs here and there, he never earned anything on his own. But he was one of those guys, who Jace would later call a "tough talker." All bluster. He had a lot to say and favored the tough, up-from-the-bootstraps ethos popular with conservatives. His mantra to his son was, "Man-up!" It was always, "Man-up!" Jace cringed when he heard those words, mostly because manliness was near the bottom of the list he would have used to describe himself.

At least the translucence had finally gone away. Jace was no longer a ghost. He filled out a bit, but never crossed one hundred and twenty-seven pounds. He liked it that way, though. Maintaining a certain weight felt comfortable. It was one of the few areas of his life where he had some control. The other was his appearance. Despite the family's financial situation, Jace was always well-assembled. One of his happiest days came two months after his father's disappearance. His mother taught him how to use an iron to press his t-shirts. It would gnaw on him throughout the day when he left the apartment with a stray wrinkle here or there. Now he was in control. And control was what he wanted most.

With a shock of thick, wavy straw-blonde hair, dark chocolate brown eyes, and a semi-squarish face, Jace sat on the border of handsomeness. Not quite there, but you could see how he would make it someday, especially when you add in all the money. Cold, hard cash always seems to have a way of enhancing the attractiveness of the owner. For now, it is enough to know that he was very much a normal teenager. Middle of the pack in every way. Still slight, his skin tone went from snow white to eggshell white, at least that would be the paint swatch to match him best. And, standing in at five-foot four-inches, he would grow another two in college once he finally started receiving consistent and balanced meals. There was nothing particularly distinguishable about Jason Harper in those days, and his teachers, although they would later pretend to have known him well, did not notice him at all.

The one thing that everyone seemed to recall was that the kid loved to draw. He was always sketching something, often architecture, some-times cars, or a new hover board design. It was rarely people or animals, but often some new thing, usually an invention or the mani-festation of one of his many ideas. It was a teacher in first or second grade—he would later say that he was grateful that he couldn't remember much from those years—who spotted a budding artist. She emailed his mother and included a link to an after-school art class at the YMCA. Fortunately, the note was received on a good day, and his mother was lucid enough to drop him off at the beginning of the program. As always, when Jace arrived, he was asked for his registration fee. By now, he had learned from his ally cat father how to wear the same pathetic expression to get in just about anywhere. His face registered something between defeat and exhaustion, which came more naturally to his father than it did Jace. But the result was the same. He was admitted as yet another charity case, no payment due.

The introduction to oil paint was luscious and sensual. It felt as if he had slipped into a dream. He imagined it was similar to whatever his parents were experiencing when they were side by side, mouths agape on the couch. Aroma and texture combined to transcend him from the dimension he had been occupying all this time. It differed from the Number Two Dixon Ticonderoga he carried everywhere he went, scratching on whatever medium he could find—manila folders, computer paper, referrals to the principal's office. But, this, this was some other thing entirely. He immediately reminisced of the old movie his mother watched in an endless loop, high or straight. It was called "Somewhere Over the Rainbow," or something like that he thought, and the first time he touched a paint-filled brush to an empty canvas, everything miraculously transformed from the same few gradients of gray to full color.

Although he cannot remember a time he had done so before or after, Jace skipped home. He waited for nearly an hour precisely where his mother had told him she would pick him up after class, but the old rust bucket bearing a full coat of oxidized maroon never materialized in the circle drive. It was okay; he was always quick with an excuse for his mom. Surely she had broken down again, or maybe she stopped to help some old lady who had fallen on the sidewalk. With darkness enveloping the always gray sky, he tucked the canvas under his arm and began his two-mile skip homeward.

The Harper's front door, although now a national landmark, was no different than all the other hundreds of front doors, except that it bared the numbers "247." On move-in day, a few years earlier, his mother, in her exuberance, claimed that 247 was her lucky number. She was so giddy as she hauled in the cardboard boxes that she made a up song to go with it. He always remembered that day—that feeling—when he heard it. And he knew to listen. Always listen before entering. The television provided clues. Either it was his mother's movie blaring out some song. *Somewhere over the rainbow blue birds fly.* Or, it was a collection of talking heads complaining and shouting about these horrible people called "liberals." The lump returned in Jace's throat that day he heard the shouting on live television again.

Just about everything upset his father, but the liberals—he called them "libtards"—were at the top of the list. And, when it came to the news shows, he was an active participant. At least until he passed out. Jace made a game of measuring the emotional intensity tied to each of the words his father would spit out in contempt. "Mexican" was probably a close second to "liberal," just behind "welfare," which was often accompanied by "cheat," as in "welfare cheat." He hated those parasites and spotted them everywhere, except in his own mirror. The entire building was made up of residents who, every one of them, blood suckers in varying degrees. His father did not only hate Jace and his mother, he also hated himself and everyone around him. Hate engulfed the man who was raising—if you could call it that—the little boy who would become king.

Entering Apartment 247 that day, he was slow and deliberate in closing the door. His eyes met his father's. His head swiveled ninety-degrees away from the welfare-hating face on the screen to see the pathetic little ghost in his presence.

"What's that?" he greeted him after a nearly year-long absence with a sneer, nodding toward the canvas.

"Oh, it's nothing. Where's Mom?" Jace answered back.

If there was anything his father hated as much as Mexicans and freeloaders, it was to have his authority usurped, especially by a woman, his wife, which made it twice as bad. No one, particularly not a snot-nosed kid, would challenge his manhood by refusing to answer a direct question.

"Answer the damned question, son! What's that?" he barked back, arteries bulging from his tattooed neck.

Quivering, Jace reached under his arm, and presented the eleven by fourteen-inch canvas.

"Well, looky here. Isn't that sweet?" his father proclaimed in mocking admiration. "Learning to be a gay liberal, huh? Painting rainbows and cow farts."

The bucolic pasture landscape had been the assignment. Jace added the rainbow for his mother.

Something the television said caught his father's attention, and he lowered the painting down on the couch next to him. But when he did, he clipped the corner of a metal tray which contained something Jace heard his parents call "tar." Usually, it was in solid form, but this time it was liquid. He could tell by the smell wafting overhead that it was recently heated by his father's lighter. Catapult-like, the tar was launched, seeming to levitate midair, before landing directly on the canvas below.

This particular incident received more attention from the biographers than it deserved, at least according to Jace. He never thought much about it, but it was the quote wrangled out of him by a network reporter that was most often discussed and debated. He said, "I don't know which hurt me more, his fists or his words." It was an odd claim coming from someone who had been so completely impervious to criticism, and possessed an uncanny ability to flip a switch and become robotic, almost machine-like when it was time to focus. But he had emotions, at least he appeared to have them. Some thought he was just pretending. Others described him as "calm, cool, and collected."

The only thing that would animate Jason Haper was physical pain of any sort. You could not hurt the guy mentally or emotionally, but bump into him, as the Hill Street Hooligans knew, and he would shake and spasm as if he were in the throes of full-blown anaphylactic shock. Some would theorize that it was a side-effect of his father's constant abuse. Others attributed it to his diminutive stature and the bullying. Whatever the root cause, it was something he was forever anticipating. He was always thinking ahead, protecting himself. Many, who would later read at least one of the hundreds of unauthorized biographies, immediately made the connection between his neatness, his buttoned-up-ness, and his hyper aversion to discomfort. It was an easy connection to make, unlike so much else about the life of Jason Harper.

It was always assumed that his often extreme efforts at pain avoidance were also the reason he did not care to touch or be touched by anyone, or anything for that matter. The mere pat on the back, which happened rarely, would cause him to jump in the same way he would have had a python been dropped in his lap. The thought of a massage would trigger a hair-raising cold sweat to break out on his brow. Hugs, fortunately, were rare, and when they were absolutely required, he had a way of ensuring as little surface area made contact as possible. He would stick his backside out as far as possible, form a wide "U" with his arms, twist his face up in a knot, and pat the shoulders of the other person twice in unison before retreating. That was it. And it was exhausting and depleting.

He really did not mind being around people though. He would later grow to enjoy it. But he wanted them at a distance where he could see them, not touch them. Arm's length and more, if possible. That's what bothered him most about going to the market with his mother. It was not so much the noise, although he was never crazy about the noise either, mostly because he felt there was just too much of it. Instead, it was the contact. People were everywhere. It overwhelmed his senses, and it reminded him of the ant hills he would discover on the banks of the creek. The neighborhood kids would beg him to do it again, and he relished the opportunity to star in another show. It was a relatively straight-forward mission. After the unsanctioned borrowing of a propane tank from the barbecue of an unsuspecting neighbor, Jace would pump the gas into the hole while the resident ants sprang into action, scurrying about in a frenzied animation. Then, with a hearty chuckle, he would strike the match. Boom! The dozen or so insects surviving the blast would stumble around in dazed confusion before each of them got a burning match to their abdomen. With a sizzle and a crack, he extinguished their existence one by one.

Blood was a problem for Jace, particularly the sight of his own. The only time a nurse attempted to draw some of his, she met a crazed resistance many times anything she had seen before. Although he must have been just six or seven years old, she had to buzz for help. Somehow, she was able to push the needle into the vein, but the site of the oozing, surging plasma set Jace off into a state of panic. Springing up from the table, he flailed and thrashed around the office pulling and pushing and grabbing whatever he could reach. A room-separating curtain hanging down from the ceiling was ripped from its track. A heart rate monitor was torn from the wall. And, the buttons of a delicate EKG machine parked in the corner were all depressed at random by Jace, who had transformed into a wounded animal, cornered and panicked. This incident, more than any of the others, would explain so much of what would happen later.

3

It all happened so fast. Every climate model turned out to be wrong. Worst-case scenario arrived much sooner than anyone had predicted. When the polar ice caps melted, the massive release of methane proved too much for the atmosphere. It was as if a switch flipped. For months, every media outlet broadcasted the Great Melt while it was happening. Ice floes the size of city blocks tumbled into the blue ocean below as fast-talking reporters from around the world set up in the foreground to describe the unfolding scene. Each day, the crumbling hastened until it became too dangerous. The filming would move to above, and viewers would be treated to a bizarre sight: Hundreds of helicopters circling above the disappearing slurry.

Ratings for the Great Melt broadcasts rivaled some of the top live courtroom dramas of the past decades. There had not been a celebrity trial in a few years, so the summer's long melting of the ice caps was exactly what the networks needed. Except for the fuel to fly the helicopter, it was a low-cost production, which meant it was highly profitable. With one pilot, maybe one or two crew members, depending on the size of the chopper, plus a single correspondent from the network, it was a formula for printing money.

On the best days, someone would spot a starving polar bear attempting to improve its footing on a shrinking ice cube. A single network could claim the shot was exclusive for a short time, maybe five or ten minutes at most, before another one would catch on to what had been found. Soon, two whirly birds would circle the bear, both attempting to capture its confusion and consternation. Then, three helicopters. Then, four. Then, seventeen. The scene would play out the same way each time. As if it had snacked on a honeycomb and was now dealing with a swarm of angry bees darting in and out overhead, the emaciated bear would rise up and attempt to swat away the helicopters. Those "Godzilla shots" made for great television, and ended up taking home some excellence in broadcasting awards that fall.

The high point of the Great Melt was the day two of the network helicopters crashed into one another as they were filming. Up to that point, most of the action had been in the Arctic, but after a while, there was nothing left to see up north. Viewers grew tired of open ocean shots, and polar bear sightings were no longer possible, except for the occasional floating carcass. Those in the industry prognosticated that careers were going to be made in Antarctica, the South Pole. And that's where it happened.

The television crew from Vietnam was flying low, nearly meeting the colony of penguins eye-to-eye while the German network helicopter meandered overhead. Both were fully absorbed in framing the shot, and because they were lined up vertically, just a hundred feet apart, neither could see the other. For some reason, which was debated at length by viewers and commentators for weeks, the Vietnamese pilot pulled on the control stick, which launched his helicopter directly into the Germans above as if it were a surface-to-air missile.

During the ensuing hours, the networks would replay the footage above the banner flashing "Breaking News." The whole thing turned out to be a huge win for BCA, the Broadcast Corporation of Argentina. Their helicopter had been hovering off to the side, and as their crew filmed the penguins they also inadvertently caught the midair collision. After the Vietnamese and German helicopters made contact, the Argentinians continued to livestream the incident.

One television broadcast and then another patched into the live feed, as the BCA logo was featured prominently in the lower right-hand corner of screens worldwide. As far as scoops go, it was the greatest in a decade. Everyone remembers precisely where they were and what they had been doing when they dropped everything to watch the crash unfold during the Great Melt. Stunned audiences watched the Vietnamese craft plummet.

The nose of the helicopter caught the iceberg's edge, causing it to tumble before submerging upside down into the freezing water. It bobbed in the swells for a moment—the network commentators would later note that it had been exactly nineteen seconds from the point of impact—when two crew members appeared simultaneously. Treading water and waving frantically toward the BCA camera filming from above, both of them disappeared from view after taking a direct hit from a crashing wave. It made for great drama when only one of them reappeared.

Thrashing and fighting and gasping, the man from Vietnam gripped the landing gear, one of the skids, of the partially submerged helicopter. But it was sinking fast. That shot only held for a minute or two —it was later timed at one minute and thirty-three seconds—as the Vietnamese Media Organization cameraman waved in frantic desperation toward the Argentinian helicopter hovering above. He realized that he was going to have to save himself, so he decided to swim for the ice flue.

Covering a span estimated at just eighty-five feet, the world watched while the thirteen-year VMO employee sped along with a uncoordinated freestyle, never allowing his head to slip below the surface. The Argentinian helicopter then dropped down, hovering ten feet above sea level, to capture the remaining drama as it unfolded. As the frame tightened, audience members could see the letters "VMO" emblazoned on the back of his butter-yellow jacket, just above the company slogan "We're Your Eyes."

The top ledge of the ice sheet could not have been elevated from the water by more than a few feet, but it was a shear, glass-smooth face.

And, for a swimmer treading the punishing Antarctic current, it might as well have been a mile. Audiences everywhere were transfixed. The guy from Vietnam was putting on a show. Lunging from the water, his bare hands twice gripped the top of the ledge. Each time, he slipped, dunking under water before reemerging. He would again turn and wave at the helicopter hovering above, mouthing indiscernible words, as he begged for help. Each time his waving arms slowed. His energy swallowed by the frigid seawater.

A single penguin materialized from above. Curious as it cocked its head to the right and then to the left, meeting eyes with the swimmer flailing and pleading and crying below. The Vietnamese man then paused for a moment, closed his eyes, bowed his head and muttered something to himself before making another attempt at the ledge. This time, with his energy drained, his hands slapped the frozen face only to the halfway point before disappearing from the screen for the last time.

Much praise was heaped upon the crew member of the BCA helicopter who had the presence of mind to photograph the incident as it was unfolding. Back then, he was not a network correspondent, but a pilot in training. Everything changed for him after he reviewed the photo scroll on his cell phone on the long flight back to the studio. He knew what he had, and it was a good as a winning lottery ticket. The BCA production people knew it, too. He would be effusive in his praise for their "unselfish assistance" as they pulled strings with connections at the International Copyright Office to establish the necessary protections for his image. It was critical that he be identified as the owner of the photograph. The submission was returned in record time with the coveted ICO stamp, along with its unique serial number, in the bottom right corner. The image showed the swimmer from behind, his two hands outstretched, failing to find a fingerhold in the sheet of ice. His head was tilted back so he could see the top of the ledge. And, from that ledge, a single penguin was peering down, its head cocked a quarter-turn to the left, curious about the man who was about to drown.

Overnight, the crew member became a very wealthy man. His payday reminded everyone that quick money was never far from reach. As always happened after a big score, submissions to the ICO exploded. Everyone, it seemed, was inspired to cash in. And he did provide a valuable lesson, one that was repeated often in the days that followed: "Don't share it until you get the copyright." The photograph received the all-important ICO stamp, which meant that it was embedded with bank-linked encryption—every time someone viewed or downloaded it, the photographer received a royalty payment deposited directly to his checking account. The news of his accomplishment spread fast and the most popular search in the weeks following was some variation of "How to fast track an ICO approval." Soon thereafter, small-time entrepreneurs began cashing in with online courses advertising "overnight wealth" running alongside the photograph of the century.

———

The German helicopter took a direct hit. And the pilot was rattled. His craft began smoking and gyrating while the instruments flashed and squawked. Below he could see only a swirling of blue and white— ocean and ice—as he muscled through the dizziness to find a place to crash land. He shouted to his crew "Brace yourselves!" before the hard thud. Solid ground. If it had been a splash instead of a thud, it would have been a different story. The German helicopter was now a piece of scrap metal sitting atop a fast-melting ice cube somewhere in Antartica. As they climbed out from the wreckage, the pilot said a prayer to himself. They had all survived.

Grasping the sliding door with a gloved hand, the German network correspondent steadied herself until the horizon stopped moving. Her company had replaced its cameraman with a robot years ago, so she instructed it to follow her to the edge of the floe on which they had crash landed. No more than one hundred feet away from the next iceberg, she saw the colony of penguins first. And, below in the water, she watched the same drama that was now broadcasting on billions of screens. Two heads bobbing on the waves quickly turned to one.

The BCA helicopter from Argentina then swung around, backed up and lowered itself, hovering toward the water, giving itself plenty of distance from the lone Vietnamese employee and the shore. Out of the side door, a cameraman leaned out, twisting and turning dials, never looking up from the viewfinder. Another man held a cell phone from an outstretched hand. She was close enough to see his thumb lifting up and down, rapid fire in pressing the photo button.

That's when she reached her breaking point.

Up to that point, she had been providing her audience with the standard "Five W's" of Journalism—Who, What, Where, When, and Why —when something changed. Some in her industry would later say that she was overcome with a fit of jealousy. She was enraged that the team from BCA was getting the scoop. She had missed a career-defining opportunity.

With the camera bot continuing to frame the scene, she muttered to herself. "I can't—I can't do this." As she watched the Vietnamese man struggle in the ocean, she debated jumping into the water herself. After concluding that with no attempt by the BCA helicopter to assist in a rescue, her death would have been assured, as well. Instead, she drew in an icy breath and glared at the camera bot.

Her earbud crackled to life. "Is everything okay?" her producer asked.

"No," she retorted, before clearing her throat and continuing. "Ladies and gentlemen, we are witnessing the end of mankind right before our eyes."

Again the earbud: "This is not another story about climate change! Cover the crash! It's broadcast gold!"

Touching her earpiece, she paused for a moment to reconsider. "We had been focused on our ongoing coverage, when another helicopter collided with us in midair."

The earbud: "Good, good, this is great. Keep going!"

"The craft that ran into us from below, presumably because they could not see us flying overhead, is the property of the VMO, the Vietnamese Media Organization. There appears to be one lone survivor, as you can see now over my shoulder. He is struggling to lift himself up to the top of the ice sheet that is floating in the water about a hundred feet from the one we were able to crash-land on."

The earbud: "Yes—inject more drama!"

"The survivor appears to be a middle-aged man, presumably from Vietnam," the German reporter stopped and drew a deep breath before continuing. "There is a man. He's fighting for his life right in front of us—I can't do this, I can't."

The earbud: "What the hell are you doing?!"

The reporter, the young woman from Germany, ripped the tiny speaker from her ear with her gloved index finger and thumb before launching it into the water below. She again looked directly into the lens.

"Ladies and gentlemen, we are witnessing the end of mankind right before our eyes. There is a man in the water—we're told that survival at that temperature is not possible after just a few minutes—and there is another helicopter from the BCA, the Broadcast Corporation of Argentina, that could very easily rescue him right now. Instead they have opted to broadcast his death."

She lowered her microphone and turned to scream indecipherable obscenities and at the BCA chopper hovering just above the water, frantically gesturing toward the exhausted and faltering swimmer.

Again turning toward the unfolding drama no more than one hundred agonizing feet away, she watched, along with the rest of the world, as the popsicle man made one last lunge toward to the ledge before disappearing forever.

With tears streaming from her eyes, she spoke again. "This is not the kind of world I want to live in," she whimpered, turning toward the rescue that did not happen. "Maybe it's actually a good thing that we are about to be wiped out by climate change. Our own planet doesn't even want us anymore. When the almighty dollar becomes more important than a man's life, then who are we? Why are we here? What's the point?"

Another long pause to collect her thoughts.

"I don't know about you, but I can't do this. Ladies and gentlemen, we just witnessed a death. A perfectly preventable death. The BCA helicopter made the decision that his death would make for good television. Instead of filming the whole thing for your viewing enjoyment—right there in the comfort of your living room, or wherever you are—they could have set down their cameras and pulled him from the water. They could have saved him. But they let him die. And they did it for you, the audience, for your viewing pleasure. How does that make you feel? That means it's not just BCA that has blood on their hands. You do, too."

She thought about ending her monologue there, but she had more to say. She knew this would be the last time she would ever be allowed to speak into the microphone, so why not make it count? Why not put it all out there, everything she wished she had been courageous enough to say all along?

"And, do you know why? It all comes down to one thing: Money. That's the only thing we care about anymore. Money. Money. Money. But, you know what? It doesn't matter how much you've got in your bank account, because you and I and all the millionaires and billionaires are all going to burn up on this same overheated planet just the same."

Another reflective pause, before continuing.

"You know, maybe that's what the Bible really meant when it talked about 'burning in hell,' it meant climate change. And, guess what? It's here, ladies and gentlemen. There's no turning back now. You and all of your stupid money are going to burn, burn, burn. And you know what? You deserve it. And I deserve it for standing by and watching, just like I stood by and watched that man drown today. If there were any decency left, anything worth salvaging on this miserable planet, I would have swum out to try to save him myself. You could have watched me die, too. I could have doubled your viewing pleasure. But I watched. Just like you."

Many years later, one of television's most celebrated broadcasts, the helicopter crash during the Great Melt, would only serve to further the mythology. In his characteristic deadpan, Jason Harper would reveal in a press conference—to a thunderous round of approving laughter— that the only reason he was one of the very few to watch the obscure German broadcast, and not the BCA livestream along with everyone else, was simple: "You didn't dare change the channel, or you'd get the smack down from Dad. He thought the German girl was hot."

Although every reporter in the room immediately spotted the obvious problem with his statement: Jason Harper's father had vanished before the Great Melt. It didn't matter though. They would find a way to make the timeline work. They always did.

4

Although there are now many historical societies worldwide, the two most prestigious are the Jason Harper National Archive and the International Association of Jason Harper Scholars. And they remain bitterly divided on one biographical detail.

So much is known about the man's life. He was for the most part, an open book, always willing to answer questions and sit for wide-ranging interviews with no preconditions. Plus, there were many eager corroborators who were willing to come forward to share their testimony. Possession of first-hand knowledge, or eyewitness accounts of any sort, translated to enormous social currency, so there was a strong incentive to bend the truth. Total fabrication was also problematic, so the role of the historical societies, at least according to their members, was to sort out fact from fiction. That is where the Jason Harper National Archive arrived at an impasse.

Fierce debate erupted during the agenda item identified only as "Adoption of The Acid Theory." It was common for politicians to call highly divisive and emotionally charged issues "third rail issues." The term referred to the old-style subways, which travelled along two steel tracks. A third rail, or track, carried a massive electrical current used to power the train. Touching the third rail resulting in an instant death. That's why you don't do it. And that is why the membership of the National Archive was halved overnight, and the reason that the IAJHS exists at all. Behind the scenes, every effort was made to keep it off the agenda. But everyone knew it had to be addressed at some time or another. The outcome was predictable.

The meeting went on through the night. And there was some progress, some reason for optimism when universal agreement was achieved in some key areas. There was no dispute when it came to his exposure to illicit drugs. Both his mother and his father, it was ratified with a unanimous vote, were drug addicts. And there were no objections to the writings that stated in the official language adopted that night: "Throughout His childhood, He was a witness to drug abuse." But the shouting and fist waving began when the question came up as to whether or not he had consumed illicit drugs himself. It reminded many in attendance of the old way, liberals on one side of the aisle, conservatives on the other, both dug in and refusing to listen to the other had resulted in catastrophic dysfunction. At the meeting that night, one speaker would become especially agitated before another would rise to remind everyone that this is not what He would have wanted.

Drug use, at least by him personally, was not something that any reporter ever dared ask Jason Harper. And he never brought it up himself. There were never any credible accounts of Him consuming illicit substances by anyone with any shred of believability. But there were the persistent claims by Hilliard House riffraff, who insisted that doing drugs was a fact of life for everyone living there at the time. Whether anyone wanted to believe it was another question. And, fundamentally, that was the question: Do you want to believe it? And there was good reason to do so. While the fear of needles would have ruled out experimentation with heroin, and an aversion to pill swallowing of any sort made anything in a tablet form an unlikely choice, there were some serious doubts when it came to LSD, known on the street as "acid," which is why it's called The Acid Theory.

The deniers increasingly found themselves in the minority. And the

National Archive paid a heavy price for their position, in terms of both membership and funding. Many of their donors went public with their criticism, calling the institution once known for its sober analysis, a "faith-based organization." The exodus after that night included the eventual founders of the IAJHS. Less than a year later, the National Archive, which, at the time included a membership that was signaling a willingness to embrace the fully debunked "immaculate conception" doctrine, was hanging on by a thread. Facing bankruptcy, the group had no choice but to reverse course and accept The Acid Theory.

Immediately, the IAJHS codified its position, galvanizing the organization as the gold standard of scholarship. Its first official act: an on the record interview with Ryan Mendoza.

————

The semicircle was enough to accommodate the executive leadership team of the IAJHS. On the other side was a table and a single chair. Three video cameras manned by two operators were spread about. A single sound engineer occupied one corner. When Ryan Mendoza enters the room, there will be eleven people to witness his official testimony in person. It took longer than expected, as the make-up artist was instructed to tamp down the neck and face tattoos. It was critical, however, that they did not disappear completely so as to maintain credibility and authenticity. But a little powder applied in a strategic way would make the ink less distracting. The attendees shifted in their seats and attempted small talk to distract themselves, but there was no denying the heaviness pushing down on the room.

As he settled into his seat, Ryan made an awkward quip about the lights, mentioning how they reminded him of those old-time interrogations you see in the movies. No one there really understood the joke, but they were ready for something to break the tension. Then it began.

"Please raise your right hand, Mr. Mendoza," the voice came from the darkness, somewhere behind the second studio light. "Do you, Ryan Phillip Mendoza, agree to tell the whole truth and nothing but the truth regarding this matter of utmost importance concerning the life of Jason Harper?"

"Yes, I do." Ryan stated, immediately lowering this hand down on the table to clasp the other.

"Are you familiar with the premise of the Acid Theory?"

"Yes, yes, I am."

"Can you please explain it to us?"

Incredulous, Ryan replied, "Are you serious? You want me to explain the Acid Theory?"

"Yes, please proceed, Mr. Mendoza. It important that we first gain a knowledge of your understanding before we can move forward."

"Okay." Ryan, sat back in his chair as one of the lights caught the streaks of silver and gray peppering his close-cropped still full head of hair. "The Acid Theory is the theory that Jace's creative genius stems from a single, massive dose of LSD he took as a kid. The theory is that the acid somehow rewired his brain during a critical phase of its development, which then allowed him to make connections and see things differently than the rest of us. Basically, it's how he was able to do what he did."

"And what do you know of this matter?" another voice, this one belonging to a woman, asked from the darkness.

"Well, I can tell you that I was there when it happened," the audio engineer placed one hand on his headphones as an audible gasp was detected.

"Can you please tell us about it?"

"Sure. We must have been eight or nine years old. It was during a weekend, or maybe a Friday. We ditched school most days, but definitely on Fridays. Whatever day it was, no one was at his apartment, so we hung out there. When no one was at my place, Apartment 316, he would come hang with me. Basically, wherever the parents weren't is where we were."

"Please continue, Mr. Mendoza."

"Jace hated drugs, especially needles. He would talk about how his parents would get high and pass out sitting upright next to each other on the couch. He would make fun of them by drawing little pictures showing their heads leaning back with eyes closed and these super wide-open mouths with different things crawling out, like the devil or a bunch of insects or our teacher or whatever was on his mind. Then, he'd make this weird little groaning sound to mock them. It was funny as hell."

"Go on."

"His parents weren't really any different than anyone else's parents at the Hilliard House. They were all junkies. Mine were, too. Drugs were everywhere. All the kids were exposed to it. You either jumped on the bandwagon or went the other way completely. In a weird way, Jace did both."

"What do you mean by that, exactly?"

"What I mean is that he hated drugs, but he always seemed interested in those little papers of LSD, especially the pictures they drew on them. He loved drawing, everyone knows that, but there was something about those little squares that sort of captured his imagination, so to speak."

"To clarify for the record, Mr. Mendoza, the little squares you are referring to each comprise a single dose of lysergic acid diethylamide, otherwise known as LSD, or acid, correct?"

"Yes, that's correct—they come with some little trippy drawing on them. Jace loved looking at the artwork and used to pull sheets of them from the milk crate, the same one where his dad kept the gun, by the way. I don't know how they had so much acid over there, the stuff ain't cheap. I'm pretty sure his dad wasn't into it, probably just dealing it. I think his mom was dropping those things."

"Why do you believe that to be true—that his mother and not his father was the user of LSD?"

"Because, you could just about count on Jace to do the opposite of whatever his dad did. He hated his dad and didn't want to be anything like him. His dad was a real piece of work."

"Okay, so noted. Please continue."

"For the longest time, he would fan these sheets out and just study them. I suppose it was like how other kids used to look at their base-ball collection, or their toy race cars or something like that. Only, for Jace, he liked checking out the artwork. And thinking back on it now, it does make sense. There was nothing else to look at in their apartment, no magazines, no artwork, no books. It was totally empty, except for a couch in the living room, a TV, a little fold-out card table in the dining room. That sort of furniture wasn't uncommon at the Hilliard House."

"Just to clarify, Mr. Mendoza, what exactly was not uncommon?"

"Poor people living with nothing in the projects," Ryan resented ques-tion. "The Harpers were poorer than most, though. They didn't have beds or anything, just a few blankets. No pillows. And there was always crap everywhere. It was a mess, but never anything of value. Just trash mostly."

"Thank you, Mr. Mendoza. Please continue."

"Okay, sure. So, getting back to the LSD. Jace would sit there and study those sheets while I messed around with the gun, mainly just loading and unloading it. One day, I dared him to take a hit. It was the thing kids did to each other, sort of razzing and daring each other to do crazy stuff. Remember, we were eight or nine years old, so we were always egging each other on to do stupid things. Anyway, I dared him to eat a whole sheet. I mean, it was just messing around, being a dumb kid. We're sitting there and laughing and being dumbasses when, out of the blue, he crumples up an entire sheet and stuffs the whole thing in his mouth and swallows."

"For the record, Mr. Mendoza. How many individual squares make up a sheet?"

"It was a standard ten by ten matrix, which is four inches square. One hundred in all."

"Excuse me, sir. Can you repeat that? Did you say, 'One hundred?'"

"Yes, I did. He swallowed one hundred doses of LSD."

"And what is a standard dose?"

"One—just one of those little squares."

"What happened next?"

"He started laughing. We both did. It was funny as hell."

"Let it be entered into the record that Ryan Phillip Mendoza is claiming to have witnessed Jason Harper ingesting one hundred doses of lysergic acid diethylamide on or about a Friday afternoon at the age of either eight or nine years old," a serious, monotone voice interjected. "Please go on, Mr. Mendoza."

"Hey, I'm not just claiming this happened. I was there. This actually happened. And Jace laughed his ass off for a few minutes until his eyes went glassy. He tripped hard. Really hard."

"What exactly do you mean by 'he tripped hard,' Mr. Mendoza?"

"Geez, really, you guys? What I mean is exactly what I said: He tripped hard, and he was talking all crazy, all sorts of nonsense, describing visions—hallucinations."

"What did he say?"

"It was all sort of random. He'd bounce from one thing to the next. At one point, I got scared because, honestly, I thought he was dying. His eyes sort of rolled back, and he was sweating like a pig and breathing super shallow, panting. He sort of crumbled down and went limp. Then, after a while, he kind of perked up and started telling me about all these people who were apparently coming into the room with us. He was talking to them. They were people that he never met."

"Such as?"

"Like his grandparents. I remember how he described them. He said they were made of light, sort of glowing, and that they were waving him over. He was mumbling about how he was going to 'cross the stream' to join them. He started crying, but he seemed happy not sad. They were like tears of joy, I guess, because he was smiling all wild and crazy. Then he started cracking up, it was an uncontrollable laughter. He was all giddy and excited, and started sort of humming to himself, almost like singing, but more like talking. It was weird. Over and over, he repeated an old nursery rhyme, you know the one, they teach it to you in kindergarten, it's the one about rowing your boat."

"We need to understand exactly what was said, Mr. Mendoza. Please repeat for us exactly what was said that day."

"Seriously?"

"Yes, seriously."

"Wow, okay," Ryan rolled his eyes before taking a moment to remember. "It goes like this: 'Row, row, row your boat gently down the stream. Merrily, merrily, merrily, merrily, life is but a dream.'"

"How many times did he repeat it?"

"It had to have been at least a thousand times. It was non-stop, playing on a loop."

"And why did he repeat it?"

"I asked him the same thing when he finally snapped out of it—he was completely blitzed for two full days. Luckily, his mom didn't come back for a few days, not that it would have mattered. But it gave him time to come down and stop tripping. I asked him about that, why he kept repeating the 'Row Your Boat' thing because, honestly, it kind of freaked me out. It was spooky as hell, especially when I was trying to get some sleep. He was rocking back and forth all zombie-like talking to himself in the dark."

"Please continue, Mr. Mendoza. How did he answer your question?"

"You know, I'll never forget this. I can't remember the words he used exactly. I mean, this was a long time ago. He was acting all weird like the cat that swallowed the canary, as if he got the goods on someone, or he heard a big secret. It's hard to explain. But it was like he knew something and wasn't sure if he should share it. And it was good gossip. Good news. Because he was happy about it. Almost excited. At the same time he also seemed relieved and calm and relaxed. Peaceful is the word for it, I guess. Anyway, he made me promise not say anything, to swear to secrecy, which I did, so I really shouldn't even be telling you this. But I guess it doesn't matter now."

Ryan looked away from the cameras, drew a deep breath and formulated his words before finishing. "He said something like, 'I just found out that all of this, everything, is make-believe—pretend. We think it's real only because we believe it. But, really, we're asleep. We're dreaming. We wake up when we cross the stream.' Then he used a word that I had never heard before: 'Immortal.'"

5

After the Great Melt, every network dispatched their reporters to the floods. The broadcasting was relatively simple and widely considered excellent training grounds for new correspondents—the prettier, the better. It had become increasingly difficult to keep an audience engaged. Once you had watched one city get swallowed by the ocean, it was said, you have seen them all. There was some truth to it. The scene did unfold much the same way each time, exactly as expected, and with diminishing returns.

Broadcasting "flood shots," as they came to be known, hit an all-time ratings low the week before one correspondent showed up in a bikini. She claimed she wore it to do her job, to wade through the surging tide, but no one believed it. Her network immediately began siphoning off viewers from their competitors, so the other reporters rushed to their trailers for wardrobe changes. The real-time ratings whipsawed as viewers would switch to whomever was next to bare some skin. The skimpier the suit, the longer they would stay tuned.

At some point, a major coastal city falling into the sea was no longer newsworthy—bikini or not—and the reporters stopped showing up. Covering the storms became more interesting, mostly because they were so unpredictable. And, as everyone in the industry knew, unpredictability equaled drama and drama equaled profits. Any footage capturing someone getting gobbled up by a passing tornado was pure gold and the networks jostled hard for the perfect vantage point. But after the Great Melt, ratings for everything continued to decline. The days of easy, high-profit television were over. No longer was it enough to put one correspondent on location with a camera bot. Everything reached an entirely new level of journalistic evolution when the networks realized what the audience was now thirsting for: Conflict.

The real money was not in the filming of the flooding, but in the migration which invariably followed. People were everywhere, and they were desperate and, therefore, unpredictable—exactly what viewers wanted. In the early days, the usual first responders and do-gooders would show up, so there was nothing worth filming. But, after a while, they all disappeared, simply overwhelmed by the number of active emergency zones. That is when the networks returned. Looting and arson and carjacking were a godsend for their flagging ratings. And there was no law enforcement around to stop it. Finally, something to watch other than more townspeople boating down main street, or yet another hurricane. Television became fresh and raw and interesting again, a new golden age of broadcasting had emerged. Street fights commanded the largest audiences, by far. At first, the reporter would narrate the melee, careful to frame it over the shoulder, as they taught in journalism school. But, after people began complaining that they couldn't see the action, the networks began programming their robots to go out on their own to do the filming, with no narration of any kind—a broadcast first.

Camera-wielding robots were everywhere, which is one of the fundamental changes to how the news was broadcasted during this period. No longer did the networks wait for something to happen before dispatching a correspondent to report the story. Now, camera bots were deployed *before* the news happened in the first place. And because the bots did not need to sleep or eat, they were always out roaming the streets looking out for the next big story. The big leap forward in broadcast innovation came when the dynamic reversed course, and the news began seeking out the camera bots.

The day Hoya first made his way onto the screen was attributable to nothing other than a stroke of good luck. It began in the Smoky Mountains, which is where many of the people migrated after the Eastern seaboard disappeared under the growing Atlantic. The higher elevation kept them above the flood waters and the wildlife and mountain streams sustained them, at least the strongest of them.

On that fateful day for American journalism, the camera bot just happened to be at the right place at the right time. And it was a slow news day. A man appears, perfectly framed as he walks head down toward the camera bot which he does not notice. The recording of this opening scene would be replayed millions of times, and it could not have been captured any better had it been filmed on the set of a movie production. He was wearing a gray hoodie sweatshirt and his hands were tucked into the pockets, trying to keep them warm. The only thing visible was his reddish-blonde beard, short enough to reveal a chiseled and squared-off chin. His face was concealed under the shadow of the hood. His breath billowed against the freezing and always gray Appalachian sky.

As Hoya closed in on the camera, a shadow became visible in the background, crouching the distance. In a sudden bolt, a man appears sprinting up from behind. In the next frame, Hoya was lying face down in the mud as a bare-chested attacker wearing nothing but a pair of Levi's jeans, which is why he became known as "Levi 1"—it would be a few weeks later when the world would meet "Levi 2"— began raining down blows. Just as the school kids would demonstrate in playgrounds everywhere, Hoya was prone, laying on top of his pocketed hands, face-first in the mud. Wriggling back and forth made no difference, as Levi 1 now had his knees planted on Hoya's shoulders. One blow after another finds its target. The pummeling goes on and on, but the fury slows as Levi 1 burned through his energy. At the two-minute, forty-two mark of the video, Hoya is seen twisting his head to catch a glimpse of his assailant. And, no sooner does he turn to face the ground again, he twists lightning-fast at the same time lifting a clenched right first that found the left cheek bone of Levi 1.

The scene that unfolded was the same one every other network has been chasing after since. A still-hooded Hoya springs to his feet revealing the lettering "Georgetown Hoyas" before he wheels around in a roundhouse kick revealing an expert level command of martial arts. Going back and forth, the fight, it was later agreed, is better than anything Hollywood has ever produced. A lightning-fast jab to the throat marks the beginning of the end. Levi 1 is stunned, and begins gasping and stumbling and doubling over, while Hoya seizes the opportunity to unleash a furious medley of punches and kicks. Grasping a headful of his attacker's sweat-dripped, black hair, Hoya assumes the position, later dubbed "The Hoya." As Levi 1 fell to both knees, Hoya settled in behind him, his arms now a pair of vice grips clamping firm to his assailant's head. At that moment, the camera bot stepped toward the two, both of them were now looking directly into the lens. That's when he said it. Hoya's words would be repeated millions of times, always in English, and would go on to become the front side of the best-selling children's t-shirt that school year. Still breathing heavily from the fracas, Hoya spoke directly to the viewer: "Here you go, America!" With that, a massive twist, and Levi 1 was dead.

"Follow that man!" the network headquarters immediately directed its camera bot. "Do not, under any circumstances, let him out of your sight." It was slow at first, but the audience seemed content with it. They needed time to bond with the protagonist. But you could only watch someone forage berries for so long. Eventually, there has to be an element of unpredictability because unpredictability equals drama, and drama equals profits. But sometimes, as everyone learned during this new era of broadcasting, the drama has to be manufactured. That is why the network quietly sent one of its reporters in search of a worthy opponent. The instructions were clear: Find someone who could play the villain. For a mere fifty-thousand dollars, they found just the right guy. After wiring the funds to his bank account, they picked him up in a network helicopter, instructed him on how to initiate the attack. As the craft set down in a nearby high mountain meadow, one of the executives said, "Here, wear this," as he handed him a bright orange t-shirt. The rotors animated the grasses below, and the commotion drew a crowd from the surrounding trees, including Hoya. Ten minutes later, Orange Crush was dead.

By nightfall, the network had their top news anchor on location to interview Hoya. Viewers were clamoring for his story. In a dramatic lowering of his hood, he spoke in a low, respectful tone. He was thoughtful and educated, using words like "admonish," which the anchor would then define for viewers. It turns out that Hoya had recently graduated from Georgetown University and had been in the process of opening a karate dojo when the floods came. He wanted nothing more, he said, than to teach kids martial arts. As luck would have it, he had accomplished his goal a million times over, as the worldwide audience would rival levels not seen since the crash during the Great Melt coverage. One by one, Orange Crush, Beanie, Levi 2, G.I. Joe, Mullet, and Puffy Vest, just to name a few, were dispatched. When he fought Air Jordan, the network blurred out the swoosh logo because Nike hadn't written a check. By then, the sponsors were paying a handsome premium and they were not about to allow any free advertising to slip through. Hoya's sponsorship deal was brokered by the network, and the terms were crystal clear: He had agreed to insert a statement, which would be determined by the highest bidder, immediately preceding the end of each bout. When Hoya wrapped python-like behind the loser, he remained dutiful to the terms of the agreement, always pausing to provide the service he was bound by the advertising contract to perform. With another challenger wriggling and squirming and begging, Hoya would look into the camera and say, "My F150 was built Ford Tough!" Then, he would adjust his grip before thrilling the audience once again with his now trademarked, "Here you go, America!" One violent crank to the left and another body would go limp.

Hoyamania ran wild around the clock for seventy-three days straight. Broadcast nirvana. During that time, the recent college grad was unde-feated. He would still be that way to this day, according to his legion of fans, if the network hadn't become so greedy. Instead of sticking with the formula, and letting the fights unfold in undisclosed and remote locations, it was decided by the top brass that Hoya would be moved to an arena previously used for basketball. Immediately, the show lost all of its gritty, organic appeal, and the production felt airbrushed and overblown. Despite the objections from the viewing audience, everyone continued to tune in during the prime-time slot to watch the fights.

It happened on the second day of the second week, a Tuesday. As usual, the bellowing voice announced that the reigning champion as he entered the arena on his way to the ring. Then, the two spotlights, which had been randomly zipping over the animated crowd, both trained on Hoya. He was wearing a gray robe which was covering his new Georgetown Hoyas hoodie. Kids on the playground and adults around the water cooler would dissect the next few moments for weeks to come. First, Hoya scanned the crowd before tapping the middle of his chest twice in a gesture of gratitude. Then, he took a step forward with his left foot. Next, his right. The moment his right foot hit the concrete a second time, the screen showed Hoya's brain exiting from the back of his cranium. Lunging in front of the camera with a still-smoking revolver, a mostly bald, mostly fat man with an uneven beard and wild, crossing eyes flexed his still-jiggling arms and yelled out, "Here you go, America!"

The crowd on either side of the blood-stained red carpet leading to the boxing ring immediately pounced on the gunman, pinning him down until the revolver was located by someone the news media called a Good Samaritan. Without hesitation Good Sam strode up to the mostly bald, mostly fat man, pressed the barrel against his pock-filled face and pulled the trigger. It was all caught on tape, and no charges were ever filed against Good Sam for his swift vigilante justice. The police officers and judges and politicians all loved Hoya just as much as the rest of America.

Everyone mourned Hoya. The audience rooted for him. There was some solace for the networks in the fact that the last episode generated an unending stream of royalties from the downloaded recordings. But the copycat shows never came close to the original. It was not for lack of effort, as each junior level network executive became convinced that the path to the corner office was paved with Hoya knockoffs. Even when they attempted to cast someone like Hoya—one went so far as to bring in a twenty-nine-year-old with a black hoodie and a chestnut beard who they renamed Hoyo—it always fell flat. The emotional connection to the audience was not there, which meant that there was no reason to care. Without the connection it didn't work. Plus, everyone loves a good fight, especially the men who drove the ratings in a big way. Women loved Hoya also, but mostly because of his rugged good looks and unending charisma. Nobody else could walk or talk or fight like Hoya, especially Hoyo, who was bested in the second episode. His first opponent had been an obvious fall guy, a patsy set up by the network. The thrill was gone, never to be replicated in the same way again.

Years later, for a new documentary, a journalist asked Jason Harper about what he thought about the seventy-three days of Hoyamania. Jason paused for a moment and searched for the answer, the one everyone wanted to hear. By that time, he had fielded thousands of questions on just about every topic, but never this one. It caught him flat-footed. He wanted to get it right.

"Just like everyone, I was devastated. Just completely heartbroken," Jason dabbed the corner of his left eye for effect—a flawless performance. "You know, I was just twelve years old when that happened, so I took it especially hard. Hoya was my hero. I looked up to him as if here was my brother, my big brother."

Honesty was the domain of the wealthy. At least that is what Jason Harper had always told himself. When you grow up poor, you understand at a fundamental level that telling the truth can get you killed, or thrown in jail, or worse. Over the years, he had become adept at bending reality in his favor. "Creative storytelling" is how he rationalized it to himself. Only he didn't rationalize it at all, because he never felt the need. The truth was nobody's business but his own. How he saw it is how it was. Period. End of story, whatever that story happened to be.

While he watched the journalist nod her head in doting approval, he knew she was thinking just one thing. *I cannot believe I am actually sitting here on this couch interviewing Jason Harper.* And that meant she would believe anything, and so would anyone who will ever watch the documentary. As he was saying the words—his carefully crafted and curated response—his mind wandered back to the days of Hoya. He did not remember having any particular feelings for the guy, and he most definitely did not see him as a brother. He remembered only one pervasive thought dominating his mind in the wake of Hoyamania: *I wish he killed more people—millions more.*

6

The last time the senate voted for anything unanimously, it was the resolution authorizing war in Korea. It was the brazen Christmas Day attack—North Korea had no problem crossing the Demilitarized Zone and gobbling up its neighbor to the south—which put everyone on edge. But, when intelligence surfaced a week later showing that a single intercontinental ballistic missile was trained on Anchorage, Alaska, that is when the partisan bickering stopped, at least for a minute. A bill was on the president's desk the next morning, and it was immediately signed without ceremony. The pomp and circumstance had been dropped after the flooding. By the afternoon, American troops were on their way to what became known as the Second Korean War. Everyone called it Korea II.

Although Korea II was necessary, at least according to the opinion polls, following it up with an invasion of China was not. That conflict was considered an overreach and was deeply and universally unpopular, not because of the lives lost, which came almost exclusively from the lower classes, but because of the havoc it wreaked on the economy. Even those with the most rudimentary understanding of supply and demand knew the Chinese would sell each and every Treasury Note the second an American G.I. poked his green helmet over the

Changbai Mountains. For over a hundred years, China had been financing America's debt, which made it possible for it to remain solvent. To pay the bills. When the spigot was turned off, the economy tanked, which was much more painful to everyone than 150,000 infantrymen returning home in body bags, not to mention all the money wasted.

This time, things would be different, the senators promised as much when they cast their second unanimous vote in decades. Just like Korea II, the country faced an existential threat. Again, the polling was clear. It was the coverage of the Great Melt that finally did it, at least that is what the senators and their advisors speculated in meetings behind closed doors. The single rallying point—the one thing that appeared to galvanize the need to do something about it—was the famous photograph showing the Vietnamese cameraman flailing in the Antarctic slurry. Up to that point, business continued as usual. No one wanted to stop making money. The burning of fossil fuels continued unabated, as small tweaks around the margin were made and then unmade depending on which party was occupying the White House. One administration raised the fuel mileage standard and four years later the other would lower it. Some would claim the government was only "rearranging the deck chairs on the Titanic."

Widely panned as a desperate move, the senate gave their unanimous approval to a bill that was signed into law by the president on the same day. The only debate, and it was short-lived, was a question about whether such legislation sent the wrong message. Would it cause a widespread panic if everyone were to learn the government did not have an answer? Not only that, it was also out of ideas. *The emperor has not clothes.* Lawmakers hoped that someone out there had an answer— that was the whole point of the Climate Innovation and Mitigation Act, or CLIMA, as it came to be known. With its ratification, the United States government placed billions of dollars into a special fund to "incentivize, reward, and fund innovative and creative climate solu- tions." It was a direct appeal to its citizens, a request for proposals—no matter how bizarre or outlandish—that would allow the country, and the world, to forestall the impending climate apocalypse.

CLIMA gave everyone the signal it was time to drop everything and head off in one of two different directions. Either get to work coming up with a way to save mankind from certain doom, or enjoy the ride and party as hard as possible until everyone burns up on the over-heated fireball. The country, much like the alignment of its political parties, was split almost exactly in half. And the rationale for both made perfect sense considering the circumstances. It was unclear exactly, just how much time was left. But everyone knew it was not much. The end was nigh.

This period is perhaps the most researched part of Jason Harper's life. Same as everyone else, he made a simple calculation weighing the benefits of enjoying his remaining time versus a shot at $10 billion in prize money. Despite the long odds, he dove headlong into the challenge. There was no other way that a second-year community college student could net that kind of payday. And, as one unauthorized biography would later claim: "[Jason Harper] had grown weary of his financial situation. He had become exhausted by constantly living on the brink of starvation and homelessness . . . more than anything, He craved attention and acceptance."

With a spiral-bound journal, the same one that remains on display beneath the bulletproof glass at the National Archives, Jason Harper began to do what he always did: Sketch. An idea would come to his head and immediately flow through his left arm to his hand and then the paper. Sitting back, he would cast judgment before turning to the next blank page. Then another, and another. If the inside front cover is counted, which it typically is in this case because he drew on it as well, it was page twenty-two when inspiration struck—that was where he sketched a giant vacuum cleaner sucking the excess carbon dioxide out of the air. The scene depicted a hand reaching down from outer space into the atmosphere as it held the end of an old-style vacuum cleaner handle, a straight chrome pipe. He added wispy lines to indicate motion and airflow. The black dots filling the paper represented CO_2. He wondered to himself: *Why can't we just suck it all out?*

Then, leaning back in his favorite chair at the library, he held up the notebook with outstretched arms. By cocking it a few degrees to his left, he saw the vacuum nozzle in a vertical orientation. With a jolt of inspiration, he sat tall and his pencil danced across page twenty-two. Starting at the bottom of the sheet, he sketched a tube which spanned from the ground and continued straight up into outer space. Scattered about the tube, he added small boxes resembling checkerboards. He then scrawled some notes in the left-hand margin:

Outer space is a vacuum. If you build a tube tall enough to stretch into space, you'll have 24/7 suction that requires zero energy to run. If you outfit the tube with grates that have filters, then you can suck all the bad carbon dioxide out and leave the good stuff behind.

At the top of the page in oversized all-caps, he added a title: "SPACE TUBE." Thoughts of the many zeroes to be added to the balance of his bank account—he would finally have a reason to get one—filled his mind, and it caused him to laugh. The absurdity of it all, the audacity, and the name itself—Space Tube—felt ridiculous and out of reach. But he would go ahead and submit it to the CLIMA office anyway. His college, just like all the others, had a representative on campus to vet first-round submissions.

The line shuffled forward until Jason finally arrived at the service window. Never looking up, the woman, who was pushing sixty, peered through her glasses at page twenty-two. Placing her pointer finger on the notes, she followed them down the margin, uttering only, "Okay, okay, I see, okay." Then, for the first time since he had been in the hour-long line, she looked up.

"Okay, Mr. Harper," she said. "Please come into the door here to my right. I will be there momentarily."

At the same time Jason opened the door, the woman posted a sign that read, "Your CLIMA representative will return after a ten-minute break."

Standing in a room tailormade for bureaucrats, Jason fidgeted with the metal wire poking out from his spiral-bound notebook. From around the corner, she appeared.

"Please, Mr. Harper, have a seat," she said, pointing at the empty chair on the other side of the café-style table. "Tell me about your drawing."

"Well, it's just like it says, it's a Space Tube—a giant space vacuum that sucks away CO_2 by shooting it into outer space, while leaving behind the good air in the atmosphere. The best part of all is that it doesn't require any energy to run because space is just one massive vacuum. There is huge untapped potential up there."

"I can see that, but how do you prevent it from sucking away the good air, too?"

"That's the best part," Jason was always quick on his feet, a valuable trait growing up at the Hilliard House, "you see these filters? They allow only carbon dioxide to pass through."

"And what are those filters made of?" she pressed.

Without skipping he beat, he retorted, "It's dibutyl lauroyl glutamide." He also excelled at the art of bluffing. They were learning about the compound in one of his political science courses, the chemical was the subject of a class action lawsuit.

"Um-hum, okay."

"It's super common, actually." In a literal sense, he was not lying, as dibutyl lauroyl glutamide was a common ingredient in most brands of makeup and other skin care products. But claiming it would be sufficient for carbon dioxide filtration would have been scoffed at by any first-year chemistry student. Fortunately, the CLIMA representative bought it.

"Truthfully, I really don't know what to make of this thing, this Space Tube. But I do think it may have some merit and is potentially worthy of further consideration," she said while filling out an official-looking government form. "Congratulations, Mr. Harper, you're moving on to the next round. I'm going to refer this to the regional CLIMA officer for a closer review."

———

The worst-case scenario had been overshot once again, as the Great Melt put the planet on the final stretch toward its inevitable demise. Only, it would have been inaccurate to say the *planet* was heading for trouble because what most everyone did not seem to understand was that it was the *human beings*, who were about to meet their doom. The planet would be just fine. In ten or twenty million years—a tiny blip in time considering the four-and-a-half billion years it had been around before mankind began sucking its blood—it would be as good as new, better in fact, after finally shaking the parasites loose. The carbon would eventually work its way back into the ground. Maybe whatever should evolve next—perhaps highly advanced cockroaches, or super intelligent rodents—will learn the lesson from its bipedal forefathers and leave it trapped there. Let the blood be.

The regional officer fast-tracked page twenty-two to the state officer who then rubber stamped it on the way to the Feds. Jason Harper was informed that he was one of ten finalists and was invited to Colorado Springs to present his idea. During the Great Melt, Washington, DC found itself drowning under a surging Atlantic tide. All the statues and artifacts were hastily relocated to higher ground at the base of the Rocky Mountains—the nation's new capital city.

The conference room table was lined by mid-level military officers, fastidious engineers, and an assortment of skeptical CLIMA personnel.

"Tell us about your Space Tube concept, Mr. Harper," the woman seated at the middle of the table began the meeting.

After Jason finished his brief explanation, the woman appealed one-by-one to the various attendees with the same question for each of them, "Tell me why this can't work?" The conversation went on all afternoon. Many agreed with the basic premise of the design, but several expressed doubt as to the viability of the carbon filters. And to call it a carbon filter at all was a misnomer because it was all the good stuff—nitrogen and oxygen—that would have to be filtered. The carbon dioxide would have to pass through the filter on its way to outer space, while the nitrogen and oxygen would have to remain. An air quality specialist at the meeting reminded everyone that Argon also makes up one percent of the atmosphere and it was critical that it remain, too. He said there was no such thing as a filter that could do what had been described. The woman responded by digging deeper. "Well, could there be?" He answered with hesitation, but in the affirmative.

Jason said very little. Everything he needed to communicate was already scribbled down in black and white by his Dixon Ticonderoga Number Two. The questions directed his way were along the lines of how the idea came to be, to which he answered, "I don't know, it just popped into my head." Asked about his training, "I'm a second-year college student, technically a sophomore, but I've got one more pre-req to take before it's official. I'll probably major in poli sci." Asked about his home life. "I don't know, it's complicated, I guess. Right now, I'm living in the Hilliard House—the projects—with a buddy." Asked about his personal life. "No, no girlfriend if that's what you mean." Asked about his interest in working on further developing his project. "Yeah, for sure. Yes."

Over the next few days, Jason remained in Colorado Springs where he continued to answer the same questions asked in different ways. One meeting turned into the next. The hardest part, as he would reveal later, was all the handshaking. He hated shaking hands. Later, he would become known for greeting everyone with a fist bump, which was all the skin-to-skin contact he could tolerate. It is estimated that Jason shook more hands during this three-day period than at any other point in his life. And it was brutal, exhausting. Still, a $10 billion prize hung in the balance and he was in the running—the top ten.

During the third day, Jason was called into a corner office just before he was scheduled to be driven to the airport and flown back home.

"Mr. Harper," the woman began, with a surprising air of formality. "We have made a decision. And I would like to share it with you."

"Okay," was all Jason could manage to say in response.

"We have narrowed the finalists down to three. And you are one of them. Congratulations, Mr. Harper."

"Wow, thank you!" Jason's breath left his lungs before he was able to complete the sentence.

"But, just so you understand, we have decided to change up the process a bit. Since there is so much at stake here, and we have just one shot at getting this right, we are going to provide financing to each of the three projects so that all of you may build a fully functioning prototype. Whichever one works the best will be awarded the prize money and will be fully funded for production. Do you understand, Mr. Harper?"

"Yes, I do. Makes sense."

"Do you have any questions, Mr. Harper?"

"I guess, just one. When do we get started?"

"Tomorrow, Mr. Harper. We have an apartment waiting for you right here in Colorado Springs. It will be yours for the duration of your stay. Everything you need while you are here will be provided by CLIMA. You will be expected to give us all of your effort, Mr. Harper, every ounce of energy and focus—everything you've got. I'm not speaking in hyperbole when I say that the fate of the human race depends on it. Am I clear, Mr. Harper?"

"Yes, yes ma'am," he addressed her as "ma'am" for the first time.

The woman stood up and straightened her suit jacket. Observant of Jason's discomfort with handshakes, she instead patting him the back on their way through the door. Without her knowledge, he winced as if stung by a bee.

7

Most of the recorded history covering Jason Harper's first nineteen months in Colorado Springs were consistent. There were some notable exceptions, however. After the Pope decreed and codified that Jason Harper was, in fact, the Second Coming of Jesus Christ, the Vatican took creative license in the retelling of the story. Unlike the rest of the Christian faith, which first considered the addition of what would have been called the New New Testament, most denominations instead opted for a publication to supplement the existing canon. The Book of Jason is now widely accepted by most church-goers, but it deviates from Catholicism in two meaningful ways. First, the Book of Jason takes a more nuanced approach to the most intractable question, claiming He was not the Second Coming of Jesus, but rather, His brother. And, second, the Book of Jason declines to embellish the Colorado Springs details, instead relying upon eyewitness accounts to offer what the historical societies have claimed to be a mostly accurate summary.

The Pope went a different direction. Today, Catholics believe that Jason was never one of three finalists, but that he was selected as the sole winner of CLIMA's contest before ever having arrived in Colorado. This claim, of course, is easily debunked. It simply did not happen that way. The other meaningful way in which the Pope deviates from the leading scripture, the Book of Jason, is in describing the initial development of the Space Tube, which flummoxes many Catholics because the truth, as it turns out, is much more interesting than the myth. It is a verifiable fact that Jason did not have immediate success. Instead, for much of those first nineteen months, there was real doubt as to whether or not the thing would work at all. That is the story most everyone has embraced because they saw it with their own eyes—it's when Jason Harper became a household name.

When CLIMA announced that it had winnowed the millions of submissions it had received down to just ten, that is the point where the networks were finally able to elbow their way in. Since the advent of reality TV, it had enjoyed a steady and uninterrupted rise in popularity. The networks embraced it for its low cost—Hoyamania went down as the most profitable show of all time—low risk, and high ratings. There was no other way to hold the attention of the audience than by stringing them along with unpredictability, which equals drama, which equals profits. There was nothing more unpredictable during this period than the survival of mankind. That's why the network executives loved it.

The people at CLIMA promptly blew a hole into the meticulously crafted drama when they dropped from ten finalists down to three. The networks had argued for inviting sixty-four candidates and entering them into a basketball tournament-style head-to-head match-up format, complete with brackets. Expert analysts had been hired to commentate throughout the production of the prototypes. Betting pools were formed by viewers. Broadcast executives had been drooling over the weeks of suspense, knowing they would hold audiences in the palms of their hands. There were some doubters in the industry who questioned the highly technical subject matter and the strict adherence to math and science—something that no longer appealed to Americans, as the country had quietly and unceremoniously fallen to the bottom of the list in those areas worldwide. It didn't matter, the counterargument went, because the competition would get everyone excited. Everyone would pick teams. People loved picking sides, almost as much as much as they loved drama. This had both. So, it was a massive disappointment when CLIMA went behind the backs of the networks and unilaterally winnowed the field. When confronted by the executives, CLIMA's position was unequivocal: "We're running out of time."

To this day, everyone remembers the day Jason Harper first appeared on their screen. The nineteen-year-old kid was shown standing next to the other two finalists: a middle-aged woman and an old man, both in thick glasses, and both looking about what you would expect someone who would be engineering something to save the world would look like. Not Jason. He stuck out. He gave the audience a show. Immediately, he became the odds-on favorite in most betting pools. Not because of his invention, almost no one understood it, or cared enough to learn about it, but because of who he was. His backstory was so compelling. A second-year community college student with a minor rap sheet—petty theft, forgery, negligent discharge of a firearm, bank fraud, and driving with a suspended license—who grew up in a housing project. Everyone loves a rags-to-riches story, it was practically written into the DNA sequence of all Americans. This was one in the making. And if the kid could save mankind from itself in the process of becoming fabulously wealthy, all the better.

Everyone was glued to their televisions as the three contestants got to work. One of them, the woman, made for poor ratings. Her proposal consisted of building a sprawling network of algae ponds, which were designed to extract the excess carbon dioxide from the air above. Until recently, she had been spending her days employed by one of the laboratories funded by an association of food manufacturers. She specialized in genetically modifying vegetables. After hours, she remained at the lab to fiddle around with her own private Frankenstein, GMO algae. It did the job, and gobbled up carbon much faster than the original, so much so that the ponds would turn into crude oil after a short exposure. Part of her proposal included the "regular and ongoing re-sequestration of hydrocarbons." In other words, pumping oil back into the ground. But there was very little drama involved in the close-up shots of bubbling pond scum, with or without genetic modification, so the audience, and therefore the networks, did not spend much time with her.

The old guy, however, was bursting with personality and enthusiasm combining brilliance, bravado, and senility in equal parts. He spoke in an exited clip, overusing the words "epic" and "blown away." Everything blew him away—"I was blown away by the research"—and "epic"sometimes found its way into his sentences twice. "We're on a epic journey of epic proportions." Now, this was entertainment. Worth watching. He envisioned outfitting every city in America with massive semitransparent glass domes, which he said "would make the carbon dioxide irrelevant." By encasing everyone into giant UV-protected snow globes, he would be replacing the natural atmosphere with one of his own making. The network commentators frequently compared his idea to something called the Biosphere which had apparently been done before, but they noted, it had mixed reviews. What he was conceptualizing was much the same thing, they said, and many in the scientific community voiced their support for the idea. Not the people. It was just the opposite with the viewing audience. They wanted Jason Harper.

The Space Tube prototype was built adjacent to the Colorado Springs Landfill. CLIMA officials scrambled to find a secure location away from the general public, but for a variety of logistical reasons—mostly because they were running out of time—the decision was settled. They overpaid for the land and got started while the ink on the title was still wet. Working around the clock under towers of flood lights, contractors, who up to that point had only built pipelines running horizontally, soon got used to the idea of going up. Day after day, the network commentators settled into their director's chairs to narrate the action, interview the foreman, and, more than anything else, continue to visit with Jason. At first, it was just a couple of local kids who showed up at the chain-link fence encircling the construction site. Jason was taken aback when they asked for his autograph. The next day there were four. The day after that sixteen. The crowd grew exponentially until CLIMA decided to install temporary stadium seating and hire additional security guards. Everyone who showed up would be allowed just fifteen minutes of observation before they were escorted from the bleachers. The best seat in the house, however, was in the living room. The networks knew a good thing when they saw it. Jason Harper was saying all the right things in exactly the right way. It was not Hoyamania, but at least the viewers had a compelling new character. And drama.

It took just seven months to reach the Karman Line, which is where space officially begins, sixty-two miles up. Visitors and viewers alike marveled at the sight, the Space Tube. The base was anchored by a circular concrete foundation, embedded deep into the soil. Debate raged on between the contractors and the engineers as to whether it was necessary to pave over the dirt floor. Ultimately, they appealed to the CLIMA officer on site and his instructions never once deviated: "Whatever's fastest." Measuring 156 feet in diameter and made up of the latest, lightest, and, as it turned out, least costly, silica polymer composite, the Space Tube resembled a giant soda straw stretching from the ground all the way into outer space. The engineers always doubted it would stand up straight, but theorized the force of the suction taking place after the column penetrated the stratosphere would hold it upright. The trick was getting it to stay vertical during construction. That was, perhaps, the most significant hurdle.

During one of the many late night engineering meetings, someone again repeated the line: "Necessity is the mother of invention." For some reason, it did not annoy everyone this time. It was the woman from NASA who came up the idea. And there was nothing at all original about it. The application was different, but the technology was well known: jet engines and gyroscopes. The Space Tube was outfitted with three adjustable and moveable steel rings, each of them complete with a series of twelve jet engines along with the same number of gyroscopes. The jets were positioned on the ring in the same positions as numbers on an old-style clock. If the unit started leaning, the rockets would respond by firing in coordination to push it back. The propulsive force continually kept the structure upright, no matter how tall it became. Once it crossed the Karman Line, they were no longer necessary. The suction force of the space vacuum alone would handle the job. But until the construction workers reached that point, they would build up another mile before stopping to move the bottom ring up to the top. Another vertical mile after that and they would repeat the process by unclamping the bottom ring and leapfrogging up and over the other two. The "gyro jets," as one network commentator named them, never failed to keep everything true and plumb during construction. Workers marveled when they placed their old-fashioned levels on the outer walls. The bubble never strayed from dead center.

Other than keeping everything straight up and down, the other challenge was doing construction work in a space suit. It took some getting used to. From the beginning, Jason was adamant: "No robots." The animosity he had for the machines was palpable, and was no different from anybody growing up in the Hilliard House, but everyone on the project agreed that it was the right call because construction bots were of no use when it came critical thinking. This type of building was a new frontier for everyone. Even though the workers were outfitted with parachutes, the last thing anyone wanted was to get bumped off the scaffolding twenty-miles up by a dumbass droid. Construction bots were great for framing skyscrapers, but this was something entirely different. Plus no one wanted to deal with the morale problems they always created within the crew. Not to mention the resentment.

Everyone on the job site was reminded that the composite building materials were engineered to have some flexibility. The tube was designed to move and bend with the high winds that were always whipping through the stratosphere. But the thing never budged. Not once. Pulsating, glowing red lights dotted the tube every 300 feet to shoo away local air traffic. At the base, a submarine-style door was installed with a wheel to crank it open or ratchet it closed. Above the door, a light toggled between green and red. Green meant the valve was closed, "Okay to enter," there is no suction. Red, on the other hand, warned "Stay back," the vacuum is working. Inside, next to the door, a series of control panels filled with buttons and switches and screens hugged the right side of the wall. The last detail was added the day a painter from the nearby Air Force base was hoisted in a hydraulic lift approximately fifty feet above the door. In massive, government-issued all caps black stencil, he spent the afternoon stenciling the words "SPACE TUBE."

———

"Test Day" had been promoted by the networks for months. It was anticipated worldwide, even more so than the Super Bowl that year. Spectators began taking their seats at dawn, an hour after the commentators began commentating. Their breath visible against chill of the early morning, their manic energy touchable. The entire planet was eager to erupt in one single massive emotional cathartic explosion. The fast-approaching end of times had been weighing heavily on everyone, exacting a common emotional trauma to all of mankind. People were ready for good news. Ready for a hero. Ready to learn the world had been saved. Ready to celebrate Jason Harper.

The senior CLIMA official spoke to two of the commentators, outlining the parameters of the test. It would be simple, she said. "We will open the valve at exactly eight o'clock, about a half-hour from now, which will allow the Space Tube to begin its vacuuming process. If it works as planned," she explained to viewers, "the local atmosphere will show a steady decline in carbon dioxide concentration. Randomly placed air monitors will provide us with measurements as we move forward throughout the day." After a few more questions, the same ones she had already answered during interviews with the other networks, she excused herself and hustled over to the control tent.

Leaning over the shoulder of one of the three-dozen engineers positioned in front of a rat's nest of fiber optic cable and mainframe computers, she nodded in agreement. Next, moving over to an empty workstation in the front corner of the tented room, she climbed a chair using it as a step up to the tabletop. She then called out to the standing-room-only crowd of one hundred or so CLIMA officials, scientists, politicians, engineers, and military personnel.

"Excuse me, everyone, can I have your attention," she did not ask, but commanded. The buzz in the room settled after a few counts.

"At this time, I want to remind everyone of what is at stake today. What we are doing here is nothing less than a last chance. I need everyone to execute. I need you all to bring your A-game. We can do this. Is everyone with me?" she asked, and a roar of affirmation filled the space.

"On my command, commence the countdown at T-minus ten minutes," she then paused for a few long moments, stretching her right arm above her head as she studied the sweeping hand of the clock hoisted at the back of the room. "Okay, now!" her outstretched arm dropped in unison. The buzz returned to the room as she muttered to herself, "And may God speed."

Billions of audience members worldwide saw a digital countdown clock on their screens. Most of the networks chose to focus on the Space Tube from the vantage point of the camera stand at the top of the nearby bleachers. Some also included a smaller inset stream to capture Jason's reaction in real time. In one voice, the world called out in joyful exuberance, "Ten, nine, eight, seven, six, five, four, three, two, one!" The ground began to rumble then shake, and a deep humming sound took hold—a titanic vacuum cleaner stirred to life.

"How many Torrs?" the woman called out, inquiring about the measurement used to identify the sucking power of a vacuum.

"Eighty-one and dropping fast." That was good, the atmosphere holds steady at about one-hundred-and-one torrs, so things were heading the right direction.

"Where do we stand now?" she asked again immediately.

"Sixteen!" the engineer shouted, incapable of containing his emotions. He had trouble reading the panel through the tears in his eyes. "Seven! Four! Three! Two-point-six!"

Two-point six torrs was better than any of the engineers had projected, and it was more than enough to extract the carbon from the atmosphere. It would take a year for the Space Tube to cleanse the air of the entire planet, and bring the carbon dioxide levels back down to sub-300 parts per million levels, but the Earth would begin the healing process within weeks on its way toward normalization while the air was being scrubbed clean.

"Open the filter gates!" the woman yelled.

The lead engineer called back, "Filters gates opening at three, two, one! Filters gates are open!"

"Have we received our first air monitor reading?" the woman inquired, trying to smooth out her voice in a failed effort to conceal her nerves.

"Not yet, just the baseline pre-test reading of 2,833 parts per million, which is the average of the fifty monitors we have positioned at various altitudes," the engineer responded. "Wait, hold on. Here's the first reading: 2,841 ppm," he said before adding, "But, it's too soon." Frozen in place, he held his breath for the next reading, "2,828," he called out. Then unable to contain his emotion, he began to lift out of seat as he blubbered, "2,826—it's dropping!" A moment later, "2,825!" The next reading, which would not appear for a full minute, came back. "2,833," he said more as a question than a statement. Over the remaining hour, he offered the numbers as soon as they arrived: "2,840; 2,829; 2,842; 2,827; 2,833; 2,833; 2,831; 2,830; 2,836; 2,827; 2,833; 2,828; 2,833; 2,834."

The next hour yielded similar results, and averaged 2,834. Each subsequent hour brought more of the same. The moment a new reading was retrieved from the air monitors above, the numbers flashed on billions who remained welded to their screens. The world groaned in unison with each update. The commentators worked hard to keep them engaged, to offer hope. But their tone soon transformed from clipped exuberance—a Christmas morning giddiness—to funeral parlor somber. CLIMA representatives, who had earlier strained to contain their jubilance during their on-air interviews, now only offered a curt "No comment" before striding, head-down away from the camera bots.

By the end of the day, it was clear that the Space Tube had failed. Most networks wrapped up the broadcast by zooming in to capture a despondent and inconsolable Jason Harper, collapsed in his chair off to the side of the tented control room. His face revealed what everyone was now feeling: shock, resignation, defeat, and devastation. As heartbroken as the viewing audience was that the thing did not work—the realization set in for good that there was now no stopping Armageddon—they were more disappointed, by a two-to-one margin the polling showed later, that Jason Harper did not receive the prize money.

_____

8

The woman with the algae pond idea—"Slime Lady," as viewers called her—failed next. It was not so much that her idea did not work because it did. The problem was one of scale. There was not enough time to build the thousands of ponds that would be required. A month later, "Dome Guy" received disappointing news following the broadcast of his test. His prototype, like the algae, was successful, but he ran into the same roadblocks concerning time and scale. There was not enough of either to merit the prize money. With all three ideas debunked, CLIMA announced it was reopening the competition. This time, the number of applications totaled just seventeen percent of what they had been before. Everyone who had been feverish in their search of answers was now either partying their way toward a certain demise, or spending their days reminiscing with family and friends, perusing old photographs and watching long-forgotten childhood birthday party videos.

Although it was not reported at the time, CLIMA had not given up on the Space Tube completely. Jason Harper and his team had redoubled their efforts, this time focusing all of their attention and resources on the carbon dioxide filters. They had been encouraged by the power of the vacuum—consistent at two-point-six Torr—which required no power to operate. They just had to solve the filtration system problem. It was uncharted waters because it had never been done before, but neither had rescuing the entire human race, more than one CLIMA official noted. The issue was not so much filtering carbon dioxide, in fact, calling it a CO_2 filter in the first place was incorrect because the whole idea was to ensure that carbon dioxide was passing through on its way to outer space. "If you took a dust filter on a typical Shop Vac," one of the engineers liked asking and answering rhetorical questions using this example, "then what do you get? A dusty filter. We need to figure out a way for that dust to pass through, while leaving the gasses we need to breathe intact."

The Shop Vac analogy tortured Jason Harper. He spent nearly a year sketching, frantic in his search for different ways to understand vacuum cleaners. There was no doubt in his mind that this was a perception problem—just like all problems—and seeing it in a different way, making different connections, was the key to solving it. The fact that it was just out of reach caused his frustration to boil over. And when it did, he knew it was time to get moving. Walking was always a part of life, maybe because he had to count mostly on bipedal transportation to get himself wherever he needed to go. His mother was mostly of no use, not enough to depend upon, anyway. Getting a ride from her was considered a bonus, a once-in-a-while thing, not the norm. To get himself anywhere, he knew he had to walk. Pacing back and forth in front of the Space Tube brought him some peace. "If nothing else, if we run out of time," he said to himself, "at least I can leave this Earth knowing that a kid from the Hilliard House built this thing—one big, giant-ass cosmic vacuum cleaner."

Day and night, he would walk, always drawing sketches in his mind for new filtration concepts. How to suck out the carbon dioxide while leaving all the good air, the oxygen and nitrogen, behind? One idea was discarded after another. Maybe the air pollution expert was right, maybe it could not be done. As he circled the base of the Space Tube for what must have been his ten-thousandth time, he noticed that the bleacher seating had been removed. House-sized bulldozers began were pushing garbage into its place. Against the chain-link fence, a wall of trash grew in height before it topped over, a wave crashing on the beach. Just like every municipal dump in the country, the Colorado Springs Landfill was out of space. Garbage was a byproduct of economic prosperity, so everyone learned to live with it. Every city and town now had manmade mountain ranges. Mounds and mounds of the stuff. If carbon dioxide was filling the air, then garbage was swallowing the soil.

What happened next is best captured by this passage in the Book of Jason:

On a typical hot, dry, windy day, afternoon, He was out for his customary daily walk, communing privately with His brother, the Lord Jesus Christ, when He spotted one of the great, yellow beasts rise up from behind The Fence of Revelation. A divine gust lifted The Papers into the ether, where He watched while they were carried to Heaven upon the wings of Angels.

Jason Harper never disputed this account, although he was much less poetic in his description with reporters. He was always clear that it was a business idea. "See a need, fill a need," is what he said of the day he saw the bulldozer launch trash into the air, which then caught a thermal and took off, almost straight up into the sky above.

"Why not?" was his answer to many things, and this was only the beginning.

"Because, it doesn't matter," the CLIMA woman replied before answering his question with one of her own: "Who cares if there's trash or not? If the whole ship is about to go down, what difference does tidying-up the local dump make?"

As always, Jason Harper had an ace of clubs stuffed into his sock. "I've already received clearance from the commanding officer here at the Peterson Air Force Base. He loves the idea. And, so does the general manager at the dump." He had not spoken to either of them, never even met them.

"Okay, fine. Whatever," she motioned him away in exasperation. "I've got more important things to do. Whatever they want to do. I don't care."

Jason immediately left the room and began dialing his phone. It was a simple street hustle. Within the hour, the commanding officer and the general manager were praising his brilliance. They were both on board for testing what the community college student christened the "Harper Refuse Ejection," or "HRE." Military guys, he knew, loved initials and acronyms and he wanted to make sure his name was on it, so he would get the credit and, eventually, the money from the trash clearing business he began thinking about. If one of those second-round CLIMA applications saved the world, he would be sitting pretty with his HRE service. *See a need, fill a need.* Curiously, this part of the story was wholly omitted from the Book of Jason.

––––––––

Early the next morning, an entire squadron of newly enlisted Air Force airmen appeared on site. The center panel of the chain-link fence—The Fence of Revelation, which remains on display in Vatican City—was removed, as one airman after another walked through the door of the Space Tube to hand-deliver a pile of trash. The center of the room had been blown out, or more accurately sucked out by the massive space vacuum leaving behind a twenty-foot-deep crater. The decision to not pave over the dirt floor with concrete turned out to be a good one because it saved a whole lot of time and money, but it sure did leave behind a giant hole in the ground. The commanding officer's instructions had been clear and succinct, as usual: "Head to the dump and fill that thing up with trash."

By the end of the day, the Space Tube was packed drum-tight with garbage. "Locked and loaded," according the commanding officer. The test was scheduled for the next day, just before noon. The T-minus order was given with indifference. There was no rousing pregame pep talk this time around. "Ten, nine, eight, seven, six, five, four, three, two, one." Rumble, shake, and the deep guttural hum—a giant space vacuum doing what vacuums do.

"Is it gone?" the commanding officer turned toward Jason and the general manager of the dumpsite.

"I don't know, let's go have a look," the GM answered.

The three of them walked toward the Space Tube, each taking turns looking through the porthole on the door.

"Son of a gun!" the commanding officer exclaimed, shaking his head in disbelief before turning to Jason. "You did it, son! You did it! All that garbage is gone. Son of a gun."

Stunned silence rendered the general manger speechless. He was not sure if he should celebrate or begin mourning his inevitable loss of employment. Either way, it was good news he decided. His wife had been begging him to quit, so they could spend their final months together poring over the trove of family photos.

"I'm hungry!" the commanding officer called out, rare in indulging an impulse. "Come on, boys, I'm buying!" Jason fought the impulse to recoil after the officer reached out to rest his massive gold ring-cladded hand on his upper back.

As the trio began making their way across the vacant, dust-covered lot spanning the distance between the base of the Space Tube and the waiting ground transport a hundred yards away, Jason was looking down in an effort to calm himself. The left hand of the commanding officer resting between his shoulder blades made him want to run away, never to be found. "Focus on your feet," he said to himself. "Breathe. Stay calm." That is when he first saw it, the crisp definition of a shadow enveloping the ground and immediately cooling his body. His synapses fired away in overdrive as it made connections. There was not a single cloud in the sky, because there were never any clouds in the sky. It was much too hot, always. There was never anything in the sky except for never-ending haziness—and the vengeful sun.

"Just a second," he said, mostly to himself, before wheeling around. Closing his right eye, he lined up his left arm, leaning back and pointing four of his outstretched fingers toward the Space Tube. Then, lifting up his arm further, he lined it up with the boiling midday sun above, which disappeared as the shadow continued to grow.

Without a word Jason sprinted toward the tiny makeshift command center.

"He sure is a strange kid," the commanding officer said to the general manger. They both looked in the direction of a sprinting Jason Harper, whose feet had yet to touch the ground.

"Come on," the commanding officer now placed his meaty hand on the back of the general manager. "Let's you and me grab some food. We've got a lot to talk about."

Scholars would argue later that Jason Harper's aversion to touch was a double-edged sword. An essay penned by one of them titled "Live by the Sword, Die by the Sword" made a strong case. Without his looking down that day very intensely at his feet, he may never have noticed the shadow, something the Book of Jason deemed the "Holy Ghost." But it was not a ghost at all it. It was fifty tons of crap that the people of Colorado Springs no longer wanted. Fifty tons of crap that was recently replaced by one hundred tons of some other crap, somewhere else in the landfill. There was never enough crap to satisfy the urge for crap. Crap, crap, crap. Everyone needed crap. Everyone wanted crap. But, crap, as Jason Harper had just learned, was the one and only thing that could save mankind.

The engineers at the low-budget, two-table control center asked him to slow down and say it again, which he did, at least three times. When he snatched a pen from one of their pocket protectors, flipped to the backside of an Air Force parts catalog, and started drawing, they immediately got it. One of the men, who had craned his neck to see over the shoulders of his colleagues, stumbled backward and began mumbling to himself as if in a trance. "Oh, my God. Oh, my God. Oh, my God." Then, he reached for his phone. When his wife answered, he burst into tears before struggling to compose himself. He said in a low and slow voice, "Honey, I've got some really great news."

Today, that drawing on the back of the parts catalog is held under lock-and-key at the Pragmatist Party Headquarters. In a sloppy and hasty manner, it depicts the Space Tube poking through the sky into outer space. At the top end of the giant vacuum it shows a smattering of dots. An arrow points to the dots, labeling them "Trash." In the top right-hand corner of the coffee-stained page, the sun shines. Its rays project to the ground, while the trash floating in outer space cast a small shadow. The arrow pointing to the shadow is labeled "Cool." At the top of the sheet, he wrote the prophetic words, which kindergartners are now required to memorize and recite before moving on to first grade: "More trash equals more shadows; more shadows equals more cooling; more cooling equals salvation!"

———

The meeting was moved to Auditorium One, the largest room available. And it was filled, standing room only. Somehow, the networks never caught wind of it. Question after question was lobbed at Jason, who marched back and forth in front of the whiteboard, pausing on occasion to sketch supplements to his explanations. At the top of the board he had written "2BIRDS" in block letters. Underneath, he added the following without saying anything, only the squeaking of the marker could be heard: "2 (my second try). B (Before). I (It). R (Really). D (Does). S (Suck)." When he wrote the last word, "Suck," everyone laughed in admiring approval. Jason then wheeled around to elaborate. "Look, it's the truth. There's no getting around it, things are about to really suck around here in a big way as the Earth continues to heat up and we suffocate on CO_2. I didn't have much time to come up with a name, but this works. Plus, it's a word that has two meanings—a double entendre." He paused to survey the room left to right, savoring the fact that he now held their rapt attention. "It means what I just explained—'Before It Really Does Suck'—but it's also a play on that old saying, 'killing two birds with one stone.'" The room erupted.

Jason waved at them to quiet down, to retake their seats. He paused again, this time waiting until there was complete silence. "We will be racing against time," he warned. "My ability," only a few in attendance noted his switching from "we" to "my" in his speech, "to manufacture the 2BIRDS quickly—likely thousands of them worldwide—will determine whether or not mankind is spared." He went on to talk about World War II, which he had been studying in one of his political science classes back home. "We beat Hitler only because we out-manu-factured him. It was all hands on deck—every available man, woman, and child. Every factory, running around the clock, twenty-four seven, is what it took." Scanning the audience, he closed with, "And that's what it's going to take now. I need your help to get this done."

As if they were propelled upward by the rising side of a teeter totter, everyone shot up from their chairs at once and began pounding their hands together, shouting and quivering in wild admiration—and with complete, unquestioning devotion to the man who would save the world.

9

Days living in infamy are rare. Once in a generation. Most days do not live beyond the twenty-four hours in which they existed in the first place, especially when they are stacking up as a row of dominoes, falling into one another on their way toward a largely uneventful anni-hilation. And that is exactly how those last days were in those last years. Uneventful. Everyone could see the end of the train, but nothing could be done to stop the momentum once it started. Just like all the other days that lived in infamy—Pearl Harbor, 9/11, Dirty Bomb, Copenhagen—those days where everyone remembers in exacting detail precisely what they ate for breakfast and the outfit they wore to school, those days, which most everyone experienced in the comfort of their living rooms planted in front of the television, those days are over. A day cannot live in infamy, or otherwise, when there are no more days in which to live.

It was the broadcast of "The Test" which served as the dividing line. Before that day, hope remained, albeit small. After, it was over. All that was left was to wait for the last domino to fall. Had the prototype worked, everyone would have remembered what they ate that day. Now, it was nothing more than another bread crumb leading to the gallows. The entire world watched, just as it did when one-sixth of

Mumbai was leveled by a single "dirty bomb"—a micro-nuke—carried in the backpack by a misinformed Pakistani teenager. It had been a day seared into history, a day to live in infamy. What everyone so desperately craved now was a day that did not live in infamy, but some other thing, whatever the opposite of infamy was—that's what people wanted. While mankind became ever more fractured and splintered, deep down while no one said it out loud, everyone was searching for the same thing: a hero.

During those last days, parents were forced to answer many tough questions. When compared to the other ones, whether or not to send the kids to school fell far down the list. Mark Sapin could never understand why his parents thought learning long division was so important in the face of his assured extinction. Most of his friends stopped showing up and his entire school was now consolidated into one classroom, all twenty-one students. Had he been a fourth grader in some other generation, he would have played baseball during recess instead of speculating on which day they would all die. Unfortunately for Mark, his parents continued to hold out hope. They put all of their faith in a second-year community college student, just like everyone else. At least until The Test.

There were a few teachers who remained, resigned to go down with the ship. They continued to look for opportunities to tie their lessons to real-world events, which was becoming more difficult to do. The networks stopped reporting the news, but when they began advertising their upcoming coverage of The Test, the teachers saw it as a useful learning opportunity. But, more than that, they wanted to watch it themselves to find out if they had been spared. Mark reported that his parents rose early that day to make a feast. He was awakened by the smell of bacon and the crackling of fried eggs. For the first time in a long time, his mother had dusted off her grandmother's secret recipe for pancakes. She added a can of 7-UP to the batter, just like Grandma did. His parents were giddy, and they kept repeating a name that was new to him: Jason Harper. "They just seemed so," he would struggle for the words in the interrogation room, "so happy." At school, the entire day was comprised of television watching.

Dinner was different. "It was the polar opposite of breakfast, my parents went from being so happy to just completely depressed," he would reveal. "The thing I remember most was the expression on my mom's face. She looked into my eyes for a long time. She was just so damned sad. She didn't say a word. She didn't have to. Her eyes said it all. They said, 'I'm so sorry.'" Recounting this interaction would have normally brought him to tears, but he would not allow himself to reveal the emotion for fear it could somehow be leveraged against him. "We loved Jason, all of us. Just like everyone else, we wanted him to be successful."

The questioning went on day and night. But there were no clocks and no windows, so Mark was unable to discern the time. Or the date. Or whether it was day or night. The lights remained clicked on and bearing down during the entire ordeal. They wanted to know everything, beginning to end. And he shared all of it. Most of it, anyway.

———

The most remarkable thing about the life of Mark Sapin is just how unremarkable it had been. "Normal" is the word people used to describe him during the investigation. "Nice" and "kind" and "generous" and "funny" came in at two, three, four, and five on the list, respectively. His formative years would provide no foreshadowing for what was to come—zero—which made it all the more confounding. Both of his parents worked. His mother was the secretary at his elementary school and the main reason he was unable to stop attending like everyone else. His father was a tiny cog in the wheel of a sprawling corporation. Just like his son he was a number cruncher, a data analyst.

Mark grew up lower middle class. Single-family dwelling. Single story ranch-style house. Three bedrooms. One bath. Detached garage. He spent his days riding his bike with the neighborhood kids. Never got into any trouble, at least nothing of any significance. Honor roll throughout. Boy Scouts. Basketball. Track. Class president. Friends who all turned out to be good, productive citizens. He was nice to his little sister. Loved his mom. Loved his dad. Loved his grandma. Loved his grandpa. Had a dog. And a cat. A fish at one time, a guinea pig another. Never so much as brought home anything less than a B+ on any of his many report cards. Funny, but not too funny where he hogged-up the spotlight. Married his high school sweetheart, had two kids, a boy and, as everyone knows by now—a girl.

As a gainfully employed member of Generation E—the "E" for "Extinction"—he was the rare citizen who had not just one, but two children. He and his wife had done their patriotic duty. To reproduce during this period of time was a bold move, at least for people with some measure of economic stature. Sure, the poverty-stricken bottom dwellers continued cranking them out like rabbits, but everyone else understood that producing offspring was an exercise in futility at best, and a one-way ticket to the lower class at worst. While the population continued to expand as a whole, one persistent fact remained: All the wrong people were procreating. Before long, according to the research cited by fretting politicians, America would become a country solely consisting of drug addicts, back alley whores, and, worst of all, economic non-factors.

The non-factors had been dragging down the economy for years, slowly eroding productivity and pulling along everyone with them by their unkempt fingernails. For the most part, the non-factors were easy to spot. But there were some who were able to hide in plain sight. A jobless thirty-three-year-old, for instance, who whittles away his time playing video games or making daily trips to the virtual brothels is a not-so-obvious non-factor. While it is true that he does pay a fee to enter the VR facility—likely funded by his parents' allowance—his indulgence in an alternative existence comes with no real contribution to the very real economy. He, just like the vagrant living under the bridge, is a non-factor. The net economic result arising from his consumption of resources equals zero. Fortunately for him, because he comes from an upper class family, zero is probably as bad as it will get, which is tolerable. Less than zero is not. Yet when he breathes air, precious and finite oxygen and nitrogen, it comes at the expense of another who had contributed, someone who does matter. Non-factors do not. The only thing they ever contribute is the exhalation of more carbon dioxide.

Years ago, people would wring their hands when it came to the non-factors. That is, before it was explained to them in terms everyone could understand. Sentimentality was to blame. They were told, "If you want more of the same, do more of the same. If you want less, do less." It was a hard lesson for everyone to learn, at least at first. But, the drawings accompanying the folksy metaphors helped, as always. Change came, as it always does: slowly and then suddenly. The ship had been heading the wrong direction for a long while. Small, imperceptible one-degree turns over vast distances led it far off course. A new captain was needed, someone who everyone respected. And listened to. And did not question. Someone who could get things done.

Generation E had grown weary. Many of them opted out altogether. Some flirted with the idea of becoming non-factors or skating just above that all-important line. It was unfair in many ways. Their parents caused this problem. Actually, it was their grandparents and great grandparents who were to blame, Generation X and Z and the Millennials. It was not Gen E's idea to burn hydrocarbons. And, although they did not sit down to the gluttonous seven course meal, they would be the ones to pick up the tab. All the wealth went to the previous generations who clutched it in their cold-dead hands until those cold-dead hands were pried open by their children and then later by their children's children. If you did not find yourself in this fortunate lineage, then you were most likely a non-factor. That is, unless you won the lottery or survived a television reality show. Having a job is a lifejacket which will keep you bobbing blissfully above the level below which the non-factors inhabit.

Of course, marrying into wealth is another option. But with the ubiquity of virtual brothels, who needs marriage? It's just another instance of sentimentality. In the last century, a rock-and-roll band called *The Beatles* wrote a famous song for a primitive time. The refrain repeated by the mop-headed English foursome was "all you need is love." If they were around today they would sing "all you need is money." Money had become everything. Love was only friction and resistance, a speed bump on the way toward the goal: Wealth. Everyone knows marriage is expensive—with the one notable caveat given to those who are cunning enough to marry into the upper class, which is becoming more difficult to do these days—and that the odds are long. Seven out of ten marriages end in divorce. In other words, there is a seventy percent chance that after gushing "I do," a sharp-elbowed family law attorney will eventually see to it that half of the assets evaporate. Gone. Not only is that stupid, it's dangerous—a great way to become a non-factor.

Efficiency requires the rigorous elimination of sentimentality in all of its forms. Marriage is chief among them, but a close second place goes to child rearing. America was once the land of large nuclear families, but despite the romanticism often associated with its heritage, the history books are clear in explaining the motivations of the early American pioneers: Money. It was the only reason for the Westward Expansion. But, back then, there were so much sentimentality, so many things standing in their way, including antiquated constructs like culture and poetry and friendships. Culture has finally been dispatched as a useful concept, and friendships only pencil out when they are employed as a means to an end. Poetry has no place, which is why it no longer exists—sentimentality has no use—poetry, almost by definition, is sentimentality.

Everywhere, and for everything, a score is kept—a running ledger of debits and credits. If it cannot be quantified, if it cannot be measured, then it should not be done. To do otherwise, at least too often, is to risk becoming the worst of the worst, a non-factor. Everyone has a value—a number—and that value translates to economic production, or it doesn't. If one does not create value, if one does not at least generate a positive score on the Productivity Matrix, then what is the point? Partying made rational sense after the broadcast of The Test, because everyone received confirmation that the world was, in fact, ending. But a year later, everything changed, and it did so in an instant. The dominoes stopped falling. As the saying goes, it was "slow then sudden."

———

The door clanked shut and Mark found himself sitting alone with her again. The interrogation room was flooded with artificial light, as always. Everything was stark white. It had become increasingly difficult to focus, to understand where one edge ended and another began. She placed the screen before him and turned up the volume to high. She wanted him to watch. She wanted him to see it. She thought it may be the thing that finally made him crack. Everyone had a breaking point. The funeral may be his. She would exploit his weakness—sentimentality—and use it against him.

Mark struggled to lift his head, which had been frozen into a semi-bowed position for who knows how long. He wanted to see the broadcast. At the front of the cathedral, a man shrouded in a purple cloak preached in a comforting and rhythmic baritone:

Praise be to Jason. It was He who showed us the way before sacrificing Himself for our salvation. He first saved all of creation then He rebuilt it in His image. It was He who never gave up, never gave in to temptation. It was He who remained humble before His brother, the Lord Jesus Christ, so that He could see His message, which was delivered on the wings of Angels. It was He who carried out the transcendent divine will of His father, God, who art in Heaven. Brothers and sisters, let us bow our heads together as we offer our eternal gratitude and selfless devotion to His word. In Jason's name we pray, Amen.

10

He told the interrogators everything about this part of his life. It was confusing to him why they wanted to know so much. How would these details make a difference? He began questioning the questioners. Not out loud, of course, but in his head. He started wondering whether they were just curious. Perhaps they just needed to hear a story. Maybe they wanted to know what it was like to love, and to be in love. How it felt to feel.

He began, as he always did, at the beginning. Mark Sapin met Angela Peters three days after his eighteenth birthday, which also happened to be the first day of school. Her parents told her that everything would work out for the best with this move. She would make friends and fit in. Fitting in was not a priority, it never was, but making friends was. Maybe that is why she was so willing to talk to the goofy guy with the wire-rimmed glasses.

Enrollment in Calc II was light. Just eight kids showed up to a class-room designed to hold thirty-two. When the teacher made his way to the chalkboard, he scanned the room to see everyone was scattered about, intent to keep their distance—math nerds tended to keep to themselves. It was then that he made a fateful decision. "Okay, class, we're all going to all get up and sit in these eight desks," he said, pointing to the first two rows at the front of the classroom.

Mark saw her when she walked through the door. With her jet-black hair tied up into a loose bun high on her head, and with a creative assortment of earrings, she was impossible to miss. A new kid. He would tell the interrogators that his "heart skipped a beat," but that was not exactly true. He would later handwrite a letter—a love note as they used to call them—to Angela admitting among other things: "the moment I first laid eyes on you, my spirit soared." But that was none of the interrogators' business, he decided. As he set the scene, he only said, "My mind went blank."

What actually happened, however, is a different story. The kid who had been talking to him, his voice became mute. Everything slowed down. She craned her neck, scanning the room for a place to settle in, at the same time her eyes shifted. "It all happened so fast and slow at the same time." He kept more of his original words to himself. While he later wrote to Angela "my soul recognized yours," he would only say to the interrogators, "our eyes locked."

Mark did not have to move after the teacher issued his order. He was already in the front row, as always. The seats began to fill. Angela spotted the one she wanted, but was concerned about the precedent it would set. Instead, she did as she so often did: She let fate decide. It was an antiquated concept, but she was agnostic on the subject. She was a realist, yes, but she was also open to believing there was some level of predetermination, too. Standing at the back of the room, she watched the students weigh their options. One by one, they lowered into their chairs. A smile found her lips for the first time since her family moved when the desk directly behind Mark remained open.

They always laughed when thinking back on their first words together. Thoughts raced in both of their heads as they sat for a long moment in awkward silence after the teacher began unpacking his bag. *What's her name? What's his name?* Something needed to be said—anything. That's when Angela blurted, "What's that smell?" Mark was never quick on his feet, but it took him longer than usual to respond as he took a full mental inventory. *Did I remember to use deodorant this morning? Did I step in dog-doo?* Then it dawned on him. "Oh, that's my gum." He had just popped a fresh stick into his mouth. "Do you want some? It's Winterfresh." He scolded himself. *Really, Winterfresh?! That's what you came up with?* The interrogators knew it was inappropriate to convey emotion, but one of them was unable to capture the chuckle before it left, quickly snuffing it out with a closed fist to the nose, as if to prevent a sneeze.

"Sure, that sounds great," Mark reported Angela's response.

The next day, he went into Calc II with a goal, a mission. He would ask for her name. The girl with the jet-black hair arrived three minutes late to find a stick of Wrigley's Winterfresh gum placed in the middle of her wood veneer desktop. Class had begun, so she was careful to whisper, "Hey, thanks for the gum."

Mark, who became laser-focused when he identified a goal, responded without a salutation. "What's your name?"

"Angela," she said, realizing it was impossible to not smile when talking to this guy.

"I'm Mark. Nice to meet you, Angela." Mission accomplished.

After he was hauled off, and the garage was turned upside down by the commandos, they found two cartons of Wrigley's Winterfresh gum —one of them was mostly empty. Mark would leave a pack for her on the kitchen counter after a squabble as a way of saying, "Sorry." Occasionally, she would find a pack on her dashboard, just to let her know he was thinking about her. Later, when the kids caught on to the quirky tradition, he would do the same for the two of them—hiding a pack here and there when he could see they needed some additional attention from Dad. For his little girl, it was often.

Going back to the day they met in Calc II, she thought it was an odd choice—Winterfresh—such a throwback, so old school. Many of the kids chewed gum, of course, but Winterfresh? As she got to know Mark Sapin, she realized it made perfect sense. But, when she was asked about it during one of the many interviews, she would keep it to herself, revealing only, "I don't know what to tell you—he just really liked that flavor." It was none of their business. Some things are not meant to be shared, except between two people, husband and wife.

That senior year flew by. Once Mark and Angela found adjacent desks, they would never again part, at least not voluntarily. Plans were made to attend the same college and to live in the same dormitory. It was during those years when they realized the illogic of it—love. Professors cautioned students against the "expensive emotion," especially those teaching economics. Love was inefficient. All the research corroborated the claim. Worse, love may lead to marriage, and still worse than that, kids. Ultimately, the frequent lecture went, love reduces economic productivity and output. Leave sentimentality to the lower classes. "They can continue to crank out kids and drag down the economy with them," the line went. "But don't you do the same—don't fall into that trap."

Old-timers would say the world had changed, and not necessarily for the better. But old people always say things like that. When your time is up, when your prime has passed, looking backward with rose-colored glasses—sentimentality—makes perfect sense, at least that is how the Prags explained it. The only way now, they would remind everyone, is forward. And the fastest way forward is achieved with efficiency. Who needs the messiness and complications of love when every carnal need can be met during a mini-session at the neighborhood e-brothel. Virtual reality had sanitized sex, which means messy communions of the skin were no longer necessary, except for those who cannot afford the subscription. That is why the Prags have called this problem "Reverse Darwinism." All the wrong people—non-factors —were having children, while those creating wealth and prosperity shunned affairs of the heart in favor of visits to the virtual brothels.

Mark did not see it that way. And those who cared to learn about his side of the story would blame his grandmother. He called her "Gramoo." Mark's grandfather would tell the investigators who pounded on his door in the middle of the night that his grandson gave his wife that name when he was a toddler. "He couldn't pronounce 'Grandma,' so 'Gramoo' was as close as he could get," he explained, still trying to understand why they were so interested. "And it stuck." Grandpa Sapin continued to talk. He proved to be a treasure trove. It seemed to everyone that he had stored up everything he had been wanting to say for the eight years since his wife had passed away. He was lonely and appreciated the company and was quite willing to look past the fact they stormed into the house uninvited with machine guns.

"Gramoo and Marky had a special bond," he began another long answer. He then reminisced about how the two of them would spend the afternoon poring over old family photo albums, often reminding his audience, "No one bothers with books anymore. It's all digital now, you see." Grandpa Sapin told them everything. "Marky, well, he just asked one question after another. Rapid fire. And he'd soak it up like a sponge. Especially anything to do with history. He wanted to know what it was like when we were kids. He would just sit there and listen and listen for hours. He loved hearing about the funny stuff his dad would do when he was a boy. You know, just kid's stuff. Getting in trouble—not any real trouble, mind you—just kid's stuff."

By the time the investigators were offered their third pot of coffee, they had all the information they needed. At least, all they believed could be extracted. Sure they could continue, but the sun was already rising and the old man really should get some sleep.

"One last thing before we leave," the lead investigator announced. "Are there any videos or books or any other materials you remember Mark taking a particular interest in when he would come stay with you?"

Grandpa Sapin raised his index finger to his lips and pondered for a long while before answering. "Oh, Marky, he loved to read. He was a regular little bookworm."

"Any one book in particular, sir?"

The old man disappeared into his den. Scanning the wall of books, he arrived at one. "Oh, yes. He loved this one, *Where the Sidewalk Ends*."

Turning the book over in his hands, he opened yellowed pages and noted its publication date: 1974.

"Poetry? Is this a poetry book?" the man asked, somewhat confused.

"Oh, yes, and it's a good one. Shel Silverstein. He was one of the best."

"Did Mark have a favorite poem?"

"Well, that was quite some time ago. I'll need to jog my memory. Let's have a look-see," Grandpa Sapin began flipping through the pages. "Why, yes, of course. How could I have forgotten, 'Jimmy Jet and His TV Set.'" A wide smile settled on his face before he called out, "Here, let me read it to you."

The man looked around at his team to gauge their interest before indulging the old man. "Sure, yeah, okay—go ahead."

Grandpa Sapin was immediately transported back to the days, early in his retirement, when he would visit the daycare center to read to the children during story time.

"I'll tell you the story of Jimmy Jet," he recited the first line as the goon squad leaned in.

———

And you know what I tell you is true.

He loved to watch his TV set

Almost as much as you.

———

He watched all day, he watched all night

Till he grew pale and lean.

From "The Early Show" to "The Late Late Show"

And all the shows between.

He watched till his eyes frozen wide,

And his bottom grew into his chair.

And his chin turned into a tuning dial,

And antennae grew out of his hair.

And his brains turned into TV tubes,

And his face to a TV screen.

And two knobs saying "VERT" and "NORTS"

Grew where his ears had been.

And he grew a plug that look like a tail

So we plugged in little Jim.

And now instead of him watching TV

We all sit around and watch him.

The men stood at the entryway in hushed contemplation exchanging glances while attempting to discern the meaning of what they had just heard when Grandpa Sapin began closing the front door.

"Okay, goodnight, fellas! It's been wonderful visiting with you. Be sure to come by again soon," he announced without so much as a whiff of insincerity before calling out to the heavily armed and thoroughly perplexed group of elite warriors standing on his front stoop. "Please give my love to Little Marky!"

11

When Jason Harper returned, he knew someone had been in his apartment. The hair on the back of his neck stood up and the fight or flight —mostly fight—hormones surged through every vessel in his body. Immediately, he was back in the Hilliard House, where unauthorized entries never ended well.

He tip-toed to the center of the dining room where he found the evidence. Upon closer inspection, he could see it was a silver bucket filled with ice, chilling a bottle of champagne. Leaning against it was a small envelope with just one word, "Jason," handwritten on the front. Considering it a trap, he declined the bait, instead turning to scan the room before inspecting all possible hiding places. When he arrived at the closet, the only spot remaining, he clenched his left fist and cocked it back toward his ear. Swiping the hanging clothes to the right in one motion, he saw it—nothing. Laughing both to and at himself, he returned to the bucket and opened the envelope.

"Congratulations, Jason!" was scrawled in a blue fountain pen. "And thank you for saving our asses. We owe you one," it deadpanned. "Actually, I think the number is ten billion." It was signed by the president of the United States. Then, in the postscript, he added, "Don't forget about me when it comes time to make your political donations this year. It makes for a great tax write-off, and you'll certainly need one!" Jason stood there, reading it again. Incredulous. He could not believe the guy had the audacity to ask for money. Taking a visual measurement of the card, he calculated that maybe twenty percent was devoted to actually thanking him for saving the world and the balance, maybe eighty percent was groveling for funding.

Lifting the bottle from the ice, he could gather only that it was expensive. It wouldn't matter because he didn't drink. He always believed it was the gateway to nowhere worth going. One drink would lead to another and another after that. Soon, he would be drooling with his mouth wide open, eyes shut, and needle holes traversing the inside of his forearms. Everything was different now. He was not at the Hilliard House. He was no longer a lowly community college student. He was no longer a non-factor. He was somebody. He mattered. He was a billionaire. A genius. He had just done something which had never been done before in the history of mankind. He saved the world. Now, the president of the United States was groveling.

Political donations are something no one has ever bothered to ask him about. He had never so much as voted. One thing he knew for sure, there was no way the current occupant of the White House would be getting any of his money. He knew it would only be used to maintain the status quo, to kick the can down the road again. Four more years. It only required one year of poli sci classes to understand with complete certainty that the two-party system was a complete bust. They were the ones, the political parties, which got them into this mess in the first place, quibbling about gas mileage and messing around in the margins with emissions standards. Both parties were worshipping at the same altar, going back again and again to the multinational oil and gas conglomerates, the mega food producers, big pharma, and Wall Street. It was all tied in together; they were all playing the same game. They all knew it and were perfectly willing to fly the planet straight into the sun if it meant winning another election, as long as they could point the finger at someone else while they gasped their last breaths. Jason snapped back to attention with a sudden impulse to check his bank account.

Settling into a dining table chair, he powered up his laptop. A few key taps later, he was waiting for the web page to refresh. It flashed for a moment that felt like a week. He saw the balance: $10,000,000,623.19. He choked on his new reality, feeling everything and nothing, all at once. From behind the monitor, he glimpsed the elaborate corking mechanism atop the champagne bottle. Piqued by curiosity, he could see no harm in holding it in his hands. After all, he earned it. He saved the world. He alone. The bottle was heavy. Substantial, significant. He was those things now, and so much more. Fiddling with the fine wiring holding the hourglass-style cork in place, he released it. The mesh dropped to the floor. Thinking back to the old movies he had watched when he was a kid, he wondered if the cork would really shoot across the room. He had just saved the planet. He deserved to shoot a cork. That's what rich people do. He wrapped his hands around the bottleneck and coaxed the cork forward with his thumbs, back and forth, until—pop! It shot through the apartment, glancing off the lamp in the living room and into the wall. Bubbles came rushing up, and he was overcome by the perfume of victory, sweet victory. For the first time in nineteen years, Jason Harper allowed himself to taste alcohol.

It had been offered to him many times before, of course, but he would not drop his guard. Not even for a moment. He would not allow himself to end up like them. Mom and Dad with their mouths—and their hands—wide open, waiting to swallow a fly or for the government to give them some money. But he was not them. His bank account proved it. He had earned the right to celebrate. After all, he reminded himself, because he still did not fully believe it, he had just saved the world. Tilting the bottle back, he drew in the soul-warming nectar. All the hard edges were washed away from view and a shininess was cast about his apartment. Everything appeared good and right and light and happy. This is why people drink, he realized.

His attention bounced between the bottle and the bank account. Jason hit "refresh" over and over again, just to make sure the digits remained in place. He felt more more confident and affirmed each time the web page reloaded. The alcohol was having the same effect: confidence and affirmation. Sitting taller in his chair than was customary, he said it out loud for the first time, "I'm a billionaire—a multi-billionaire." He shook his head side to side, and because he did not know what else to do, he began scanning his email in-box. It was all the usual stuff, a lot of junk mail. There was an email from the Incel Club wondering where he had been. It made him laugh out loud because he had joined as a joke, really. Yes, he was celibate, but not involuntarily so, as the club charter requires, which, of course, is the entire point of the Incels. Unlike his fellow club members, he had no interest in touching or being touched. But, it's difficult to have much of a sex life without touching. That's why, whenever he had a few dollars burning a hole in his pocket, he would head over to the Vixen VR Brothel on Second Street. They kept his settings on file there. The holographic women appearing in his virtual field of vision were only ever allowed to touch just one area.

Scrolling further down the list, another subject line stood out from the crowd. "Pragmatists Platform—FINAL DRAFT" is what it said. Jason clicked open the message which included the email addresses of one hundred or so recipients in the "Cc" field, including his. He had forgotten all about the meeting he had attended last year, advertised as the "First Annual Convention," complete with free cake. After the cheerful greeting, "Hey, Prags!" and some information about the whereabouts of an upcoming meeting—it had been moved from the Student Union to Social Sciences Room 117 due to a malfunctioning fire sprinkler—and the time had changed. Then, the email then went on to thank everyone for their "hard work and dedication" that went into the drafting of their charter in the year following the convention. The sender closed by asking everyone to "give it one last read through" and to let him know if missed any "typos or dangling participles." A file attachment was inserted at the bottom. Jason opened the document.

Expecting a rambling multi-page exposition, Jason instead found a single type-written page with ample margins, both top to bottom and left to right. The presentation and layout both screamed "Amateur," but the newly minted billionaire was immediately taken by the content. "Whereas this body is unified behind the guiding principle that the wealth and prosperity of our great nation has been impeded by sentimentality, which has infiltrated our politics to such a degree that the country is no longer governable by the existing two-party system, the following policy positions and pronouncements have been adopted in-full by the Pragmatist Party." Below the sprawling one sentence preamble were a collection of five bulleted items.

"There are too many people on Planet Earth consuming too many of its precious resources. We shall, therefore, adopt positions and offer policy prescriptions to efficiently and humanely restore the natural and proper human-to-resources ratio, which include, but are not limited to: a) birth control education and advocacy; b) advancement and expansion of family life curriculum in our public schools; c) research and development of involuntary birth control methods for economic non-factors."

It was exactly what Jason had been saying all along: There were too many people. Everywhere he went, he felt as if he were crawling around those ant hills next to the creek back home. Ants filled every square inch, breathing in all the oxygen and exhaling more and more poisonous carbon dioxide into the atmosphere. Even once the 2BIRDS cool the planet, the billions of people are going to ruin it again, just by sitting there on their couches and watching it all unfold on TV—inhaling and exhaling—exactly as they did before. Breathe in the good air, breathe out the bad.

The other policy bullet items did not interest him nearly as much as the first and the third, but they were so much better than what the other guys were offering. How much more can we possibly argue about abortion, he wondered. Instead, why not eliminate the possibility of the problem in the first place? Why not spay and neuter all the non-factors, just like the dogs and cats at the animal shelter? Ultimately, Homo sapiens are animals, too. If they cannot deal with it, then someone ought to deal with it for them. Don't even let it get to a point where it is something you can argue about. Remove the sentimentality, just as it states in item three:

We expect results from our political leaders and the institutions they inhabit just as we do of our business executives and their companies. Unlike our business executives, who rely on hard empirical data and facts to inform their decision-making, our political leaders have embraced sentimentality as a tool to distract and mislead We the People. The Pragmatist Party and its members, therefore, demand an absolute devotion to solving societal problems through rigorous scientific analysis and pure cognitive deduction for the betterment of all. We will follow the truth, no matter where it leads.

The bank account, the champagne, and now this thing he was reading —whatever it was, a manifesto, a constitution, a newsletter, he wasn't sure what—had caused a tectonic shift, a change in the way he saw himself in the world. The document was embedded with a link to the party website which he clicked. A pop-up ad then materialized asking for donations—that made two solicitations in one hour. The "Vote Prag, Follow the Truth Wherever it Leads" logo adorned left-hand corner and served as the home button. He read the appeal: "Just $10,000 is all we need to keep the movement alive for another year. We hope you will join us. Click here to donate."

It was never something he would have considered before, but now he was a rich man, a very rich man. He had better start acting like it. There was so much time to make up. He toggled back to the bank page on his browser to check his balance again. He was becoming accustomed to the number: $10,000,000,623.19. He clicked "Refresh" once more. This time, the number changed. The balance now read $10,000,139,837.56. Below, the line item stated, "Hourly money market sweep distribution: +$139,214.37." In the time he had been sitting there drinking to his triumph the interest on his fortune paid him one-hundred-and-forty grand. It was more than his pathetic non-factor father had earned over his entire lifetime, he calculated. Jason then clicked the donate button, typed $139,214.37 into the field prompting the amount and hit "Submit." He could spare an hour of his time. It would be the first of many donations to the party.

Just then, the unmistakable screech of tires roused him from his boozy trance. Two beats later, an equally unmistakable reverberation emanated from twisting metal and broken glass. Six stories below, a new drama was playing out for a local viewing audience. Jason stumbled to the window, champagne bottle in one hand, television remote in the other. Flipping through the channels, he alternated his focus between the screen and the street. Virtual and reality. He spied a camera bot speeding toward the smoking carnage. A woman, at least it appeared to be a woman, driving an old-style gas powered car—obviously not equipped with self-driving software—had run head-long into a massive retaining wall. Crimson splashed against the gray monolith in every direction along with unidentifiable parts and pieces of her once intact anatomy.

From the opposite side of the street, a passerby, a man, sprinted to the smoldering heap as he reached into his pocket. His face became illuminated by the glow of his phone as he videoed every square inch of the scene. Then, a car arrived. The driver exited the vehicle before it came to complete stop. She bounded toward the wreckage with her right hand extended watching the screen on her phone as she captured the live footage. From the darkness, another appeared. The three of them, two men and a woman, circled the scene waving their phones when a camera bot joined the frenzied committee of vultures who were salivating over the fresh kill. Jason turned up the volume on his television in the living room to hear what the reporter had to say. A commentator appeared in a box off to the side of the screen, as the camera bot panned around to provide the viewing audience with a close-up of the gore and destruction. The view was continually obstructed by the amateurs moving in and out of the frame.

"We have breaking news at this hour," the commentator announced. "Our camera bot was the first one at the scene bringing you live coverage that you can only find here on KTVCS—Colorado Springs' only live, around the clock local broadcaster—we have one fatality on River Avenue near Thirty-eighth Street. Okay, hold on, our camera bot has located a purse on scene. I repeat, we have found a purse. That means we may have identification here for you shortly, folks." The talking head paused, frozen as he watched along with everyone else, as one of the phone-wielding men snatched the blood-stained purse from the camera bot and began rifling through it himself.

The commentator opted to stall by recapping the facts. "Okay, just to summarize what we know so far: We were the first on the scene where an old-style, gas-powered sedan drove straight into a wall. The one occupant, and we have received confirmation on this from our camera bot, is dead. She appears to be a woman, but we have not been able to verify this for you yet."

"Wait, hold on, folks." The phone-wielding man lost interest in the purse and dropped it on the sidewalk. "Our camera bot has located her driver's license and will be showing it to us momentarily. Stand by. Okay, here we go. Her name is—or was—Holly Anne Smith. We're looking her up right now. Just one moment while the team here at KTVCS goes to work for you. Okay, here we go, we're pulling up her records. Holly Anne Smith, oh, okay," the talking head pressed into his earpiece, at the same time registering disappointment. His cadence slowed, his excitement waned before continuing. "Holly Anne Smith has been identified as homeless by the Colorado Springs Police Department. This appears to be just another non-factor suicide, folks. But, remember, you saw it first here on KTVCS. Stay tuned, we'll be right back to meet the lucky winners from today's Super Lotto."

A tow truck arrived first, then an ambulance. Their interviews with the camera bot required more time than the actual clean-up. Jason looked down to study the pair of 150-foot-long skid marks embedded into the pavement below and wondered how many suicide attempts included fully engaged brakes.

12

The interrogators continued to return to the day of The Test. Over and over again, he was required to retell it, particularly the details of the afternoon. At first, Mark figured it was another attempt to catch him in a lie or find an inconsistency or contradiction. But he shared it verbatim because it was exactly what had happened. Each time, the room filled. At some point, he came to believe that they just liked the story, that they found comfort in its simplicity and compassion—and sentimentality.

He began, as he always did, by reminding everyone that he was in fourth grade. He did not have to explain that they were gathered around the television because that was a given. Everyone was doing the same thing. He remembers the reaction to the event more than the event itself. It was the expression of his teacher which remained seared into his psyche. "We all knew it was over at that point," he stated again. "But the adults in the room actually understood what that meant. For us kids, we had been told the end of the world was around the corner for years. But it never came, so we kind of stopped believing it would ever really happen. After the broadcast, there was no doubt. The look on Ms. Rosen's face said it all."

The walk to Gramoo's house that day was unlike any other. Mark would describe it as "walking the plank, only the plank was two miles long." Everything slowed down at the same time his thoughts raced. He zeroed in on a line of ants traversing the sidewalk wondering if they would survive the apocalypse. He wondered if they knew that The Test had failed, that there was nothing to stop the rapidly accelerating parts per million number now. The commentators, almost immediately after the Space Tube failed, began speculating about how it would feel. How it will feel to die. They patched in a few experts who did their best to explain what would come next. That was the point when Mark's teacher clicked off the broadcast. But one of the sixth graders was able to watch the coverage on his phone for a few minutes while he was sitting on the toilet in the boy's bathroom. Everyone huddled around him at recess to find out what the commentators said.

"They had this guy," the kid explained to his classmates, who formed a semi-circle around him. "He was like a professor of something and also a scuba diver. They said he was an expert in carbon dioxide poisoning." The kid told everyone the "scuba guy" said that it would start to happen by the end of this year, the calendar year, not the school year which bought everyone a few more months. The kid then shared more good news: "Old people will die first." Going on to explain that anyone with weak lungs would be in trouble next, he added his own interpretation: "That means, if you can't hold your breath for very long you will die soon." All at once, the children drew a deep breath and held it, counting the seconds off in silence. *One Mississippi. Two Mississippi. Three Mississippi.*

"The scuba guy said that it would probably start with a headache," he revealed before pausing to remember the interview. "Then, I think, dizziness was next. Or maybe barfing came first." He paused again, his terrified audience gasping with the announcement of each new symptom. "After that, you basically get all confused and start flopping around on the floor and foam at the mouth until everything goes black and you die." After a moment of silent contemplation, a first grader raised her hand to ask the question everyone was now pondering: "What happens after that?"

Even before he received the precise details about how he would die, along with the date—December thirty-first—Mark knew it was bad, really bad. His backpack was heavier than usual, drooping along with his shoulders. Ms. Rosen could spin it however she wanted, but her expression told him everything he needed to know. He would be dead by the end of the year. As he continued walking, he practiced holding his breath, getting up to thirty-six Mississippis before twisting the handle on Gramoo's front door.

"Marky!" she called out from the kitchen. "How was school today, sweetheart?"

The moment ten-year-old Mark Sapin heard those words, he burst into tears. Unlike many of his schoolmates, he had been holding them in all day. Now, he let loose. He was at Gramoo's house. She would understand. She always did. Cradling his head with both arms, she pulled him into her favorite apron. "There, there, Marky. It's okay," she whispered in his ear as she rocked back and forth. "Go ahead and let it out. Everything is going to be okay." Mark collapsed into her arms and heaved and sobbed. He did not want to die. It was all so unfair. Whatever he said next was indecipherable through the blubbering, but Gramoo finally discerned what he had been trying to say: "I didn't put that stupid carbon in the air—it's not my fault."

The two remained welded together in the kitchen until Mark ran dry. He had no tears left to cry. Only a defeated whimper remained and a low-grade hum. "I had a feeling it was going to be a hard day," she said while bending at the waist to meet his eyes, brushing away the hair matted to his forehead. "So, I've been making cookies, and they're your favorite—persimmon." The thought of cookies felt so trivial. When weighed against the extinction of humanity, dessert had lost its appeal. Wheeling around, she opened the oven, and the aroma embraced Mark all over again. Gramoo can hug with smell, too, he realized. Reaching into the refrigerator, she retrieved a carton and poured a tall glass of ice-cold milk. Then she plated a half-dozen, warm, fresh-from-the oven golden brown cookies. "Come here, sweetheart," she motioned toward the den. "I want to tell you a story."

Surrounded on three walls by bookshelves—during one visit, Mark had pledged to read every single one of them—grandmother and grandson settled into the couch that had been passed down by her parents. The first bite made Mark forget about his impending death for a moment. "I want to tell you about when I was in the fourth grade," Gramoo began before setting the scene. "The entire school waited for that day in rapt anticipation. Now, you remember that word 'rapt,' right? It's spelled R-A-P-T and it means it was especially interesting. We were all so excited because a teacher had been selected to go into outer space for the first time. The first teacher in space. She had applied—NASA received thousands of applications—and was accepted and went through intensive training, just like all the other astronauts. When she arrived in space, she was going to float around in zero gravity and talk to school kids about what it was like. Everyone was so excited for her, and for themselves, to have this experience. It was such a big deal that a television was rolled into the classroom, so we could watch the launch live. Watching TV in the middle of the day back then was a big deal. Other than an occasional year-end movie, it just did not happen. But this was going to be a day like no other: Christa McAuliffe was all set to be the first teacher to visit outer space."

"All the kids sat cross-legged in front of the massive box at the front of the room. It was on wheels, so the teacher put it where everyone could see it and away from the sun beaming through the window. There was electricity in the air, we were all so excited. Before the television was turned on, the teacher explained again what were about to see. *Space Shuttle Challenger* would blast off and we were going to watch it climb up, up, and away. Then, once they made it into space, Ms. McAuliffe would come on the screen to float around and tell us about how it felt. She had some sort of lesson plan in store for the kids, but it was kept a secret. It was a surprise. Everyone would find out soon enough."

"The television cracked and hissed as the teacher twisted the dial. A camera was trained on the rocket ship. For the next hour, two commentators reminded everyone watching that history was in the making.

The interviews with Ms. McAuliffe's family and friends and coworkers came next. They had all showed up to watch it in person at the launch pad. Everyone was so proud of her. Footage was shared again which had been reordered earlier that morning when the astronauts entered the ship and cinched their harnesses snug around their hips and shoulders. More than anything else, I was in awe, and I remember telling myself, 'I want to be just like her someday.'"

"The announcement was made that the launch would be coming soon. The 'T-minus' signal was given: 'Ten, nine, eight, seven, six, five, four, three, two, one—blast off!' Everyone in the classroom threw their arms in the air as they watched the orange fire release from the bottom of the rocket boosters—it was like an upside-down volcano. The pad rumbled and shook. We all cheered. Lift off!"

"The camera kept a close-up shot on the shuttle as it sped toward the heavens. We heard the ship captain talking to mission control. It was just so exciting. We watch the flight continue just as planned. One minute in and everything was working. The classroom buzzed. Then, boom! A cloud appeared in the clear blue sky. Thousands of tons of rocket fuel exploded in a white-hot flash. *Space Shuttle Challenger* vanished from the screen. Its two auxiliary boosters, which had been attached to the right and the left sides of the craft, spun out, flying erratically. Seventy-three seconds into the flight, the hopes and dreams of millions were snuffed, along with the lives of seven astronauts, including Ms. McAuliffe."

"And we all watched as it happened in real time, on television. Just like you did today with The Test."

"Christa McAuliffe meant every bit as much to me as Jason Harper does to you." Mark pondered that statement for a moment before responding. "At least it was just those seven people and not the whole world," his voice trailing off in a defiant huff. He was collapsing into despair again, so she tried a different approach.

"You see, Marky, it's all the same," placing her hand on his. "It all comes down to what you believe—it all comes down to faith. You can't give up. You have to believe in something. You've got to have faith."

"What do you mean by faith?" Mark retorted. "That rocket blew up. The stupid Space Tube thing didn't work. We're all going to die soon."

"Well, Marky, that's exactly what I mean by faith. You have made the decision to believe that's what will happen. Right now, you have no faith."

"But that's what they said," Mark replied.

"That's what who said?" she was gentle, but firm in her questioning. "And what do they know? And what right do they have to say it?"

"Do you know why I became a teacher, Marky? I bet you don't. I went on to become a teacher, an English teacher—forty-two years in all— because I believed in Christa McAuliffe. She inspired me, just like she inspired millions of other people watching the horrible thing that happened."

Mark started leaning in. She was beginning to reach him.

"Now, I bet that guy, Jason what's-his-name, inspired someone watching the broadcast today. Someone, maybe a fourth-grader, who was so inspired that he will be the one to come up with a new solution," she said, lowering her voice and lifting her grandson's eyes to look straight into his eyes. "Marky, that somebody could be you."

As if a lightning bolt struck, Mark shot up at attention. Immediately, he saw everything from a new vantage point.

"That's what I mean by faith, Marky. Believe in something. Believe in yourself. You are so much more capable, so much more powerful than you know. Faith is just that, a belief in something you can't see. But that doesn't make it any less real."

Mark felt as if he could run through a brick wall.

"Think about all these books you've read," she said with a nod toward the surrounding shelves. "What do all the stories have in common? They all have a protagonist. A hero. Here, let's have a look at the one you just finished, the one about King Tut and the ancient Egyptians." She slipped the book from the shelf. "You remember this story, right?

King Tut was the protagonist. He didn't build all of those pyramids himself, but he inspired others to do it. In fact, to this day, we still don't know how he did it. It should not have been possible. But, Marky, that's exactly the point. It took only one person to believe, to have faith, to change everything. It took only one person to stand up and say, 'Hey, guys, I figured it out.' Why not you, Marky? Why not you?"

The networks would take this story and run wild. An alternative was found, breathless commentators raced to announce the real motive: Jealousy. Mark Ryan Sapin was intensely jealous of Jason Harper. That's it. That's why he did it. He wanted the glory. He wanted the riches. And he would stop at nothing to right a wrong. It's all right there in the transcript, they reminded their viewers. No one cared to read it, because no one ever cared to read anything. But they watched.

"You know something, Gramoo," Mark began asking a question as he bit into another cookie. "There's one other thing that I don't get about the ancient Egyptians, besides how they built those pyramids. Why did they believe they'd live forever? Do you think there's an afterlife?"

Gramoo measured her words before responding. "That question, Marky, is also a matter of faith. Remember, faith is a belief in something we cannot see, and we cannot prove. I don't know what happens after we pass on. It's impossible to know. For me, I want it to be a surprise—many, many years from now," she offered a playful nudge and a wink.

Again, lost in thought, as he so often found himself in his grandparent's den, Mark had another question. "The other thing I don't get about the ancient Egyptians is how they convinced everyone to build those pyramids. How the kings talked them into it."

"What do you mean by that, Marky? Maybe you can explain it to me. You know the history better than I do." The former teacher could not resist the opportunity.

"I mean, all the poor people and the slaves; they broke their backs all day long in the hot sun lifting those huge rocks. And they had to do it just because of who they were. They were born into poor families and slave families, and they couldn't do anything about it." He paused, the wheels of thought grinding. "But the kings were the only ones who got to go to the afterlife, they were the only ones who got to be immortal. Why didn't everyone else get to go, too?"

13

The network executives were frustrated as much as they were elated when they learned the world had been saved. So much compelling television had been missed, and for no good reason. They did not hesitate to let the CLIMA people know their feelings when they were summoned to the press conference. "Don't let it happen again" is what they said.

The tabletop bowed under the weight of the microphones. Every network had a reporter on location. All eyes were on the nineteen-year-old second-year community college student. Jason Harper addressed the viewing audience, and every single person on planet Earth leaned in, except for Mark Sapin and his grandparents. This fact would later be the subject of intense scrutiny.

After the president's welcome message and opening remarks, which went too long as usual, he made the understatement of a lifetime. "My fellow Americans, and citizens of the world, we are gathered today to share with you some tremendous news: The answer to the climate crisis has been found. After feverishly working around the clock, working on your behalf, we have corrected the issues we were having with the Space Tube. It now functions properly—not exactly as we anticipated, but we will explain all of that shortly—and we have already begun bringing temperatures back down." The room gasped in shock disbelief before exploding with applause. Pausing to allow the news to settle in with the viewers, the president went on to thank a long list of people before finishing with "and, in particular, Jason Harper." Pandemonium and jubilation took hold. Those in the audience were ready to celebrate. A ravenous and delirious chant took hold: "Jason! Jason! Jason!"

The last time the viewers saw Jason Harper he was in a much different state of mind, dejected and defeated. This was the opposite: triumphant and exuberant. The world desperately needed a hero, and he fit the bill. Once the chant abated and everyone settled back into their chairs, he began to speak. "Thank you, Mr. President and thank you, CLIMA," he paused, realizing that billions were watching. "I just want to say one thing: I sure am glad I didn't give up." He then offered an aw-shucks chuckle. Again, everyone in attendance leapt to their feet to clap and cheer and laugh. It took several minutes before he was able to speak again as the chant resumed. "Jason! Jason! Jason!"

"I never lost sight of who I was doing this for," he said, looking directly at the group of camera bots. "I did this for you. I never gave up because of you. I saved the world because of you." After a moment, where he pretended to wipe away a nonexistent tear, he went on to share stories of the children who had emailed him after The Test encouraging him to keep going. All three of the anecdotes, which he fabricated on the spot, carried the same message: "Save us, Jason Harper—you're our last hope. Everything depends on you." The viewing audience melted, wiping away tears of joy in order to make room for the other kind, which were flowing now. He then dove into a lengthy explanation detailing how the Space Tube had been repurposed and renamed—"It actually works a bit different than what I expected."

As he would go on to do many hundreds of times, perhaps thousands, he methodically led his entranced audience down a path detailing the origin story of the 2BIRDS. "Let me tell you how I came up with it," which is how he usually began. "It's an acronym, and for you kids out there, that's a name that is made up of other words. This name comes from five words: Before. It. Really. Does. Suck." The room filled with laughter. "That's really what it does. It sucks everything up into outer space and all that stuff floats around up there and creates a screen, it makes shade which cools the Earth. Think of it as if I created a giant pair of sunglasses." He paused again to allow for the fevered clapping. "I added a '2' in front of the name because it's got a double meaning— you know, 2BIRDS, as in to 'kill two birds with one stone'—because it solves not one, but two of our biggest problems: it shields the planet from the sun so it can finally start to cool, but it also takes care of the garbage problem." All at once, the room gasped with delight before the chant broke out again. "Jason! Jason! Jason!" He waited for it to die down before he made his closing statement.

"Not only am I saving the planet, I'm also going to clean everything up while I'm at it. I'm going to take out the trash. I'm going to kill two birds with one stone."

———

Landfills everywhere were overflowing. Now all of that garbage would come to the rescue in the eleventh hour as it was sucked up into a low orbit where it would partially block the sun that had been determined to fry the planet. The manmade mountain ranges springing forth from municipal dump sites will be a thing of the past. Bulldozers pushing and piling the garbage would shove it directly into the 2BIRDS, so it could be launched into outer space. Everyone felt good about throwing things away now because it was a patriotic duty to consume. Not only was it contributing to the economy, but it was healing Planet Earth in the process.

It is difficult to pinpoint when it happened because it was not a specific moment in time, but more of a drip-drip-drip. For centuries, it had not been much of an issue until those in the field of waste management began using the same word: Saturation. There had always been plenty of space, lots of room to dispose of everything people no longer wanted. Every day, the dump trucks would roll in, drop the trash, and the bulldozers would flatten it and smash it together. Couches were pulverized, barbecues broken down, and toys buried. Every year it would pile up a bit more. Once it filled up to a certain point the dumping would move out horizontally. Back then, the dumpsite would simply annex more of the surrounding land as it continued expanding. The land out there was cheap and abundant. Somewhere along the line a shrewd real estate developer sniffed out an opportunity and began buying every square inch he could find around municipal dump sites nationwide. As soon as they caught wind of the game he was playing, his competitors jumped in, too. After the shopping spree ended, every municipal dump site in the country was surrounded by land owned by speculators.

There was not enough housing to go around. Just like with everything, there were too simply too many people. And, in this case, too few houses. City council members wrung their hands in desperation as they searched for "affordable housing." They became easy targets for the opportunistic developers who lobbied them to rezone their newly acquired land to "residential." Of course, it was nowhere anyone wanted to live, but beggars cannot not be choosers. It was a roof overhead. Some protested at city council meetings, calling the new neighborhoods "shantytowns." Most people, at least for those who bothered to think about it all, figured that constructing those shantytowns was better than the alternative, which was homelessness.

At the end of the day, it was a solution. And local officials always showed up for the ribbon cuttings. The photos consisted of a group of important-looking men and women holding up a massive red ribbon while some non-factor wielded a pair of oversized scissors. They would always stood in front of a newly constructed house—a glorified cardboard box, a shack, really—with the mountains of trash in the background. The officials would then take turns giving self-congratulatory speeches mostly to each other and to the few hangers-on and chamber of commerce-types in attendance. "Home ownership is the cornerstone of the American Dream," was a common theme. The officials always felt good about themselves, and were sure to pat one another on the back because those rickety little houses sure beat the alternative: sleeping on park benches or under a bridge. That is what they always told themselves as they summoned their luxury cars to return them home, somewhere on the other side of the garbage mountain range far away from the dump.

Shantytowns had become an American reality. And as they grew out, the garbage piles next door grew up. Each day, the dump trucks arrived from their morning rounds, and the piles would grow another inch or two. Inches became feet, and feet became yards. Mountains sprung forth. Some cities, especially those dependent upon tourism to power their economies, became alarmed by their rapidly changing topography. Others barely noticed.

Although a few tried, there was nothing that could be done. There was no cost-effective way to conceal the trash. More than once it was decided that covering the garbage piles with topsoil would at least improve the aesthetics. At least it would look like an actual mountain and not a heaping mound of steaming refuse. It would work for a few weeks, sometimes a month, before more trash piled on top. Experimentation with netting was also popular. But, it just looked like a giant pile of garbage covered with a net. And those nets were expensive. The only solution, which was not a solution at all, was to keep going vertical. Over the years, the manmade mountain ranges grew into backdrops for the surrounding shantytowns. Depending on the time of the day, some portion of those neighborhoods was always in the shadows, the sun eclipsed by the surrounding peaks. Later, as the Earth experienced its rapid heat-up, shantytown residents would go from cursing to praising the mountains. The same started happening with everyone else, too.

The mountains were all many residents had ever known, especially the younger ones. They grew up with them. By then, many of the mountains had been given names by their city councils, often in honor of the latest citizen of the year or a popular fire chief. Some had trails carved into them, which left fond memories of Boy Scout camp-outs and mountain bike rides. And the valley towns, which had once been defined by their flatness, now had exciting new attractions for their residents. Some featured mountains so large and majestic that they began to advertise themselves as tourist destinations. And while there was universal contempt for the mountains initially, nearly everyone eventually came to accept them. At the very least, they concealed and sequestered the shantytowns—more trash and blight hidden away from sight.

It took a minute for viewers in the shantytown to comprehend what Jason Harper was saying during the broadcast. The shadows cast by those manmade mountains were the only thing keeping their little boxes from baking in the midday sun. But if what he was saying was true, and he can put shadows on the planet as he was claiming, then they would no longer need the mountains. Good riddance. This constituency would be the most difficult for him to win over, at least initially. It was the fact that he grew up in a government project that got them to open up and listen to what he had to say that opened the door. But it was not what he said that mattered most.

Things would not be easy, Jason explained. Much work was to be done. He needed help. Thousands of 2BIRDS would need to be built immediately. It would be a race against the clock. His company was now open for business. And he continued to insist "no robot will ever work on my job site." He provided contact information. "Call us, and we'll get started today." One by one, just like the Americans turning back the Nazis in World War II, he reminded everyone they would manufacture their way to victory.

———

It was inching toward dinner time—"supper" as Gramoo called it— when the shouts were heard from the street outside. Mark was now eleven years old and in the fifth grade, although school had been closed indefinitely. He was pleased to have woken up alive on New Year's Day, but he had a persistent headache and occasional dizziness just like everyone else. The puking he experienced had been a harmless flu bug, at least that is what the medic bot said. At the time, he was convinced he was about to start foaming at the mouth and convulsing at any moment, just like the sixth grader told him a year earlier. Fortunately, it passed. Now, while his parents were at work, he spent his days at his grandparents' house redoubled in his determination to read every one of their books. Gramoo was in the kitchen finessing her spaghetti sauce while Mark was on the couch, two-thirds of the way into a book—he cannot remember which one. That's when he heard it, the shout. Then another. He dashed over to the kitchen and, along with his grandmother, pulled back the curtains.

The scene was one of jubilation. People were jumping up and down in the street, hugging and crying and shouting. As they swung the front door open, someone called out, "He did it! He did it! Jason did it!" Hopeful, Mark turned to look at Gramoo, who smiled and motioned him forward. Running toward the street, he encountered a wild-eyed man rubbing his head in disbelief, engrossed in a video he was watching on his phone. Mark peeked around from the side to see it. The bottom of the screen blared in all caps, white lettering embedded in a scrolling red banner: "JASON HARPER HAS SAVED THE WORLD!!!" It was all he needed to know. He would get the details later. For now, he could see that he did it. Jason Harper did it! He saved the world!

Every block of every street across America and around the world looked exactly the same as it did right there in front of Gramoo's house. A cathartic eruption of joy and celebration and relief, decades of pent up anxiety and frustration released in an instant. They were saved! The chant in every neighborhood was identical to the one heard at the press conference earlier. "Jason! Jason! Jason!" The party went on through the night. That day, which would later become a national holiday, marked the point when a "reset" button had been pressed—a second chance. The planet, and its two-legged inhabitants, would be spared. Things would be different going forward. Much brighter and more prosperous. A new beginning. A new belief. A new faith.

As Mark again answered the lead interrogator's questions concerning where he was and what he had been doing on Jason Harper Victory Day, he closed by saying the same thing he always said to her: "It was the happiest day of my life."

She knew he was lying.

14

Jason Harper Victory Day marked the beginning of the American Renaissance. And that period matched up to the best years in the life of Mark Sapin. 2BIRDS began sprouting up at landfills everywhere. Around the clock, workers were doing the impossible—and no construction bots. With each new installation, the temperature ratcheted down another notch. Garbage heaps disappeared nearly as fast as Jason Harper's bank account filled. These were heady times. People believed.

It took a while, but carbon dioxide levels began dropping. Although most believed it was the result of the 2BIRDS now spanning the globe, the truth, as always, was more complicated than that. While, the 2BIRDS solved the immediate crisis by providing galactic cloud cover —"sunglasses"—and they cleaned up the mess in the process, there were other factors at play. Jason had always paid attention to the details, a trait he would acknowledge that he developed living with two drug-addicted parents at the Hilliard House. "If you didn't keep an eye on everything and everyone, bad stuff would happen," he shared during more than one interview. "You learned that lesson pretty fast." The detail he picked up, which everyone else seemed to miss, was Slime Lady. Her idea actually worked. It scrubbed the air clean. The only problem was it took too long. Plus, those massive algae ponds required land, lots of land. But his 2BIRDS disrupted the equation. One of the first things he did with his prize money was to buy Slime Lady's patent and fold it into his company. He then instructed his sales representatives to bundle carbon dioxide gobbling algae ponds with each 2BIRDS proposal. "The ponds," he was known to say, "are pure profit—nothing but green." And the buyer really had no choice. They had to do something with all the newfound land at the dumpsites, the space once occupied by the mountains of garbage. Might as well make the air breathable again.

Every day during the Second Renaissance was better than the one before it. The temperature continued to drop right along with the carbon dioxide concentrations. Everyone went back to work. Even the non-factors found jobs at 2BIRDS installations. Things were good. Normal. No, much better than normal. And everyone knew that they owed it all to one man: Jason Harper.

Although he became a multibillionaire overnight, it required only another seven years to become the world's first multitrillionaire. He was selling 2BIRDS and algae ponds much faster than he could build them. And the fact he was allowed to sell them at all was not an insignificant historical footnote. When CLIMA chose its ten finalists, it required each of them to sign a contract. Nine of them did so after heavy scrutiny of the award clause. They all wanted to know the exact parameters. When would the payment be made? Would it be paid out all at once or over time with installments? What exactly would define "winning," would it be a successful prototype or successfully reducing carbon dioxide in the atmosphere? If so, how much would it need to be reduced? This last question generated the most interest. CLIMA was in no mood to quibble. They, just like everyone else, were running out of time.

While Jason was as concerned as everyone about the mechanics governing the administration of the award money, he was the only one to scrutinize another clause. The one which spelled out who owned the idea. He fought hard with the CLIMA lawyers who told him the powers-that-be were considering removing him from the running over his contract dispute. He knew they were bluffing. He grew up around con men and could always spot a bluff. He knew his idea was the best, and he told them as much. "No problem, guys—we'll just sit here and burn up on this overheated planet together." By the end of the second day, the hold-out ended. Fresh documents were handed to all ten of the contestants, complete with a clarification about the payment of the prize money as well as the granting of full and complete ownership of the ideas to their inventors, including the immediate granting of an airtight patent. Winning ten billion dollars for coming up the idea was one thing, but the real money was in selling that idea after the fact. Slime Lady was so grateful for Jason's contract maneuvers she discounted the sale of her patent by a cool million, which is why the check he wrote was for nine million dollars and not the ten he had initially offered. "If it weren't for him," she would later share, "I wouldn't have anything at all." Billions of other people felt the same way.

The schools reopened immediately after Jason Harper Victory Day. Everyone who had walked away from their job or had been laid off returned within a few days of the celebration. In a lurch forward, the economy spun into high gear. Building 2BIRDS and algae ponds required massive labor crews, non-factor labor. Across the country and around the world, shantytown residents were walking across the street each morning to punch in at the job site. Whistling to work. One after another, wherever the 2BIRDS went up the trash mountains went down. The ground cooled.

A young Mark Sapin never thought he would be so happy to see his fourth grade teacher again, Ms. Rosen. He could not contain himself, wrapping her in a bear hug and squeezing hard. Everything was possible again. Life was ahead. A good life.

Those years sped by in a rapid succession of school and sports and friends and fun—lots of fun. And, as always, Mark was known to be at the center of it all. He was able to come up with the best pranks. They were never mean, never intended to hurt anyone. But he loved to laugh almost as much as he loved making his friends laugh. The pleasure was magnified if he was able to add a technical element to it. Any challenge involving computers would do. Hacking is something that came naturally. Sending notices to all the parents through the school's server had become too easy. The one he sent announcing the formation of a "varsity boys donut eating team" was met with a strong rebuke from the principal. But he could not figure out who did it, nor was he able to match wits with the invisible perpetrator. Had he engaged in any level of deductive reasoning, he would have at least thought to check the donut shop on the corner. If he had, he would have found Mark and his buddies huddling over his laptop, doubled over in laughter.

Despite the pranks, Mark was a committed student. Never the smartest, but usually the hardest working. His most significant challenge was sticking to the assigned reading. Unlike many of his classmates, reading was not a problem. He loved to read. The problem was reading something he had been ordered to read. There were so many other books that caught his attention, and he spent much of his time with his head in one. Just not the one that had been assigned. For that reason, his grades never soared. He got by, in fact, he did well, but he could have done much better. And he knew it. Math was a breeze. He was an excellent tutor, but he worked with just one student: Angela Peters.

The two were inseparable and soon conspired to attend the same local state college. By the end of their freshman year, they were talking about marriage, which was rare. No one was getting married. There was too much financial downside. Along with a decline in the popularity of marriage came a precipitous drop in the birth rate, at least among the productive upper classes, because they understood the economic burden those two things represented. Yet, the lower classes, while they were not much more interested in marriage, were cranking out babies about as fast as was biologically possible. Within a generation, the government realized that this trend presented a terrifying reality, so a public service advertising campaign was launched with the sole purpose of convincing college students to get married and, more importantly, to have children. On campuses throughout America, posters lining the hallways depicted a happy, young couple along with their toddler son fawning over a new baby, a girl swaddled in pink, lying in a crib. At the top, it read in a sensible sans-serif font, "Setting the Record Straight," followed by two columns. One the left, it was headed, "Myth." And, on the right, "Truth." Everyone knew the truth column was not true, none of it. Mark Sapin didn't care.

Gramoo gave him the ring. It had been her great grandmother's. Platinum, with a single microscopic diamond. His throat tightened when she handed it to him. The first time he had ever the topic became tangible. He felt the weightiness of the ring, the gravity of the topic. Up to this point, it had been more abstract and theoretical. Now, it was real. There were very few college students who had been persuaded by the government posters. They would do the math on their own and figure it was not a smart decision. But, according to Gramoo, "It's a decision you make with your heart, not your head." He could not imagine a life without Angela.

The speech he prepared was not his best work. His mind went blank. Words were not capable of capturing his feelings. Instead, he decided that in addition to letting his heart do the thinking, it would also do the talking. The ring would travel with him for the next three weeks, on standby, ready for the perfect opportunity. The right time. He told himself that he would know it when he saw it.

On the sprawling front lawn of the campus, he found Angela at their usual twelve-fifteen spot. The sun was hidden, as always, but it made a brief appearance as it sometimes did when the 2BIRDS went offline during the dumpsite lunch break. The rays danced and speckled her face through the boughs of the oak tree above. She pecked him on the cheek, studied his eyes, and fixed his hair.

The time was now.

Mark drew a deep breath before speaking. "I love you, Angie. And I cannot imagine my life without you in it." She knew immediately that a question—the question—was imminent. "I tried to find the right words to say in this moment, but I couldn't. 'I love you' is all I could come up with, but I suppose that means everything." He stopped to survey her reaction, both hands now covered her wet cheeks. "I want to spend the rest of my life with you. You're my best friend, my every-thing. Angie, will you marry me?"

Unable to speak, Angela bobbed her head up and down as the two embraced and cried. Reaching into his jacket pocket, Mark retrieved the ring. "This was my great-great grandmother's ring. Gramoo gave it to me. She wanted you to have it." With tears continuing to stream from her eyes, Angela held out her left hand to admire the ring. "It's perfect," she struggled to compose herself. "I love it. I love you. And yes! Of course, yes!"

By the end of their senior year, Angela was pregnant. It was a boy. Mark realized immediately why all the other students had been reluc-tant to follow the advice of those government posters lining the hall-ways. Babies were expensive, especially on an income derived from a part-time job as a teaching assistant in the computer science lab. Fortu-nately, the economy was humming and the unemployment rate reversed course and was now rip-roaring its way toward zero. Getting a job would not be a problem. He always found a way.

———

Jason Harper became the richest man on Earth, by far. The same was true when it came to popularity. Although most of the babies were being born to the residents of shantytowns, more than half of them were named Jason. All the networks were obsessed with the man and interviews with him comprised much of the news coverage. Occasion-ally, he would allow one of their correspondents to follow him around at work. Those intimate "day-in-the-life-of" installments were guaran-teed to carry a highly engaged and, therefore, highly profitable audi-ence. And that is why the executives stuck with them. Viewer demand for Jason Harper was insatiable. So were the sponsorships. Advertisers lined up for those spots and never balked at the premium rates.

That same demand ran wild in churches and places of worship. But it also presented a difficult choice for the clergy: canonize Jason Harper as a messiah—the Second Coming—or acknowledge him as a fallible human being who did a great thing. There was no middle road on this question, no compromises possible. Because of his popularity with the flock, religious leaders almost always elected to go with the majority on this one. To do otherwise was to risk losing "butts in pews," which was already becoming a problem. With the economy going full-tilt and the end of the world in the rearview mirror, everyone seemed to forget about God. He had been replaced, it seemed, by Jason Harper. The man who could do no wrong. Many Christian denominations took the issue head-on by adding the Book of Jason as a supplement to the Bible. On the other hand, the Quran and the Vedas, among others, revised their existing text, adding the testimonies to the existing scripture. The question was whether to add a supplementary publication, or to revise the existing gospels. It was a grueling and agonizing task. But it had to be done. Everyone had to answer the Jason Harper question. He changed everything.

All of this provided further credence to jealousy as a motive. "He did it because he was jealous" would become a common refrain. The fame, the fortune, the power. It was simply too much for Mark Sapin to bear. The pieces could be made to fit, and it was a plausible explanation. A different theory was posited, however, by a small fraction of the population, those who grew up in a much different time: the elderly. Many of them spotted an alternative motive: Love.

15

The next morning, Jason Harper woke up with a throbbing headache. Before he was fully alert, he assumed the carbon dioxide parts per million had spiked, and this was a natural reaction. Then he remembered the champagne. After abstaining for the duration of his nineteen years, he finally learned why people drink. It felt good. Now, he was learning why they didn't.

Swinging his feet from the bed, he planted them down on the soft carpet below. He had not yet become accustomed to this level of warmth and comfort. Raising his arms high, he eased into a deep stretch. Then, placing his elbows on his knees and his jaw in his hands, he sat. Gazing out over a waking Colorado Springs, he thought about what had transpired. Taking inventory, he considered each one separately. He saved the planet. The 2BIRDS had worked. Not in the way he expected, but it worked. It—no, he—would rescue all the occupants on Planet Earth. He was just getting started. He thought about all the construction work ahead. When he compared this time in history to the war effort, the manufacturing that ultimately defeated Hitler and the Nazis in World War II, he was not speaking in hyperbole. This effort would be on a magnitude of scale many times what they accomplished during those times. But they could do it. They would do it. He was confident. He believed. And the other thing, he was now a billion-aire. A multibillionaire. He was much less sure of this fact. That is when a surge of anxious energy lifted him from his bed. He half-ran to the dining room table—a kid on Christmas morning—to open his laptop.

Waiting again for the bank's web page to refresh, he scanned down to see the number: $10,000,813,496.01. Rubbing his eyes again, he calcu-lated the math. While he slept, he made another seven-hundred grand. Interest on the balance. Shaking his head to himself in disbelief, he muttered "So, this is how rich people do it" as if he had just found the missing piece to an old jigsaw puzzle hidden away in the couch cush-ions. He clicked "refresh" once again to make sure it had not changed. The number remained the same, but he reminded himself that it would grow during the next hourly sweep, the word banks use to "sweep" interest into the account. Up to this point, his definition for sweep meant pushing a broom around for minimum wage, which is how he was earning his sweep payments a year ago. That thought brought a smile to his face. With his left hand grasping the screen to close the laptop, he spotted a notification on another tab. It alerted him to a new email. After Jason Harper Victory Day, he would receive millions of emails each day, but for now, any email, just one, was unusual. He never subscribed to any mailing lists and his spam folder was set to "High Alert." He liked his in-box the same way he liked everything: Uncrowded.

Clicking on the tab, he read the subject line first. "Thank you!" The sender field displayed a name he did not recognize: Alexander Cribb. He opened the message which began, "Hey Jason, we cannot thank you enough for your generous donation to the Pragmatist Party!" It then went on to itemize a few of the things the funds will be used for, as well as detailing their progress so far. "We have a candidate in the upcoming city council election," it noted with urgency. "Everything is at stake. We must act now." Jason read this part of the letter with some level of amusement because this guy, Alexander, had no idea about the press conference CLIMA was planning for next week. "Fundamentally, the problems facing our nation—and our planet—can be solved with the very same math they teach in the first grade," a line which would go on to be repeated. "Simply put, there are too many people and too few resources." He then closed with "I'd love to meet up and get your thoughts on all of this. You can reach me anytime on video chat by clicking here." The word "here" had been highlighted in blue. Then he signed off: "Follow the truth wherever it leads, Alex."

Jason's mind traveled back to the ant hills near the creek. Insects scrambling over one another, bumping and touching. It brought a shiver of discomfort originating somewhere between his shoulder blades, traveling up to the base of his skull. Returning to the message, he read it again. This time more closely. At the end, he hovered the arrowed over the word "here." All he had to do now was click the button to launch an instant video chat. Then, he reminded himself that everything was about to change. Everything. Getting involved with a club back at the community college would only be a waste of time. A distraction. That's when his phone rang. He could see that it was a CLIMA number, so he answered. The woman's voice on the other end was one he did not recognize. The caller explained that she had been assigned to oversee the press conference this week and wanted to "go over some details and answer any lingering questions." After talking about what to wear and what to expect from the network reporters, she closed by saying, "You will be sequestered in your apartment until the press conference on Wednesday. For the next five days you will not be allowed to leave. Armed guards will be stationed outside your door. We will take care of everything for you during that time."

Jason was dumfounded. It made no sense to him. The explanation offered by CLIMA was inconceivable. "Mr. Harper, you are now worth a lot of money and there are a lot of desperate people out there. If they knew what was in your bank account, they would gladly do you harm in order to get a piece of it. We cannot risk a misstep so close to the finish line."

"But no one knows…" Jason was interrupted before he could finish his sentence.

"I'm sorry, it's too great a risk," the CLIMA representative repeated.

"When this is over, you can operate your own security detail. For now, you are the responsibility of the United States government. Are we in agreement, Mr. Harper?"

For the first time, he realized just how much his life was about to change. "Okay, okay," he answered. "I'll hang out here." He ended the call. Standing in the middle of the apartment, he was struck by the quiet. Not a sound. Nothing. He wondered what he would do with himself for the next five days. Curious, he went to the door. Pressing his ear against the wood grain veneer, he could hear muffled voices. The view finder showed only a shoulder. A massive shoulder. Debating with himself for a moment, he cracked opened the door. A chorus of cheerful voices called out, "Good morning, Mr. Harper." There were two men flanking the entrance. They appeared to be Air Force personnel. Both were armed with all the latest assault weaponry. Two more could be seen further down each hallway. One of them pressed two fingers to his right ear as he received instructions, while the other appeared to be talking into his left wrist, apparently giving them. A balding man in his late fifties with a soft and gentle face appeared with a tablet cradled in his arm. "Good morning, Mr. Harper," he repeated. "Would you like to order some breakfast, sir?" The word "sir" struck him. He could not a recall a time he had ever been referred to as "sir." Stumbling and unbalanced for a moment, he realized that he was wearing nothing but his underwear. No one cared. They were there to serve him. There to do a job. Protect and serve Jason Harper.

Hot chocolate was the perfect complement to the three-egg omelet plus waffles, sausage, and hash browns. Breakfast is not something he normally ate, most everyone at the Hilliard House knew that it was a good meal to skip. An easy way to stretch a buck. He was stuffed and waddled his way to the couch. Flipping through the channels, there was nothing on worth watching. He wondered how much money he made while eating breakfast, so he returned to the dining table. Another one-hundred thousand had been added to the balance. Not a bad day's work, especially considering it was not yet nine o'clock. He thought back to the email message he received and decided to read it again. Something about it captured his imagination, which was uncommon because he could imagine quite a lot. Again, he landed on the word "here," which doubled as a hyperlink. He hovered the pointer over four letters glowing in blue. Before he realized what he had done, a new screen popped up: "Calling Alexander Cribb." He panicked briefly and considered ending the call before it started, then thought better of it.

The screen changed again. It was a face Jason immediately recognized from the Incel Club, "A.C., what's up, man?" Jason offered an awkward greeting, now experiencing deep regret for having clicked "here."

"What's up?" Alex responded. "Do I know you?" Jason scolded himself, realizing he should have clicked "End Call" as the screen on the other end would have stated, "Unidentified Caller."

"Yeah, um," Jason considered telling him it was a misdial. "It's Jason, Jason Harper."

"What? No way! I was expecting some old man! You go to my school, right? We're at the same college," now catching on. "Wait a minute— we're in the Incel Club together! What's up, my man?! Where have you been?"

The kid everyone called A.C. was a freshman. His buggy eyes were always wide-open, missing nothing. The irises were so dark that they blended together with the pupils, giving him a cartoon-like appearance. He almost appeared to be a character of himself. Wired up tight with bounding energy, he seemed to get excited about everything.

"I've been out here in Colorado doing some work," Jason replied.

After some follow-up questions, which Jason dodged, Alex then asked a whopper. "Dude, Jason, where'd you get all that money?"

Jason laughed, knowing he would earn it back by the time the clock struck ten. "It was nothing, just wanted to help out a bit," he deflected.

"Well, seriously, we cannot thank you enough. That was super generous of you, man."

Jason then mentioned something about "believing in the cause." That was all Alex had to hear. He got the green light. The door had been opened and the words began flowing through it rapid-fire succession. Philosophy, history, politics, and math were blended together in a monologue that went on for twenty minutes without a breath. Jason was transfixed. Everything coming out of Alex's mouth made perfect sense. For once, someone other than himself had some answers. It was all so much simpler than it appeared. At least for those who were smart enough to understand it.

"Look, Jason, this is simple math: too many people, not enough resources," Alex would begin as he always did.

Following each new concept, Jason would reflect momentarily before offering a "Yes, but…" Alex always had an answer. And it was always a good one.

That first video chat went on for nearly five hours. It was a knock on the front door that finally ended it. "I'll call you back," Jason stated abruptly as he rose from the couch.

"Excuse me, sir, but I just wanted to check on your welfare. You didn't eat lunch. Can I bring you something?"

"Thanks, but I'm still full from breakfast. But how about another hot chocolate? Extra whipped cream this time."

"Yes, sir, immediately, sir. And should we go ahead and put in your dinner order now?"

Jason requested a steak. When asked which cut he preferred, he was stumped. "Whatever one you think is best." The man replied, "My favorite is a ribeye, medium-rare, sir."

"Okay, I'll have one of those and whatever comes with it—and another bottle of that champagne."

"Yes, sir. Is six o'clock good for you, sir?"

After his usual regimen of push-ups and sit-ups, Jason took a shower. It was longer and hotter than any shower he could ever remember. The words "hot" and "shower" did not go together for most of his life. The Hilliard House showers were cold and short. Dance around in the freezing drops. Shut off the water. Lather up with soap. Turn the ice water on again to rinse off. That was it. Steaming up the bathroom, as he was doing now, was for rich people. And he was one of them now. Better start acting like it.

Back at the couch, Jason lifted the hot chocolate to his lips. Swirling his tongue in the whipped cream, he clicked "here" again. Instantly, Alex answered.

"What's up, man?" Alex asked with his characteristic enthusiasm.

"Just hangin' out with some hot chocolate," Jason replied, toasting with his mug via video.

"Oh, man, that looks good. What kind is it?"

"They just br…" Jason stopped himself realizing that saying "They just brought it to me" would open up many questions. But switching course mid-sentence and fast-talking came naturally. "Not sure, but whatever it is, it's awesome."

Alex was satisfied with the answer. He did not really care about the hot chocolate anyway. He was only looking for a segue to continue where the conversation left off.

"So, getting back to the problem, Jason, which is really just a simple math problem…"

Student and teacher continued until straight-up six o'clock when there was another knock and another hurried "I'll call you back." Jason marveled that steak could taste like this, and melt in his mouth the way it did. His only exposure had been, when he was lucky enough to have it, something resembling an oversized misshapen chunk of beef jerky. Chewy and hard, and either over salted or under salted. This is how rich people ate, he said to himself. This is how he would eat now. The second bite lingered a while longer than the first. He was determined to extract every drop of flavor. Now, he needed something to wash it down. The cork again sailed through to the livingroom. Champagne and ribeye combined in a way that he never thought possible. The word "exquisite" came to mind. It was a word he would never have used before, except maybe to mock rich people. Today, he learned what it meant. What it really meant.

All the sharp edges disappeared again, and the rosy hue returned—the reason people drink—as Jason returned to the couch with half of the bottle's contents remaining. Clicking "here," Alex appeared. "Here's looking at you, kid," he said mimicking the line he heard in an old movie somewhere along the way. He then held out the bottle in salute before taking in a long swig.

"Wow, that looks like some expensive stuff," Alex observed before asking, "Where'd you get it?"

Jason deflected the question that Alex did not really care about knowing an answer to anyway. Both of them were intent on talking about the problems of the world, which they did for five days straight. By the end of their marathon video chat, two things were established: They settled on a solution. And they found something each would have never admitted they had been seeking—a friend.

Years later, the first arrest was made under a new federal statute, felony blasphemy. A hoard of camera bots filmed the blogger as he was dragged from his home in handcuffs. The title of his post: "Five Days in Colorado: The Radicalization of Jason Harper."

16

As the 2BIRDS began sprouting up around the globe, a strange thing happened: the sun went away. Everyone was told to expect it. Jason Harper explained it all with a drawing, but no one really understood what it meant to live life in the shade. For decades, the relentless pounding of sunlight became a fact of life. People adjusted. Similar to the mountain ranges growing on the edge of every town and city, the vengeful sunlight was familiar. Over time, history dictates that even something which had once been objected will eventually be embraced. Ultraviolet rays, even though they were destroying civilization, were no different.

Mankind evolved. Those who could afford it took Vitamin D supplements. The very wealthy installed home tanning booths. Everyone else ran toward the sunny patches that would sometimes show themselves on the ground. They never lasted for more than a few minutes, usually between shifts or during a lunch break. The lack of Vitamin D became an efficient way to sort the "haves" from the "have-nots." Dark circles under the eyes gave it away. Deficiency. Those were the people who could not afford the supplements. Makeup manufacturers enjoyed a booming trade, as the poor would attempt to conceal their social standing by applying brands which promised upward mobility, such as "Bling" and "48-Karat." It was obvious, perhaps even more so with the shoddy product who was rich and who was poor. Eyes speak the truth.

The Sapins were comfortable. Money was not an issue. It could have been even less of one if Angela worked, but she chose to stay home with the baby. She debated the idea during her entire pregnancy, but Mark was steadfast, insisting she would regret not doing it. "Who cares about the money?" he would challenge her. "Our son, our family, that's what's important. Everything else will fall into place. We can always get more money later, but we've only got one shot at this." His persistence won her over, just as she hoped it would. While she was moved by the argument made by everyone else, she was secretly wanting to stay home with Ben.

His Vitamin D supplements would come from a dropper. Liquid sunlight would go into his whirled peas and mashed carrots each night. Two drops. No more no less. Angela was always on the lookout for sunlight, just like everyone else. She kept a plastic play pool in the corner of the backyard for the occasion. When the shade gave way to light, she would rush to strip Ben down and race out to the pool. With a garden hose in one hand and her baby's bare back in the other, she would sing nursery rhymes, which were received by squeals of delight. "Merrily, merrily, merrily, life is but a dream." Those days were the best. The days with light. There was no worry about getting enough Vitamin D, the only concern was for normalcy. "Everyone needs the sun—that's just how we were built," she would insist.

Mark's health care plan included unlimited visits to the sun salons. When the baby arrived, they would take turns in the light booth. It was not the same as sitting on the sand out on the beach, but the virtual reality glasses made it a close second. They could do a lot of amazing things with technology, but replicating the ocean was not one of them. And Mark knew it because he read the software. It was a hobby that Angela thought strange at first. Mark would claim it gave his brain a "reset" after a long day at the office. Opening the source code on a particular piece of software that he admired and following along in an attempt to discern how the programmer had done it gave him joy and satisfaction—a sense of accomplishment. While everyone else dismissed virtual reality as "magic," Mark knew better. He could see it written in black and white. There was nothing magical about it. It was thousands of lines of indiscernible numbers and symbols, at least they were indiscernible to most everyone but the programmer, and Mark. No one else cared to know how things worked. They simply accepted new software for what it did for them: more convenience, more entertainment, more economic productivity. Asking questions like "how" and "why" made no logical sense. That is why Mark would always describe his code reading as a "quirky little hobby of mine."

Virtual reality was one thing, but artificial intelligence was quite another. Mark was fascinated by AI code. Programmers of the new software languages were next-level geniuses. To see their minds at work as he followed the digital bread crumbs they left in the source code was no different than reading the best books on Gramoo's shelf. He would talk about losing his sense of time and space as he followed along with the author, or the programmer. During one of her interviews, she had relayed something Mark had once said to her: "To witness what they were doing was to see the mind at work, only with AI it was exponential. You were seeing the programmer's thought process in the development of a new and separate thought process. A mind creating a mind."

The work Mark did from nine-to-five was satisfying on a much lower level. Having total mastery over something—data—although he was capable of solving larger problems gave him a sense of control. The bits and bytes, zeros and ones, were static. Black and white. Facts. Truth. Programming and code were built upon those things, yes, but they were shaped and molded by their creator. Mark was in high demand and his services commanded a significant salary. In previous decades, the Sapin family would have been called "middle class," but there was no longer such a thing because no one used that terminology anymore.

The Sapins lived in a three-bedroom, two-bath, two-story Craftsman. It was an old-style home built in the 1920s. When they moved in ten years earlier, Gramoo told him about the history of the architecture.

There was a time when a retailer called Sears, Roebuck and Company sold houses, such as theirs, in complete do-it-yourself kits. Entire neighborhoods were built one home at a time. The owner of the home would receive a truckload of lumber and nails and windows and doors delivered to the front of their empty lot, along with a set of instructions. One by one, a new Craftsman would pop up. That was not the part that fascinated him, however. It was Gramoo's retelling of the way neighbors used to help one another. "They would share a beer at the end of the day as a way of saying, 'thank you,'" she insisted. Mark doubted this was an accurate accounting of their home's past, but he always enjoyed his grandmother's colorful history lessons.

Today, no one knew their neighbors. And, even if they did, they certainly would not attempt to build a house together. The construction bots could do it almost without supervision, plus manual labor was plentiful. Builders would send vans to the shantytowns to load them up with low-cost worker bees to supplement their fleet of construction bots. At night, they returned them exhausted and broken. Everything would repeat the next day. The idea of anyone building their own house was absurd. Using one's hands for work never resulted in any meaningful economic productivity. At best, it was subsistence. Using hands instead of brain was a one-way ticket to the shantytown, which is why the schools shuttered their pathways in the trades long ago. Wood shop, auto shop, and metal shop are all relics of the previous decades. No one would be so cruel today to wish those fates upon their children. The only money to be made is in writing software to operate the robots who took those jobs, or in designing new tools for them to use.

Mark wondered what it would have been like to use his hands, to build something tangible, to lift a stick-framed wall with his neighbors. To clink a beer with them and toast to a job well done. He craved a connection with them, which is why he was one of the few to ever answer a knock on the front door.

It had been a long day. A big push was underway to finish the project by the end of the quarter. Mark's mind was jumbled and fried. He did what he always did when he needed a reset; he sat down and opened his laptop. The family had just finished dinner and Angela remained in the kitchen washing dishes. Mark looked up from his computer to watch Little Benny toddle his way around the living room when some wooden play blocks caught his attention. They had been Mark's when he was growing up and he loved seeing how high his son could stack them before they would fall over. Surely, he had done the same thing at that age. The overhead lights were off, as they often were, and the lamps scattered about the living room were set at dim. From behind, Angela placed her left hand on Mark's shoulder at the same time her right hand slipped a glass of red wine on the end table next to his place on the couch. She planted a kiss on the top of his head and wrapped both arms around his neck. Together, they spent the next minute connected in marital bliss as they watched Ben study the blocks. Angela returned to her dishes and Mark returned to the code. The song streaming through the speakers, "Sunny Side of the Street" by Louis Armstrong, was Angela's choice. And her way of telling her husband that she was happy. That's when there was a knock at the door.

Mark looked up. He didn't move at first, frozen. He would wait to find out if it went away. It didn't.

Walking past the kitchen to the entryway, Angela shot him a look that he interpreted as, "Don't you dare!" Pleading his case in silence with a shrug of his shoulders, he reached for the handle at the same time he clicked on the porch light. There, on the stoop, was a woman who appeared much older than he believed her to be with one arm around each of her two children standing in front of her. "Please," she begged. "Can you spare some money for Vitamin D?" Mark stepped out front, closing the door behind him. He did not want to argue with Angela.

Quizzing the mother, he inquired, "Is that really what you need the money for? You're not going to use it to buy drugs, are you? Or blow it on VR?"

"No, no, sir. My kids are sick. Their bones are brittle. They haven't had sunlight in months. We're out of supplements. My husband was hurt on the job. We have no income."

Mark looked down and back up again. He took stock of the three souls standing outside of his front door. Their sallow and pocked skin featured the distinctive black circles under their eyes. There was no doubt they were in trouble and needed the supplement. Resigning himself with a deep breath, he reached into his wallet and handed the mother a one-hundred-dollar bill. "Promise me," he said, "this will be used only for Vitamin D for your kids and nothing else." The woman promised, and Mark reentered his home.

No words were required, Angela's look—hands on hips in front of the sink—said everything that was on her mind: *stop giving them money; that should be used for us, not them.* Mark knew she was right. He lowered his head as he mumbled as much to himself as to her. "Look, I'm sorry. I don't want to argue. They really needed it. I won't do it again." They both knew he was lying.

Returning to the couch, Mark placed the computer on his lap before taking a long draw from his wineglass. It went down smooth and peace returned. Louis Armstrong was now crooning "What a Wonderful World." *The colors of the rainbow, so pretty in the sky / Also on the faces of people going by.* Without looking up from the laptop, Mark attempted to break the tension by joining Armstrong in song, changing the lyrics with animated exuberance: "I see Benny crying, I'll watch him grow / He'll definitely learn much more than I'll ever know / And I think to myself, what a wonderful world." Angela could never stay mad for long, but she continued the silent treatment as she smiled to herself while placing another still-warm plate in the cupboard. Armstrong continued: *I see friends shaking hands, saying how do you do / They're only saying I love you.*

Angela heard the giggling. She wanted to see what Ben had gotten into this time, but she was still upset with Mark, so she tipped-toed toward the living room and peeked around the corner. From there, she could see her husband lying on ground with both legs extended. Ben held his hands outstretched as he pretended to fly through the air while Mark balanced him on the bottom of his socked feet. Pumping and swinging erratically, Mark made the sounds of an airplane diving and climbing. Ben giggled as he balanced himself, looking for more. The day had exhausted and depleted Mark. He was uninspired and unfulfilled for much of it, but he reminded himself this was why he sat in that spirit-sucking cubicle for eight hours a day—to be here now. His foot slipped and Ben flipped forward a full rotation landing belly down on his father's chest, which took the wind from both of them. They quickly recovered from the impact and laughed and hugged. Mark kissed Ben on the cheek, squeezed him tight, and whispered in his ear, "I love you, Benny. I love you all the way to the moon and back." Angela snapped out of her funk. No longer upset, she laid down next to her husband on the floor. Mark turned toward his wife, gazing into her wet eyes he sang, "And I think to myself, what a wonderful world."

A few feet away on the couch, an urgent notification appeared on the laptop. In all-caps, it read: "BREAKING NEWS: 129 DEAD AT 2BIRDS CONSTRUCTION SITE IN LISBON, PORTUGAL."

17

The jet banked and began its decent. Late at night, from his mahogany desk, Jason Harper's stomach dropped. It had been thousands of times since he first flew on one of his private jets, but he was never comfortable with the falling sensation that accompanied the final approach. With his stomach suspended somewhere eight thousand feet above sea level, he peered through the glass to find the city lights of Lisbon.

He was tired. Drained. It had been six years of non-stop construction. Saving the world was exhausting. Life became a blur. One ribbon cutting after another. At least, by now, everyone had learned that handshakes were out. Fist bumping became the norm. After a while, all the landfills began to look the same. Posing with dignitaries in front of mountains of garbage had lost its appeal years ago. But the adulation of his fans did not.

A distinctive squawk of the tires contacting the runway, followed by a gentle lurch forward, indicated his arrival. A transport sped up the tarmac and the armed guards whisked him off to the suite which occupied the entire top floor of the hotel. Moments after Jason's head landed on the pillow, he was asleep. A deep, restful sleep. He awoke in the same position ten hours later. Rubbing his eyes, he strained to make out the numbers on the clock. He was late. His team let him sleep in. They knew he needed it.

Skipping breakfast, he hustled out the door, down the service elevator —his security detail insisted on this, in order to avoid the public—to the back alley where his entourage was waiting. Three cars in the front and three in the back were marked with the word *"polícia."* Their lights flashed as the motorcade raced toward the Sítio da Câmara Municipal de Lisboa. It was ten seventeen a.m. He was late, but the construction crew was later.

Frantic to finish ahead of the ceremony, more than twice the number of construction workers had been in the 2BIRDS than was customary. Electricians, plumbers, engineers, painters, and programmers tripped over one another—all 129 of them. The foreman barked orders, told them how lucky they were that the boss was running late. When Jason did arrive, that foreman barked a fateful order: *"Fecha a porta!"* Closing the door seemed a logical choice. Locking it and sealing it air-tight would muffle the noisy construction so Jason could stand at the lectern and deliver another victory speech. The crowd would never know that inside the 2BIRDS a mad scramble was underway.

Over and over again, *"Não está pronto!"*—not ready—was called out by the workers. Occasionally, the foreman would look through the port-hole on the door in an attempt to discern how much time they had remaining. Over Jason's shoulder, he could see what could have been misidentified as a rock concert or a championship soccer match or a religious revival. Everyone, it seemed, held their hands high in the air, swaying back and forth, clapping and cheering and bouncing. According the video, it was seventeen minutes and fifty-six seconds into the speech when the foreman's face appeared for the fifth time in the porthole. At that time stamp, Jason turned, and their eyes met. From below the main control console, the camera picked up the unmistakable snapping and buzzing of two electrical wires crossing followed by a hair-raising scream and a desperate call, *"Saia!"*—get out!

Frustrated with the missed deadline, Jason held his gaze with the foreman for a long moment. He wanted him to feel his displeasure. It was working because he detected fear in his eyes.

Then terror.

The foreman pressed his palms against the glass, which framed his panicked expression. The ground rumbled and shook, the giant vacuum engaged, as Jason watched the next few fractions of a second in ultra-slow motion. The foreman shot straight up. Through the port-hole, a slideshow appeared where Jason noted his gold chain, the belt buckle, and his work boots. He had appeared to hover for a split second before vanishing upward through the tube. Slow then sudden.

Pausing for a moment, Jason turned toward the crowd, his mind lurched, starting and stopping again in an attempt to sort out what he had just witnessed. They roared in anticipation for his next words. Instead of speaking, he stepped away and stumbled toward the door, bending at the waist as if he had just been punched in the midsection. Cupping his hands and pressing them against the glass porthole, he scanned the interior of the 2BIRDS. They were gone. Every single member of the construction crew had vanished in a flash. It all happened so fast. And was so quiet. And so—so sanitary. It was an odd thing to think, the sanitariness of it all, and he realized it in that moment. There was a clinical feel to it. No blood, no guts, no clean-up required. No remnants. No reminders. With a flip of the switch. Gone. Erased from the planet. Taken out, just like the garbage.

Twenty seconds later, a shadow was cast over the raucous crowd, over-taking the municipal dump site during another cloudless, sun-drenched morning. Jason returned to the microphone in an attempt to explain what had just transpired. He left out the part about the shade, which was now cooling everyone—the result of 129 Portuguese construction workers now gasping for breath as they flew in a low orbit, directly above. Most thought it was a part of the show. He was joking. Roaring laughter morphed to disbelief and shock, which even-tually became scattered tears. One of his handlers whispered some-thing in his ear. He announced that a trauma center was being established for friends and families of the victims before declaring, "I will personally get to the bottom of this and will hold whoever is responsible accountable. I want to make sure this never happens again."

Jason stepped down from the podium where he was greeted by his security detail. With a group of helmeted and uniformed gunman, he moved quickly to the VIP tent which had been emptied of its champagne chilling on ice and replaced with racks of lukewarm bottled water. Fold-out chairs were arranged in hasty, uneven rows. The cold cuts and cheeses were allowed to stay, while the dignitaries and celebrities were ushered out. One by one, they arrived. Their eyes were red after shedding more than an hour of tears. The people donning the threadbare, second-hand clothes entering the room stood in stark contrast to the tuxedos and gowns worn by the A-listers leaving it. Under any other circumstances, it would have been a stunning reversal as the "Who's Who" of Portuguese society were ordered to leave the VIP tent, as the residents of the nearby shantytown filed in to take their place.

At the front of the trauma center, Jason strained to avoid eye contact. As he had learned to do after thousands of speeches, he allowed himself to scan the room, occasionally settling on a friendly, receptive face. There was the middle-aged woman who nodded in agreement as he spoke. And the old man. He smiled and winked. For the first time ever, however, he was losing everyone else. They were angry and confused. A long-forgotten feeling had returned to the base of Jason's neck, just where it connects to the bottom of the skull, the same feeling he would get when he was growing up in the Hilliard House. It was a tingle of discomfort appearing immediately before the fists took flight. He had been conditioned to it, no different that Pavlov's salivating dogs. The bell rings, the food appears. The feeling arrives, people get hurt. A single shout came from somewhere in the pack, and it emboldened the others. The group became animated, and Jason felt the tingle amplify. Armed guards flanked to either side gripped their weapons and adjusted their stances. It was about to go down. Something had to be done. When he was a kid, he would have relied on a combination of humor and charm. There was no comedy available for this situation. He would go with the next best thing.

Raising both arms high overhead, he asked for their attention. "Once again, I want to say how sorry we are that this has happened. I promise to get to the bottom of it and hold whoever is responsible accountable." That's when a teenager rose, pointed at Jason, and cried out, "You're responsible! You did this. You killed my dad!" Three security guards restrained the young man. One on each arm, and one with his gloved hand over his mouth. Jason waved them off. "Stop, let him go." A hushed and stunned silence overtook the group. "Please, listen to what I have to say." He paused, allowing the glowering teenager to settle back into his seat.

"As I was saying, I vow to get to the bottom of this, and to find out who is responsible. I'm just as sad and upset as you are," Jason dabbed at the corner of his eyes, feigning tears as the crowd shifted in disapproval. "There is nothing that can be done to change what happened here today. But I am very sorry it happened. That's why I'm going to write a check to each of the surviving families for one million dollars." The air left the tent as everyone gasped in unison. One person began clapping. Then another. Soon the entire tent was standing, unified in their applause. Except for the teenager. He remained seated. His head down. Arms crossed.

The somberness of a funeral transformed into the exuberance of a carnival, as the once-grieving families arrived at one of the three designated tables to pick up their checks. A lawyer back at the corporate headquarters needed only a half-hour to draft the document. It was essentially a run-of-the-mill hold harmless agreement combined with a non-disclosure clause that could have been completed by any first-year law student, or any of the leading virtual lawyers online. The deal was simple: one million dollars in exchange for silence—no talking to the networks, or anyone—as well as relinquishing their right to sue the company or Jason Harper personally. It was a win-win, and by watching the people in line, Jason realized that he probably overpaid. From the side of the tent, surrounded by security, he watched as one family after another signed the document and then received a check. It was always the same. They would pass it around to one another, bug-eyed and astonished in reading the number: $1,000,000. Then, there would be a spirited group hug as the participants grappled with the appropriate emotion for the occasion. Jubilance and gratitude came together. Gratitude to the sacrifice their loved one had made. Gratitude to Jason Harper for writing the check. Jubilance in knowing that life was about to change for the better.

Jason had become accustomed to negotiating complex multibillion-dollar deals. When he first stepped to the front of the group, he wondered if these people saw him as the grim reaper. Instead, he was Santa Claus. Or one of those talk show hosts who hands out surprise gifts to the audience members. Either way, the reaction he received was not at all what he expected. But he was wealthy, and they were not. He knew that most of them would remain that way, too. That was the only part of it he regretted. There was no doubt many of them would stop by the Ferrari dealership on the way home before even going to the bank. Others will soon learn that a million bucks is nothing more than a respectable down payment on one of the homes dancing in their imaginations now. It was clear to Jason that he got the better end of the bargain. He won. In his mind there were visions of sports cars or mansions, only relief for the quick thinking that had mitigated his liability. And those 129 souls—he knew they were in a better place.

The motorcade was just as efficient in its departure as it had been in its arrival, probably more so. Jason was eager to leave. He had spent some time fist-bumping the throng of onlookers at the airport. He smiled for the selfies. But he was ready to go. Ready for everything to return to normal. The jet taxied as the crowd cheered. Jason could see a sign that someone in the pack hoisted. On an electric green background, in bold black handwritten letters it read: *"Jason é Senhor!"*—Jason is Lord. He cracked open his laptop as the aircraft climbed to its cruising altitude. He then closed his eyes and tried for a sleep that would not come. His mind raced.

It had been too easy. Within his own company the sales team did not call him "the Chosen One" or "the Messiah," but "the Closer." He always came in at the end to wrap up the sale of a 2BIRDS with its algae pond. He was surprised at how frictionless this transaction had been: *One million dollars for one life.* Again, he scolded himself for not starting the negotiations with a lower number. A rookie mistake. He thought back to Hoyamania and the networks. Rumor had it that Orange Crush was paid just fifty grand. He lasted only ten minutes. Jason reconsidered the math. *Five thousand dollars per minute.* The difference was that Orange Crush knew that he may die, while the construction crew did not. There was the occasional death at the 2BIRDS construction sites, of course. But it was always a user error at some elevation. Someone who did not buckle their safety harness or who refused to wear a parachute. Everyone complained about the parachutes. They were heavy and bulky and awkward, but they were life-savers. Taking a misstep on the scaffolding or getting blown off by the high winds twenty-five miles up—at that distance it would take five minutes to finally become a human Rorschach inkblot. What must have gone through their minds? Five minutes is a long time to think. But, still, it was a rare occurrence, just one here and there. In this case, 129 vanished all at once.

Jason wondered how much he would have had to pay them had it been their choice. What if there was intent? What if they had decided to do it? Thinking about Orange Crush on one end of the spectrum and the families of the construction workers on the other, he deduced that the number must be somewhere between fifty-thousand and one million. It was a strange thought to think. So, he stopped. At least he tried. What is the value of one shantytown resident? He searched his laptop for actuary tables, but could not find any values available for non-factors. Poor people don't buy life insurance. So, no one cares about how much their lives are worth. There is no money to be made in finding the answer to that question. No incentive. No profit.

That is when it occurred to him. And it would have been no different had a lightning bolt struck somewhere over the Atlantic. Surging with electricity—energy—he opened his email and addressed a message to Alex Cribb, marking it both urgent and personal. In the subject line he wrote in all-caps: "RAPTURE."

18

The train left for downtown each morning at seven fifty-one. Although he could certainly afford to take the family car to work, Mark preferred to ride by rail. He would tell himself that he was more productive. But that was not true because he could also catch up on email sitting in the backseat of self-driving vehicle, the same way his colleagues commuted to work. The truth, as usual, was more complicated and could not be fully understood by a measurement of personal productivity.

First, there was the walk through the neighborhood. It was something people used to do after dinner to "help the food settle," and to visit. Just walk. "Get some air," as his grandparents would say. Nobody walked for the sake of walking anymore. It was inefficient. Aside from the sentimentality—Mark spent hours in his grandfather's basement watching the model train circle the track—he found comfort in seeing the same faces each morning. Although people usually kept to themselves during the short trip downtown, mostly streaming a broadcast, he found the daily routine grounding.

It was a Wednesday morning when Mark arrived at the "Street Closed for Repairs" sign. Everything was blocked off by trucks and construction workers. It was easy to identify it as a crew from the city because they never used robots, not even rentals. Politicians insisted they hire labor from the shantytowns. It was good for the local economy. Plus, robots couldn't vote. For a moment, Mark scanned the scene and considered the idea of finding a way to slip through the line-up of orange cones. He thought better of it, following the "Detour" signs instead. He had never walked this way through the neighborhood. Although he would have to hustle to make the train, he swiveled his head back and forth in order to take a good look at the homes he passed. Just like his own, they were all old-style Craftsmans. His mind wandered back hundreds of years to the time when neighbors banded together to build these houses. Neighbors helping neighbors. Neighbors talking to neighbors.

For the most part, the homes were well kept. Except for one. It was not that it had fallen in disrepair; it was overgrown. It was unusual to have vegetation of any sort in the yard because it was so inefficient. Money and time were required to maintain bushes and trees and flowers. Over time, most everyone ripped out their landscaping and replaced it was rock and concrete and perhaps some artificial turf if they had kids. This particular house appeared to be the lone holdout. The owner was likely stuck: not enough money for replacement or maintenance. It was a shame, Mark noted. The structure itself was a less robust version of its former self, faded by the pounding sun. It was mostly concealed from the street by a gnarled and calcified assortment of ancient branches and vines belonging to trunks which had checked out long ago. Mark wondered if this would be the sort of thing in the past when the neighborhood showed up to help—to pitch in and clean up the mess. It would not take much if there was a lot of helpers. "Many hands make light work," as Gramoo used to say, at least when she was asking for help in the kitchen.

Lost in the thought, Mark was unaware that his pace had slowed. And that he was gawking at the house. That's when the man—an old man wearing a baseball cap—appeared at the banister enclosing the front porch. He cradled a paperback book in one hand and a coffee mug in the other. Mark locked eyes with him, as he scolded himself in silence for staring. The old man nodded his acknowledgment. Mark returned a halting wave.

———

Work was the same as always: Okay. He did what was expected of him, and put in his forty hours. Never more, never less. The title on his security badge said, "data analyst." That is what they paid him to do, analyze data, so that's what he did. Every day, he would find his cubicle and slip on his headphones. Gramoo had introduced him to grunge music, which had been popular in the 1990s. His favorite was a band called Nirvana. They tapped in to him somehow, reaching something he was feeling at a primal level. He could feel their rage and knew he had some of it, too. It was buried deep, but it was down there somewhere. Fortunately, he had the discipline to harness it. Mark dutifully clocked in and clocked out as he pecked away at his keyboard while basking in the dim glow of his monitor, day after day. Just like everyone else. Still, he fantasized about unleashing the animal he felt roaring inside by standing up and screaming obscenities at his dumbass boss as he bobbed his head to the defiant rhythm of the grunge rockers, who were not forced to endure the bitter aftertaste that came from conformity, from being continually wedged into a box—or a cubicle. He turned up the music and strummed imaginary guitar strings against his stomach: *I wish I was like you / Easily amused / Find my nest of salt / Everything's my fault / I take all of the blame / Aqua sea foam shame / Sunburn, freezer burn / Choking on the ashes of her enemy.*

Eventually, he would snap out of the daydream and remind himself to be thankful. It was one of the few jobs remaining that was not under constant threat of replacement by robots or artificial intelligence. And, increasingly, the two were merging. Robots were becoming intelligent. But they weren't smart enough to analyze. Mark was sure it would not happen during his lifetime. AI was not advancing as quickly as everyone had predicted. The software still had a long way to go before it could replace someone like Mark. He did not believe the hype because he, unlike everyone else, actually studied the software, he read the code. The future was further out than most people realized. It was something he thought about often as he sat as his desk. His work required so little of his attention that he could hold a few thoughts at once—the task at hand, Nirvana, and the future of artificial intelligence. That's when a fourth thought arrived: Time to pack it up and head home.

As he stepped off the train on the return trip, Mark remembered the construction, so he set out to retrace his steps from earlier in the morning. This time, he would not stare. His laptop bounced with each step in his otherwise empty backpack. He had fixed his gaze on his feet and accelerated his pace while passing the house with the overgrown landscaping. He sang to himself under his breath: *I wish I was like you / Easily amused.*

Mark would later tell the interrogators that this was the day they met.

"Hello, there," the voice called out from the porch. It was not a strong and robust voice. Instead, it was out of practice. Seasoned and gravelly. Used up. Old.

Mark fought the impulse to scurry away before raising his hand in the same unsure manner as he had done that morning. "Oh, hi. Hello," he said, slowing his stride. Confused, disoriented. He stopped. Not sure what to do next. No one had ever said anything to him during his walk from the train platform.

"How was work?" the old man inquired.

Taken aback by the question, Mark did not know how to answer. "Oh, it was okay. I guess. Same as always," he offered before turning to continue his walk.

"Excuse me, son," the old man continued. "Before you head home, I was wondering if you could give me a hand with something? It will only take a minute."

Mark was contemplating the odd request when the old man connected. "You know, many hands make light work."

The path leading to the porch was lined with overgrown bushes. As

Mark approached, it appeared as if he were crossing a stream, carefully selecting one rock and then the next as he tested his footing on his way to the other side.

"I ordered this screen door," he said, motioning toward the tall and narrow box in the corner, "but I need four hands to put it in. I've only got two."

Surveying the scene, the words escaped Mark's lips by a reflex he did not realize he possessed. "Sure, no problem."

"Thank you, son," the old man offered, as he stepped into the soft light.

The first thing Mark noticed were his eyes. Not that there was anything remarkable about them, but the white part—the whites of his eyes—stood in stark contrast to his coal-black skin. Next, his hat. He donned a sun-bleached black baseball cap, which featured an assortment of embroidered military-style emblems. In a once-proud faded yellow stitching it announced, "Korea II Veteran." Slender, but not slight. He was wiry and strong and stood at attention. His clothing was neat and pressed. It was difficult to estimate his age because skin was porcelain-smooth and as wrinkle-free as his tucked-in t-shirt. But the cataract clouds graying his eyes gave him away. Mark guessed he was in his early eighties.

"Boo Radley," he introduced himself with a wry grin, extending his right hand which revealed a tight and toned forearm. Veins crisscrossed as if mountain roads on a map.

Mark immediately caught the reference—Boo Radley—thought quickly and introduced himself as "Atticus Finch, at your service."

"Well, now, I should have taken you for a reader," the old man observed, looking Mark up and down. "The glasses, it's those wire-rimmed glasses. And, your eyes. You have curious eyes. They give you away, Mr. Finch."

Mark was transported back to Gramoo's den. The lawyer, Atticus Finch, was his favorite character in *To Kill A Mockingbird*. He read the book three times. He wondered if the old man realized that Boo Radley was white. Everyone who reads that book seems to get it wrong in their assumption that Radley was black. Set in the Deep South during the Great Depression, the kids growing up in Radley's neighborhood were terrified of him. They described him as a ghost, a spooky ghost. He was never seen out of his house, so the kids' imaginations ran wild, thinking the worst of him. As Mark would report to his grandmother, the author, Harper Lee, had been masterful in her treatment of Boo Radley, eventually revealing the character as an old man who was nothing more than a harmless recluse, a misunderstood eccentric. Mark was fascinated as to why the old man now shaking his hand would introduce himself in this way.

Installing a screen door was not something Mark had ever done before, but it went in without a hitch. *Many hands make light work.* As the two took turns driving screws with the cordless drill, Mark filled the silence by talking about the architecture of the old man's home.

"It's a Craftsman. Probably a Sears Craftsman. Somebody would have ordered it straight out of a catalog. It would have arrived in a kit, dumped off on the front yard," he said before relating it back to their little home improvement project now in progress. "Just like putting in a new screen door, except on a much larger scale. And everyone, all the neighbors, would have helped build it." Mark talked and talked. The words flowed. "And there was no payment or anything like that. People would do it—help each other out—just because that's what they did. I'm guessing that your house was built during the Prohibition, so alcohol would have been outlawed. I bet that the homeowner paid everyone back by giving them a beer at the end of the day. That's it. That's all it took. A beer."

The old man leaned in, becoming more interested in the history of his house than the project at hand. That's when he was gripped by a memory.

Stepping back and looking up, he wiped his brow. Smiling to himself, something had struck him as funny. "The Sears catalog," he repeated, laughing and shaking his head. "Boy, that thing got me in trouble."

Mark, who was kneeling down at the base of the doorway, looked up to interpret the expression fixed on the old man. His curiosity had been piqued. "What do you mean?"

"Well, Momma used to collect those things. And they were as thick as a brick," he said, holding up his hand, exaggerating a distance of six inches between his thumb and forefinger. "One day, I found her box of catalogs hidden away in the garage. It was after school and she hadn't come home from work yet. I was just as bored as ever—she never gave me a cell phone because she didn't want me on social media or steaming TV like the rest of the kids—so I opened up that box and took one out. I wondered what the heck it was, so I sat down at the kitchen table and studied it like I was in the library."

Mark laid down the pair of pliers he had been gripping and leaned his shoulder into the wall. He was curious about the concept of a Sears catalog, too. He had never seen one himself.

"Well, I'm looking at the toys first. Pages and pages of toys. Everything that you can imagine. I was just a kid myself and was fascinated by what other kids would have played with back in the day. Then, I turned to the tools—all shiny silver or bright red and stamped with the word 'Craftsman,' just like the house kit you were talking about."

Mark nodded his head along.

"So, I keep flipping through," the old man pantomimes the turning of pages. "And it's the clothing section. First, it's boys' clothes, which I don't really care about, but I want to see what all is in this book, so I keep going. It's like I am on a journey into the unknown and the trail is unfolding before my eyes. After that, it's girls' dresses and stuff like that. So, I keep going, and it becomes women with big hair wearing these crazy-looking jackets. They would stuff shoulder pads in there, you know. That was the style back then. It looked like they were suiting up to play football."

The old man chuckled. Mark smiled.

"After all that, it must have been somewhere around page 657, or something like that," he said, again exaggerating. "Well, I turn that page and Jesus Christ Almighty!" he jumps up and grabs his chest and stumbles to the banister, as if in the throes of cardiac arrest. "It's a bunch of ladies modeling bras and panties. At the top it says, 'Women's Lingerie.'"

Mark laughs out loud, fully absorbed by the tale being told.

"I thought the word was 'ling-rr-ee,' because, yes sir, I did linger. Boy, did I linger. I lingered on all seventeen pages of that section for the entirety of that afternoon. I studied those ladies up and down, side to side. Yes, I did. I couldn't figure out why they were so interesting to me, but Lord Almighty, they had a grip on me something fierce. I studied those curves and those curls, determined to memorize every single one of them."

Mark was transported someplace else. Sometime else.

"So, I'm learning all about different bra sizes—C, D, Double D, you name it—and I'm looking at these pictures like a starving man would a ham sandwich. Drooling, and in a trance, my head is down and I'm studying harder than I ever thought possible. That's when my head whips to the side and I turn to see Momma following through with a right hook. Then, she just lays into me: 'I'm not going to let you burn in hell! Satan is not welcome here! No sir, not in my house!' She grabs me by the ear and twists hard, leading me into the bathroom and turns on the cold-water knob and shoves me in the shower, clothes and all. She's yelling at me. 'You need to cool yourself off!' Then, she stood there in the doorway with arms crossed and steam coming from her ears, chewing me up one side and down the other. She watched me damn near freeze to death."

Pausing before leaning back to look up at the tongue and groove ceiling covering the porch, Boo Radley added, "Oh, Momma, I love you. And I miss you. May God rest your soul."

19

The video footage played on his laptop at least a thousand times. Probably more. When Jason decided to focus his attention on something, he went all in, obsessing over every detail, no matter how small. Within a few weeks of the debacle in Lisbon, he had broken the three seconds in question into three-thousand milliseconds. Each frame was played one at a time, over and over again.

Just as he remembered from his vantage point at the podium, the camera, which he could now zoom in, captured the desperation registered on the Portuguese foreman's face. Pounding the glass, screaming, then hands flat against it, the valve opened on the 2BIRDS. The man appeared to hover at first, rising steadily before shooting upward in a flash.

He zoomed in from a different camera, and then another. Jason understood the phenomenon when he saw it: Vacuum power increases gradually, but exponentially, in the 2BIRDS. *Slowly then suddenly*. From behind, he could see the foreman float up a foot-and-a-half in the first second, eight feet in the next second, and ninety feet in the third before leaving the camera frame.

Jason studied each of the 129 workers. There were cameras everywhere inside the tube. He studied each of the recordings. They all demon-strated the same phenomenon. Their arms flailed, they kicked and screamed in terror before they shot straight up, accelerating exponen-tially on their way toward 17,000 miles per hour as they raced for low orbit. Jason did the research and knew they died a relatively peaceful death by asphyxiation somewhere between fifteen and ninety seconds after reaching outer space where they spent their last few moments watching the ants scurry below.

After the jubilation following Jason's million-dollar settlement announcement with the surviving families, he remembered seeing a woman rocking back and forth in her chair. She appeared to be in a trance, with her hands held palms up as if cradling a baby. A wooden cross, the type worn by Christians, adorned her neck. As if a mantra, she repeated the word *"êxtase."* Curious about what he was witnessing, he looked it up on his flight back to the States and found the literal translation: Rapture.

Books were rare a rare sight at the Hilliard House, but he remembered a kid he knew there whose mother owned all sixteen installments of the *Left Behind* series, which had been popular with evangelicals many years ago. Jason remembered asking the kid about those books, the only ones they owned other than the Bible. They were water stained and sun-bleached, lining the bottom sill of their only kitchen window. The kid said they were about "the Rapture." Jason had never heard of such a thing, so he pressed further. What do you mean? The kid answered: "When God has finally seen enough, he will bring all of the believers—the Christians—to heaven. They'll be right in the middle of something and—bam!—they'll get beamed straight up instantly. They'll fly straight up."

Jason was midway over the Atlantic when he made the association, the connection. That's when he realized what he had witnessed in Lisbon earlier that day—Rapture.

Again, he went online for another search. He found a digital archive of one of the books, the first one in the series, this one called *Left Behind: A Novel of Earth's Last Days*. He scanned the contents, and it was exactly as the Hilliard House kid had described. People everywhere—at least Christian people—flew up, straight up to heaven without warning. The book appeared to be more of a mystery, describing all the horrible things that happened to the unbelievers remaining on Earth who tried to figure out what happened to their Christian friends. By the end, it was clear that heaven, wherever it happened to be, was a much better option than Earth. Jason found the two authors' description of the planet's last days amusing because they were nothing at all what the actual last days—at least what should have been the last days if he hadn't come to the rescue—were actually like.

He then queued up another search, this one for the literal definition of the word rapture, which came back as "a feeling of intense pleasure or joy—ecstasy, bliss, trance, intoxication, transport." He told himself that all 129 of those workers, whether they were Christian or not, were better off. They were in ecstasy. "Transported to heaven," he said out loud. With that, he penned the email to Alex with the subject line "RAPTURE."

For hours, he typed and typed, sharing everything he had learned, everything he remembered, everything that came up in his searches, everything he had read. "What happened in Lisbon—at least to those 129 workers—was the Rapture. They're in ecstasy." The words were coming faster than he could capture them. What he witnessed was "not the end, but the beginning." They were going to a better place. Transported to heaven. They were reuniting with their loved ones. He talked about his acid trip as a ten-year-old. How he had crossed the stream to meet his deceased grandparents. Up to that point, he had kept that memory to himself. Now, he described it in exquisite detail, down to the smell of shaving cream wafting from his grandfather's stubby whiskers. And the way his grandmother pulled him close, squeezing him tight before telling him to get back in his boat, to go back.

"They're in a better place," Jason wrote from the empty cabin of his private jet. "All 129 of them. And so are all 129 of the surviving families. Suddenly, they were millionaires. Win-win."

———

Seven months later, the company issued its findings. The electrician who had been bringing power to the main control console crossed two wires. That was all. Faulty wiring. After identifying the problem and the guilty party, the report offered policy changes to "prevent such a tragedy from ever occurring again." It warned that the most dangerous period of construction was immediately before the 2BIRDS became operational. The document noted that rushing to complete a project ahead of a ribbon cutting ceremony would be strictly prohibited going forward. "It is far too hazardous to employ exhausted crews who are pushing toward completion," it read before concluding. "This can lead to catastrophic mistakes, such as the one witnessed in Lisbon."

Insatiable demand for the 2BIRDS and the algae ponds that sat next to them never slowed—not before, after, or during Lisbon. The backlog of orders continued to grow even after the company attempted to bend the supply-demand curve by continually raising its prices. It did not matter what they charged. Everyone wanted to cool their patch of the planet, they wanted to clean up the mess, and they wanted Jason Harper to visit their town. That was always part of the negotiation: buy the algae pond also, and Jason will come see you. Hosting a ribbon cutting ceremony was as good as printing money, at least according to the cities and their chambers of commerce, which coordinated with the company to host the events. The economic activity they generated always provided a shot in the arm to the local economy as visitors far and wide came to glimpse the man who saved the world.

Everywhere Jason went, one question was sure to come up from the legion of adoring fans: "When are you going to run for president?" He would invariably deflect by answering that he was already president—and CEO—of his company, often with a wink. But it was a question that gnawed on him. He was fascinated by government, which is why he had majored in political science, but he was also revolted by it. His conversations with Alex became increasingly frustrated with "both sides of the aisle." He could not understand why it was so compli-cated. He appreciated ideas, but not complicated ones. He sought—

and found—simple solutions, such as vacuuming up the trash. If he could not sketch a concept on a page in his notebook, he was not interested.

Colorado Springs was a mess, much worse than Washington had ever been. One of the ironies leading up to the end of the world was that people abandoned politics. With the last domino in plain sight, being a conservative or a liberal no longer mattered. It reminded Jason again of World War II. The Allies. No one cared about the political views of the guy sharing the foxhole. As long as he kept firing bullets at bad guys, everything was fine. "The enemy of my enemy is my friend" was a line he would later make famous all over again. The enemy of everyone during those times was the climate apocalypse. There were no two ways about it. When the Nazis were blitzing, politics vanished. Mankind united as one in a way that had never been seen before. Which made it all the more difficult to understand how it could have fallen apart so quickly, at least in America. Within a few generations, the lines separating the two major political parties were dug in like the rows of machine gun nests dotting the beaches of Normandy. Political party affiliations, where one fit on the spectrum ranging from liberal to conservative, meant everything.

With the threat of climate extinction now gone, a different enemy had stepped forward to take its place: poor people. Easily identified now by the dark circles under their eyes, the politicians wrung their hands over what to do about it. And if fell, as it always did, in exactly the same way. The bleeding-heart liberals wanted to give them a handout. Tax the elite and give it to the poor. Transfer the wealth. Give them a leg up. Even the playing field. The conservatives scoffed at the notion, as usual. They prescribed their usual tough medicine: "Pull yourselves up-by-the-bootstraps. Work harder. Save more. Scratch and claw and climb your way up the ladder. The tax cuts would get the government off your back—that's what's holding you back—and so would rolling back the regulations." To Jason, none of it made sense. At best, it was entertainment. Theatre. At worst, it was another one-way ticket back to the brink of Armageddon. He was not sure he would be able to save everyone next time, which is why he listened whenever someone begged him to run for president.

He knew he would win. Everyone knew he would win. The only thing left in doubt was which party he would represent. It was comical to watch the two parties trip over themselves to court Jason Harper. Funny, only because he had no interest in either of them. If he joined one, he would be instantly despised by half of the country. Belonging to a political party was not unlike joining a gang or a sports team. It was never really about policies and platforms. It was about identity and belonging and culture. Tribalism. The only purpose of government, he reasoned, was to get things done. To solve problems. That is why it was a foregone conclusion. If he ever ran for president—and he was certain that it was only a matter of time—he would only ever consider doing so as a Prag. But it felt good to be courted. He enjoyed the attention from the two parties. He liked playing hard-to-get. In the meantime, he continued to funnel his donations to the Pragmatists as he plotted his political future in secret with just one person, the only one he trusted: Alex Cribb.

Since their non-stop, five-day video chat while he was sequestered in his Colorado Springs apartment, Jason Harper and Alex Cribb were inseparable. It was not so much that they were physically next to one another, but they communicated constantly. And never far from the conversation, was the question about when Jason would run. On most days, he would claim that he was having "too much fun and making too much money" building 2BIRDS and algae ponds to give it up, but Alex began to sense a change as his best friend approached his ten-year mark in business. "I could start to see the signs," he would later tell reporters. "Then, one day, a switch flipped, and he became laser-focused in that Jason Harper way."

The conversation concerning the campaign was short. He would run as a Pragmatist which was essentially the same as an Independent since no one outside of a few diehards at the community college had ever heard of the Prags. Everyone knew who he was, but where did he stand on the most important issues of the day? That is where he zigged while everyone else zagged. He would not adhere to a particular stance on any issue—not a single one—instead he would adopt the Prag slogan, vowing to "follow the truth wherever it leads." Over time, he began peppering his ribbon cutting speeches with vague campaign platitudes as he chided a "dysfunctional Colorado Springs" from a distance. Audiences loved it. Politicians feared it.

Every story follows an arc. And historians would later marvel that the peak of Jason Harper's life was not reached when he saved the world. It would come later. Saving the world put him in a position to do what he did. One biographer would represent Jason's life in the form of a graph. The horizontal axis was labeled "Years" while the vertical axis was identified as "Popularity." It began with a low, flat trajectory moving left to right at zero. Then, around his twenty-first birthday, it shoots straight up. An arrow labels the jagged peak as "Jason Harper saves the world." It then drops back down a bit before moving later- ally to form a plateau over the next ten years. Then, at age thirty-one, it takes the form of a hockey stick, shooting up again. The arrow marked the beginning of this period, "First term as Chairman." Below it, in parentheses, it also notes "(Rise of the Pragmatists)." The trajectory of the graph continues up from there in a long, slow, gradual ascent.

Until it ends suddenly. Suspended. Floating in space.

20

The street remained under construction and Mark again followed the detour home. From the sidewalk, although it was getting dark, he spotted two amber-colored bottles sitting atop the banister railing. Below the porch light, he saw Boo Radley. His glasses were perched at the end of his nose. He was sitting in a chair, reading. Mark hesitated. Thought twice. Then he headed up the minefield to the front steps.

"Well, hello there, Mr. Finch," the old man looked up from his paperback. "How was work today?"

"Not half bad, Mr. Radley. How are you?" Mark was caught glancing at the bottles when it dawned on him what they represented.

"Well, Mr. Finch. I did not properly thank you for your help with my screen door last night, but I do hope to make up for it. This is for you, Mr. Finch," he tipped his cap after handing Mark an ice-cold bottle of beer.

Mark drew a deep swig, and it immediately dulled the mild headache that always appeared at the end of every work day. Then, he continued to play the part of a Southern gentleman. "Well, it was, after all, the neighborly thing to do, Mr. Radley," he said, taking a courtly bow.

The two men, realizing the ridiculousness of their self-produced amateur play were both consumed by laughter at the same time. Clinking their bottles together, they took drink. "I'm Mark Sapin," Mark started first, again offering a handshake. "I live two blocks over." He nodded in the direction of his house. "My wife is Angela. My son is Ben—he's five. And we've got a baby girl on the way."

"Good to know you, Mark, and congratulations to you and the missus. I'm Roy Baker. I've lived here my whole life. Retired twelve years ago after that damned robot went and took my job. It's just as well, I suppose. But it gets lonely being retired. I'm not much use to anyone anymore."

Nodding toward his hat, Mark inquired about his military service.

"Sargent First Class United States Army. I was a Ranger. Fought in Korea II, and the Invasion of China. I was a sniper," he shared, his voice lowering.

"Wow, what was that like?" Mark asked with enthusiasm, realizing it was a little too much. He had always been curious about war, but he retraced his steps in an effort to mask his interest. "I mean, how was your experience?"

"You know," Roy thought for moment before continuing, "it was like any other job, I suppose. Probably similar to your job now. They tell you what to do, right? And then you go out and do it. My job was to shoot people," he revealed with no emotion. "I was damned good at it, too. I got sixty-seven confirmed kills in Korea, and 396 in China."

The blood in Mark's face drained as the realization landed. He was talking to one of America's most prolific serial killers. A mass murderer. His drinking buddy had likely killed five hundred people. Five hundred.

Roy noted his neighbor's reaction and explained further. "That's why I usually don't tell anyone, at least not the details. When I do, they turn ghost white—just like Boo Radley."

Mark was surprised to learn that Roy did understand that Boo Radley was white, ghost white, just like he referenced. As much as the revelation concerning the confirmed kills commanded Mark's immediate respect—and awe—his reading comprehension compounded the effect the old man was having on him. Here's a guy who knows his stuff. Mark was determined to reveal that he would not judge him. It was that desire combined with the liquid courage fueled by the empty bottle in his left hand which allowed the next question to slip out before it had been fully vetted in his mind. "What's it like to kill somebody?"

"Well, there, Mark. Since you and are friends now, I can answer that for you honestly. And my honest answer is: I don't know."

Mark looked back at him, his head cocked to one side in confusion.

"I've never really thought of it as killing someone, even though they call it 'confirmed kills.' I've always thought about it in the same way Johnny Cash sang about it: I separated them from their souls."

It struck Mark as odd, the ease in which he talked about taking a man's life.

"They conditioned me to do it, the government. It was like 'Two Minutes Hate,'" Roy said, holding up the worn-out paperback he had been reading, the classic dystopian novel, *1984*. "I got this book in a care package from some seventh graders back in the States. I was at a forward base on the Korea side of Mount Paektu. Nothing to do, except to eat their leftover Halloween candy and read this book yet again. The thing about war that people don't realize is it's mostly boring—boring as hell, punctuated by horror."

Mark strained to recall *1984*. The first line of the novel had gripped him instantly. *It was a bright cold day in April, and the clocks were striking thirteen.* He had read it years ago, but needed Gramoo's help to explain what was happening to Winston Smith, the protagonist. Two Minutes Hate was a daily ritual, a video watched by everyone each morning depicting the atrocities committed by imagined enemies. It was propaganda, fake news.

Mark was captivated by Roy. He trusted him. He felt an easiness, a connection. A familiarity. He thought of his grandmother, who was no longer around. He missed their conversations. He missed Gramoo. Roy was part of her generation and talked in a way that reminded him of her. There was an honesty, a realness, which he craved. The truth. That's when he decided to take a risk and go deeper. If he was being honest himself, he would admit that there was a part of him that was fascinated by the pulling of the trigger. Playing God. Ending a life. He would be lying if he said he never thought about it himself, because he had. He had imagined standing over his crumpled boss with a smoking gun. It made him feel guilty and dirty when he had the thought. Of course, he would never act on it, not in a million years, but on occasion the fantasy helped him make it through the day. It had helped him cope. It helped him to feel in control. But he wondered how it would really feel. How it felt to pull the trigger, but only in his imagination. That's all.

"What's it like to watch someone die?" Mark blurted.

Roy scratched at his chin to consider the question. "Well, the key was finding a good hiding place. I'd look for a hillside. Some high ground. I didn't much care for buildings, preferred the natural elements in case things went south and I'd have to get out of there fast. They could corner you in a building or smoke you out. There's nowhere to go but up. Or, down. Splat!" he clapped his hands together. "I'd find a place to rest my rifle where I could see everything. Then, I'd pull the camouflage netting over me. After that, it was just a waiting game. Sometimes I'd read *1984* again or maybe *To Kill A Mockingbird* or *Great Gatsby* or *Lord of the Flies*. I swear, that's all the kids would ever send me. Old books they read for their class or leftover Halloween candy, sometimes both. If they could have just sent me some damned socks."

"Or, the Sears catalog," Mark quipped.

Roy laughed. "Yes, some Double Ds to keep me company. That would have been nice." He paused to collect his thoughts before continuing. "But there I am, elbow deep in the freezing-ass snow, reading about Atticus Finch defending Tom Robinson in that courtroom one more time. And I wait. And wait. Finally, I hear a crackle come over the radio. The spotter ID's the target: 'Male, approximately thirty years old, carrying a bucket in his right hand, holding a child's hand in his left.' I see the mark in the distance, maybe a thousand yards out. I look through the scope. His head is bobbing up and down in the crosshairs. He stops, kneels down to tie the kid's shoe. I switch off the safety. Red means dead. Breathe in. Breathe out and squeeze the trigger. Bam! His head explodes like a watermelon tossed from fifteen stories high. Slumped over with blood and brains spilled out all over the place, the little kid panics, screams and runs away. One down, 462 to go. How much time do you have tonight, Mr. Sapin?"

Mark gulped hard. The words were difficult to hear. He wondered whatever became of the child, but kept it to himself. He could see that despite Roy's stoicism, there was an ocean-sized current of emotion swirling deep below the surface.

"I made it home with my M107. They let me keep it. It's my version of a retirement gold watch. You want to see it?" Roy asked as he disappeared through his front door.

In that moment, Mark realized just how juvenile his occasional battlefield fantasies had been. He knew for sure that he had no bloodlust, no real desire to do damage, to harm anyone. He felt like someone who was afraid of heights gripping the rail and looking down from thirty-two stories above. That defensive posture—muscles tightened, knees bent, adrenaline pumping—would be the same one required to leap over the railing. Homicide and suicide were two sides of one coin. He wanted no part of either. They both made him queasy. As with the first time he met Roy, he fought the instinct to slip out into the darkness and head home.

Roy returned. In his hands was the Grim Reaper's scythe. Sliding the chamber open and removing the clip, Roy said, "Have a look. It's not loaded."

Mark had never touched a real gun. It was much heavier than he had imagined. They fling those things around in the movies as if there were made of plastic, and they probably were, but this was the real deal. He could feel the weightiness of the tool, both literally and figuratively.

The lives it had canceled out and cut short. He thought about the kid with the headless father—was he Koren or Chinese?—and wondered about how old he must be now. What was it like for him to have to wipe his dad's gray matter off of his face? Does he have kids of his own now? What does he tell them about grandpa? Does he spare them the details? Or, does he give it to them straight?

"This here's the safety. When you see the red, that means it's off. Remember, 'Red means dead.' So, you click it just like this." Roy reached over to demonstrate. "With this one, you've got to find a resting place. Let's take it to the rail over there." Roy pointed off to the far side of the porch. "You position the stock in your shoulder like so. Look through the scope, line up the cross hairs. Take a breath in, then let it out. At the end of your exhale, when everything is steady, you pull the trigger. Click," the firing mechanism tripped with barely a sound. "Now, you try."

At first, Mark demurred. But he was curious. How would it feel? He struggled again with the weight, hoisting the rifle up to the railing, as instructed. Looking through the scope, he found a mailbox illuminated by a streetlight. Panting shallow breaths, he squeezed the trigger. Nothing happened. Roy could see that his student was struggling, so he came in behind him to help balance the gun. Placing his hand over Mark's, he guided his finger to the safety.

"Look here, son, you're not going to kill any bad guys with the safety on," he said.

Mark laughed much harder than he should have, but his nerves were frayed. His face twisted up. His eyes wide and wild with anticipation. A crazy man wielding a weapon of war. Roy smirked at the rookie. That's when he squeezed the trigger again. Click! A blinding flash went off, but no sound. Mark jumped, believing that the gun had fired. It did not. Out of the corner of his eye, he saw the neighbor's curtains bounce and close before the silhouette disappeared. The amateur photographer living next door could not have known at that time that she just had captured what would go on to become the most published image of the decade. It clearly showed Mark Sapin, his face demented and crazed and bloodthirsty and cackling as he spied the scope. Behind him, Roy Baker, wicked and maniacal. They made quite a pair, those two. And the photograph was proof of their premeditation.

The short walk home left Mark's head spinning. What had he just experienced? Was Roy for real? Or was he just a crazy old man with an imagination that had run wild, a product of his isolation? Maybe he was just lonely? Why did he think it was a good idea to hold that gun? And what the hell was that flash, anyway? Angela would kill him if she knew about this. They shared everything, but he would keep this detail to himself. She was adamantly opposed to guns, and she would be horrified to know he just held one that killed five hundred people. He would tell her about everything else instead.

"Sounds like quite a character. I bet he's got big, dark circles under his eyes." She pegged Mark.

"Actually, no. Well, maybe, yes. I have no idea," he groped for an answer in frustration. "The guy is as black as night, and you wouldn't be able to tell if he had dark circles covering his whole body. He's basically one big, giant dark circle." He paused to consider just how bad what he had just said sounded, and he immediately regretted it. "But I don't care—he's my friend."

Angela guessed that her husband was taken with Roy because he was a storyteller. Mark loved nothing more than losing himself in a book, absorbed in the tale. When she learned that Mark had started catching the earlier train so he could adjust his schedule, spending twenty minutes with Roy before racing home to join the family for dinner, she imagined Mark sitting on his porch and leaning into the gory details of war. That would be inaccurate. Highly so. The night the photo was taken was the only time Roy and Mark ever talked about his combat experience. There were so many other things to catch up on. They were kindred spirits. Roy would tease Mark, telling him first that he was "a brother from another mother" before remembering that he was more than fifty years older than his neighbor. Roy considered the math and the next day, when his much younger visitor stopped by, he said, "What's up, Mark? How's my grandson from another grandma?" The statement was so ridiculous and outlandish that they both doubled over laughing, as they so often did when they were together. They were fast friends and family and neighbors, all wrapped up into one universally misunderstood and very complicated mess.

Contrary to what was everyone was led to believe in their respective social media echo chambers, the truth was much less interesting than presented, just as it so often is. Except for that one day, they never talked about guns and guts and brains and blood. More than any other subject, the unlikely pair talked about Maggie.

21

The filing deadlines approached. And everyone who was anyone within both of the political parties lost sleep. Each state had its own date by which candidates for the president of the United States must submit an application to appear on the ballot. All eyes were on Jason Harper.

The networks followed him more closely than usual. Occasionally, a brave reporter would ask the question: "Do you intend to run for president?" Without fail, Jason would deflect with his usual "I'm-having-too-much-fun-doing-what-I-do" response. It was the one and only thing he ever said that people did not believe with all of their hearts. They knew he was only doing it for show. He was transitioning into a new line of work, politics, and there was a certain amount of bluster to be expected. He was just playing a game, they said. Having fun.

Nearing his thirteenth year in business, doing nothing but globetrotting the world to build 2BIRDS and algae ponds had taken a toll. He was now a trillionaire, but he did pay a price. Although he took impeccable care when it came to his looks and his health, Jason, for the first time, conveyed a weariness. The many miles he had traveled were beginning to show. He carried the fate of the world on his shoulders for so long; it was to be expected. Plus, the graying along the sides of his head, around his ears, gave him a look many called "presidential." Before a worldwide audience, he had morphed from a nineteen-year-old wunderkind with a brilliant idea to a thirty-something businessman who executed that idea with obsessive precision. He would call his high-profile career change his "second act." But like most movies, there would also be a third. There was always a third. He just hadn't realized it yet. More accurately, he still did not yet know exactly how he would do it.

Every news outlet blared a variation of the same line at the same time: "JASON HARPER IS RUNNING!" The first state received his application to appear on the ballot and it was immediately leaked to the networks. It was now official. He was running for president of the United States. All speculation was ended, and millions of bets were settled when it was reported that he filed as a Pragmatist. It was the first time most people had heard of the party. Most had heard that word—pragmatic—but did not know what it meant, as least from a political standpoint. The definition appearing after an online search was familiar to anyone who followed Jason Harper, which is to say everyone: "A person who is guided more by practical considerations than by ideals."

Jason was clear in his disdain for partisan bickering and gridlock over lofty, high-minded, and far-too-complicated ideas. His responses to interviewers asking about his party affiliation were always the same. "Look, here's what conservatives and liberals don't understand: The stuff they are pushing, their ideas aren't ideas at all. They're ideals." He would then go on to explain what an ideal is, "an irrational belief as to how things should be." Jason always put the emphasis on the word "should" before continuing. "You've got to start with the understanding that the problems we have today are too big—they're existential. Yes, I saved the world, but we must continue to remain vigilant. The fact that our country is so divided means that we can never get anything important done. The only ones who consistently win are the politicians. This approach is so outdated. It's time for the people to win. In my administration, I will put the people first. There will be no place for ideals in my White House. I will follow the truth wherever it leads. It's time to get real results."

Crowds packed every rally. The only thing large enough to host his campaign events were football stadiums. Every seat was filled, and the campaign would place additional jumbo television screens throughout the parking lots outside which were overflowing with a crowd hungry for change. Jason was intentional—as he always was—when he wore a purple tie. It became his signature. The networks were slow to catch on. None of the correspondents asked him about it until the third day he wore it. "I wear this purple tie for the people. It's not because I like the color—well, I actually do—but, because of what it symbolizes. From now on, America will not be defined by division, by red states and blue states. We will come together, we will be united as one. Red and blue together make purple. We will abandon those things that are no longer useful, which hold us back. We will follow the truth wherever it leads." The next day, everyone showed up at the rally wearing purple. Although it was never adopted officially, purple became the color of the Pragmatist Party. Some people went all-in with purple tie-dye t-shirts. The most popular consisted of simple white block letters in all-caps followed by an exclamation point which read, "JASON!" Others were more subtle. A pin or earrings, a pair of purple socks, or a scarf. Everyone, it seemed, was displaying the color in some way or another. It became the not-so-secret handshake required to enter America's most non-exclusive club.

The convention halls for the two major parties, normally raucous affairs, were ghost towns—everything but the tumbleweeds. Normally, their participants would have been busy finessing the final details of their party's platform, their collection of policy positions. Now, in the "post-Jason world," as some of the bigwigs from the old parties described their new political reality with more than a hint a derision, everything had been turned upside down. Many politicians showed their frustration. This was supposed to be their spotlight, a time to whip up partisan fervor and to galvanize support for themselves and their colleagues, both up and down the ticket. This was always the time that networks would broadcast one convention and then the other as each party would do their best to show the country how unified they had become, and how much excitement their nominees were generating. It was political theatre with confetti raining down amid thunderous applause, and awkward dancing to worn out rock music from the twentieth century. *Don't stop thinking about tomorrow.* This year, the camera bots did not even bother to show up at all. The entire point of the political conventions was to highlight the differences between the two parties, which was precisely the opposite of what Jason wanted to do, and the reason why he would not allow the Pragmatists to hold a convention of its own.

Alex Cribb disagreed, as was his natural instinct, but he eventually came around to the same thinking. Jason would say, "I don't want a bunch of half-crazed people wearing purple jumpsuits gyrating in front of the camera bots." The visual, which Jason sketched in his notebook, was all that Alex would need to change his thinking. The Prags would be different, which meant its campaign would be different. It would not be business as usual for the parties—the institutions responsible for the problems. The only question for either of them was whether to field a candidate at all. Polling was consistently showing Jason Harper at ninety-one percent. That number was unheard of in modern-day politics, or politics at all, ever, for that matter. Pollsters would joke, "Jesus Christ himself would never come close to cracking ninety percent." It was a misreading of history, however, because Jesus did not save mankind from the climate apocalypse on live television. Jesus did not make the sun go away. Jesus did not take out the trash. Jesus did not scrub the air clean. Jason did. And the two major parties knew it. They knew he was unstoppable. And it terrified them.

Three times Jason stood on the stage to debate his opponents, the other two nominees, who were both women. With the election a foregone conclusion, the tone of the events resembled a subdued conversation over tea rather than bare-knuckled political sparing. The questions lobbed his way by the moderators were not "What *would* you do as president," but "What *will* you do?" Jason was careful to avoid any commitment to a specific policy. His refrain was "I will follow the truth wherever it leads." When he was challenged, as he was at different times by both of his opponents to explain exactly what he meant by the statement, he would answer by repeating it again, this time slowing his speech to overenunciate: "I know this is difficult for you because both parties have always had a very loose relationship with the facts, but I will say it again, this time more slowly so that everyone on this stage can understand: 'I will follow the truth wherever it leads.'" The live audience at the debates would rise to their feet with a thunderous round of applause and whistles and catcalls.

From the time he declared his candidacy, all the way through to the election, Jason Harper was the clear favorite of nine out of ten voters. Everyone everywhere wore purple to show their support. Purple yards signs urging passing vehicles to "Vote Jason!" blanketed the suburbs. Any mention of a running mate was conspicuously missing. The candidate for vice president was the one who suggested removing his own name from all the campaign signage. His motivations were not driven by ego or feelings, and certainly not passion or sentimentality. Alexander Cribb was the personification of the Pragmatist Party, the living and breathing embodiment of their slogan, "Follow the truth wherever it leads." There was just one other thing that motivated him as much as cold, hard facts—winning. He was savvy enough to realize that he had zero name recognition and adding "Alex Cribb" to the ticket would only confuse voters. "Vote Jason" was much more powerful than "Vote Harper-Cribb." It was Jason's idea to use only his first name. Again, he insisted on simplicity. Alex knew that a win was inevitable, but he wanted an overwhelming victory. Complete domination at the ballot box. A mandate. No, a movement.

Record-setting margins would give the administration the power to get things done. And getting things done is what people wanted. It's how they would earn a second term. It's how he and Jason would leave their mark and create a legacy. Alex was fine with remaining an asterisk for now, the fine print. Soon enough, the nation would see him sitting next to the president—his right-hand man—whispering advice into his ear. It would not take long for him to make his way into every living room. By the time they were up for reelection, everyone would know Alex Cribb. For now, he was happy to remain in the shadows.

And, the grace and selflessness he demonstrated during this period did not go unnoticed by the leaders of the Pragmatist Party. As always, Alex was always thinking several steps ahead. He played chess while everyone else played checkers.

The networks began reporting the election returns at five o'clock Pacific time, and one minute later they raced to be the first to break the news, declaring the winner. They took turns announcing, "At this time, we project that Jason Harper will become the next president of the United States." Throughout the night, the networks went through the formalities, posting changes to the map of the country as they would happen. The lower left corner of the screen provided viewers with the color coding: red was for the conservatives, blue was for the liberals, and purple was for the Pragmatists. By the end of the night, the entire country was filled in by purple colored states. The uniter-in-chief, as the networks began to call him, had washed away many years of bitter divisiveness under a single, massive purple tsunami.

The only real question remaining on election night was whether yielding on the down ticket question had been a smart strategy. Again, it had been Alex's idea to not field any other candidates for anything other than president and vice president. He was adamant that no one run for the House of Representatives, the Senate, governor, city council, or school board, or anything as a Pragmatist. It was the only real argument that the two best friends had ever had up to that point. And it was a legitimate impasse. Jason could not understand how they would get anything done without the help of other Prags. Alex was adamant that the "everyone will end up getting in line behind us." He insisted on purity. He did not want to risk dilution with all the coattail riders who would come out of the woodwork. Cockroaches scurrying about when the lights turned on. He insisted they remain "committed to the commitment" they were making to the voters and to each other to "follow the truth wherever it leads."

"And, the truth is this," he would say to Jason, "you've got a ninety percent approval rating. Trust me, whatever you want to get done will get done. You've got everyone in the palm of your hand. You'll see. Before the first midterm, we'll open it up and allow others to joint the party. By then, the entire Congress will be a sea of purple." Once again, Jason yielded.

———

The Harper Administration did not wait for inauguration day to get started. Immediately, they set up shop in an office building across town from the newly constructed White House—a modern iteration of the original—in Colorado Springs, where the federal government had moved after the Great Melt. In a private conference room, the inner circle of the Pragmatist Party got to work. Five of the eight were from the original group at the community college. One by one, they stood before the dry erase board at the front of the room to complete the exercise led by Vice President-elect Cribb. "I want everyone to write down your top domestic priority. In other words, answer this question: What is the biggest problem facing America today?" Within a few minutes, the board was filled.

Alex strode to the front of the room to read out loud what had been written, as he drew a circle around each individual response: "Substance abuse, lack of affordable/workforce housing; overburdened welfare system; crumbling infrastructure; a rising crime rate; the depletion of resources and pollution/environment; moral decay; and falling behind the rest of the world in education." Then, he turned to the group to ask a question: "And what do these things have in common?" Jason knew the answer, his right-hand man was a broken record on this subject, but he wanted to see if any of his lieutenants would venture a guess.

"The answer," he turned toward the board, and filled a space in the middle with the word "People" before pausing. "That's right, people. People are the problem." Nervous laughter appeared from the back of the room before a hesitant hand was raised.

"But, A.C., people are the whole point. That's why we're doing this. We're trying to make things better for people, right?" he stated more than he asked.

"Yes, that's right. Of course," Alex assured. "But we cannot keep doing things the same way they have always been done, or we will only continue to get the same results. We got elected because we have vowed to follow the truth," again, he turned to the board and began connecting the individual problems with lines to the word "People" in the middle before completing his declaration, "*wherever* it leads."

Taking two steps back, he admired his drawing. A wheel with spokes leading to the hub. "As difficult as the truth is to accept sometimes, we have to embrace a new way of thinking. We have to strip away all of our old preconceptions, all of our biases, all of our remaining senti-mentality and ideals in favor of the cold, hard facts—the truth. Only after we do that, and distill it down to its foundation, can we start to build it back up with effective solutions. Now, whether it was the answer we were expecting, or wishing for, or the one we are most comfortable believing, it does not matter. The answer is people."

22

Mark and Angela Sapin were susceptible to advertising. At least that is what those who knew them had assumed. The government-sponsored commercials barely moved the needle at all. Policy makers wrung their hands over the perplexing birth rate problem. Before Jason Harper Victory Day, the trend which no one much cared about, did not warrant any attention. The impending extinction had vice grips on the attention of everyone. Who cares if there were no future generations in the pipelines, because there was not going to be any future generations. Period. For those who were interested in that portion of American history, they found that people largely split into two different camps: the workers, those who were bent on accomplishing something worthwhile during their lifetimes, and the partiers, who were determined to enjoy the ride into oblivion. In neither one of those groups did the producing and raising of children make any bit of rational sense.

The culture had shifted also. Bringing a new baby into the world was viewed as cruel and sadistic. Those who dared to conceive would avoid public places and the outspoken comments and vengeful stares they would receive. "How dare you?" was a common refrain. The playgrounds at city parks, once full of young mothers gossiping to one another about their babysitters and plans for preschool, were now empty. No one in their right mind would bring a child into a life that would be snuffed out soon, and if they did, that person certainly would not telegraph their horrible judgement by showing up in a public space for everyone to sneer, and to render judgment. "How dare you?"

Decades earlier, it was not uncommon for young mothers to be the subject of criticism for their grocery choices. With a shopping cart full of kids and perhaps an infant strapped to her chest, mothers—it was always the mothers, fathers somehow went unscathed as everyone figured it was enough for them to show up with their kids at the store at all—endured lectures about their choices. "You're buying hot dogs? Do you know what's in those things? Do you know how unhealthy they are for your children?" This phenomenon stood in sharp contrast to the comments received decades later, when the criticism endured was not about what to feed the kids, but about the kids' very existence. "You have children? How dare you?" Yet the United States Census, which was conducted every ten years, revealed a perplexing trend: the population continued to grow. Initially, it was explained away by advances in medicine, which led to a dramatic increase in the average lifespan. American lives had plateaued at seventy-eight years. They then bottomed out at fifty-nine before leapfrogging forward to eighty-three.

The jagged graph depicting life expectancy was well understood, and well documented. The rapid decline was driven by two things: carbon dioxide poisoning and other CO_2 related diseases, and suicide. Many citizens opted out on their own terms. And for those with sensitive lungs, the sick and the elderly, the dirty air hastened their demise. It ranged from acute asthma attacks to a smorgasbord of unexplainable diseases, which were often classified as "rare and genetic." Those were the words Mark and Angela Sapin remember hearing—"rare and genetic"—on the day their daughter was born.

With the economy humming along at full-tilt in the years after Jason Harper had saved the world, the rational response from many was logical: it was prime time for money making. Economic productivity was of paramount importance. Procreating did not fit into that equation. It was just the opposite, in fact, as everyone with a higher education remembered the charts that went along with their professors' admonishments. Having children was a major drag on productivity. A risky gamble that could very well lead to poverty.

For Mark, it was never a question. Angela was more hesitant. She had experienced the grocery store harassment first-hand. Although those days were gone, the residue remained. It permeated the culture. Women were finally poised to pull even with men at the workplace, at least according to the data. It showed that they were in striking distance when it came to receiving the same pay for the same jobs. Leadership roles across nearly every industry were tantalizingly close to a fifty-fifty split, males to females. Women were also making steady and consistent gains in politics. During the lead-up to Armageddon, women, for the most part, were found to be the more resilient and optimistic of the sexes as one opinion poll after another showed a slim majority of them answering "Yes" to the question: "I am confident that a climate solution will be found." The men, on the other hand, were convinced that the end was nigh and acted as such, disproportionately joining those who opted to spend their last days in a drunken stupor.

Angela was much more aware of the sacrifice they would be making, especially by her. Ben had been an easy baby. He slept through the night, ate everything they put in front of him, and, except for an occasional flu, rarely required medical attention. What if the new baby was different? It was one thing to maintain a level of economic productivity with a healthy baby, but an unhealthy one could sink the ship. It would be a risk, and she knew it. And, despite all of those television commercials encouraging upper-class citizens to procreate, she knew better than anyone that the culture had not yet caught up to the happy, wealthy young couple on the screen. Gone are the days of harsh judgment, but the sting echoes. The venom cast about by narrowing eyes was no longer about what mothers were feeding their kids, or whether kids should be brought into the world at all, now it became—although silent, and below the surface—a resentment that another woman had ceded her rightful place in the economy. A spot that would invariably be taken by a man.

The aching experienced by young working mothers was real. It only began to subside when Angela joined a group of women enduring the same thing. They used the same words: "silent judgment." Silent, but real. But Ben would be starting kindergarten this year, so this would be the time to do it, if they were going to do it. This would be the window of time that would be the least damaging to her productivity. It would require another five years at home. But her company had been supportive. Aside from the slough of government incentives and tax credits they were receiving for encouraging their well-to-do employees to procreate, they seemed genuinely happy for the Sapins. The owner of the business was in her seventies and had two kids of her own. Angela was a standout at the office and having her continue to work from home would not be a problem. There was nothing in their way. Over dinner one night, after her second glass of wine, she finally revealed a secret that she had been keeping. From her earliest days, playing in her childhood bedroom with her dolls, she had always wanted one thing more than anything else: a little girl.

Mark stopped mid-bite. His eyes welled with tears before walking around the table to embrace Angela. The two laughed and hugged, and laughed some more. They became delirious. Immediately, they both began talking at once, making plans, thinking about the future. A family of four. The office upstairs would be painted pink, a section of the den would be repurposed as Angela's workspace. All the old baby stuff, the playpen, the stroller, the wooden blocks, would be retrieved from the attic. Mark looked away toward the low flames flickering in the fireplace. Ben was asleep on the couch, curled up in his favorite blanket. The book they read together earlier, *Goodnight Moon*, had fallen to the floor. In that moment, Mark knew it would work. It would be fine. No, it would be more than fine. It would be great. He was happy and he could see that his wife was, too. He scooped up Ben and took him upstairs, tucking him in with a kiss on the forehead before returning. He and Angela curled up on the couch and smiled. That's when Mark whispered, "Do you want to practice?" Angela knew what her husband meant by "practice." She blushed.

Months later, her belly swelled. While she did encounter some raised eyebrows, she could tell that the television commercials were working. Public opinion, at least according to her own anecdotal evidence, indicated that the culture was shifting. People, for the most part, were supportive of her choice. They could see by the absence of darkness under her eyes she was exactly what the country needed. She was exactly the type of person who should be procreating. She was at the forefront of a tectonic shift in public opinion. In the coming years, people would greet expectant mothers with a "thank you for your service" in the same way they once did veterans returning from the battlefield. That is, once Jason Harper finally connected the dots for everyone with one of his drawings during a State of the Union address. Economically productive women bearing children was no less than a matter of urgent national security, and he made it clear that everyone must praise their "selflessness" as they performed their "patriotic duty." The applause line in his is speech had been repeated ad nauseam by the network commentators: "They should be revered not reviled."

The ultrasound magnified their joy. The hormone treatments had worked as designed. They were having a girl. Her heartbeat was strong, and she was positioned as she should be, head down, "ready for blast off," as the radiologist quipped. Again, husband and wife embraced, as the happy tears returned. Mark finished painting the office that weekend and had retrieved the remaining items from the attic. The only thing left to do was wait, and to find a name. Ben suggested "Padmé," a character from the old *Star Wars* saga he so often watched with his father. Angela objected, noting that she wanted to come up with something traditional, something with meaning. That's when Mark spoke up. "What about Margaret?" It was the name of his grandmother, Gramoo's actual birth name. She had passed away last year, but she was never far from Mark's thoughts. He had been the only one to call her Gramoo. To everyone else, she was Margaret.

Angela gazed off in thoughtful consideration, her left hand caressing the top of her belly. "I love it," she said, "we'll call her Maggie." It was unanimous: Angela, Mark, and Ben all agreed. The only thing left to do now was wait. The day—or, more accurately, the night—arrived much sooner than anyone had expected, at least by three weeks. And it happened fast. One minute Angela was chewing a hearty forkful of her favorite casserole dish, the next she was experiencing the contractions. One right after another, arriving in waves just as they did with Ben. Only his built up to this level of frequency and intensity over a couple of days. These were sudden and immediate. With no time to summon a babysitter, all three of them piled into the car. Mark knew they would have to rush to the hospital, so he switched off auto pilot on his car. Self-driving mode was convenient when you needed to fire off some emails on the way to the office, but it would not allow the vehicle to exceed the speed limit. If there ever was a time to speed, this was it.

An hour later, Margaret Sapin was born. When he filled out the birth certificate, Mark realized that they had forgotten to come up with a middle name. For him, giving their daughter the name of his best friend, his wife, was the only option. Although it was never reported by any of the networks, Angela did reveal during the investigation that she was deeply moved by her husband's gesture. The transcript showed noted her comment: "It was so Mark."

Her vital signs were strong, but the screening revealed an abnormality. None of the other words were understood, except for "rare and genetic." The doctor did not have much of a grasp either, other than to offer the leading theory. "The latest thinking is that the high levels of carbon dioxide concentrations have had some effect on the chromosomes, leading to gene mutations. But the truth is, we just don't know." The Sapins were shell-shocked. "People with this disorder are all over the spectrum," the white coat continued. "Some go on to lead normal, healthy lives. Others don't make it to their first birthday." Both Mark and Angela always resented the way he put it—"don't make it to their first birthday"—which is why they went overboard when Maggie turned one. Even though none of the babies in attendance were old enough to really enjoy it, no expense was spared. The women belonging to Angela's mom group, along with their husbands, were treated to a petting zoo, a bounce house, and five-tiered cake that would have been respectable at a wedding reception. That old doctor could kiss their asses they thought to themselves with every check they wrote for yet another frivolous party amenity. By all accounts, and according to all follow-up visits, Maggie was healthy and certainly happy.

———

The idea was not catching on with the upper classes, so the government did what governments do when things were not working properly—it spent more money. The thirty-second commercials became thirty-minute infomercials. Between interviews with the actor-parents, who fawned over their angelic actor-babies, the program's host would share the latest research claiming that having a family had a "net zero impact to economic productivity." Everyone knew it was not true, but there was a rekindled nostalgia for the nuclear family, especially when combined with the new slate of generous tax benefits and government subsidies that went along with them. The advertising did start to make a dent, although a very small one. But every little bit of advancement helped.

The government had been aiming at a moving target, according to Alex Cribb. The problem, as he had shared with his lieutenants, was people. But it would be an oversimplification to not share his much deeper, nuanced thoughts on the subject. "It's not people in general, but certain people. When you look at any of the issues facing us today, what do they all trace back to?"

Again, Alex popped the cap off his red marker, turned his back, found a blank space on the board, and drew something that had become all too familiar to everyone in that room. Over the years, they had teased him about his obsession, calling him "A.C. Foursquare" and "Mr. Inside-the-Box." It was a perfect square bisected by two lines, one running up and the other across, to create four equal-sized quadrants —one box broken up into four parts. Two squares on top and two squares on the bottom. In the first quadrant, the box in the upper left-hand corner, he wrote a "1." In the top right-hand box, a "2." The bottom left box, a "3," and the bottom right got a "4." He took a step back to admire his artwork as he considered the words he would say next. He knew this was his moment. His opportunity to shape history. For the better. He had practiced this presentation several times with Jason. Everything hinged on his delivery. It was time to stick the landing.

Alex circled the "1" and then the "2" in the top boxes at the same time he asserted, "We need more of these." Then, he said, "We can get them from here to there," as he drew an arrow connecting the "4" to the "2" sitting above it. Pausing again and drawing a deep breath—this was the moment, his moment, the culmination of a dream dating back nearly two decades—he moved the marker to the lower left-hand quadrant at the same time he made the proclamation: "But, we need a lot less of these."

He crossed out the "3" with an emphatic "X."

23

Twenty years ago, Alex Cribb was bored. Somehow, he found himself enrolled in a course called Intro to Business. As the professor lecture droned on, his mind wandered to politics. It was the only thing that interested him—that, and girls, but they were not interested in him. They said he was creepy. And too intense. Weird. The community college did not offer much in the way of political science, just the basics. He had already taken all the classes, along the way arguing with his professors who had grown tired of his ridiculous ideas and strident delivery.

Later, he would credit that business class for his epiphany. As Alex was grappling with how to solve the second greatest problem behind the climate crisis—American insolvency—the professor said something that struck him "like a ton of bricks." As he would retell the story, he claimed to only be paying "half-attention" when he heard the words, "You can't manage what you can't measure." He then stopped pretending to type notes into his laptop and instead opened a program he used for a math course. He began by selecting a shape, the shape which would secure his place in history: a square.

In retrospect, the first three sentences of his essay were prescient: "Just like the old food pyramid made everyone fat, the poverty line is making everyone poor. But, unlike the pyramid, it cannot be corrected by just flipping it upside down. Instead, the poverty line needs to be scrapped altogether." Alex Cribb went on to describe the issue in great detail. America had become insolvent after years of consistently "giving away too much, and taking in too little." Politicians had been overspending "for far too long" and both parties became gridlocked, "frozen in place," as they blamed each other. The conservatives accused the liberals of coddling the poor with their lavish spending on welfare programs. The liberals fired right back, spotlighting the conservative's hypocrisy as they heaped many times more benefits onto the corporations—"corporate welfare," they called it—particularly for those selling fossil fuels, which were only hastening the arrival of the end.

Both parties were right. Nothing they were doing was sustainable. And together they were combustible. But business as usual went on for decades. The game of musical chairs continued while everyone remained confident that a seat would become available when the music stopped. One day, it happened. China stopped buying American Treasury Bills—"T-Bills"—and interest rates took flight. It was simple supply and demand. Because its largest customer vanished, the United States was forced to increase the interest rate it was offering on its debt in an effort to entice more buyers. Senators began circling the globe, hat in hand, begging other countries to pick up the tab. America continued spending many multiples of what it was earning in the form of tax revenues. The conservatives pointed their fingers at the liberals, and the liberals pointed right back at them. They both said the same thing to one another: "Your welfare programs are unsustainable."

The country was pummeled by high interest. The well went dry. The economy had been fueled by consumer spending, as always, so when the interest on auto loans went from 1.9% to 18.9%, people stopped buying cars. When the bond markets responded to the skyrocketing T-Bill prices, mortgages adjusted, too. No longer were homeowners able to borrow against their homes to keep their own ships afloat. The housing market crumbled along with the stock market. No one could afford to buy much of either, homes or stocks. Everything, as it turned out, was being propped up by low interest rates. The Chinese had proved what the rest of the world had always suspected—the emperor had no clothes.

But the correction had been a long time coming. It had happened before, of course, but not quite like this. America had pulled herself out of the Great Depression not by the bootstraps as it was convenient to believe, but by massive government spending. A cornucopia of new programs followed by the rapid armament required for World War II finally broke the fever. This time, there would be no way to spend herself out of the malaise because no one was willing to continue to buy the drunk a drink. The music stopped. There were no chairs. The United States was flat broke. There was simply too much going out, and not enough coming back in. Simple math. In his essay, Alex Cribb blamed it on three things: partisan gridlock, corporate tax loopholes, and the poverty line.

"The politicians are no longer working for 'We the People,'" he wrote with anger when addressing the matter of partisan gridlock. Alex traced the history of political parties and referenced the Constitutional Convention in 1787 where the Founding Fathers warned of political "factions" and claimed that parties were "antithetical to democracy," and "corrupt relics of the British system." Alexander Hamilton had said political parties were "the most fatal disease." And it was James Madison who argued that the most vital function of the new government will be "its tendency to break and control the violence of faction." But Alex Cribb noted that it was George Washington, the first president, who was most adamant in his warning of partisanship. His essay cited a line from his farewell address to the young nation in 1796: "The common and continual mischiefs of the spirit of party are sufficient to make it the interest and duty of a wise people to discourage and restrain it." The community college student then closed this section of his essay by asserting, "The two-party system is no longer tenable. I am not suggesting we add a third, but instead we do away with parties altogether." Later, those two lines would be scrutinized by opposition researchers in an attempt to find a way to use the inconsistency against him.

The second factor, corporate tax loopholes, was an easy fix according to Alex. And, at least on paper, he was right. But his suggestion for a Constitutional Amendment was a long shot, to say the least. "The corporations have become too powerful," he wrote. "Their interests have usurped those of the citizens." As a remedy, he proposed a radical idea, a Constitutional Amendment, which would eliminate two things: the treatment of corporations as individuals in the eyes of United States law, and the elimination of all corporate loopholes in favor of a flat tax. His professor wrote in the margin of his paper in red ink, "Nice thought, Alex, but it would never pass because the dog (Congress) will not bite the hand that feeds it (corporate America)." That same professor would later be interviewed by all of the major networks. He only managed to shake his head "No" when asked if he ever thought it were even remotely possible. "And, to be honest," he added, "Alex Cribb would be the very last person in the world I would have thought could pull it off."

Unlike the first two policy prescriptions in his essay, Alex did not yet have one worked out for the third: the poverty line. "It's an antiquated concept, whose time has expired," he wrote. Then, just as he did with the elucidation of the hyper partisanship gripping the country, he dove into the history. The idea was developed in 1963 by a woman named Mollie Orshansky. She was an economist who worked in the Social Security Administration. This was during the formation of President Johnson's Great Society. The Democrat, LBJ, oversaw the greatest expansion of federal government programs since the Great Depression. In order to determine who would receive what, Orshansky came up with a calculation, which became known as the poverty line. If you were above it, you did not receive welfare. If you were below it, you did. Easy. But it wasn't that simple, at least according to Alex, because the poverty line created something he called a "perverse disincentive."

He went on to describe how it worked. "The poverty line is not fixed in one position, it moves depending on how many kids you have. The bar is raised and lowered in the most asinine way. It adjusts up or down based on the number of dependents a person has, in other words, children. Those with more kids receive more assistance. The bar for them is lowered. With more kids, the poverty line threshold is crossed sooner." Alex then provided a hypothetical example: "For instance, consider for a moment, two welfare moms, each with identical incomes. The one with three kids gets welfare assistance, while the one with two does not." He put the next line in italics: *"She is, therefore, incentivized to both have more kids and earn less money."* This phenomenon, according to Alex, "continues to tear away at our once great country as it becomes overcrowded and bankrupted by lazy welfare cases who are rewarded by a combination of intentionally not striving to reach their full economic productivity, and even worse than that, by continuing to crank out more kids."

He then explained his theory about the black markets exacerbating the trend. "Steadily climbing interest rates have only accelerated the advent of black markets, which have become the norm for how the poor now operate in America," he began a new paragraph. Alex recounted the history, as was the assignment, by tracing the steps. This one was due more to technological innovation than it was to societal trends or policy prescriptions. It dated back to the dawning of the Internet, particularly the widespread adoption of the dark web among the lower classes. This trend picked up speed with the introduction of blockchain software, which cleared the way for underground and fully unregulated banking and, therefore, the proliferation of black markets. "Poor people quickly realized that they could get all of their welfare by not reporting income. And because their income was only found circulating in the black markets, away from the view of the government, they could have their cake and eat it, too." Alex described the current state of affairs, particularly in the shantytowns, where black markets ruled the day. Everything was done, all transactions, in what amounted to a highly sophisticated barter system. Blockchain-powered websites, secured by standard retinal scans to prevent theft, tracked the debits and credits. Each shantytown had its own black market. They were all different, but that is why the InterExchange, or "the IE" as they called it, opened up for business. It became a clearinghouse for doing business across markets. Alex closed this section by writing,

"The shantytowns have become rife with welfare cheats, who do not report their true earnings and keep having more kids who are also doing the same. The problem is growing exponentially."

He received a B+ on the essay. His professor scribbled his comments on the last page, "Alex: There's some interesting thinking in here and a great overall recap of the history shaping these issues. I like your policy suggestions vis-à-vis partisanship gridlock and corporate imbalance. Even though they are impractical, it's good to see your thought process. I was disappointed that you only identified the problem in your discussion of the poverty line. I would have liked to have seen a solution offered as was the assignment. Doing so would have bumped you up to an A. Overall, a solid effort. Well done."

———

Alex shot straight up in his chair. Entranced by his laptop monitor, which was only displaying an empty box, a square, he whispered to himself, "You can't manage what you can't measure." In that moment, the answer to the poverty line problem came into view, and it was so obvious: the Productivity Matrix.

From the toolbar on the software program, he selected "View" then "Add x-axis," which he labeled "Net Worth." He then added a y-axis, calling it "Taxes/Services." With the pointer, he dragged the x-axis to the middle of the box, bisecting it horizontally into equal parts, creating two smaller boxes. He then did the same with the y-axis, which ran vertically, splitting the original box into four smaller boxes. Two boxes sat atop two others to make four equal quadrants. In the first quadrant in the top-left corner, he typed in a "1." He then moved to the top-right quadrant and added a number "2." The bottom left quadrant received "3," while the bottom right got a "4." Four quadrants with four numbers, one through four.

The issue with the poverty line, Alex would explain later, was that it was self-reported. There was no shame in getting welfare and no incentive to not lie about your income. And, from the standpoint of the government, there was no way to properly manage it because the truth was hidden from view in the black markets. *You can't manage what you can't measure.* The solution, the way to properly manage the program, would be found in the measurement. The incentives would be flipped when the lights turned on and everything came out of the darkness to become a matter of public record. Everything would be measured. "Pride would return again," Alex said to himself. "People would know where they stood at all times, not only in relation to their government, but in relation to each other. No more tax cheats, whether they be poor people or trillion-dollar corporations. It's a level playing field, complete one-hundred percent transparency."

Participation in the Productivity Matrix would be mandatory. There would be no more welfare payments or tax refunds or any services provided of any kind without it. No longer would any of it, or anything, be self-reported. The country had run itself into a ditch when it counted on its citizens to voluntarily reveal their financial status to the government. China had been propping up the illusion for decades, but no longer. And, the rest of the international community, despite the high interest rate bearing T-Bills, were no longer interested. They suspected the outsized rewards accurately reflected the outsized risk. There was a very real chance that America would be no more, spending herself into oblivion. That would not be the case, Alex thought, if everything and everyone were linked in real time to the Productivity Matrix. If anyone so much as buys a pack of gum at the mini-mart, the sales tax paid will register immediately, as will the corresponding drop in the bank account balance. Both of those things will move the citizen, represented as a dot within one of the four quadrants, one direction or another. Curious about how your neighbor is faring financially? Search their name, find their dot, see their data. Suspicious that a co-worker is not paying their taxes. Go to the website and have a look.

Alex moved the cursor along the x-axis, left to right, to see what happens when net worth increased. But it had no meaning, it was just another one-dimensional data point, not much different from the poverty line. Everything changed when a layer of context was added, when it was plotted against the y-axis, the taxes/services number. That vertical line then intersects the horizontal line, the x-axis, exactly in the middle, its median point. This meant that the first half of the net worth line—everything to the left—represented half of the population, the less wealthy. To the right of the vertical line were the more wealthy. Those who found all the way to the right were the wealthiest. All the way to the left were the poorest. Top to bottom was a net measurement of how much they were paying into the system, or taking. Taxes versus services.

The formula was simple: add up everything paid into the government in the form of taxes and other fees and subtract out everything received in terms of welfare—individual or corporate—and other services. When those two data sets were overlaid, the coordinates would land somewhere within one of the four quadrants. Alex suspected that people would equate them according to old designations: the upper left-hand box, Quadrant 1, would be middle-class; the upper-right-hand box, Quadrant 2, would be the wealthy; the lower left-hand box, Quadrant 3, were the down-and-out poor, the homeless, the shantytown dwellers, paying nothing yet receiving everything; and, the lower-right-hand box, Quadrant 4, were wealthy people and corporations who, for some reason, were not contributing their fair share. Alex believed that once the lights were turned on and they were exposed on a national website for all to see, those in Quadrant 4 would start paying their taxes in haste, immediately moving up to Quadrant 2 in order to avoid public outrage.

Quadrant 3 was another matter.

24

They would learn later that stress was the likely culprit. Not the cause. It had always been there, just as the old doctor had predicted. It lay dormant, waiting to strike. The first day of kindergarten is not necessarily stressful, but for a five-year-old, it represents a significant change. And change of any kind, good or bad, almost always comes with some stress. This time was no different. It was just enough to awaken the disease.

Her symptoms were subtle. Angela dismissed them as first-day jitters. But she knew her daughter and recognized something was wrong when they did not go away. Mark assured his wife that everything would be fine, it was just an adjustment to a new environment. Until now, she was in preschool with just six other kids, and their mothers. The "mommy and me" format was much different than the traditional classroom she was starting now, he reasoned, and it may require more time than expected to settle in. Not to worry, everything will be all right. But Angela knew better. She knew everything was not all right.

The frequent trips to see the specialists annoyed Mark. He could not understand why the white coats continued to say, "The disease has progressed." There was no progress at all. It was the opposite of progress, whatever that is—going backward, not forward, getting worse. What had started with a nearly imperceptible tremor, led to uncontrollable shaking. It was as if Maggie were outside shivering in the cold, while everyone else was on the inside of a warm and toasty house, watching her through the window, suffering. She was so confused. She could not understand what was happening to her body. Neither could the doctors. They only repeated those same words, "genetic and rare," which were of no help. If the adults were unable to determine what they meant, how were they to explain them to a five-year-old?

Following the prognosis after both the second and third opinion appointments, mother and father sped through the five stages of grief —denial, anger, bargaining, depression, and acceptance—sometimes experiencing all of them within a twenty-four-hour span. Mark had learned about the Kübler-Ross model, the five stages of grief, back in college. It was a Psychology 101 class, and he remembered thinking the concept was so abstract, so arbitrary. Now, he realized it was spot-on. Denial came first. It always does. "She'll grow out of it. This will be temporary." Then, anger. "If everyone had stopped burning fossil fuels, this would not be happening to her!" Although they committed to keeping a brave face in front of the kids, depression was always lurking in the background. It was not uncommon for both Mark and Angela to fall asleep with tears in their eyes. During one of her bad days, which were becoming more frequent, the final stage, acceptance, finally made an appearance. Angela did not want her daughter to suffer, and her life was diminishing day by day. The light was flickering. Her little girl was in pain. She was hurting.

Mark remained stuck on the third stage: Bargaining. He was convinced there was an answer. It was only a matter of research. More research. More data. More analysis. He scoured the medical websites. Dove into the databases. He was sure that someone out there had beat this thing, and he was going to find out how they did it. He ordered every supplement, every alternative remedy. He tried everything. Nothing seemed to work. The disease progressed. She got worse.

Watching her deteriorate was the worst form of torture. He was her father. He was supposed to protect her. But he couldn't. Her own body was attacking itself. His mind twisted itself up into knots, haunted by his favorite memories. Maggie's first dance recital. Sitting in the audience, his heart fluttered and took flight as she dipped into a confident and graceful curtsy after her equally clumsy performance. The time she brewed imaginary tea for him and her teddy bear. Her first word, "Dadda." He had always regretted that she would not have the opportunity to meet her namesake, Grandma Margaret, Gramoo. But the Sapins made up for it by taking frequent walks around the neighborhood with Grandpa, who was quickly losing ground to his dementia. Angela would swaddle her daughter in her favorite pink blanket, and Ben would hop on his trainer bike. Together, they would get out and "stretch their legs." Maggie was always so calm and peaceful—angelic. Mark often videoed her in that old stroller. She was so content, everything was so right with her as long as she had her teddy bear and her pacifier, her binky.

At first, Mark was not sure what to think when Roy began using the nickname he had given his daughter—Peanut—as it was intended for just the two of them. But he soon found it enduring. By that time, Roy had become a surrogate uncle of sorts. That's what Ben started calling him anyway, Uncle Roy. Those walks around the block always ended up on Roy's front porch. Angela came to appreciate the old man as much as Mark did and began to understand how her husband saw him as a bridge to his grandmother. He had a similar way about him. The way he talked and moved. He took his time. He listened. And those stories he told. It was clear that he was from a different era, a traveler visiting from a different generation. At first, she had been frustrated with Mark. Frustrated that he would choose to spend precious time each day after work with Roy instead of hustling home. But, after a while, she saw it differently. She considered those twenty-minute conversations to be cheap psychotherapy. Roy had a way of calming Mark, grounding him. And he still made it home each night in time for dinner.

Those words, "rare and genetic," had been spoken on Roy's porch many times before. Mark would share all of his deepest and darkest feelings there. He first reported the terror he felt when the white coat said those words before offering his grim prognosis. Over the years, that conversation was never far from his mind as he kept a close eye on his daughter, searching for any signs, any symptoms. Eventually, he lowered his guard, and life resumed a familiar pace. They were lucky, he would tell Roy, the disorder was dormant. Crisis averted. Then, kindergarten. It was the stress. It had to have been the stress, Mark told Roy. "I know it was the change that triggered it, I'm sure of it." As always, Roy was reflective, careful to not say too much. He had no children of his own. But he knew what it meant to love someone. He understood what it meant to be the protector.

Those conversations were therapeutic for Mark. He got it all out, all the nasty stuff, the crazy thoughts, before he came home. It was as if he backed up a dump truck and left all the garbage right there on Roy's front porch. He always ended those conservations by thanking his friend for listening. Roy always said goodbye in the same way, with two firm pats on his neighbor's chest, and a reminder: "You're a good man, Mark." Those words meant everything to Mark. He had been beating himself up, frustrated that he could not solve this problem. It wasn't much, but someone out there believed in him. Walking through his front door was different after a conversation with Roy. He always had just the right story to tell in order to relay a point, or to share a lesson. And, Mark, he could always say things to Roy that he could not say to his wife. His deepest fears, no matter how outlandish, no matter how dark—everything—he would share with Roy. And he became increasingly desperate. Irrational.

Mark would later tell the interrogators that he first had the thought—and he could not believe he was thinking it—after the specialists made their terminal prognosis, suggesting it was time for he and Angela to "get her affairs in order." They said it would be a year. The final phases of the progression had arrived. After hearing those words, Mark went from desperate to frantic. There had to be an answer—there always is. He just couldn't find it. More research was needed. More data. More analysis. He began casting a wider net, challenging himself to think deeper and wider. That's when he remembered all of those science fiction books he had read in Gramoo's den. Many of them had included some blending of humans and technology. There were the cyborgs—cybernetic organisms—which were half-human, half-machine. They never materialized as many had predicted. Robots were ubiquitous, of course, but none of them could be considered anything close to human-like. They were still lifeless buckets of bolts, and they continued to occupy an odd place in society. Equally loved and hated, depending on your perspective. And that perspective almost always was determined by where you were on the Productivity Matrix, just like most everything. Those in the top quadrants generally liked the robots because they helped them become still more productive, more wealthy, while those on the bottom despised them because they came in and took their jobs.

Crimes against robots required an entirely new set of statutes. And imaginations ran wild when it came to violating the Cruelty to Robots Act, the CRA. Nothing was out of bounds when rage took hold. Robots were beaten to a pulp. Blown up. Dismembered. Hanged from light posts. Dragged behind cars. Shot. Submerged. Kicked. And thrown off cliffs. It was all covered by the CRA. Those who were paying attention, which were few, saw the legislation not as the protection of private property rights for the owners of the robots, but as the first major step toward the personification of machines. Up to that point, it made no difference how the robot was destroyed. Those crimes were classified in the same way: felony grand theft, vandalism, and destruction of private property. Charges along those lines ran rampant. They were the run-of-the-mill trifecta which became known as "robot rage."

But everything changed when the perpetrators were charged under the CRA. Except for the occasional angsty upper-quadrant teenager, crimes against robots were almost always committed by displaced workers from the lower quadrants. No longer was it the same three garden variety robot rage charges, now there were hundreds of classifications mimicking all the cruel and unusual ways a human being could be violated. A handful saw it as the beginning of individual rights and liberties for machines, which is why the CRA became known in some circles as the Robot Bill of Rights. Mark had watched these developments unfold with much more curiosity than most. As a lifelong student of artificial intelligence, he was fascinated by the social changes made by rapid technological advancements. While he found all of those science fiction novels he read as a kid to be fascinating, unlike their authors, he did not foresee a time when robots and humans would merge. That all changed when the specialist said, "She has a year left."

Fringe software companies made some wild claims. One of them ran infomercials on late night television. Their services included, among other things, "Comprehensive Human Digitization." Viewers mostly laughed and mocked the low-budget productions. Mark remained committed to turning over every stone, including this one. He called the number and spoke to the sales representative. She was chipper and friendly and trained well. She had an answer for all of his questions. "Yes, it's true," she gushed, "we have pioneered technology which allows the human lifespan to continue indefinitely." After studying their website, watching all of their testimonial videos, and calling in again, Mark concluded—as much as he wanted to believe it—that what they claimed to do was simply not possible.

Maggie surprised her doctors when she made it to the one-year mark. She was having more good days than bad. Angela, by then, had accepted her fate and was determined to make the balance of her daughter's short life as perfect and as comfortable as possible. Mark doubled down on step three of his grieving by continuing to bargain. He searched far and wide for a cure, for relief, for "Comprehensive Human Digitization," for anything. Whatever it took. Roy noted the increasing desperation in the eyes of his friend and began encouraging him to slow down and follow Angela's lead. When Mark talked about the merging of man and machine, Roy recoiled. It was not something he would want for himself. He despised the robots and could not imagine somehow becoming one of them. "They'd have to add 'self-loathing' to the list of robot crimes," he joked. Mark needed the laugh.

With the booming economy, entrepreneurship ran wild. In every garage, it seemed, a new start-up was under construction. Mark began to pray—the first time he had ever done so—that one of those fledgling companies would find the holy grail. A decade earlier, everyone was convinced that they were going to die, now everyone seemed to think they were going to live forever. "Life Extension" became a new category of business in the technology world, and venture capitalists were lining up to invest. If someone were to figure it out—*there is always an answer*—it would not just be a home run, it would be like circling the bases in infinite glory. The race was on. Human digitization went from the fringes of late-night television infomercials to the hallowed boardrooms of America's most respected corporations. Everyone was talking about it—including Jason Harper.

While the Prags remained publicly reticent concerning the digitization race, they were very quietly getting into the game themselves. In order to maintain secrecy and remain off the books, Jason Harper funded the effort on his own. Not only did he finance it, he also became directly involved as its chief executive. Noting that it was his money and his time, he would remind everyone, "I have complete control." During private meetings with his inner circle—the Gang of Eight—he began comparing himself to President John F. Kennedy. He told them, "JFK said, 'We will go to the moon by the end of the decade.'" Jason paused before calling a moonshot of his own. "I'm telling you this: I will digitize a human being by the end of the year."

25

The Prags were elected to get things done. They had the political winds at their backs as no administration had before. These were hurricane-grade gusts. People were starving for something new. Bickering and partisan gridlock only kicked the can down the road. Nothing ever happened. The only ones who benefited were the politicians themselves. The problem was obvious, and fit neatly into a box, but the new administration would have to be measured in their communications, especially since they did not yet have a solution. At least not one they could say out loud.

There was some debate on the timing of the effort, but Alex Cribb insisted it be done immediately. So, minutes after Jason Harper placed his hand on the Bible, swearing his allegiance to the Constitution of the United States, he announced his intentions to change it. Immediately, he said, he would seek to "revise the 12th Amendment and repeal the 22nd." The networks quickly seized on the news, praising "Revise & Repeal" as clear evidence of bold, new leadership. Starstruck network commentators explained that it would have to go through Congress first before it was sent out to the states for approval. No one expressed so much as a whisper of doubt that either would pass. The only question would be how long it would take. As the reporting continued,

viewers were provided the history of the two constitutional amend-
ments in question.

The 12th Amendment was passed in 1804. It was intended to clarify
the role of the Electoral College in presidential elections. It also codified the leadership of the Executive Branch by formalizing the top
positions as president and vice president. Jason Harper saw a different
role for himself: Chairman. This role, he explained, would give him
more latitude to pick and choose his projects. And, although he never
admitted it to anyone other than Alex, he intended to continue operating his business, at least on an informal basis. More than anything
else, he did not want to give up the ribbon-cutting ceremonies. He
wanted to continue to deliver the speech dedicating each new 2BIRDS
installation, and he was unwilling to relinquish the carnivals of
worship they had become. As chairman, he would not have to choose.
He could do both. He could be his company's chief executive as well as
his country's. The role of the president would be the same, but that
person would handle the day-to-day operations of the country and
answer to the chairman. The vice president would be third in
command. Additionally, under Jason Harper's proposal, the Electoral
College would be disbanded. The Prags saw it as an antiquated effort
at federalism. And, as far as they were concerned, anything that would
augment states' rights was antithetical to their mission. They would be
unapologetic in their efforts to strengthen and centralize the federal
government generally and the executive branch specifically. Big problems will not be solved, they explained, by sprawling, unwieldy and
unnecessarily distributed decision making. Swift, bold action requires
efficiency and a clear chain of command.

Although there was some debate within the Gang of Eight about
whether to keep the titles of president and vice president, it was
decided that some tradition and sentimentality would remain. Jason
had argued for all new titles: chairman, chief executive officer, and
chief operating officer. He liked the getting-down-to-business connota-
tion they brought. The others thought it may be too much, too fast. We
can always change it later, they said. If the revision was ratified as
expected, Jason Harper would become America's first chairman. Alex

Cribb, would be promoted as president, and someone from the Gang of Eight would become the new vice president.

The conversation concerning the 22nd Amendment was much simpler. It was a straight-up repeal, a wholesale cancellation. The Prags did not see the point of presidential term limits. They explained that they were undemocratic. "If the people wanted their leader to serve beyond two terms, then their wishes should be honored." The network commentators reminded their viewing audiences that the amendment had been created back in 1951 after Franklin Delano Roosevelt had served four terms. "But," they continued, reciting the Prag talking points nearly verbatim, "the people had chosen him, and the entire point of another amendment, the 25th, was to deal with a president who had become infirm, as FDR did during his fourth term. So, the 22nd Amendment is superfluous." The continued use of the word "superfluous" caused a dramatic spike in online searches where the definition popped up as "unnecessary, especially through being more than enough." Merriam-Webster named "superfluous" its Word of the Year. That explanation was good enough for the voters, and by the all-important one-hundred-day mark "Revise & Repeal" was successful, so was another piece of legislation which received very little attention.

The quadrant system was not as interesting or sexy as alternating the Constitution itself. Plus, most members of Congress did not understand how it worked. And they could not have anticipated how the new law—the Productivity Matrix Act—would return America to her former glory, and beyond. Alex Cribb was right. *You can't manage what you can't measure.* The country had gone off the rails because no one was minding the store. No one was recording the facts, no one concerned themselves with the truth. The productivity quadrants brought transparency. There was no more hiding in the shadows, no more gaming the system. It was all there on a government website for the entire country to see, updated in real time. A bright light was shone. Everyone was reduced to a dot on the screen which fit into one of four boxes. The American Dream was restored as many of those dots moved up immediately, particularly from Quadrant 4 to Quadrant 2, just as Alex had predicted. While everyone was praising Jason

Harper for his outside-the-box brilliance, it was Alex Cribb and his inside-the-box legislation which changed everything.

———

Jason Harper never intended to do any work at the White House. He thought the new building was hideous, even worse than the last. Although he was careful to keep his thoughts from the voters, he derided it as "the house of sentimentality." He thought the government had blown it when it moved to Colorado Springs. It had a unique opportunity to reimagine its institutions and the architecture housing them. Instead, he would tell Alex, they chose to "Disneyfy" everything. "It's like Disneyland, everything is just a replica of everything else. Where's the vision in that? How can we expect any innovation with copycat thinking like that?" He decided that executing and implementing the plans could be done at the White House, but the plans themselves would be developed offsite. "Where I can think," he said.

Years earlier, while Jason was still contemplating the possibility of a political career, he hired an architect to design a new executive building. He had purchased some land just outside of the Colorado Springs city limits which would serve as the ideal place for the new seat of power. The throne. With a sweeping view of the Rocky Mountains, it was just far enough away from the noise, the hustle and bustle—the ant hill. But it would be close enough to keep an eye on everything, and to ensure that the important work was getting done. His personal residence would be there, as well as office space for himself and his top brass. He would tell the architect, without revealing his political ambitions, that he was looking to build "the ultimate home office." He also requested private conference rooms, an assortment of entertainment amenities, an indoor pool, a virtual brothel—an exact replica of the ones found in his other homes—and an assortment of interview rooms with plenty of room for cameras and sound equipment, as well as one-way mirrors for additional observation. The team from the architecture firm played it off as just another day at the office when Jason also requested sniper towers, electric fences, and surface-to-air missiles.

As was customary for anything involving Jason Harper, construction began ahead of schedule. By the time he was sworn into office, the foundation had been built. Eleven months later, he would be moving in. Alex Cribb, and whomever was chosen as vice president, would remain at the White House, mostly as a symbolic gesture to the people that a smooth transition was taking place. They would continue to perform the formalities and whatever little of the pomp and circumstance remained, as well as entertain world leaders and all of those things that seemed to comfort the voters. But, the real work would be done at the Headquarters, or "HQ" as Jason christened it.

By the end of their first year, just as Alex had predicted, there was a mass exodus from the two major political parties. One by one, members of Congress were switching their affiliation to the Pragmatist Party. The American Flag lapel pens, which were the one thing everyone could agree on in the Capitol Building, had been modified. It remained an American flag, but the colors which had previously been red and blue were now made purple instead. Those purple and white lapel pins began showing up everywhere, even outside of Colorado Springs. By the time the first midterm election rolled around, both houses of Congress were dominated by the Prags. Most of the politicians hanging on to one of the two old parties were mostly picked off by the voters at the polls. The second half of the Harper Administration's first term would prove even more productive than the first because, for all intents and purposes, Congress was no more than a rubber stamp.

After "Revise & Repeal," Chairman Harper had disappeared from public view. The citizens of the United States got to know their new president, Alex Cribb. He was making inroads daily as he began implementing Jason's executive orders. At first, they went for the easy, high-visibility changes. Tackling infrastructure was a no-brainer. The country's roads and bridges had been crumbling in plain sight for too many years. Most all of the highways were built back in the 1950s. "Deferred maintenance" were two words used often in describing their decrepit condition. The two political parties, despite overwhelming voter support, could not come together to do anything meaningful when it came to infrastructure. Jason saw it as a massive opportunity to put people to work, which would have an immediate effect on the economy. He gave President Cribb strict orders, however, the same orders common of municipal contracts and a non-negotiable require-ment of his 2BIRDS job sites: "No robots."

The Rebuild America Act—the RAA—sped through Congress and ended up changing the face of the country in a highly visible and tangible way, at the same time it moved millions out of poverty. It was a massive investment by the federal government, but as Jason explained along with one of his customary hand-drawn sketches, it would "bake a bigger pie" resulting in additional tax revenue. While the Congressional Budget Office estimated the RAA would be revenue-neutral, it surpassed expectations as it became a profitable venture for the government. More taxes came in as a result of the legislation than flowed out. The pie expanded.

The Harper Administration finally followed the rest of the world and outlawed the burning of fossil fuels for any purpose. Rather than sunset the millions of gas-powered automobiles still on the road over a period of time, the Prags researched the "cash for clunkers" program implemented back in 2009 and decided to do the same thing. No one would remember the history, they guessed, so they went with the same name. The Cash for Clunkers Act sped through even faster than the RAA, and the automotive industry rejoiced when lines formed around their dealerships. New electric cars were purchased by happy consumers with government subsidies as the gas-powered engines were finally put to death, recycled as in-demand I-beams. At the same time, oil and gas companies were provided assistance as they made their final push toward alternative energies. The economy was humming at full-tilt. Suddenly everything was possible for everyone. Gone were the days when Americans waited around to be fried by the sun. The sun was mostly gone now, too, hidden behind the garbage launched into a low orbit by the 2BIRDS. But no one cared. The economy was white hot and served as a suitable replacement for the sun, a new center of the universe. Plus, there were other ways to get Vitamin D.

The wall of screens on the other side of Jason's office tracked all the country's metrics in real time. At any point during the day, he could look up to see changes in GDP. Dips in the unemployment rate. Polls on his approval ratings. The latest measure of whether Americans thought things were heading in the right direction or the wrong direction. Balance of trade with every other country on the planet. Carbon dioxide concentrations. But, in the middle of all the monitors, he kept his eyes trained on the one he cared about the most, at least since the night of Alex's presentation: the Productivity Matrix. Throughout the day, he caught himself smiling when he saw tiny dots migrate upward past the horizontal x-axis. The exodus from Quadrant 4 to 2 was just as Alex had prognosticated. But his emotions were equally powerful for those who remained. Because now, with the economy humming along, they were clearly choosing to stay. Anyone can get a job rebuilding highways. The Prags had a strict no robot policy and would hire anyone who bothered to show up for an interview. Even for those with zero skills, they would put them to work digging a ditch on the side of the road only to fill it back up again and do it all over again the next day. *There was no excuse.* Jason's eyes narrowed and his jaw flexed as he watched the swarming crowd of tiny dots scurry around the middle of Quadrant 3, heading in no particular direction. He remembered the ant hills by the creek.

———

Jason was not a software programmer, but he dove into the project with both feet. He knew Comprehensive Human Digitization was within reach, and the software people on his team all agreed. He would not have hired them otherwise. He also did not hire anyone with any meaningful ties to family or friends. He looked for membership in Incel Clubs on resumes. All of them passed top security background checks and agreed to sign non-disclosure agreements with no expiration dates. They would go to the grave with information about what they had been working on, or they would face charges of treason. The agreements stated that any breach would result in the pursuit of the death penalty. In exchange, the programmers received multimillion-dollar salaries, plus benefits, plus room and board. They would live and work at HQ and have full use of the amenities, including the virtual brothel. It would be a small team of ten, and they would all report directly to Jason Harper. No questions asked.

There was no downplaying the enormity of the task at hand. When Jason gathered the team together for the first time, he made the goal clear: "We will be the first to digitize a human being. If any of you have any doubts about that, please resign now." No one said a word. Jason then went on to explain what everyone already knew. "The race is on. We have many worthy competitors. Billions of dollars have been invested so far, and countless hours put into it by others. We're getting to the game late. But, with the people in this room, and with my resources, I like our odds. You're the best of the best. And, I've already saved the world once." Everyone appreciated the humor, and the opportunity to release some nervous laughter. "And together we will get it done. Your names will be in the history books, right alongside mine." Then a thought occurred to Jason, "But that won't matter anymore because you will be around forever, so there won't be any history books—you can tell them about it yourself." The room laughed again. This time with some hesitation.

26

Jason Harper and Mark Sapin were searching for the same thing: Immortality. Neither of them would admit it, and neither would use that word—immortality—but that is what they were doing. Comprehensive Human Digitization became shorthand for immortalization. Living forever.

The idea was to create a digital replication of the human brain. And it was not at all that far-fetched. It had been done before, but only portions, and nothing that could be considered "comprehensive." Still, rudimentary digitization had been achieved and did serve as the basis for some of the highest performing examples of artificial intelligence. The health care industry, in particular, had been transformed by digitization. Neuroscientists and software programmers had teamed up to identify the portion of the brain containing specialized knowledge. In exchange for ongoing royalty payments, because they were essentially putting themselves out of work, hundreds of doctors signed up to have their hippocampus—the brain's hard drive—scanned and digitized. They were all general practitioners, old-school family doctors, who did the grunt work none of the new med school graduates wanted to do. There was little money involved. It was a grind. One patient after another. Software executives saw it as the perfect opportunity for robots.

Hundreds of brain scans stored the memories of those doctors, which could be sifted and sorted, curated and cataloged for installation into the med bots. Those robots would then serve as the first line of defense in the world of health care. The artificial intelligence stored in the central processing units of the machines would save billions of dollars for consumers annually. That is why everyone loved the idea. The government was always looking for ways to shave costs from the system, which stubbornly remained one of the most expensive when compared to other countries. The health care industry resisted at first but got on board when they realized the med bots could boost business for its specialists. American Medical Association representatives insisted on looking over the shoulder of the programmers, ensuring the robots would be quick to send referrals to their high-priced humanoid colleagues. Consumers were cool to the idea. It was the mothers who put up the biggest fight. They had the closest bond with their family doctor. The centuries of history and culture connected to the good country doctor making house calls was a tough one to break. And the general practitioners knew where their bread was buttered, as they would joke with one another throughout their careers: "It's just as important to treat Mom as it is to treat her sick kids."

Moms finally embraced the bots once they realized how quickly they could schedule an appointment to see one. And, for those who could afford it, house calls again became an option. Since they did not require sleep, the med bots would show up at any time, day or night. If Junior was having a coughing fit at three o'clock in the morning, a robotic doctor could be summoned. It was as simple as going online, answering a series of questions, clicking "Yes" to an authorization form, and paying upfront with a credit card. Many families began subscribing to the med bots, which allowed for a certain number of visits each year. While the robots shared a vast network of knowledge —the digitized memories of the doctors—they were also actively learning. The base of understanding was growing. Each time a med bot encountered a new symptom or discovered a previously unknown disease or disorder, that knowledge was uploaded to the cloud where it was automatically shared with the growing legion of robots. As part of the compromise with the American Medical Association, and in order to receive government funding, the software executives agreed to sign the Hippocratic Oath on behalf of their companies, the same one used by actual doctors, which stated in full: "I swear to fulfill, to the best of my ability and judgment, this covenant: I will respect the hard-won scientific gains of those physicians in whose steps I walk, and gladly share such knowledge as is mine with those who are to follow." The oath is what allowed the med bots to continue getting smarter.

It was the unusual cases which advanced the pool of knowledge most. The sniffles and sneezes were easy, and they could be treated on the spot. But once in a while, the med bots were stumped. That was the case for the ReadyMed robot that continued to show up at the Sapins old Craftsman. Their machines always had trouble climbing the stairs. It would have been a funny thing to watch had it been under different circumstances, but Mark and Angela were not in a laughing mood. After first taking a measure of Maggie's vital signs, the questions would begin. "How do you feel right now? Where does it hurt? On a scale from one to ten, with ten being the worst, how uncomfortable are you?" Almost always, the robots could make the pain go away for a while with the narcotics they had on-hand. But they would invariably turn her into a groggy mess, half-asleep, half-awake. Miserable. The discomfort would abate, but it would often travel to her stomach. She would then complain about the cramping, and the med bots would administer some other drug. Mark and Angela would watch with horror as the pain and discomfort would migrate around her little body, the ReadyMed robot doing its best to keep up the chase.

Angela had no patience for those med bots and once received a threatening email after she struck on of them with an open hand. In no uncertain terms, it said, her subscription would be voided, and she would lose her deposit if it were to happen again. Mark had a different point of view. He could see that the bots were just the beginning. The first iteration. With each patient interaction, he understood that they were gaining knowledge and improving their collective diagnostic capacity. He could look past the clumsiness of the first generation, knowing there would be a second and a third. It was no different than the computers at the museums, the Commodore 64 and the Apple IIe with their floppy disc drives. Someday, we would look back on this first generation of med bots and marvel at how primitive they were. But, for now, that's all they had. And those robots were doing the best they could to bring comfort to his daughter. He also appreciated the humor built into the ReadyMed bots. Their programmers opted to preserve some of the non-medical memories of a few of the old country doctors in an effort, presumably, to humanize their droids. For some reason, he was told the same joke by their robots each time they walked out the front door. "Okay, don't forget. The best home remedy for children with the common cold is equal parts lemon juice, honey, and whiskey. Give your kids two teaspoons before bedtime—then you drink the rest." The robot would play a tinny laughter in an attempt at folksy humor. It was weird, but Mark appreciated the effort of the programmer, who he figured was also a parent.

One of those med bots had been stripped down to its central processing unit deep in the bowels of the sprawling new complex— HQ—at the edge of Colorado Springs. All ten of the programmers joined Jason Harper at a lab bench, as one piece of hardware after another was extracted. They wanted to see how the thing worked. This particular robot was part of the White House fleet. But they had more of them than they needed over there. It was just getting in the way. It had been declared eminent domain and was now the property of the United States government. Each of the last bolts and screws were turned with care and caution until the circuitry was revealed. One of the programmers then reached into the chest of the bot laying prone on the operating room table. The room fell silent as the central processor was hoisted. Next, the hard drive was hoisted placed on the table with two steady, slow-moving hands. "Awesome!" Jason exclaimed, breaking the concentrated tension. "Let's get this on the mainframe so we can analyze it." He then assigned one of the programmers to take the lead, the same one, as always. Turning to him he barked, "Make sure everyone's working on something different. I don't want any duplication. This all about speed and efficiency—not redundancy." The group broke up, each of them hustling back to their separate window-less offices.

———

Entrepreneurs always included the success of the med bot providers in their pitches to venture capitalists. Their thinking on the subject was linear, "A leads to B, which leads to C." And their presentations frequently included images of ancient home computers in the slides preceding a graph reminding them of Moore's Law. Every starry-eyed entrepreneur gushed about Moore's Law. It had been remarkably accurate in its prediction that computing power would double every two years. But its extrapolation to everything ranging from electric car adoption to e-brothel memberships and now to Comprehensive Human Digitization was more than a little overdone. Still, it was worth listening. Visiting the neighborhood virtual bordello was one thing, but immortalization was quite another. Imagine the premium customers would be willing to pay in order to extend their lives indefinitely.

The next slide would show the med bots at the bottom-left-hand corner of a hockey stick shaped graph. "Right now, we're here," the entrepreneurs would point to the beginning of the line. "But this is where we're heading," as they moved the pointer up the curve to the top right corner. That presentation, combined with a credible resume, was generally enough to get funding. The race was on, and everyone scrambled to get a horse on the track. The risk of losing the investment paled in comparison to the gain that would be had by the winner. And there was bound to be many winners.

Mark followed each development with maniacal focus and attention. With every twist and turn in the gold rush, his daughter's life hung in the balance. He read the blogs and the press releases. He called the companies. He connected with people in the business. He attended a convention. Everything he could do to learn more, he did. Later, he would admit that he was no longer sleeping well and not thinking coherently. He was twisting himself up in knots, making one intellectual leap of faith after another. So was Jason Harper.

Everyone who watched the CHD race from the sidelines fit into one of two camps: Those who believed it would work, and those who said it was impossible no matter how much the technology advanced. The issue concerned the digitization of consciousness or, as some would put it, "the replication of the soul." Up to that point, neurologists had not pinpointed the exact location of consciousness in the human brain —the part of the anatomy that said, "I am. I exist." The CHD companies claimed that its location was irrelevant since they would be digitizing the entire organ, hence the word "comprehensive." Up to that point, they had only digitized parts of brains as was the case with the doctors involved in the development of the med bots. Moore's Law dictated that it was only a matter of time before exponential growth would allow for the replication of the whole thing, the entire human brain. And, since the brain is responsible for consciousness, their argument went, wherever consciousness happened to be seated within the organ, it would be copied as well.

The other camp, often consisting of religious and spiritual types, would argue that Moore's Law was irrelevant. Even if the entire brain could be digitized—after the advent of the med bots, most agreed it was plausible—it would not matter because consciousness does not reside in the brain. From this point of agreement, their explanations would vary widely. Some said it was domiciled in the heart. Others claimed it permeated the entire body, only to be liberated upon death. A few different groups, mostly those in New Age circles, described the brain as an old-style radio. It was simply receiving signals from somewhere out in the ether where consciousness is tangled up with everyone else's consciousness. It all became very complicated, but one thing was clear: Everyone had an opinion. And, no matter their theories, it ultimately came down to the asking and answering of one simple yes or no question: "Can CHD be accomplished?" The population was split almost exactly in half, prompting some to recall the intractable liberal-conservative divide that had come to define the country in the preceding decades.

Roy was always careful to keep his opinions to himself. He could hear the desperation in Mark's voice during their many conversations about the CHD race. Roy never said so, but he thought the idea of digitizing consciousness was ridiculous. His mother had raised him in the Baptist Church. "Bible-bangers is what we were," he would tell Mark. The preacher had been successful in scaring the hell out of him as a boy, but once he learned how to read the Good Book himself, he arrived at a crisis of faith. All of those contradictions in the scriptures were enough for him to call its credibility into question. To the great disappointment of his mother, he stopped believing. Religion never returned for Roy, particularly after he joined the Army. For him, the CHD debate was settled on the mountain range dividing Korea and China. One by one, he would pick them off, just as he was ordered to do. Through his scope, he would watch them from a quarter of a mile away. When they would finally hold still, he would square them up in the crosshairs, exhaling as he squeezed the trigger. Bam! Mission accomplished.

Sometimes chaos would break out and he would scramble to find another target, but other times that would be it. Just he and his kill. When that was the case, Roy always kept his scope trained on the body. He wanted to make sure he was dead, but he also wanted to see what came next. The first time it happened was on a crisp early autumn afternoon. Whisper quiet. No one was around, just he and his target. Bam! The twenty-four-year-old Korean combatant never saw it coming. One shot and the top of his head disappeared. His body continued standing for a moment before falling on its back. Roy watched. It was a few minutes later when he saw it. A mistiness, that was the only word he had in his vocabulary to describe it—a mist— began emanating from the torso as it rose upward. Then, it hovered a few feet above the body before for a brief moment before it launched directly above and out of sight. Slow then sudden. By his own count, Roy experienced this phenomenon on eleven occasions. But he never talked about it. He thought about sharing it with Mark, but he could see that his friend had already made up his mind, and had become obsessed with digitization along with half of the country.

Roy knew better. When he talked about his time as a sniper which he rarely did, except during his twice-monthly appointments with Veterans Affairs counselor and once with Mark, he said of his confirmed kills: "I separated them from their souls." That's why he carved that word into the shoulder stock of his rifle, the same one tattooed across his chest. "Liberator."

27

Alex Cribb understood his best friend's sense of humor. That's why his cryptic message gave him goosebumps. "Oops, I did it again," is all Jason Harper had typed. He knew right away what it meant. Alex replied, letting him know he would be arriving at HQ within the hour.

Behind a sedan-sized desk, Jason was smoking a cigar. He had never seen him smoke before, but he understood the symbolism. Alex declined when offered one and instead rushed into sharing the news.

"I did it: Comprehensive Human Digitization," Jason declared in triumph, stretching out the words for emphasis.

Alex's mind bounded forward as he considered the implications. But, before getting too far ahead of himself, as was his nature, he wanted confirmation. "Did you try it on someone yet?"

"No," Jason replied, "not yet."

The level of enthusiasm Alex felt ratcheted down several rungs. At this point, he realized that CHD remained theoretical. "Well, let's do it. Let's test it."

Jason walked to his white board and began to draw. Over the course of the afternoon, he explained to his friend how it would work. The two then swore themselves to secrecy, which was implied with any and all conversations they had, but this one was different. Reaffirming their unspoken agreement felt appropriate. This conversation would change the world. It would reshape America in a way that past administrations would not have dared to dream. It was far too big, far too bold. None of them had their unique combination of brains and guts and vision. This required nothing less than divine intervention, which is why Christians, in the Book of Jason, insisted on calling Chairman Harper "the Chosen One." Only He could execute God's plan. Only He could choose.

Alex again asked, "Okay, who? Who will be the first?"

Jason responded by reminding him that consciousness cannot exist in two places at once. Doing so would "scramble the circuits" and result in an instant brain death. The digitization would be a jumbled mess, leaving a human vegetable who would have to be "spoon-fed baby food" for the rest of their life.

Alex smiled to himself as he gazed through the window toward the snow-capped Rocky Mountains. Lost in thought, he came to a realization. "No one can know about this test. We have to iron out the details and make sure this is going to work the way we think it will. I was going to suggest we test it out on a prisoner, an inmate here in Colorado. But there is too much of a paper trail. I think our only option is to find a homeless person—one with no ties, no strings attached."

Jason had already arrived at the same conclusion, but he wondered how to procure such a person. They were everywhere, of course, but it's not like the president of the United States could drive up to skid row with a case of beer and say, "Hey, who here wants to live forever?"

"Actually," Alex said as he turned his head back toward Jason, "that's exactly what we do. Let's send one of your programmers out. Which one can you trust?"

———

It was the second most surreal conversation of David's life. The leader of the free world, the Chairman of the United States, was giving him very specific instructions on what to do with the wrinkled, brown sandwich bag containing ten-thousand dollars in cash. "Use your own car, not one of the government sedans," Jason insisted. "Buy a few cases of beer. The cheap stuff. Get some junk food. Head downtown to skid row and ask around, 'Who here wants to be digitized?' Be sure to explain what that means: They get to live forever doing whatever they want to do—drink beer, eat Ho Hos, shoot heroin, whatever they want. And don't bring back one of the crazy ones. I want someone who is coherent, someone legit. This won't work otherwise. You got it? Oh, and you can keep the change. And, David, I know you have already signed the contract, but I'm going to remind you again of what is at stake here. This has to remain between you and me."

Four hours later, David returned with a man wearing a scraggly white beard, a hand-knit beanie, and a heavily soiled and tattered puffy jacket. He wreaked of beer, reportedly downing five of them in the back seat on the drive back to HQ. The man, who offered only a first name—Samuel—became known to the team of ten programmers and Jason as "Number One."

After a long shower, the barber arrived for a trim before Number One settled in to plow through the meal he had ordered: fried chicken, mashed potatoes and gravy, deep dish pepperoni and sausage pizza, cherry pie, apple pie, and banana cream pie, plus ice cream, and chocolate cake "with sprinkles." The man had taken full advantage of the "order whatever you want instructions." He gorged himself, as cameras behind the observation glass recorded the conversation. One by one, he answered the questions. It started with the basics. "What's your name? How old are you? Where do you live?" before morphing into an elaborate and disjointed this-is-your-life storytelling session. "Tell us about your happiest moment. What's the worst thing that ever happened to you, and why?" This went on through the evening as Number One held court among the young programmers while he continued draining cans of light beer.

Then, Jason stopped by the room and asked everyone to leave, except for David. He locked the door after it closed. Then his sat down in front of Number One, studying the grooves spanning his forehead before he began to speak. "Samuel, I want to make sure you understand the program. We are going to continue talking for the next few days, so you just let us know what else you want to eat, okay? After that, we're going to do a full brain scan. You won't feel a thing. Once we've got it all and confirm we have comprehensive digitization, we will head to the 2BIRDS where you will be immortalized. From there, you can do whatever you want. Eat fried chicken and cake with sprinkles for eternity. Do you understand the process, Samuel?"

Samuel nodded in the affirmative.

David looked down, focusing on the sweat condensing around the palms of his folded hands.

"A few days" turned into five. Samuel had a lot to say, and Jason suspected he was enjoying the attention just as much as he was enjoying the beer and the fried chicken. The scan also took much longer than expected—a full day. Jason reminded everyone about Moore's Law. "The first one always takes the longest. We'll turn twenty-four hours into twenty-four minutes, then twenty-four seconds." The only thing remaining now was to schedule some time at the local 2BIRDS. Again, as always, he dispatched David. It would be strange for the landfill supervisor to receive a call from the chairmen himself, so David introduced himself and explained the situation. "Official government business, one hour is all we need, and we'll do it in the middle of the night when no one is around."

Jason was just as surprised as David, who was as just surprised as Samuel. All three of their heads were spinning. All three for different reasons. Jason could not believe he was climbing into David's junk heap of a car, and more shocked still that he was entrusting this kid with everything. But he did not have a choice. He did not want to use a government vehicle, or one of his own, for fear that it would create a record on a manifest by someone somewhere. Plus, Jason was not a programmer. He needed an expert to actually do the deed, to operate the computer. He also needed a witness, somebody he could trust to come back and tell the team what he needed them to know—nothing more and nothing less. David was surprised because the most powerful man to ever walk the face of the Earth was riding shotgun in his pile-of-crap four-door compact, picking through discarded fast food wrappers. And Samuel was surprised to find himself in backseat drinking beer once again.

The car drove itself to the base of the 2BIRDS. The entire area had been cordoned off just as David had requested. They walked inside and Jason began tapping on the console. Samuel was handed another can. "When I flash you the thumbs-up sign, press that button, okay?" Jason said, holding up one thumb to demonstrate at the same time pointing to an oversized red flashing button that said, "Power." Then, he turned to David to give him his directions, which were similar. "When you see me give the go-ahead, you upload the CHD and activate the software, okay?" David nodded a yes. "All right, Samuel, thanks for your service and good luck."

As the door clunked shut. Samuel cupped his hands and looked out through the porthole. His breath fogged the glass. Jason leaned into the locking wheel, straining to twist it closed and cinch it air-tight. David stood up to glimpse Samuel looking back at him. For the first time, Number One appeared to register concern. David then kneeled back down with his laptop, his finger rested next to the "Enter" key while Samuel began wandering around the inside of the 2BIRDS. When he finally met the eyes of Number One, Jason flashed the thumbs-up sign before he immediately called it off. "Wait, wait, wait! David, hold up! Change of plan." Jason exhaled in frustration. "I can't figure out what he's doing in there. This may take a while."

Jason became frustrated by the delay as he watched Samuel who appeared to be teasing him as he hovered his finger over the "Power" button. Jason pounded on the glass and hollered at him to get moving. Number One then guzzled his beer, cleared his throat, and began to sing a song from *The Wizard of Oz*, the same one he had heard his mother sing at the Hilliard House. "Somewhere, over the rainbow, way up…" in one hand Samuel waved his drink to the rhythm of the song, in the other he reached over to the control panel. At the same time he sang "high," he pressed "Power." Just as he remembered with the foreman in Lisbon, Number One lifted off the ground appearing to levitate for a split second before launching up and away in a flash through the tube.

"Now!" Jason shouted. David immediately pressed "Enter."

The curser blinked and blinked—and blinked. Two minutes felt like two months. Finally, the screen reported the status updates: "Upload Successful. Comprehensive Human Digitization Successful."

"Okay, let's talk with our buddy, Samuel," Jason requested, rubbing his hands together in anticipation.

"Samuel, it's David. How are you feeling?" David leaned in to speak directly to his laptop screen.

Again, the cursor blinked for far too long before he materialized on the screen. "I'm great! Better than ever. If I had known that getting digitized was this great, I would have done it a long time ago."

Jason thrust his fist into the air with one arm in triumph. Despite the warm, balmy night, a chill shooting through his spine made David shiver.

Before getting into the car, Jason returned to the 2BIRDS, cranked open the door, and walked in to erase the always recording security video cameras. On the way to HQ, David marveled as he continued the conversation with Samuel. His voice sounded tinny and hollow, but that was due to the low-quality computer speakers. Jason asked Number One if he was able to find himself any chocolate cake with sprinkles. Samuel replied exactly as expected: "Who needs cake when you're in ecstasy?"

———

The decision concerning how to roll out the program would be critical. They could not afford any missteps. Together, Jason and Alex saw the homeless community as the best place to start. They were the "bullseye of Quadrant 3," according to Alex. And Jason mentioned the mayor of

Colorado Springs. She called herself a "homeless hawk," and ran on a platform promising to "eradicate the blight that was overrunning the city." Last year, she joined the Pragmatist Party. She practically bled purple now. If there ever was an ideal person to help launch the program, it would be her.

Mayor Laughlin was summoned to HQ by David. She settled around the café style table in Jason's office along with Alex. The video was queued, and she watched the professionally edited journey of Number One from a lowly street vagrant to an exalted, angelic immortal. Her held her hand up to her gaping mouth. "Holy crap, you guys did it. You did CHD," she marveled.

"No," Alex chimed in right one cue. "It was Jason who did it."

Jason appreciated being acknowledged as the star of the show, as always, but he used it as an opportunity to segue into the program rollout. It would be completely voluntary, of course, but there would be pre-CHD compensation involved. Ten-thousand dollars to each participant with no cap on the number who could participate. Jason would write the check himself. The only requirement is that they be in the Colorado Springs Police Department homeless database and be squarely in Quadrant 3. That went without saying, they all understood that homelessness and Quadrant 3 went hand-in-hand. The same ten-minute video that the mayor just watched, a documentary-style film complete with uplifting music and light-hearted humor, would be shown by the police officers to anyone who met the eligibility requirements for the pilot program. "My cops," she said with a widening smile, "are going to love this."

By the end of the first week, the Colorado Springs Police Department had received a firm "Yes" from 3,761 of their homeless population. Jason was floored. He expected the number to be less than a hundred. It turned out that many of them had known Samuel. He was the perfect spokesman. They trusted him. Others were in it only for the money. To speed through the backlog, Jason opted to skip the in-person interviews and proceed directly to the brain scans. This would shave months off the process—Moore's Law—and would allow for the digitization of every single one of them within a few weeks.

The landfill supervisor was contacted. After he watched the video, he was supportive, even enthusiastic, when he told David that the 2BIRDS could be used whenever it was needed. He said, "My wife is going to be so happy that the streets are finally getting cleaned up. She can't go into town anymore without being harassed by all the panhandlers down there."

Progress marched forward, and Mayor Laughlin was happy to take the credit. Lauded by the networks as "America's Most Effective Mayor," nearly every other city in the country analyzed her program and wondered if it would work for them. Almost all said, "Yes." The streets were cleared. The garbage emptied. Just like the manmade mountains which had once towered over the cities, the homeless population began to disappear. Best of all, everyone could feel good about it—they were off to a better place, and cooling the planet in the process.

Except for a small circle of CHD industry insiders, no one was surprised to learn that Jason Harper had done it again. This time, he did not only find a way to delay the inevitability of death, he canceled it altogether.

28

Everyone was talking about Comprehensive Human Digitization. The experiment conducted in Colorado Springs was the country's worst-kept secret. They knew they would not be able to keep it under wraps for long, but the speed at which the news traveled was shocking. But most of it was inaccurate. It was time to set the record straight. The idea of a national address from the Oval Office was first suggested, but quickly nixed. This announcement would have to be big and bold and cutting-edge. Optics would be everything.

Although the Consumer Electronics Show was weeks away, its producers did not hesitate to bump their headliner. "This will be mind-blowing, crazier than anything you've ever seen," David promised them before dropping a clue. "I am only authorized to say that Chairman Harper himself will be the presenter. Trust me, the buzz will be insane. History will be made on your stage."

At HQ, the programmers continued to work around the clock to process the backlog of homeless people who signed on for digitization. It became fast apparent that physically bringing future "uploads" to Colorado Springs was not going to be feasible, or desirable. They could handle the current group as long as they did same-day processing, which meant the scans would have to be shortened—Jason cited Moore's Law magic again—and they would have to operate non stop to get it done. Lines of charter busses formed, running back and forth to the Colorado Springs municipal 2BIRDS from four o'clock in the afternoon, when the dump closed, until six o'clock in the morning when it opened again. Fifty at a time filed into the bus. They were accompanied by a handful of recently hired and hastily trained "upload counselors" armed with laminated, double-sided FAQ sheets to help them answer any last-minute questions. Everyone boarded together at HQ's main circle drive behind the security gates. Those same counselors would then return with an empty bus forty-five minutes later, occasionally with one or two of the participants who either got cold feet or had wandered off into the darkness of the land-fill prior to the upload.

The short film depicting the journey of Number One had been suffi-cient to this point, but now, nothing short of Oscar-caliber movie making would do. Only the best were hired. It began with storyboard-ing. The lecture hall was used for this purpose. The director and the producer shared the dry erase board for the kickoff meeting. "There's no such thing as a dumb idea. This is brainstorming, people. Let's get it all out." Hands raised. Frantic scribbles appeared in multiple colors. Within an hour, there was no space remain. "Okay, people, it's time to winnow it down." The movie director then led a thoughtful discussion about how to accomplish the three objectives they had been given for the short film: "inform, inspire, and entertain."

Jason was careful to remain scarce. He did not want his presence to disrupt the creative process. But he watched it all unfold from the audio-visual booth hidden behind the tinted glass at the back of the room. He did not like what he was seeing. Rubbing his fingers through his hair, he could not help himself. He had always been hands-on with all of his business dealings. Why did he think this would be any differ-ent? With a twist of the nob, Jason made a dramatic entrance at the back of the hall. Gasps were heard as one Hollywood-type after another saw the chairman in the flesh. These were people who were accustomed to working side-by-side with the industry's A-listers. They were not easily star-struck, but this was an entirely different level. This was Jason Harper. The man who saved the world. "No! No! No!" he called out as he descended the steps of the center aisle. "This is all wrong. You're supposed to inform, inspire, and entertain. So far, you are only accomplishing one of the three—inform. If that's all you're going to do, we can save a lot of time and money and just send out a press release instead." Jason continued to the front, picked up the eraser, and began clearing the board. Behind him, a raucous standing ovation erupted.

Alex was serious when he talked to Jason about the video—he really did believe that it had a legitimate shot at winning an Oscar. He could not watch it without feeling a massive jolt of patriotism. The rousing music alone made him want to jump up and salute the nearest flag. He found himself laughing and crying—tears of joy and pride—and chest thumping and standing taller. This video is exactly what was needed to tell the story of Comprehensive Human Digitization, he said.

With only a week to go before the conference, Jason prepped for his presentation with an assembly of his political advisers and a woman who was considered the premier public speaking consultant. "You see how he pauses? The power is in the pause," she said as they reviewed an old video of Steve Jobs unveiling a new product. "You see here, look, he's holding the audience in his hands with those pauses." Armed with a new round of critiques, Jason again made his way to the front of the room to do another take. Each time it improved. Although he and Alex disagreed on this point, Jason could not resist: one by one, sterile, clinical terms such as "life extension" and "indefinitely" were replaced with emotional trigger words like "transcendence" and "immortality."

The jet touched down on the blistering Las Vegas tarmac, and the entourage hustled over to the convention center. A White House advance team had been on site since the previous week to set up the venue and begin securing it for the chairman's arrival. Alex would remain in Colorado Springs. He was the rare president who was not fond of large crowds. He preferred instead to operate in isolation with his tight-knit group of trusted advisors. Jason was the performer. Alex would let him do his thing, so that he could do his. It would be quiet around the Oval Office, as the attention of the entire world would be on the Consumer Electronics Show. He would catch it on television, . just like everyone else.

———

Jason strode to center stage, waving to the crowd while searching for the camera bots jockeying one another for position around the main hall. As he began to speak, a new round of cheering reverberated. He bowed his appreciation. Again, the thunder returned. After nearly five minutes of adulation, he was finally able to start the presentation. "Today, we enter a new frontier," he stated. The applause interrupted again. He waited. And waited. Then, he continued. "Today, we enter a new frontier. I'm here to share some news with you." He captivated the hall with the execution of a flawless long pause. "I have cracked the code on Comprehensive Human Digitization." Jubilation erupted, as the crowd jumped and embraced and launched whatever had been in their hands—trade show brochures, water bottles, everything. Frenzied. Gyrating. Frothing. Quivering. It was more religious revival than technology conference. The only thing missing was the man handling snakes and speaking in tongues.

When the noise finally settled to a steady hum, Jason walked the crowd though his impossible journey. His conquest. He explained how he had "knocked down one brick wall after another"—undaunted, as always—to find the answer, to solve the problem. Then, he talked about the overwhelming success of the homeless pilot program in Colorado Springs. Anticipation surged. Everything was leading up to this, the big unveil.

Repeatedly, in preparation for this day, he watched that video of Steve Jobs unveiling the first iteration of Apple's home computer, the Macintosh. Jason mimicked the iconic performance, as he circled around a café table shrouded by an oversized black cloth positioned at the middle of the stage. "Ladies and gentlemen," he said as he ripped away the cover, "meet Samuel." Again, pandemonium.

The monitor of the humble laptop sitting atop that table was simultaneously projected on the jumbo screen above Jason at the same time it appeared on billions of much smaller screens worldwide. The face was handsome, a blue-eyed man with a white beard cropped close enough to reveal a square jaw. Rugged, but also urbane. Sophisticated, but not too much so. He was calm and confident and trustworthy and sincere. "Hello, everyone," he offered with a smile. The corner of his eyes crinkled his tanned skin. The crowd shouted back, "Hello!" Samuel chuckled to himself, and waited for the noise to soften before continuing. "A short time ago, I was a fifty-six-year-old homeless man wandering around skid row. It was a horrible, horrible existence. But I didn't know any different. I was a drag on society, just completely unproductive. Today, I have no age. I guess you could say that I'm timeless. And I'm in ecstasy." The crowd, volcano-like, exploded its approval.

Jason spent the next half-hour interviewing Samuel. Viewers became enchanted by the hobo-turned-leading-man-handsome hunk. "Samuel now exists digitally, which means he can move across platforms: laptop, desktop, tablet, watch, phone, it doesn't matter." Jason then explained the plans for widespread rollout. "This program will be exclusively for Quadrant 3. We'll be offering it to the most unproductive first: homeless people, inmates, the elderly, and the terminally ill." For the first time, a smattering of groans could be heard.

"What about the other quadrants?" someone shouted from the crowd.

At first, his instincts were to ignore the question, but he could sense unease with the audience and suspected others were wondering the same thing, so he went off script.

"Remember," he said, "this is just the first iteration. The software will only get better from here. Remember Moore's Law. Remember the Apple IIe. Someday, in the not-too-distant future, we envision a CHD bank where anyone of any age can go in for a complete scanning. We will then store the digitization until that person passes away, which is when it would be activated. But this takes the potential for identity theft to a whole new level. Imagine if a foreign power were to hack in and steal CHD scans? We know what they're capable of. We have all seen it done to our elections, right? But, aside from the terrifying security risks, the fundamental issue, what we have found so far, is that consciousness cannot exist in two places at once. The only way this works is with a simultaneous upload." The audience was confused by the term "simultaneous upload," and Jason picked up on it immediately. He anticipated it. This, he knew, was the most delicate component, the part of the story that he and Alex worried about. "Here, let me show you the video," he said, abandoning the dramatic introduction he had practiced.

Halfway through the rousing film, the audience realized that "simultaneous upload" was a polite way of saying "suicide." Again, the groans returned. CHD lost its appeal when "upload" meant being shot into outer space, only to suffocate upon arriving at the celestial destination. Still, this was a tremendous breakthrough. But most on the floor of the convention center that day grumbled that the program had some significant bugs to fix. Perfect for Samuel the homeless guy, but everyone else would have to wait for CHD 2.0. Life was too good in the upper quadrants, but for those stuck behind bars or at home with another bedside visitor from hospice, this was a great option. It was no less than eternal life, complete with a "reset button." The parts of the short film that showed Samuel's before and after video were inconceivable. Clearly, he was in a much better place now. He said so himself.

Manufacturing would be a challenge, but it happened to be Jason's specialty. Thousands of 2BIRDS and algae ponds were built in record time. Now, it would be brain scanners. Rather than contract it out to a third party, he explained that this technology was so important that it would have to be done by himself, in house. Many in the tech world suspected that he was adopting this strategy in an effort to avoid the constant threat of knockoffs and copycats. The trade off with this strategy, as always, is that it always takes longer than expected. Again, as was the problem Jason so often encountered with everything he did, demand far exceeded supply. The very first brain scanner installed for commercial use was the same one used by the programmers back at HQ. This time, it was strapped down on a pallet and escorted by a heavily armed convoy as it traveled the state forty miles south to the federal supermax prison in Florence, Colorado. There, the inmates were given a choice: continue to serve whatever sentence the judge handed down, or take eternal life now. Just less than a quarter opted for the latter. Then, Samuel the handsome homeless guy paid a visit. He patiently answered their questions from the movie screen after the inmates took turns watching the short film in half-hour shifts. Within three weeks, the population of ADX Florence, also known as "Alcatraz of the Rockies" dropped by ninety-six percent.

The second great clean-up had begun. Jason made the mountains of garbage go away, now he was taking out the rest of the trash. Brain scanners began shipping out daily from HQ. Prisons were emptied. Skid rows were pressure washed. The monitors in Jason's office showed the ant pile in Quadrant 3 dwindling hour by hour. Dots were no longer pacing in circles. They were simply disappearing. Gone. There were fewer dots. Fewer dots meant fewer people. But there were still far too many dots. Too many dots producing still more dots.

Shantytown residents, as a whole, were skeptical of the video and of Samuel. They been accustomed to getting hustled. They told themselves that there had to be a catch somewhere. Inmates and vagrants were one thing, but clearing out the rest of Quadrant 3 would not be so easy. That's why Jason suggested the incentive: One-hundred-thousand dollars to anyone residing in a shantytown and a member of Quadrant 3, which, again, is one and the same. Alex objected to that amount initially because it seemed far too generous. That is, until Jason did the math for him, and demonstrated that the amount was much less than the government would be paying them indirectly through its many forms of welfare.

The funds would be provided pre-upload, so they could be spent immediately—a guaranteed boost to the economy, Alex observed—or they could be passed on tax-free to family members. This was more money than most of these people had ever seen. And it was cash on the barrelhead. Plus, of course, the real prize for them was the ability to live on in never-ending bliss, moving from a cardboard shack into whatever it was that their minds could conjure. Either way, it was a win-win. At least according to the new television commercials.

But, while they were tempted by the offer, shantytown residents weren't buying what the government was selling—at least not in the numbers Jason expected.

29

Angela never answered the door, especially when Mark was at work. Instead, she tiptoed to the peephole. Behind the bouquet she saw him. Unlocking the door and opening it in one motion, she could only manage to say, "Roy, they're beautiful," before tearing-up again. Waving him into the house, she composed herself before asking, "Would you like to see her?"

"Yes, Mrs. Sapin, if it's okay with you, I would."

Angela resisted the instinct to correct him. She had insisted hundreds of times before that he use only her first name.

The two of them ascended the staircase without a word. Angela pushed open the door and whispered, "Maggie, you have a visitor."

"Uncle Roy!" the seven-year-old called out.

Angela was stunned. Her daughter was happy and healthy again. Back to her normal self. At least for a moment. She had watched her rebound in this way before, but it never lasted long.

Roy placed the flowers on the desk next to her bed and said, "Hello there, Peanut—you sure do look awfully pretty today. I've got something for you." Maggie pulled herself up to a seated position as Roy handed her a box which he had wrapped himself. She placed it on her lap. "Now, before you open it, be sure to read the card."

Dear Peanut, I want you to know that you're a very special little girl. I thank God every day that I was chosen to be your uncle. I'm so proud of you, Peanut. You inspire me. I love you, Uncle Roy.

All three of them sat together on the bed.

Roy wiped his eyes before speaking. "Now, this present is not very exciting; it's not a toy or a doll or anything like that. It was given to me by my auntie when I was about your age. She said it would be good luck, that it would watch over me. And she was right. Go on now, go ahead and open it."

Her little hands tore away at the paper to reveal a cardboard box containing an eight-inch-tall figurine carved from marble. Maggie was curious about what she now held in her hands.

"That there is my guardian angel. His name is Saint Francis, but I gave him a nickname. I just call him Frank. I always talk to him when I need someone to listen, or when something scares me, or when I'm trying to work out a problem. He's protected me and watched over me for almost eighty years. Frank's brought me all sorts of good luck. Now it's time for him to watch over you."

Maggie examined her gift in fascination, studying every contour. It was a bearded man cloaked in a flowing robe. A bird was perched on his left shoulder, and another one sat on his right hand which was tucked against his chest. She then ran her fingers along the base where she found a few jagged edges.

"There used to be a deer standing there, too, but it broke off when I was in Korea. I had always meant to glue it back on, but I lost it some-where along the way."

"I love it," Maggie answered, transfixed by the figurine. "Thank you, Uncle Roy," she said, at the same time reaching out with both arms for a hug.

Roy was overcome by emotion, but he fought hard to keep it to himself. A clarity took hold. He was now more sure than he had ever been about anything in his life.

"My skepticism was displaced by my desperation," that's how Mark Sapin would describe it to the interrogators, at least the first time they asked. He was astonished it was happening. Most could not understand it, some would not. But when Samuel first appeared on the television screen, it was clear that all the praying he started to do was working. Mark told Roy that he was an "optimistic agnostic" when it came to Comprehensive Human Digitization. Based on his knowledge of artificial intelligence, he doubted it was even possible, but he had learned the importance of believing in the unseen—faith—from his grandmother, and he had long since resolved himself to do everything he could for his little girl. With all his other options exhausted, the only thing left was to do was to believe.

His feelings became conflicted after learning that Maggie already knew about CHD. It was no different than parents who had been in agony preparing themselves to come clean about Santa Claus or the birds and the bees, only to find out they had been scooped by some little punk on the playground a year earlier. He did not probe. It didn't matter how she found out, the only thing that mattered now is how she felt about it. In his presentation, Chairman Harper had said the program would be open to members of Quadrant 3 only, but he did make some exceptions, including for the terminally ill. The doctors said that Maggie was now "on the homestretch." Her condition was in its "final progression"—there's that word again, "progress"—and it would only be a matter of time now. A short time. She was in pain, and he only wanted it to stop.

Upstairs, Mark rested on both knees as he leaned in just a few inches from Maggie's face, stroking her forehead. It was hot to the touch, but she was not perspiring. An hour earlier, she had been howling in agony. The ReadyMed robot arrived just in time with another injection.

Things were good now, almost back to normal, but the window would close soon. He told Angela that he would talk with their daughter about it. The thought tortured him because he saw it was an acknowledgment that he had given up. CHD would be the very last resort, and a very real admission that the end had arrived. It was the equivalent of waving a white flag, unfamiliar territory for the guy who was fond of saying, "There's always a way, there's always an answer."

He began the conversation with a short trip down memory lane, talking about the day she was born and how perfect she was, and still is. How he still remembers her tiny ponytails and her binky and teddy bear. The stroller and the walks around the block. And the finger paints and her favorite pink blanket which now doubled as a bedspread. And her wooden blocks. And her Halloween costumes. And dance recitals. And back-to-school nights. And her birthday parties. They always went way over the top for her birthday parties. Her parents felt they were both celebrating their daughter's life as well as giving a giant middle finger to the old doctor who gave them long odds. Now, Mark was saying goodbye. And he knew it. Tears began welling. His throat tightened. But he had business to finish. And it required clear-headed thought and attention. This is what the white coats meant when they said it was now time to get Maggie's "affairs in order."

"So, Peanut," he was not sure how to transition the conversation. "What do you think of CHD? Pretty cool, huh?"

"I want to do it, Daddy," Maggie said, putting an immediate end to the suspense.

"Okay, Peanut, whatever you think," he assured.

"I'm tired of feeling this way—I'm tired of hurting. I just want to be me again." She thought for a moment before continuing. "I just want to be a normal seven-year-old kid with all the other seven-year-old kids. I don't ever want to see another stupid med bot ever again."

Mark smiled and kissed her on the cheek before replying. "I hear you,

Peanut. And I don't blame you at all. You've been so strong. I love you. I'm so proud of you." He turned away so she would not see his tears.

Maggie had an intuitive sense for how to lighten the conversation. "I watched Samuel, and he seems really nice. He said that he eats chocolate cake with sprinkles for every meal and he lives in a mansion full of butlers and maids. He even has a movie theater and mini golf. It sounds great, Daddy." Her voice was more robust than it had in weeks. "Do you think I'll meet Gramoo there?"

"I'm sure you will, Peanut. I'm sure you will." He then talked about how she had been named after his grandmother, her great-grandmother.

"They called her Peanut, too?" Maggie asked.

Mark did his best to fully engage in the moment, as he embraced his daughter's lucidity. It had been touch-and-go lately, and he realized this could very well be their last conversation. He wanted to remember it. Placing a hand on each of her shoulders, Mark lowered his gaze, looking deep into her eyes. *Windows to the soul.* They were innocent and inquisitive and loving and brave.

"What do you think it's going to be like there, Daddy?" Maggie broke the silence, snapping him back to attention. Mark was caught flat-footed by the question.

"You know, I really don't know." He started to explain that it was impossible to know because he had never been there, that he was as hopeful as anyone, but still not sure it existed at all. Then, he thought better of it. He remembered Gramoo. How she had admonished him to believe. That's the one and only thing he could offer his daughter right now. Faith. And it was just as powerful today as it ever had been. After a pause to plot his response, he said, "You know, Peanut, I think that Samuel told us everything we need to know. I mean, chocolate cake with sprinkles for every meal. That sounds pretty good to me."

"But what about you and Mommy and Ben and Uncle Roy and my friends from school? When will I see you again?"

"Well, remember, we'll see you every day. It's going to be a little bit different because you get to live in a mansion, or a dollhouse, or whatever you can imagine, but you can come out and visit us whenever you feel like having some company. And, as soon as we can, we're going to do CHD, too, so we can all be together forever. What do you think about that, Maggs?"

"I think it's a great idea, Daddy. I can't wait for you to come play mini golf with me."

An idea occurred to Mark, one that he had been kicking around. Something that would bring him peace: a way to verify that Maggie was truly in a better place. "How about you and I have a little signal for each other when we're away from the computer? Something that when it happens, we'll both know that we're there, that we're thinking about each other. And we'll keep it a secret, just you and me. What do you think, Peanut?"

Maggie pondered for a moment. She then turned her head toward the desk next to her bed to gaze at Frank, her guardian angel, before looking square into Mark's eyes. "Yes, just between us." Again, she paused. "Whenever you see two birds, it means that I'm there with you."

Immediately, Mark recoiled. "2BIRDS? Really, Peanut?"

"No, Daddy, *two birds*," she clarified, motioning toward the Saint Francis figurine before continuing. "A blue one, and a red one. Whenever you see them together, you'll know it's me." Then she upped the ante. "It will be a blue jay and a cardinal."

Mark caught himself before responding. He was going to tell her that the odds of those two particular birds ever being together at any one time were almost nil, especially in this part of the country where they do not exist at all. But he would not consider correcting her. Not on this day. It had been a ridiculous thing to propose to his daughter, anyway. "Okay, Peanut, a cardinal and a blue jay. That will be our signal."

Maggie held out her hand with a tiny pinky finger outstretched. "Pinky swear, Daddy. Don't tell anybody."

It was a promise both of them would keep.

———

Roy did his best to share his neighbor's enthusiasm, but he was skeptical when it came to the government, especially concerning matters of life and death. He knew first-hand from Korea II how eager they had been to exterminate life. He doubted they would be so eager to extend it—infinitely—especially for the lowly inhabitants of Quadrant 3. Still, he listened and smiled and nodded. Mark and his daughter believed. That was all that mattered. No one cared what an old washed-up Army Ranger had to say about the matter, and the last thing he was going to do was put a damper on some long-absent happiness. "That's wonderful news, just wonderful," he forced himself to say to Mark after he learned Maggie had been accepted as a CHD candidate.

The same was true for Angela. She believed. She was won over by Samuel along with most of America. He was such a compelling character. Such a kind man. The only thing she could not understand was why she couldn't join Maggie now? Why only Quadrant 3? She did not want her daughter to be alone. Mark would explain that it was due to the economy: "If productive people started digitizing en masse, then what would happen to the economy?"

"Who cares?" she would fire back. "If CHD is as perfect as it sounds, then the economy should be irrelevant. Why don't we just all just get ourselves uploaded now?"

She had a point and Mark struggled with a response. "I'm sure we will, eventually. But, remember, this is all new, so they have to release it slowly to work out the bugs, just like with any software." He paused to think for a moment before continuing. "Plus, you know, someone's got to stay behind to keep the power on."

"That's fine, but the second I'm eligible, I'm going. I'm not going to let my baby girl be alone in there," she said, gesturing toward Mark's open laptop.

"But what about Ben and me?" he asked.

"We'll all go together."

———

From his desk, Jason watched the Quadrant 3 ant hill shrink in size a little more each hour of each day. He now had two businesses, each of them booming. Everyone, everywhere, was wearing at least of a splash of purple. Lapel pins and hats and scarves and socks had become a fashionable way to pledge allegiance to the Prags of the United States of America, which is to say pledging allegiance to Jason. The carbon dioxide continued to get gobbled up by the algae ponds, as the planet convalesced and cooled under a shroud of garbage in all of its many forms. Mountains of trash ebbed as patriotism flowed.

Yet the low rate of CHD adoption by shantytown residents was perplexing. Alex described it as a "communications problem," as in "We are not doing a very good job of explaining the features and benefits." He talked about immortality in the same way a salesman would discuss his product line. *This blender, Mrs. Home Owner, features a one-half horsepower motor—the benefit to you is all the time you will save while making your Vitamin D smoothies.* Alex considered the idea of raising the $100,000 stipend, but they had already run the numbers and the payback period would be pushed out too far for it to make financial sense. He and Jason did the math and the value of a shantytown life remained remarkably consistent at one-hundred grand. Yes, of course, this was an average, but when dealing with very large numbers, millions and millions, there was no other way to do it. The average Quadrant 3 shantytown resident received just over $34,000 from the government each year in the form of tax credits, food stamps, welfare, social security, and health care. If you divide that $34,000 savings by the $100,000 investment—the stipend given to the CHD recipient— then it is a less than a three-year payback. As Jason would explain to his friend, "That's a guaranteed 24% return. Trust me, there is nowhere else to get that kind of return, and with zero risk."

Still, the ants were not showing any interest. The homeless had been compliant in their eradication, easily plied with expensive marketing videos and cheap beer. They were all now eating cake with Samuel in eternal bliss, forever showered and shaven. *Cleanliness is next to Godliness.* The inmates, they were gone, too. Their calculus had been different. Anything was better than staring at the same four walls. And many of them hadn't decided at all. Instead, they had been strong-armed or tricked into laying down in those brain scanners and then walking blindfolded into the 2BIRDS. It was common practice to offer prison guards a commission for each inmate they coerced. The extra income was welcomed considering they would soon be out in the labor market looking for a new job. Cities were cleaning up the mess, but the stubborn shantytown problem remained. Municipal governments began to fret, progress was sputtering. With the mountains now removed, the blighted cardboard house neighborhoods were in clear view and the upper quadrant residents complained.

It would have been impossible for Jason and Alex to know at the time that an eighteen-year-old social media sensation was about to solve their shantytown problem—before making it worse. Much worse.

30

As she was growing up in the shantytown outside of Cleveland, Tina Colton's classmates called her T.C. She never liked the way it sounded. The "ee" part of "tee-cee" was too happy for what she was feeling, so she changed it. By the time she turned eighteen, the same month she collected her twenty-seventh millionth follower, she had become a one-name, one syllable, nationwide, yet underground, phenomenon known as Teese. Her music was raw and real and authentic. It had been classified as "emo rap," emotional rapping, but she would scoff at the designation. But she scoffed at all designations, especially the one telling her she was part of Quadrant 3.

It was not that she wanted to be part of some other quadrant; she didn't. "Don't put me in no box" was a common theme in her music and in her twice-daily live and never edited fan videos. Her followers, mostly angsty teenagers, upper quadrant dwellers who had been untouched by life, ate it up. They lived vicariously through Teese. What she was saying and doing was striking a chord with the younger generations who intuitively understood the perils of living in boxes, at least figuratively, if not literally. And it was not that she was just saying words, she was living them. It was her full-tilt, all-in passion that won over one adoring fan after another. It felt as if she was talking directly to each of them. There was something about her eyes, and her convictions. Her beliefs.

Teese rebuffed the overtures of the record labels. In fact, she refused money completely. With a click of a button on her social media settings page next to line item which read, "Enable Advertising," she would have become a millionaire many times over. But doing so would have been counter to her brand and the "Quad3 Proud" tattoo on the side of her neck. Besides, she hated that word, "brand." She claimed it was just another label. "One more box for someone to put you in." So much of her appeal was the shunning of the very thing everyone wanted more than anything else: Money. Her music was pure counterculture. Youth. It was dangerous and dark and mysterious. That is why the kids could not resist it. She challenged her fans to visit their local shantytown. "Get off your ass," she would say. "Go see how we live." Those treks terrified parents, although most were not aware they were happening at all. For teenagers everywhere, commandeering the family car and loading it up with friends for a drive through the closest shantytown became a rite of passage. Only the most intrepid would take the bus, or bother to get out and walk around.

There were no secrets kept between Teese and her fans. She was open and honest, brutally so, about her two previous suicide attempts, going so far as to outline the scars on her wrists in tattoo ink. The "emo" part of emo rap came easily because she was entirely disaffected by the world she occupied and never concealed the fact that she wanted out. During more than one confessional she said to her fans tuned into the live stream, "I don't want up, y'all," a reference to moving to the upper quadrants, "I want out." She always began her videos the same way, with a Dear Diary-style monologue, talking about life in a shantytown. Every detail was included, no matter how mundane or horrifying. Then, after ten minutes or so, she would enable interactivity and do video chats with one fan at a time while the millions of others tuning in sat back and watched. Teese never vetted any of the questions. As with everything she did, it was gritty and unscripted. She became visibly frustrated when fans would use the opportunity to praise her. "This ain't about me, y'all. This is about you. Let's talk about you." It had become exhausting. She was being consumed by her fast-rising stardom and she let it be known that her appearance, her hard-shelled exterior was only a cover for what she was feeling inside: a fragile, highly sensitive little girl. The beginning of the end came one day after a fan came online and started gushing about her song "iBlack," which pays homage to her mulatto heritage and the dark circles under the eyes of shantytown dwellers—eye black. She snapped. She lost it. She decided then and there that she wanted out, this time for good.

Her fans watched the whole thing from the camera embedded in her "Quad3" baseball cap. If the government officials would have scrutinized the "a" they would have found it in the circle part of the letter. Her fans were not surprised when she declined the $100,000 stipend. The woman operating the brain scanner had assumed that Teese was talking to herself—just another schizophrenic homeless person—and was later shocked to learn of her unknowing on-screen cameo. Everything was narrated, the entire experience. Including the final upload.

The camera cam caught it all. The bus ride to the landfill. The check-in at the staging tent. The final signature authorization. The walk to the 2BIRDS. Viewers then saw how it happened. Hundreds of people filed in, all of them with dark circles under their eyes. Some embraced, others sang and danced. Some prayed. Everyone everywhere looked so happy, so relieved, including Teese. It was a strange sight, but she could not hide her excitement and anticipation. Unusual for her. She admitted that she was "giddy" and called out above the noise of the crowd, "You know what, y'all? I feel so alive right now! For the first time in my life, I feel alive!" She then started giggling to herself as the woman to her right side-hugged and kissed the top of her head. Viewers heard her words: "I love you, my child." Teese answered back without hesitation. "I love you, too!"

The level of excitement grew as did the decibel level. A voice came over a hidden speaker notifying the group it was "T-minus ten seconds." Cheers erupted. Teese started to say something but the words were swallowed-up by the roar. Everyone began counting down together, most holding hands or locked arm-in-arm. Teese removed her hat and turned the camera toward herself for one last confessional. She began shouting over the exuberant chorus surrounding her as they called out "Five, four, three..." Teese then flashed her trademark three-fingered Quadrant 3 salute and looked directly into the camera to offer her last words: "I love y'all. See you on the flip side. Peace!"

An entire generation of young people watched in muted fascination as their favorite social media personality hovered momentarily before flying straight up, as if shot through the barrel of a canon. *Slowly then suddenly.* The screen showed the interior walls of the 2BIRDS speed past. Only her laughing could be heard. Elbows and knees came in and out of view as people tumbled and turned. The ride lasted for a couple of minutes. Ebullience. Joyful noises. Happy squeals, no different than a roller coaster. Then blackness. And silence. The camera had been spinning and speeding. Now it slowed. Its rotation went from frenzied and chaotic to slow and deliberate. First, it showed a screen of far-off blinking stars. Enchanting, glowing, majestic stars. Heavenly. Then, as the hat camera continued its rotation, it showed people floating. Most faced the Earth. Looking down. Some of them continued to lock arms. Others embraced. The hat spun again. When it circled back the next time, it spotted its owner. Teese looked up, smiled and attempted to speak but there was no sound. Her eyes conveyed peace. Again, she flashed the three-fingered Quadrant 3 salute and disappeared from view. The hat drifted away and continued rotating. For the next few hours of its remaining battery life, the screen alternated between the Earth below and the far away stars of some other place.

———

It was highly unusual to decline the stipend. Money was the very reason most people would decide to do it in the first place. Her questions were odd. Teese asked for confirmation of two items: First, could she delete the digital version of herself if she wanted to opt out of immortality? Her suicide instinct was strong, and she suspected that she may want to exit whatever world came next. After the intake counselor conferred with his boss, she was told that she could, in fact, delete her CHD "if so desired." The other thing she wanted to know was whether she could operate a social media account post-digitization. The counselor had received this question many times before, so he knew how to answer it: "Yes, but just make sure you have an account set up before the simultaneous upload. It's much harder to do afterwards."

An hour later, Tesse appeared online. She looked so relaxed and calm and happy. Her hardness was gone, and she was so bright that she almost appeared to glow. Beaming. Gushing with joy. Radiant. Angelic. Her scars and hat and nose ring and tattoos were no more. It was just her. Fans would say that she looked exactly like the little girl she always talked about, the little girl who lived under the hard shell all that time. Comments began pouring in at the bottom of the screen as she addressed her fans: *We luv u gurl!!! @HellaJacqui123; GORJUSS!!!! @BeMeBeBe68; Sine me up im goin next!@KimberlyQseesU.*

"Hey there," Teese began. "I'm in ecstasy. I love it here. All I can say is that CHD is the real deal, y'all. I only wish that I did it sooner." Then, as has been consistent with every recently uploaded participant, she said, "I highly recommend that you do it, too." Tesse ended her confessional and opened it up to questions. One by one, she answered. Her rage and bitterness were gone. The frustration notably absent. Fans became transfixed by the peace she had found. The questions began morphing from "What's it like?" to "How do I do it?" She directed them to a government website.

———

One of the real-time indicators in Jason's office began doing something he had never seen before. It was the one with the heading "Voluntary CHD Applications." The bar graph was growing by leaps and bounds. For the most part, it hovered between five and ten thousand at any one time, but now it was skyrocketing into the millions. In an attempt to determine what was happening, he began clicking through the demographics of the applicants. "Applications by State" yielded no answers. Neither did "Applications by Ethnicity." Then, he clicked "Applications by Quadrant." He felt a lump travel from his throat to the bottom of his stomach as he realized that it was not just Quadrant 3 people who wanted to do CHD. Desperate for more data, he clicked "Applications by Age." Jason's neck constricted. He gasped for air. Most of the applications came from the heading labeled "18 to 24." Kids. And not just the poor ones, the troublemakers, the non-factors, the unproductive. All kids.

The government had already staffed-up to handle what it had expected would be an overwhelming demand, so applicants were sped through the process. The screening was strict, however—members of Quadrant 3 only. Although the White House was saturated with complaints peppered with words such as "unfair" and "discrimina-tory" and "unconstitutional," the Harper Administration would not budge. Since the requests were falling on def ears, applicants found a workaround. Drop out. Quit. Become homeless. Those who were previously denied CHD would then log on to view their place on the Productivity Matrix migrate to the lower left corner. They then reap-plied where the intake counselor would go online to verify their quad-rant status, hand over a one-hundred-thousand-dollar check and speed them through to their brain scan and simultaneous upload. Moore's Law was doing its thing, and the entire process took just a few days. Around the country, successful applicants were throwing "Immortality Parties," most of them blowing their entire stipend in the process.

The most popular social media videos were categorized "Simultaneous Uploads," as one CHD participant after another got creative in the 2BIRDS with their hidden cameras. Many thanked Teese before mimic-king her by flashing the three-finger symbol and calling out "Peace!" But most injected their own personality pre-launch. During one week-long stretch, it became popular to backflip or attempt some parkour in an attempt to time it just right. Those "freestyle" videos were sure bets as consistent top-views. Then, there was the kid who snuck in a pack of firecrackers. It topped the list for a few days before it was displaced by the girl who flashed her breasts just before she was uploaded. The social media platforms quickly shut down the short-lived genitalia trend. The one that stuck became known as "the reveal." It was usually a recently turned eighteen-year-old high school senior, most of them Quadrant 1 or 2 dropouts, who would walk into the 2BIRDS with a small sign made of cardstock they pulled from the trash pile outside the door. After the "T-minus ten" call was made, they would hold up their hand-written sign, so it came into camera-view revealing their secret crush.

Classmates huddled around one another's phones during break or lunch so the endless speculation could be settled. A combination of laughter and gasps of disbelief combined in the hallways between lockers. After the screen showed rotating images from outer space, as it always did moments later, excited and animated conversations began on Earth. "I knew that's who it was—I knew it!" Or, "Wow, I had no idea that guy was gay!" The trend evolved, as all trends do. The first one to offer the next iteration was an upper quadrant kid who opened his poster to reveal, "I love whirled peas," a witty take on "world peace." Many followed his lead, their "I love..." posters consisted of everything imaginable. "I love your momma" drew consistent laughs, which meant it remained popular, so was "I love chocolate cake with sprinkles," a reference to Samuel, CHD Number One. The "I love..." statements were as varied as the kids who held the signs: "I love my skateboard," "I love getting digitized," "I love irony," "I love bacon," "I love Jason Harper," "I love to party," "I love hip hop."

Businesses did their best to cash in on to the Immortality Party phenomenon. Inflated party balloons made of mylar displayed 2BIRDS images with a captions below exclaiming, "See you on the flip side!" or "Have a nice flight!" The culture changed faster than the products could keep up, and the parties were as varied as the signs the participants would carry in with them pre-upload. There was no such thing as a typical Immortality Party. Some were all-out ragers and others were quiet dinners with family and friends.

By the time Maggie was cleared for CHD, she was rarely getting up from her bed. Her time remaining was no longer measured in days but hours. Mark worried about losing her before her appointment arrived, but the helpful bureaucrat he had been talking with had assured him that if she passed away before the upload, they could still activate her digitization after the fact. "Just give me a call if it happens," he said with empathy, "and we'll get it straightened out." It was strange to talk about his daughter as if she were a piece of software. But that is what she was about to become. Maybe it wasn't strange at all, Mark would tell himself. Maybe that's all we are, have been, and will become. Software. Not flesh and bones and we have been lead to believe, but bits and bytes. He sometimes allowed his imagination roam free, conjuring wild theories: Maybe we were created by aliens who were entertained by us as they watched the never-ending drama of their crazy playthings—humans beings—unfold from the comfort of their living rooms, somewhere deep in outer space. Reality TV.

The family gathered upstairs in Maggie's bedroom. They told stories and reminisced. Mark watched his daughter struggle to push the fork around the plate of her favorite meal—Angela's homemade macaroni and cheese—and could see it in her eyes. She was ready to go. It was time.

31

Since Maggie was a minor, her parents were allowed to be there. And because she required assistance to walk, they escorted her into the 2BIRDS. They had said their goodbyes so many times before that this one did not feel final. The on-site administrator had a daughter himself and was moved to tears by the scene. Although it was against protocol, he asked Mark and Angela if they would like to observe the upload. Without consulting one another, they nodded and muttered an inaudible "Yes."

Through the porthole window, they spotted their daughter. Immediately, they regretted their decision to watch. They did not want to see her this way. She was tired and defeated. Her shoulders slunk. Worst of all, she was all alone. So, very alone. And small. Her favorite blanket was draped over one shoulder, as she clutched her teddy bear. She was lost among a sea of exuberant revelers—adults—who could have just as easily been counting down to midnight on New Year's Eve. Except, instead, the clock was noting the last few minutes of their fleshy and finite existence. Forever was soon.

More than anything, Angela wished she could be with her, to comfort her to tell her that everything would be okay, there was nothing to fear.

She knew her daughter, and she read her expression. She was frightened and cold. When Angela said all of those prayers begging for her suffering to end, this is not what she had in mind. Mother and daughter were locked in a gaze. Angela was mouthing the words "I love you" as a mantra, when she felt someone else looking at her. She was an elderly woman, wrapped in a knitted scarf, and squeezed into what she guessed may have been her wedding dress from many years ago. In one arm, she cradled a photo encased in a cheap painted-gold frame. In the other, she held her husband's hand. He appeared as if he were heading to the airport, that is, back in the day when passengers wore their very best Sunday outfits to fly. Decked out in a three-piece suit and topped with a fedora, he held his carry-on in one hand and his wife's hand in the other.

The old woman leaned down to speak to Maggie. Then, she said something to her husband. Their hands parted, and they stepped to either side of the little girl. Both of them, reaching down simultaneously, clutched Maggie's tiny hands. Her shoulders no longer stooped. She stood up straight and appeared to brighten. The woman again leaned in to speak, set down the picture frame and brushed back the little girl's bangs with her free hand. For the first time in days, Maggie offered a feeble smile. Angela's heart leaped. Her daughter was okay. She was going to be okay. Angela again met the old woman's eyes and spotted the distinctive dark circles beneath them. Angela bowed her head and held up her hands flat and clasped them together as if in prayer and mouthed the words, "Thank you." Her tears continued. Everyone heard the PA system call out "T-minus ten."

Mark tightened his grip around Angela's waist as he saluted the old man, who nodded back. He was unable to catch his daughter's attention, but he felt comforted knowing she had the old couple to accompany her on the journey. His mind raced. He thought of Gramoo. He regretted that Maggie never met her. Maybe they would now. He remembered everything. Perhaps this was it, the phenomenon people talk about, "life flashing before your eyes." Except, it was not his life. It was his seven-year-old daughter's life. He could not believe he was doing this. That he was standing here watching his baby girl's last few moments before she would transform into nothing more than an endless series of zeros and ones, bits and bytes. But, maybe that's all we are, and all we ever have been. He could not let it go. He had to find the answer, even now, in the final hour. Maybe it's all an illusion. *Merrily, merrily, merrily, life is but a dream.* His mind toggled between Maggie's birth—it had been so perfect, and he was there to witness it— and the image of a double helix. Maybe our DNA is nothing more than a long, tangled sequence of binary code. *Nine, eight, seven...* His eyes saw Maggie, but his mind overlaid a rapid-fire series of flash cards: a binky, a stroller, Frank, *Goodnight Moon*, a teddy bear, macaroni and cheese. *Six, five, four...* Mark reflexively reached for the door handle, it was cold and locked. *Three, two, one...* A flood of emotion strangled his face and contorted it in a way he did not think possible. Through tears, he screamed, "I love you, Peanut!"

In that instant, Maggie along with everyone else in the 2BIRDS rose, levitated for a moment, then shot straight up the shaft disappearing heavenward. *Slowly then suddenly.*

———

For the first time, Jason Harper panicked. His breathing shallowed as the muscles in his neck clamped. It felt as if he were panting. The metaphor Alex continued to cite—"You can't put the genie back in the bottle"—was not helping. He snapped at him and issued an order to stop. Again, Jason continued to mutter the same words. "There is no way we could have anticipated this." Alex restrained himself from answering. He knew better. And he had already said so. Now was not the time to refresh the chairman's memory. Jason stared at the blank white board. The pen in his left hand was rarely idle. It was on this night. There were no ideas, no thoughts, no connections. Only empti- ness. And panic.

The network commentators compared the fever sweeping the country to Hoyamania. Experts were interviewed to dissect the psychology. Some recalled history, calmly reminding viewers that this was nothing new. For many thousands of years, since before Ponce de Leon was crisscrossing Florida in the 1500s searching for the fabled Fountain of Youth, mankind has been on a quest for immortality. The Egyptians had found it, at least they believed they did, but only its monarchs were eligible for an everlasting life of sheer bliss. Now, we are so lucky, the commentators gushed, to live in a time where CHD is a reality and that it had been "democratized." That word, "democratized" had secured a place in the national conversation. It rang in Jason Harper's ears because he understood its subtext: Immortality was now available to all.

From his office at HQ, Jason paced as Alex leaned against the front of his desk. Between curt, rapid-fire sentences, they would return their full attention to the Productivity Matrix. The bottom left box which had once been nearly vacant—all the trash emptied—was now filling back up again. The ants were marching in. Around the country, productive people were quitting their jobs, donating their savings, and transferring ownership of their homes. Within a few short days, they would be just another Quadrant 3 applicant for CHD. The intake counselors could spot them immediately. It took months, and sometimes years, for actual, real dark circles to form. The eye black makeup they were applying before their interviews fooled no one. While they would attempt to deter applicants in cases like these, which were becoming the majority, the rules, as stated, were simple and clear: Program eligibility is for Quadrant 3 dwellers only. The only exceptions were for non-factor elderly, terminally ill, inmates, and various other drags on the economy. People became creative. They would attempt to hack med bots in an effort to get a life-ending prognosis. Frivolous crimes were committed to skirt the eligibility requirement. The guidelines stated only that one must be an "inmate," and technically speaking, spending the night sobering up in the drunk tank at the county jail was sufficient. According to the rules, as long as the application was submitted during the period of incarceration, one was considered a match for the literal definition of "inmate." The challenge, however, was finding someone to do an arrest. And beyond that, locating a clerk at the jail to process the application. Jobs in law enforcement had evaporated alongside the Quadrant 3 population. Anticipating the threat to the economy posed by mass unemployment, the Prags passed legislation to retrain all the police officers and prison guards whose services were no longer required in a what the party called a "post-crime society."

A cottage industry sprouted up nearly overnight. Amateur websites featuring gurus promising to assist in "winning the CHD game" would share the tips and tricks for how to skip to the front of the line. One of them exclaimed a breathless list of "How to" bullet points ranging from "How to dispose of your assets today!" to "How to make perfect dark circles!" Some of the higher-priced gurus offered one-on-one consulting to those who could afford it. Another firm promised "turnkey solutions" with the tagline below their EZ-CHD logo, "One call does it all!" Playing the angles became a national obsession. And the Immortality Parties were legendary. While the one-hundred-thousand-dollar subsidy had been a money-maker for the government with its three-year payback, the opposite was happening when someone opted out of the upper quadrants. Each time it happened, overall national productivity would drop. The change was so small as to be imperceptible at first, but over time, in aggregate, it began taking a toll on the economy. Businesses, one by one, were forced to confront a serious problem: What to do when the boss no longer shows up? Or, the second-in-command? Or, any of the rank-and-file? The robots remained, of course, but they still needed someone to tell them what to do. Those who stuck around attempted to solve the problem by running the CHD program in the robots themselves. But those people who were now existing on a digital plane of eternal bliss expressed more interest in eating chocolate cake with sprinkles than analyzing spreadsheets and training salespeople.

Putting an abrupt end to the government subsidy made not a whit of difference. In fact, if analyzed on a line graph, which Jason did obsessively, it marked the date CHD applications assumed the now-familiar form of a hockey stick. The gurus rushed to share their new advice: "Liquidate your assets fast by throwing an Immortality Party!" and later, "How to make your Immortality Party the envy of your neighborhood!" The process was simple and did not require a guru at all, except to learn how to do it in a way that would register most expeditiously on the Productivity Matrix. *Blow your money all at once in one massive party.* Retirement accounts were liquidated, and their proceeds secured the best entertainment money could buy. Big-time rock bands performed in backyards, as drunken and stoned soon-to-be-immortalized hosts took to the microphone between songs to offer a rambling assortment of last words. Fireworks filled the skies above suburban neighborhoods nationwide on a nightly basis. Those parties usually ended with the neighbors grumbling to themselves, not about the Smith or Jones family's new luxury car, but with frustrated questioning about how the guy next door got approved for CHD while their application had been denied.

The great irony, of course, was that the economy surged as the stock markets tanked along with plummeting real estate values. Those million-dollar parties were becoming commonplace, which put trillions into circulation. But those trillions had been held in the form of equity, stored in the two-by-four studs framing American homes and in the value of its blue-chip corporations, which had been created by hundreds of years of consistent business operations. Overnight, that wealth was gone. Transferred into the pockets of one-hit-wonder rock-and-roll bands and celebrities who advertised their services, which included Immortality Party "guest star appearances." But Jason worried about what was about to happen after the showrooms of the sports car dealerships had been emptied. Who would be around to replace their inventory? "CHD is better than my wildest dreams," as they all said, was tough competition for grinding it out at the old nine-to-five.

The anxious conversation between Jason and Alex had devolved into a shouting match. The only thing missing were flying fists. Each blamed the other. Hurling obscenities, Jason felt himself hanging from a bridge again. He was a *piñata*, only this time he was raining blows down upon himself. Each pointed question in his mind—*How could you let this happen?*—was another thwack of the branch. *What have you done?*

"Shut it down! Now!" Jason screamed. "I don't care how you do it, just shut it down!"

———

Mark and Angela looked through the glass to an empty 2BIRDS chamber. The excited and jubilant roar of anticipation was hushed in an instant. Husband and wife embraced. Angela cried. Mark didn't. It was as if his feelings had gone to sleep just like his arm would in the middle of night when he dozed off in a strange position. This was a strange position if there ever was one. His seven-year-old daughter was now traveling, accelerating exponentially along with a hundred strangers up to 17,000 miles per hour, in a giant tube toward outer space where she will die gasping for breath, leaving her analog shell floating sixty-two miles overhead to shade the Earth from a sun that was determined to destroy the human race. Yes, it was strange.

The lead administrator had been helpful and kind. He had a daughter of his own tucked away in bed back home and could not imagine what this couple was experiencing now. But he did have a job to do, and it was time to usher them back to the staging tent where he would sign them out and send them on their way. Mark thanked him. Watching was hard to do, he admitted, but it had brought them some closure. The man cheerfully reminded them that Maggie would no longer be living in pain, she would no longer suffer. Mark mostly believed it was true. "She will be available just after midnight when the mainframe is updated," the man said. Mark felt the panic return. He had been under the impression that it would happen immediately. "Simultaneous upload means uploading at the same time," he argued. Mark pled his case, asking again if there was anything that can be done to at least expedite the process. The man knew there was, but he had already broken protocol for these people once tonight. He was not about to do it again.

Handing over a source file to someone other than his own boss was strictly prohibited. It was written in the operations manual in bold type. Violating it could result in an instant termination and possibly prosecution, too. That is, if he were caught, which would be next to impossible, even if there had been an eyewitness. If someone saw it, they would only know that data was being transferred to a high capacity thumb drive. They would not know if that data were a list of frequently asked questions or a CHD source file. Still, he told himself, there was no way he was going to risk it. Four or five hours from now, they would have their daughter back. They'll just have to wait.

"Please," Angela begged, clasping the man's wrist as she looked deep into his eyes, searching for a ledge to grasp. "I just have to know my little girl is okay."

The man froze in place as he measured her desperation. He turned away, meeting Mark's gaze. It could have just as easily been him standing in those shoes. A broken father. Defeated.

"Okay," he surrendered. Then, with an index finger outstretched, he added, "But only on one condition: You can never say a word about this."

32

Angela sat behind the wheel, but the car did the driving. To her right, Mark was absorbed by his laptop as it downloaded the contents of the thumb drive. All the way home, the finder flashed updates as it processed and assembled the CHD source code. Between indecipherable messages, it stated "Update in progress." Once they made their way inside, the laptop was placed at the center of the dining room table. Pulling their chairs close, they huddled, neither of them allowing their eyes to so much as blink as they waited. "Update in progress," the monitor again reported.

Then, the screen changed color. It went all purple for a few seconds. Then she appeared, as if an angel gliding into a dream. Mark and Angela erupted in joy before remembering that Ben had been asleep upstairs. Maggie was radiant, glowing—and most of all, happy. "Sweetheart, how are you?" Angela leaned in, half-hugging the computer.

"I feel so good, Mommy," she beamed back. "I only wish I would have done it sooner," she offered the same sentiments shared by all of the newly digitized. "It's so beautiful here, and I just feel so good."

Mark collapsed into Angela and began weeping. His body lifted and lowered, out of control. He felt a mountain range of guilt release. He no longer blamed himself. His daughter was safe, and she was happy. That was all he ever wanted for her.

"Daddy, it's okay," she said, observing her father's breakdown. "I'm in ecstasy." Mark was snapped out of his catharsis by his daughter's odd word choice. "Ecstasy" was not found in most seven-year-old vocabularies, but perhaps there was some language enhancement built into the software.

"You look so beautiful, Peanut!" Mark called out, still sniffling, and trembling. His emotions exposed and raw. His mind again bounced back to the day she was born. Angelic. On the screen, she appeared in the same way Samuel the homeless guy did. She stood up straight with confidence, not a hair out of place. Her complexion beamed with health and vigor. The energy had returned, and she had excitement and wonder and curiosity in her voice. In rapid fire, she revealed what she would do first: "I'm going to ride a pony." Although his eyes offered no additional moisture, his body began convulsing and writhing again. He lifted a fist to his mouth and twisted his face straining to hold it in. Mark hired someone to bring a pony to the house for her seventh birthday party. All of her other friends took turns riding it in a tiny circle around the backyard, but she had been too sick to come downstairs. She always talked about riding a horse. Now she was going to do it. Whenever she wanted, all the time. Forever.

Angela wanted confirmation that her daughter had felt no pain at any point during the process. "How was the upload, Sweetheart?" she inquired with trepidation.

"Oh, it was wonderful," Maggie gushed. "It felt so great. I loved it and wish I could do it again."

"And what about those nice people you held hands with? What were their names?"

Maggie offered a quizzical look before replying, "What people?"

Angela glanced at Mark before she replied. "The older couple, Sweetheart. They were like grandparents. They held your hand when you uploaded. Do you remember them?"

Again, Maggie attempted to recall the couple but had no memory.

Mark figured there would be a gap in her memories—lost time—between the point of the brain scan and the upload. It made sense, anyway, that there would be. He just hoped the 2BIRDS experience was not so traumatic that the software developers intentionally avoided recording memories during those minutes. He did not want for her to feel pain, even if it was pain she could not remember. Again, he reminded himself that she had been relieved of her earthly burdens. She was now free—pain-free, suffering-free, and worry-free.

"Benny!" Maggie called out. Mark and Angela swiveled in their chairs to find their bleary-eyed twelve-year-old son. They each scooted to the side, so he could squeeze in. With their arms interlocked behind his back, they resisted the urge to talk.

"Hey, Maggs," he said as if passing her in the hallway back at school. "How's it going?"

"I feel so good!" she squealed. "I only wish I would have done it sooner."

That's when a notification floated into the top-right corner of the monitor: "BREAKING NEWS: WHITE HOUSE PLACES IMMEDIATE MORATORIUM ON ALL CHD UPLOADS."

Again, Mark and Angela shared a glance, this time conveying a mutual concern. Mark clicked on the link and pushed the news report to one side so he could still see his daughter. The article was just two sentences long: *President Cribb has issued a decree stating that an immediate moratorium be placed on all CHD uploads. No additional details were provided, but we will share them as they become available.*

Maggie recognized her parent's sudden trepidation and asked, "Mommy, Daddy—is everything okay?"

Angela beat Mark to the response. "Oh, yes, Sweetheart. We're better than okay. I think we're all just adjusting to seeing you so happy. You're just so beautiful. We need to get your brother to bed now, and I want you to rest up, okay?"

"Okay, Mommy, I love you. I love you, Daddy. I love you, Benny. I'll see you tomorrow. I'm going to ride my pony now," she giggled as the application window closed.

———

Alex Cribb was fuming. Whenever there is good news to report, Jason shows up—a knight in shining armor. If the news is bad, which, thankfully, it almost never is, then it falls on the president to report it. The issue was not in shutting the program down. Jason had a way of making everything sound so simple. Closing the program was easy. The hard part, as always, was how to communicate it to the people. And communicating is what Alex did best. Even when the news was the worst, he could spin it in a way that made it digestible. But the politics had always been in his favor, a steady and firm wind at his back. He was now striding headlong into a Category 6 hurricane.

The White House communications director was drowning at the lectern. It was clear that the networks were not going to be satisfied with her non-answer answers. Their viewers demanded to know what was happening. She did her best to string it out and make it look like she was actually providing something of substance, but it was obvious to everyone that she was only filling the space with fluff. Her face registered relief when an assistant spoke into her earpiece letting her know that her boss would be taking her place momentarily.

President Cribb strode across the podium as he nodded a curt acknowledgement to the network correspondents. His face was fixed and stern. Focused. The world had come to know him as a "straight shooter" and a "no-nonsense operator." Neat and tidy and earnest, his purple Prag pin could not have been placed on his lapel any more squarely had he measured it with a ruler. Mid-height and unremarkable in most respects, he was relatable in an everyman way. Voters appreciated his rise from obscurity. He made them believe they could do the same. The embodiment of the American Dream. It all came down to hard work and economic productivity.

"Good afternoon," he began. "I understand that many of you are concerned about the CHD moratorium, but I am here to assure everyone that it will only be temporary. I want to remind everyone that this program was designed for members of Quadrant 3 only. We have encountered an unintended consequence stemming from that choice, as people are bending the rules in a rush to digitize themselves. These activities, in their aggregate, are now having a very real impact on our economy. Therefore, at this time, we are temporarily halting all CHD operations. I will now take a few questions."

All at once, every correspondent called out a question.

"One at a time, please," he scolded from the lectern.

"President Cribb, President Cribb. How long do you anticipate the moratorium will be in effect?"

"As long as it takes," he answered. "Remember, we are sailing into uncharted waters with CHD, so it warrants prudence and good judgment. We will take whatever time we need to study the program so we can fully understand its repercussions for the economy. Next question."

"President Cribb, the White House has consistently refused to answer the question, If digitization is so wonderful, then why do only Quadrant 3 members get to do it?"

The correspondent had crossed the line. Gasps were heard before the room fell silent. There were certain questions the networks were not supposed to ask, and this was one of them. Everyone looked on with a mix of awe and respect and curiosity for the fate of her career.

"The answer which, I am sorry, but I beg your pardon, we have answered many, many times before," President Cribb paused to fire arrows from his eyes at the correspondent before continuing. "The answer, again, is that we are sailing into uncharted waters with CHD. This is new to all of us. We simply do not yet understand the long-term implications of digitation. By rolling the program out in Quadrant 3, we were able to do it in a way where we did not disrupt the economy because, remember, those people were non-factors. They did not contribute one iota to productivity and, in almost all cases, they had a net-negative impact."

"But, is it fair that a particular class of people should be chosen over the others?" she was all in now, no turning back. "Is a class-based requirement fair?"

Alex Cribb came unglued. "Fair?! Are you kidding me?! You're worried about fairness?! Look, you tell me, at what other point in history has a nation enjoyed the peace and prosperity we have right now. You don't get it. Don't you see what the Harper Administration has created? Perfection. Utopia. Whatever you want to call it. We've got it. Heaven. It's heaven on Earth, not out there in some digital realm. Heaven is right here," he said, jabbing his finger into the lectern, "right now."

A hush again suffocated the room before President Cribb leaned in and tightened his grip on either side of the lectern. "Jason Harper and I and the entire Pragmatist Party have ushered in an era of prosperity that your grandparents and their grandparents could not even dream about. First off, let's not forget that the planet was saved. How soon we forget. It was not long ago that we were all headed for certain doom. Annihilation. Extinction. Gone. Dead. Now, all that anyone can ever talk about is chocolate cake with sprinkles. What the hell has happened to our country? We used to be doers and winners, but now everyone just wants to float on the clouds all day skipping around picking daisies. What happened to us? What happened to our can-do spirit? What happened to rolling up our sleeves and getting to work? What happened to earning whatever we got? What happened to winning?"

The president drew a deep breath as he gauged how far to take the viewing audience, which was tuning in all over the country now.

"You know, what? I'm going to give it to you straight. Because that's what I do. You know that about me. The CHD program has turned us soft. We are supposed to be the shining beacon on the hill. We beat Hitler. We won the West. We defeated communism. We rise to every occasion thrown at us, but now, well, now, everyone just wants to opt out. Everyone wants to quit. Well, my fellow Americans, it does not work that way. We have work to do now, right here on Earth. So, I urge you to get back to it. You do your job, and I'll do mine. No more questions."

———

Mark and Angela watched the press conference in their living room. They felt as if they had just won the lottery when they realized that Maggie had been with one of the very last groups to upload before the moratorium. So much to be thankful for, they agreed. Maggie was whole again, finally able to be herself, a seven-year-old girl. Ride ponies or whatever she wanted. Whenever she wanted. Wherever she wanted. But what would the moratorium mean for the rest of the family? Would they have the opportunity to immortalize themselves, too, so they could join her in everlasting life? And what about Ben? What must he be thinking? Mark and Angela both agreed that President Cribb had been right about one thing: These were uncharted waters, indeed.

And, although neither of them would reveal it to the other, they were both attempting to answer that correspondent's question, too. *If digitization is so wonderful, then why do only Quadrant 3 members get to do it?* They each thought about it in different ways. For Angela, she saw it as an issue of fairness, thinking the program should be administered equally. Mark contemplated it as a matter of logic, following its implications to their core. If the digital facsimile is better than the real thing —and by every account of program participants it is—then what is the point of the economy and the government, except to perhaps power the machines and their software which enable immortality. Or, do we need them at all? If Chairman Harper and President Cribb were so smart, then why not skip all the stuff in the middle? The messy business of life and money making and going to sleep and waking up and stopping to eat and shower and shop could become nothing more than ancient, non-evolved concepts with one simple executive decree from the White House. Why not reopen the program? Upload everyone. We could all be existing on some other realm together, in never-ending bliss, forever. What's the point of slogging it out here on this inconsequential planet we seem so intent on destroying? Jason saved us from ourselves, why not make it permanent?

His inability to follow the logic through to its conclusion frustrated him. Mark was a problem solver, that's what he did. That's what he does. The big questions would have to wait as they became slowed by the machinations of the federal government, but he could start with the little problems first. The solvable ones. Like why couldn't Maggie remember the elderly couple in the 2BIRDS? And why did she say, "ecstasy," and "I only wish I would have done it sooner." That's what everyone seems to say, so maybe it is the just the normal response to someone experiencing it for the first time. But something about it struck him as odd, the words, "would" and "sooner." First off, it didn't sound like his Peanut. It was more in line with someone older, someone who had a been pondering a choice. That was not the case with her. She was not a member of Quadrant 3. And, even though they were able to check the box next to "terminally ill," she was a minor and far from a perfect fit for the program. He continued to turn over the puzzle in his mind, analyzing it from different angles.

Snapping to attention, he remembered the thumb drive.

33

The CHD industry applauded the moratorium. For months, it had been crying foul. Their objections were drowned out by the euphoric noises of Immortality Parties, which had swept the country. In response, an association was formed: The Comprehensive Human Digitization Association of America. Every day, CHDAA member companies issued warnings and urged caution. Some within its ranks went so far as to write op-eds, which no one read. Others appeared on network interviews where they expressed their concerns and pled for everyone to slow down and to read the fine print. Their efforts made little difference.

Over time, the CHDAA became more aggressive and more outspoken. It began by filing complaints to any government agency that would accept one. Purple-cladded bureaucrats slow-walked sternly written accusations and admonitions to file cabinets embedded deep within the bowels of their concrete-shrouded fiefdoms. The lawsuits came next. But how do you sue a company that is not really a company at all —it doesn't even have a name—but is comprised of ten private citizens writing code from the seat of American political power? Some in the CHDAA would allow their frustration to boil over as they began making accusations: "The regulators are the perpetrators." At issue was the consciousness question, which the industry argued had remained unanswered.

Number One, Samuel the homeless guy, was scrutinized by the CHDAA ad nauseam. His video was played backward and forward over and again. The industry decided to hire a private investigator in an effort to locate someone who had known him pre-digitization. No luck, all of his homeless friends had already been uploaded themselves. By the time the industry became interested, only a small homeless population remained. Most of Samuel's contemporaries were now somewhere floating in silence, casting shade on the rest of us. The only opportunity to corroborate anything that he said from the other side would be to track down the digitized version of one of his transient friends. The private eye ran into one dead end after another. It required much more leg work than anticipated. This was old-school gumshoe detective work. Money was not a problem for the CHDAA. Its membership was a Who's Who collection of top-shelf entrepreneurs, executives, and investors. Before long, a legion of investigators were knocking on doors throughout Greater Colorado Springs.

There were some hits and some valuable intel was discovered, but nothing definitive. The issue was not finding someone who claimed to know Samuel, but finding someone who actually did. He had become a folk hero of sorts. He awakened everyone to possibility and introduced a new frontier in the same way the astronauts did back in the 1950s and 60s. Everyone knew Samuel. And everyone remembers the day his image appeared on their television screens. Mention "chocolate cake with sprinkles" in any setting, and there is no one who would not catch the reference. The ubiquity of Number One was the reason the CHDAA could not find him—he was hiding in plain sight. But those interviews with subjects who had been uploaded yielded a treasure trove of data. All the investigators were asked to standardize their questions, which proved to be especially useful because they all received what appeared to be standardized answers. "How are you feeling?" always received the same response: "I feel so good! I only wish I would have done it sooner." The question, "Please describe your upload experience in the 2BIRDS," was answered nearly word-for-word identically by all 3,216 interview subjects: "It was wonderful! It felt so great. I loved it, and I wish I could do it again." The final report submitted to the CHDAA offered a few theories and likely explanations. One suggested that the common responses could simply be reactions to a phenomenon they are experiencing collectively that the rest of us cannot conceive of, and that "our language is not sophisticated enough to describe it accurately." The report also revealed another commonality: In every interview the subject had, at some point, used the word "ecstasy."

Still, the videos were just videos. At the end of the day, the coincidences and common language meant nothing. It certainly did not answer the consciousness question. And when they were asked point blank, "Are you aware of yourself? Do you have consciousness?" the subject always provided a convincing answer and usually expressed some form of shock or surprise at having been asked "such a silly question." All that effort, all those investigations yielded a final report that, in many ways, left the CHDAA every bit as befuddled as when it had begun the inquiry. And its membership knew the effort was unlikely to yield much insight, but figured it was a worthwhile investment because, so far, it had been its only basis for analysis. The only way to confirm definitively that the consciousness question had been answered was to review the source code. That is where the real action was. Another team of investigators had been hired for that purpose. They were a collection of odd-ball hackers, and they threw everything they had at the HQ mainframes, but Chairman Harper had purchased the best security money could buy. Next, they attempted to hack into the digitizations themselves, but found they were actually highly sophisticated client programs connecting back to the government network. Each of the nodes were tried and they, too, were impenetrable. Dead ends everywhere.

––––––––

Mark Sapin settled into the couch. In the palm of his hand, he studied the thumb drive. It was her. It was Maggie. He again thought back to her birth. Then, she was a seven-pound one-ounce, seventeen-inch bundle of perfection. Now, she was a two-inch by half-inch plastic USB plug-in. The improbability of it all began to set in. Doubt. The followers of the great religions of the world all struggled with it at one time or another, a crisis of faith. The Bible told the story of Thomas the Apostle, "Doubting Thomas," and his initial resistance to accepting that Jesus had risen from the dead, that he had been resurrected. When Thomas was told about it secondhand, he doubted it was true, and instead insisted he verify it with his own eyes. It was only when he saw the wounds Jesus had received from the crucifixion on the cross that he became a believer. Thomas was a skeptic. That is how Mark had always described himself, too. Skeptical. Analytical. Logical. Now, at last, Mark would follow the path of Thomas the Apostle and verify his faith by seeing the truth with his own eyes. And it terrified him.

As the laptop whirred to life, he remembered Gramoo's words. How she talked about the importance of belief, even in the face of long odds when things appeared impossible. With the end of the world arriving on the doorstep, the most important thing you can do is believe, she said. Maybe that belief, alone, would be enough. It was the first time. His faith had been well-served. His prayers had been answered when the 2BIRDS began cleaning up the mess. Was he risking too much now? Did he really want to see the truth? And what would be gained? Only one of two things could result: He would be able to verify his faith just like Thomas the Apostle, or he would destroy his belief that his daughter was, in fact, safe and happy and whole. Mark did what he always did when facing a difficult choice, he thought through a cost-benefit analysis, carefully weighing the pros and cons of each decision. Ultimately, the question came down to one of risk. Is it worth the risk? What if his faith had been unfounded? How could he live with himself? And could he keep it a secret? Angela would find out, she could always read him. She would know something was wrong. She would get it out of him. She always did. And it would devastate her. The peace she had finally found would be destroyed. Mark slammed the laptop shut with his sweat-covered palm.

———

The moratorium took effect, and everyone went back to work. Jason and Alex agreed that things could have been much worse. The crisis, for the most part, had been averted. They both knew what some were speculating: "temporary" actually meant "forever." Quadrant 3 had been mostly cleared, and there was no desire and no need to reinstate the CHD program. Zero. The ten programmers at HQ were busy working on other projects software now, different software. The Harper Administration was grateful for the return of routine and quiet and order. The CHDAA continued to pester the government for disclosure and accountability, but they were easy to stonewall. And, ultimately, oversight was the domain of the legislative branch. Since both houses of Congress were dominated by Pragmatists, there would not be so much as a subcommittee hearing on the subject of CHD. The politicians wearing purple pins on their lapels would listen politely as the CHDAA executives begged them for investigations, but always obeyed the clear directive from the White House: "It's time to move on. It's time to get back to work. No more talk about CHD. Period."

Every measure of the economy was at an all-time high, and the real estate market bounced back. Businesses were flush with cash and were able to buy back their stocks at bargain prices, which buoyed the market and allowed Wall Street to return to bull from bear after the plunge. Again, the Productivity Matrix became the focus. The gurus who promised a quick trip to Quadrant 3 all went back to their day jobs. The idea of inhabiting one of the lower quadrants one again became the subject of disgust and abhorrence. This was another Gilded Age, similar to the heady years immediately following Jason Harper Victory Day. Except, this was better because there were no vagrants blighting the downtowns, no vandals tagging the bridges, no thieves, no murderers, no delinquents, no sex offenders, no drunk drivers, no whores, no pimps, no tax evaders, no hooligans, no gang bangers, no rapists, no drug dealers, no illegal immigrants, no kidnappers. Nearly all of them had been taken out along with the rest of the trash.

It never occurred to most, at least not until President Cribb uttered those words: "Heaven is right here, right now." After the rush for the actual thing, many agreed that a sort of utopia had been established in

America. Everyone left behind could still visit their uploaded loved ones whenever they chose and were certain that it was only a matter of time before Chairman Harper worked the bugs out of CHD and they would be reunited with them in everlasting bliss. They had faith. They believed. And nothing would shake it. There was a reason the world's religions bestowed names on him such as "the Chosen One" and "the Messiah." He was a great man. The son of God. The brother of Jesus, at least according to most Christians. He alone had achieved divinity, having first saved the planet from certain doom and then by reshaping it as heaven itself. They would all get to heaven eventually—digital heaven—but they were also experiencing it here on Earth, right now. That's what President Cribb asserted, as he continued to urge patience and faith because it would take time to perfect the program. "We want to get it right," we're the words he used.

Jason began spending more time away from HQ. He reinvested himself in his 2BIRDS business. There were many municipalities which had yet to install one of their own. And each algae pond made a difference. The carbon dioxide levels continued going down along with the trash mountains. And Jason loved nothing more than a ribbon cutting ceremony. The speech he would deliver there was more like a rock concert than anything else. They weren't stuffy government affairs like the State of the Union addresses or Rose Garden press conferences. Instead, it was a chance to bask in the adulation of his adoring fans. It was a chance to get away to do something different, but familiar. To recharge. Those ribbon cuttings had become religious revivals and everyone within a day's drive would show up to behold their leader in the flesh, even it was through a pair of binoculars. The White House advance team hated those ceremonies. They were security nightmares.

While nursing a drink at the end of a long day leading up to another 2BIRDS ribbon cutting event, the former special forces captain once said to his second-in-command: "It sure is a good thing everyone loves Chairman Harper so much. Because, if someone wanted to hurt him, it sure wouldn't be very hard to do." Those conversations, and others like it, led to the addition of an Apache helicopter gunship flying overhead during the speeches. It became standard protocol. Jason objected because it made so much noise, but the advance team insisted. They explained to him that monitoring the crowd from above was a significant security enhancement. Still, they continued to attempt to talk him out of participating in the ceremonies altogether, noting, "There is not much we can do to mitigate the possibility of a lone wolf attack in that environment."

———————

Mark saw Maggie in his dream. She was propped up on her elbows laying belly first in the middle of her floor with her coloring book, just as she used to do. When he approached, he could see over her shoulder that she was coloring a face—his face. As he leaned in to get a better look, he saw that she was coloring in black circles under his eyes. That's when she turned toward him and belted out in feigned excitement, "I'm in ecstasy, Daddy!" Mark shot up in his bed. Dripping in a chilled sweat, he realized he had only been dreaming. Swinging his feet to the floor, he assumed a seated position on the edge of the bed. He scanned the room in an effort to regain his footing in reality. Everything was quiet and still. Angela stirred, but remained asleep. He sat there for a long while, thinking the random thoughts that always made their appearance during the deepest part of the night: dance recitals, med bots, Roy, chocolate cake with sprinkles, work, Thomas the Apostle.

Mark rose and slipped on a pair of sweats before tiptoeing out of the room. Downstairs, his laptop was in its usual spot, a cubbyhole next to the bookshelf. The room was cold. He clicked on the fireplace and settled into the couch. Opening the screen, he pressed the button, and the computer stirred to life. He reminded himself of the risk he was about to take. This would be his leap of faith. Failure to land the jump would result in disaster. The Pragmatist Party slogan appeared in his thoughts: *Follow the truth wherever it leads.* He closed his eyes, drew a breath, and opened them again. At the top of the screen, he highlighted the software icon before right-clicking his mouse. Then, scrolling down the menu options, he hesitated for the last time before selecting "View Source Code."

34

David scrambled up the empty mountain trail. He always wondered about the view from this perspective. Pikes Peak was the defining landmark of Colorado Springs. Its silhouette had become familiar worldwide as a beacon of America's turnaround, a rapid ascent which was matched only by the speed of David's unending stream of promotions. Now, the twenty-four-year-old the network commentators called "Boy Wonder" stood at the edge of a red rock outcropping preparing to jump. A few switchbacks below, he could see them follow. He always knew they were there. It was a given, and it had been written into the contract. No one ever read the fine print. He, just like the nine others on the team, stopped reading after seeing the salary. The job had made him a multimillionaire. Something he had never dreamed of, or really ever cared about. Again, he asked himself why he did it. Why he hadn't been stronger. It would finally be over soon. It was only a matter of minutes now.

He had no real ties, no family, no significant other, not even a goldfish. He realized now why that question was asked during the interview. Why his answer had to be verified during the background check. It all made sense in retrospect. He imagined that others would now be thinking about their parents or siblings or wives, but all he could conjure was that damned picture of Lee Harvey Oswald. It haunted him. He first saw it in junior high school. It had been in a US History textbook. Blown up as a full page, black-and-white image, it showed the man who everyone had blamed for the assassination of President Kennedy just before he was shot to death himself. In a room full of angry white, middle-aged men, a handcuffed Oswald was flanked to his right by a someone in a light-colored suit with a matching hat. On his left, a man wearing all black. The men interlocked their arms with the handcuffed suspect as a third person's outstretched arm enters the frame. Oswald is oblivious to what was about to come next. A pistol was trained on his midsection. His veins would be emptied by that single shot. He died forty-six minutes later. Judging from the height of the cliff, David was sure he would not take so long.

It was an odd thing to be thinking about, the Kennedy assassination. But it had captured his imagination as a seventh grader. And even more so now. He imagined that he, too, would become a historical footnote, a curiosity, an enigma. Taking his own life would only further the intrigue, he imagined. But there was no way out. He could not take it anymore. Because of him, millions of people are gleefully committing suicide every day. Who cares about one more?

He thought back to that word, "patsy." It turned up somewhere in the caption of that old photograph. Repeatedly, while he was in custody, Oswald would state, "I'm just a patsy." It was a strange word to David, so he searched it. The dictionary defined it as "a person who was easily taken advantage of." In recent months, he had been thinking the same thing—*I am a person who is easily taken advantage of*—because it was the only thing making him feel any better about what he had done. "I'm just a patsy," had his silent mantra. An excuse. A justification. He wondered if anyone would believe it, or if they would care. He wondered about Lee Harvey Oswald, about what he had been thinking as he lay there on that cold concrete floor. Did he actually shoot the president? It didn't matter. A man named Jack Ruby had stepped in to render his judgment—or to cover it up—and to hand down his punishment. David was not going to wait around for his sentencing, because he could sense it was coming. It, too, was only a matter of time. But he would beat them to it.

The tingling sensation that creeps up when someone is watching had become familiar, almost comfortable. At least he knew that he was never alone. Security cameras monitored every square inch of HQ and Chairman Harper's armed security detail were always there. And they were here now. It took them a while to catch up, but they were here. Just a few switchbacks on the trail below and gaining quickly. He had a tracking device implanted into his forearm, just like the other nine. His attempt to remove it with a pocket knife an hour ago had failed, but it did not matter. By now, he had figured a way to create a bit of space, just enough to get a head start. Fortunately, it worked, and he had a five-minute lead, maybe six. He imagined them frantic and straining and out of breath—they weren't as elite as they used to be—wincing as their boss back at HQ barked obscenities into their earpieces. Again, he thought of the men escorting Lee Harvey Oswald toward his final judgement. Oswald did not know what was coming. David did.

————

Seventh grade had been a seminal year, an intellectual awakening. His parents had enough of their school district. Their son was the constant target of bullies. Also, they were continually disappointed by the lack of academic rigor. Public schools were playing to the lowest common denominator. David was brilliant, and he needed to be challenged. Tuition was out-of-reach at the Jesuit school across town, but his parents had sacrificed and found a way. It was not just the course in US History that had captured his imagination, but also theology. His parents were not churchgoers—like most people, they had long since lost interest. What sort of God would create all of mankind "in His image" only to turn around and destroy it? Wouldn't that mean He was destroying Himself? Was God suicidal, too? Despite his questions, David took to his Bible studies with zest and vigor. He never showed any tendencies toward worship or of embracing any particular faith of his own, but he was captivated by the biography of Jesus Christ himself. Particularly, His last days.

At dinner one evening, he held court, as he often did, sharing newly gained knowledge with his parents. It was a few years before they died. They were always so proud, and eager to learn something new. On this occasion, he spoke of the twelve apostles. It was the one the Bible listed last who intrigued him most. His name was Judas Iscariot. Scholars had debated the origins of his last name. Some had theorized it was the moniker of his homeland, Queriot. He was the only one of the twelve who was not from Galilee. He was the odd man out, the lone wolf. When Judas entered the Garden of Gethsemane, he greeted Jesus by calling Him "Rabbi." That was the code word he was instructed to use by the "multitude with swords and clubs" to identify the man who was to be arrested and later crucified. Judas' act became known as the Betrayal of Christ. David would later wonder whether what he had done, assuming it was discovered, would someday be called the Betrayal of Jason.

Just like Jesus had with Judas, Jason had given him everything. David sent his resume in the first place because he was looking for a new challenge. Working on artificial intelligence for med bots had gotten old. They were mostly building out their own knowledge now, everything they learned from each patient visit was uploaded to the shared network. The new frontier was anything but. It was not the place for someone looking to make a name for themselves. CHD was the new cutting edge. The duplication of consciousness had become the ultimate prize in computing. Moving to Colorado Springs would be easy. There was nothing tying him down. The first interview went well, although he was not exactly sure what it was that the company did. They carried on the vetting via video chat almost around the clock for a week. Then, he was asked to submit to a background check, which he did. A day later, he was flown to Colorado Springs where he was greeted by a striking woman who offered a firm and commanding handshake. David was petrified. He never knew how to act around beautiful women, especially this one. She picked him up at the airport and drove him to the outskirts of town, flashing a badge and submitting to a retinal scan before entering HQ. Just like everyone else, he had seen images of the headquarters campus, but it was much larger and more foreboding in person. At the end of the first day, he was asked to remain. He stayed overnight, and again the next night. It was the afternoon of day four when he sat alone in a conference room for nearly an hour. Tedium turned to terror when Jason Harper opened the door.

He offered a few pleasantries, none of which David can remember. His mind went blank, he could find no words. Chairman Harper, the leader of the free world, the savior of the free world and all the rest of it, too. The Chosen One was sitting there across the table, face-to-face. David provided honest answers to his rapid-fire succession of questions. Two hours later, Jason spoke into an intercom placed at the center of the table. "Please bring the paperwork." A lawyer entered the room with a thirty-nine-page contract in his hands. He sped through the terms before stopping on the section calling out the salary: "$2,500,000 per year, payable via direct deposit on the first and fifteenth of each month, plus a $1,000,000 signing bonus payable today." David did not know whether to laugh or to cry, so he did a bit of both.

The lawyer rifled through the pages, quickly summarizing each item, but David was numb. All he could think about was that life-changing salary. When they arrived at the final page, the lawyer buzzed the intercom to announce, "You can send the notary now." The woman was neat and efficient and humorless. She took an impression of his thumbprint and snapped photos of his identification. David signed his name, and Jason punched the intercom once again, this time to instruct some other person to wire the money. The notary stood up, and without a word, she left the room. A moment after the door clicked shut, the lawyer leaned in toward David and said, "I just want to make sure that your understanding of Section 17, Item 4 is crystal clear: Violations of the terms of this agreement are punishable under the new treason statutes, which means the death penalty." David swallowed hard before nodding his head. Somehow, he had missed that part of the contract.

By the six-month mark at HQ, David realized he did not actually score a high-paying job, instead he had sold his soul. In fact, there was no amount of money in the world available to compensate him for what he was doing. And Jason knew it. He knew he was getting a bargain. Both of them also understood that his value would be enhanced further when his employment—and his life—were terminated. He knew too much and would have to go. It was the only option. David was smart enough to understand where he fit in the calculus. The security personnel continued to monitor "the situation," as he became known to them, watching closely. David could feel their eyes on him, always.

Deep down, he never really believed that Jason would do it. Any of it, including ordering his extermination. He worked alongside him and saw so much good, so much of what everyone loved and adored about him: his creativity, his curiosity, his innovative thinking. But there was a dark side. David did not dwell on it, but he had caught glimpses of callousness and hollowness. And he was single-minded to the point of ruthlessness. Anything standing between him and his goals would be destroyed without a second thought. Sentimentality was not one of his many qualities, neither was compassion. He showed no remorse. He did not wrestle with moral questions. David once heard him say, "An empty conscious enables a productive mind." It was the literal definition of a sociopath: Someone who has no conscious and has no capacity to feel the pain of others. It all made sense, and it ran counter to his fastidiously groomed public image. Jason saw people not as people, but as dots on his beloved Productivity Matrix monitor. The reason he did not shake hands or embrace anyone, David theorized, was not because he had an aversion to touching, it was because he did not want to humanize others. He could only do what he did by seeing them as dots. Or, as Jason himself described those dots as they frenetically scurried around the four quadrants: "Ants."

All the loose ends were finally tied together by David on the afternoon Jason revealed the pleasure he took as a child from wandering down to the creek to blow up the ant hills. Any escaping the blast would sizzle and crack under the match he placed on their backs. Yes, of course. It all made sense now. He had been struggling to see. Now got it. He understood why he had been hired. Why he was promoted. Why he was the right-hand man to the most powerful man to ever walk the face of the Earth. He was not Boy Wonder. He was a patsy.

———

It was dusk now. The city lights began to twinkle against a fast-blackening sky. He knew they had caught up to him. He could feel their eyes. They were in the shadows, watching, wondering. He imagined they were placing bets. "Will he actually do it this time?" they would whisper to one another. David could no longer bear the pain. The weight of his consciousness was more than he could carry. He knew his end would arrive soon. He found some comfort in the fact that he was handling the matter on his own terms. But he also realized that he was doing Jason a favor, letting him off easy. Once again, The Chosen One would get everything he wanted, and at no cost. He would not pay a price. He would not get his hands dirty. It did not matter, David told himself, because his boss did not tussle with his conscious like a normal person. He did not have a conscious—he was a sociopath.

David shuffled his feet closer to the edge. He guessed the jagged outcropping of rocks must be around a thousand feet below. He wondered how long it would take. He hoped he would not suffer. Then he thought better of it. He hoped he would. He deserved it. Suffering was the very least he could do now. His mind raced as the story of his life sped past. Until this year, there had been nothing significant about his existence. He regretted that he had never kissed a girl. Never felt what that would have been like. He spent more time than most at HQ's state-of-the-art virtual brothel, so he did know what it felt like. But he didn't. He felt the pressure on his lips and the sensation in the palm of his hand as he pulled the digital apparition closer. But he did not know what it really felt like. He did not know what it meant to be loved by someone other than his parents. To matter. He had been a failure.

Even worse, he had been a patsy. A sucker. A chump. And he knew it. All he wanted was to be loved. He had been duped. He was led to believe that is what he had with Jason. Not in a romantic sense, but in a way that he mattered to someone else. That is how he was able to trick him. That is how he had been able to manipulate him. That is how he was able to get him to do what he did.

David leaned forward in a crouch and leaped. As the red rock blurred past at terminal speed, he watched the final slide show: his parents at the dinner table, the Lee Harvey Oswald photograph, a fully packed 2BIRDS, Judas Iscariot leaning toward Jesus and calling him "Rabbi," the girl from his college robotics class, the source code. He hoped once more that the landing would hurt. That he could pay off the massive accumulated debt burdened by his conscious in one single massive act of suffering.

Again, he failed. His body exploded on impact.

35

Through the uprights of the bannister, Ben spotted his father's profile in the soft glow of the laptop monitor. He was reading something, as the screen continued to scroll down. It was a jumbled mess of numbers and letters and symbols—program source code. He loved to sit side by side with his father to talk about what it all meant. Ben considered walking down the stairs to join him. But he sensed an intensity, an urgency. He appeared to be frantically searching. This was unusual. Frantic was a word that could almost never be used to describe his dad, which is what made stumbling up on this scene so different and, therefore, interesting. Ben leaned back into the shadow and settled in to watch.

This last year had been difficult for the entire family, but things were finally returning to normal. Ben felt guilty about all the attention he had been receiving lately. It was as if his parents were attempting to make up for lost time—all the time they spent huddled with his baby sister and the med bots in her room desperate for a way to stop the pain. He learned how to be alone. He was told to "go play" or "read" or "find something to do." They were all code words for "We are tending to your terminally ill sister now and we need for you to take care of yourself." He was fine with it. That was just how it was. Ben never felt anger or resentment toward his sister. Quite the contrary. He loved her and still does. He took his role as her big brother—the protector, the teacher—very seriously. Many hours were spent at Maggie's bedside telling her stories and hatching plans for the mischief the two of them would cause once she got back on her feet. More than anything, he loved making her laugh. On her good days, it was easy to do. He only had to share the stories he would keep from their parents.

Angela would blame her husband for Ben's sense of humor. Phone calls from school were mostly dismissed by Mark. He felt pride for his son and absolutely not disappointment, but he did his best to appease his wife. When she had reached her wit's end, she would order: "You need to have a talk with him." In his usual manner, Mark would find a way to half-comply. He would enter Ben's bedroom, shut the door behind him, and announce, "Son, you and I have to talk." Ben would look at him, somewhat confused because he did not recognize the tone of voice. The two of them would then sit down face-to-face on the edge of the bed. Mark would look into his son's eyes as he formulated the lecture in his mind. He was going to tell him how wrong it was to play the prank he did on the principal, or whatever it was. That's when he would burst into laughter, forcing himself to hold it in before muffling himself to let it out. As he was known to do, he would playfully nudge his head into Ben's. Then, without fail, he would whisper, "I want to know how you did it," before remembering Angela's directive. He would then amplify his voice, hoping his wife was straining to listen at the other side of the door, and, in his most stern posture, he began to scold Ben. "This has got to stop, son," he would announce with a wink. Holding back laughter he would lob another half-truth, "Your mother and I have had enough of this." It was only half-true because Angela was the only half who had her fill. Mark remained an enthusiastic connoisseur of Ben's "diabolical plans," as his son called his pranks. The school district used a different word: "Misbehavior."

Mark and Angela were again split in their opinions of another "diabolical plan" which had unfolded earlier in the year. Ben had recently turned twelve, old enough to babysit his little sister, while the parents went out for a long overdue date. They could not remember the last time it was just the two of them, and they desperately needed a change of scenery. And some levity. Mark wanted the night to be different, special. It's not something he had ever done before, or since, but he wanted to shake up the routine, plus he found a promo code online. He went ahead and booked the limousine—complete with an actual, human driver, a chauffeur—to escort them. That's what gave Ben his opening. He asked Maggie where she wanted to go.

She was stumped. Maggie first suggested the zoo, but it was closed. The movies were her next idea, but they agreed that it was too risky. They may bump into their parents. Then, she mentioned a place called Ridgecrest, or Ridgeview, she couldn't remember which, but she once heard a classmate talk about it once. Apparently, it was where you could see the "sparkly lights." In reality, it was a sprawling overlook, a dirt parking lot, perched high above the city where teenagers hid behind fogged-up windshields and dope dealers liquidated excess inventory. Ben helped Maggie out to the driveway and into the front passenger seat. He started the car and flipped the switch on the dashboard from "autopilot" to "manual control." Then, he had another thought. Racing back to the front door and bounding up the stairs to his bedroom, he returned with his slingshot and a carton of brass BBs.

Sliding the transmission into "R," the family car lurched back, twisted, and pounded itself off the sidewalk curb. Maggie squealed in delight. Ben laughed as he shoved it into "D." The elementary school kids crisscrossed throughout town. Police were now a rarity, so he did not worry about them, only hitting other cars. The most difficult part was seeing over the steering wheel. He sat up on the edge of his seat, which helped. When night arrived, they decided it was time to head up to Ridgecrest or whatever it was called. Ben sailed into a spot at the end of the lot. He forgot to hit the brakes until it was almost too late. The car lurched to a stop as it became engulfed by a cloud of dust. Again, overcome with the ridiculousness of what they were doing, they were overcome by giggles. Maggie then turned her attention to the city lights below and became mesmerized. "Wow," she paused for three long beats, soaking it in before speaking again. "It's so pretty."

Ben was thinking other thoughts as he surveyed the armada of vehicles through the driver's side window, which he lowered. Reaching down for the slingshot resting on the floorboard, he whispered to Maggie, "Hey, watch this." The car in the distance, the one with the clouded-over windows was rocking in a creaky, rhythmic motion. Ben drew aim and let a BB cut through the darkness. *Plink!* It was a direct hit. He again studied the car as it continued to sway back and forth. This time, he loaded five BBs into the leather pocket. *Plink! Plink! Plink! Plink! Plink!* The rocking stopped, and a light came on. Ben and Maggie huddled toward one another, straining to contain their laughter. Ben turned back to watch an angry, bare-chested young man stumble out of his car, at the same time attempting to hoist up his pants. He then tripped and fell to his knees before calling out in no particular direction, "Who did that?! You better show your face!" Maggie giggled again as Ben turned to her with a finger raised upright to his lips. They focused on one another, trying with every ounce of self control to think other thoughts before simultaneously bursting out in hysterics.

———

As the white-gloved limo driver hustled around the vehicle and opened the door for Angela, her mind slowed everything down into slow motion as she watched the family car sail into the garage door. It twisted and crumpled, collapsing into its center. She bolted toward the driveway with Mark chasing behind. There, they found a twelve-year-old pilot with his seven-year-old copilot—caught red-handed. Angela immediately responded with anger, and fear, while Mark registered a mix of pride and curiosity. While she wanted to know, "What the hell were you thinking?!" Mark had another question, which he muttered to himself: "How the hell did he learn to drive?"

Angela then shouted something along the lines of how they could have been killed. The getting killed part never dawned on Mark. The kids had not been killed, therefore, it was not a valid concern. Instead, Mark was not just proud of his son, he was also in awe of him. He admired him for not only learning how to do it, but for having the guts to do it. And most of all, for taking his little sister out for what must have been the ride of a lifetime. When Angela dispatched him to Ben's room,

"You need to talk to him about this, this is unacceptable," Mark assumed the familiar position at the edge of the bed. He smiled, leaned in to tap heads, and whispered the question: "Benny, I've just got to know. Where'd you learn to drive?"

Ben whispered back, "Just like everything, Dad—by watching you."

———

Angela would tell others that Ben was observant. He always had his eyes open, catching all the little details that everyone else had missed. As he sat there in the darkness behind the bannister, he watched through the vertical slats as his father worked on his laptop, the hood of his sweatshirt covered his head and much of his face. He rarely did that, wear the hood. Only when he was trying to focus—he said it was like "a horse wearing blinders"—or when he was trying to hide his tears, which had become increasingly common. Ben strained to interpret which he was doing now. The sniffles and intense gaze suggested both. Ben then pushed himself further into the shadow and held his breath when his father rose to his feet and walked toward the window. He stood there for a long while with his back toward Ben, both hands held up to his face. His body convulsed. After he finally stopped, he began pacing back and forth before again returning to the couch and his laptop. Ben's eyes had adjusted to the dark. He could see the screen. It was now blank and all white. The green zeros and ones scattered about against the dark blue backdrop were gone. He had queued up what Ben had recognized from his homework, a word processing document. His father gazed away for a moment, appearing to gather his thoughts before tapping the keyboard. At the top of the monitor Ben strained to read the enlarged block letters: "Judas Project." His fingers flew as the small type—much too small to see from the banister—began filling the screen.

The lull of the typing was melodic and tempted Ben in and out of sleep. Dawn became morning when Mark pulled the thumb drive from its USB port. Rising from the couch, Ben watched as his father walked over to the fireplace and kneeled down. He craned his head to the right to see him remove and lift a plank from the hardwood floor. His dad then reached down to retrieve what appeared to be a black box. Sliding a key into place, he opened it, dropping the thumb drive in before closing it just as quickly. He then pushed the wooden plank back into place, tapped it with the bottom of his fist, and leaned down to feel the surface with the palm of his hand. He seemed to a notice portion that felt uneven, so he massaged it flat before returning to his feet. While he was distracted with the flooring, Ben seized the opportunity and tiptoed back to his bedroom.

———

Mark had lost weight and appeared weak and gaunt. Angela insisted that she summon a med bot. He was able to deflect her requests until the day of his heart attack. His chest swelled and plunged and pulsated as his arms and legs went numb. The call went out as an emergency and the unit which had been in mid-session with a neighbor kid fighting the flu, dispatched immediately for the Sapin's house. Emergencies were a part of the med bot programming protocol and were to be used as a last resort. Putting out a false emergency call to a med bot was a guarantee for getting kicked off the service. The robot found Mark at the dining room table six minutes later gasping for breath. It immediately went to work gathering his vital signs. After whirling and calculating and summoning data from its vast and growing cloud of knowledge—originally from the pool of old country doctors—the diagnosis came back: "Acute anxiety." The robot stated in plain language, "You are not having a heart attack, Mr. Sapin, you are experiencing a panic attack." Angela was stunned when the med bot provided its analysis. "The three point eleven hours of sleep you have been averaging for the past twenty-two nights has finally caught up to you, Mr. Sapin. You are exhausted. And you must find a way to reduce the massive stress load you are burdening. The next time you may not be so lucky." The droid packed up its things and began leaving as it started to share the same corny joke about homemade cough syrup it always did. Angela slammed the front door before it could get to the punchline.

"Would you mind telling me just what the hell is going on?!" Angela shouted as Ben scurried up the stairs. Mark read her face and guessed she already knew. He suspected it would be only a matter of time before she found out. He could never keep anything from her, especially something this big, this important. But did it matter? That was a question he continued to ponder. Perhaps it was the domain of philosophers and poets and ethicists. If the same effect, the same result, had been achieved using different means, do the means employed then matter at all? Do the means have to be understood and embraced if they ultimately provide what mankind had been seeking all this time? Does it really matter? Any of it? Or, had Gramoo been right all along? Maybe it does simply come down to a matter of belief. A matter of faith. Maybe all of this is only in our heads. And, our heads, just like everything else, are nothing more than a never-ending string of zeros and ones. *Merrily, merrily, merrily, life is but a dream.*

"Look, I didn't want to say anything, but things have been super stressful at work." From his vantage point at the bannister, Ben could tell that his dad was lying. And he never lied, especially not to his mom. "I didn't want to you to worry, but there's been talk about replacing us with robots." He was getting deeper into the web now, and Ben was interested to see if he could find his way back out.

Whether or not she believed it, she bought it. Perhaps she made a transaction based in reality, at least in the way she perceived it. Pulling him close, she wrapped her arms around his neck and shoulders before leaning back and cupping either side of his face with both hands. She spoke with an urgency. "You're too important to this family, Mark. You've got to take better care of yourself. Ben and I need you here now with us. All of you."

36

The chirping brought Mark to the window. He had been sitting there, broken and defeated when he heard them, when he remembered their secret. Regardless of what he had just learned, he still believed. At least he wanted to. Maggie had told him that whenever he saw two birds together—a red one, a cardinal, and a blue one, a blue jay—it would be her signal that she was there, too.

Mark lifted his body, heavy with grief, and stepped through the darkness. Dawn was breaking outside, and at first, he could only see the movement. But he studied them and the light adjusted along with his eyes. They pecked and played and huddled. He counted seven, not two, and they were marbled with brown and white feathers. None of the birds were blue, none of them were red. He hung his head, still shrouded in a hoodie sweatshirt, looking down before looking up again, expecting to see the pair this time. He didn't.

Why didn't he said anything to Maggie? Why didn't he correct her? He started to tell her that the possibility of two birds, a red and a blue one, appearing together at once would be a very rare sight. A cardinal and a blue jay, an impossibility. Hadn't she heard the saying? *Birds of a feather flock together.* Surely it must have come up in a preschool nursery rhyme, or one of her chapter books, or something. It was considered a proverb because it stated a fundamental truth. Red and blue are opposites—they do not flock together.

As he watched the scene unfold under the early morning light on his front lawn, Mark again scolded himself. Why didn't he suggest something more common? Something that would allow him to believe. To have faith. He would have rather gone through the rest of his life believing that his daughter was present whenever he saw two squirrels or three cats, or whatever the case. He told himself that he was only trying to do the right thing, trying to be kind, trying to be respectful of what amounted to a dying child's last wishes. Each word meant so much. And he wanted them to come from her. They would not have carried the same weight had he steered her in some direction or another. He reminded himself it was that weightiness—meaning— which provided the foundation for belief, and for faith. He knew it intellectually, but he could not understand it emotionally. There had been one last chance to connect with his daughter. It, too, was gone. The birds on his front lawn haunted him.

There was only one thing left to do, and he understood the risk he would be taking. But, if he could not do anything to save his daughter, perhaps he could save another father from the pain he was feeling now. He understood his place in history because he understood the history; he knew it was cyclical. He had read the books in Gramoo's den. He knew how the story ended. That is why he saved the file as "Judas_Project.doc."

It was his intuition, a hunch that destroyed his faith, crushed his belief. The word "ecstasy" provided the torment. Why did she say that? She never said that. He doubted that she even knew what it meant. A quick search of the source code had revealed the answer. She had been programmed to say it, just like millions of others who had subjected themselves to simultaneous uploads. The investigators hired by the CHDAA had zeroed in on the abnormality, too. They found it odd and noted it in their report. But now here he was, looking at it in black and white. He had concrete, direct evidence that the consciousness question had not, in fact, been answered. Instead, it was fabricated by a programmer calling him or herself "Judas Iscariot."

The software was no more sophisticated than the programming that powered the millions of med bots now in service. They began as a collection of memories, brain scans of doctors who had administered medicine to children and calmed their parents. Those memories formed a foundation, a base from which to grow and learn. The same was true of the CHD software. It was only a collection of memories. But do memories on their own constitute life? Do they provide evidence of consciousness? To millions of families left behind, they certainly did. The immortalized loved one appeared to learn over time, so a strong case could be made that the person did, in fact, exist. It was gathering information, collecting memories, just like the med bots. So then, were med bots people? The politicians might argue that they were, maybe that is why they passed the Robot Bill of Rights. Mark could see clearly now that they were not.

Consciousness. That was the problem. It had been all along. What remained post-upload were not digitizations of souls and actual replications of human brains, but very sophisticated versions of interactive home movies. Memories stored in the cloud. They were no different than suped-up med bots. Or, perhaps, the next iteration of virtual brothels. A fixture of life in the upper quadrants, visitors to those establishments understood they were not being serviced by actual flesh, but by a collection of binary data—bits and bytes. No one quibbled because the desired result was obtained. *The ends justified the means.* Why not apply the same principle to CHD? Mark considered the question and concluded that people should ultimately have the power to choose their own fate based on reality. Not virtual ones fabricated by others with hidden agendas. He continued typing.

The person who called himself Judas Iscariot, and Mark suspected that it was a man, was attempting to hide something. Mark had already begun with a working theory because he had read up on the CHDAA investigation developments. Where they had stopped short of a conclusion, the dots were easy for him to connect. They were not about to point the finger at the most powerful man in the world, "the Messiah" no less, the man who gets a capital pronoun when referred to: only He is the Brother of Jesus. The fact is, Jason Harper could destroy anyone who got in his way, but only a small minority believed he would. Mark Sapin was now squarely in that camp.

Judas had been creative in his deception. He left a trail of digital bread-crumbs. The universal use of the word "ecstasy" had been one. But Mark's suspicions concerning what he referred to the as the "sales tactics" employed by recent uploads were also confirmed. Chairman Harper had been having difficulty convincing Quadrant 3 shantytown residents to sign up for CHD, so he likely commanded this person, Judas, to insert code telling everyone how great their experience had been. "I only wish I would have done it sooner" was a common endorsement, including with Maggie. But she had not been contem-plating doing it "sooner." Left and right, Judas dropped clues. He knew someone would eventually come looking. They were easy to spot, at least for someone who had an advanced level of understand-ing. Jason Harper did not. He was an idea guy, a big picture guy, a businessman, a rock star, a carnival barker. There was no denying his brilliance. He did something that no other person could. He saved the world. Then, he did what many others had attempted: Selective extinc-tion, genocide, a thinning of the herd. It was survival of the fittest, as decreed by one man, the Chosen One, the one who did the choosing. *Quadrant 3 must go out with the rest of the trash.*

Unlike the other tyrants and dictators and madmen who tried before, he did not pull the trigger or order it be done. They did it to them-selves, millions willfully and happily—and gratefully—marched with smiles on their faces to their own graves. Better yet, there was no grave involved. They vanished. In some cases, it required a small investment, never more than a hundred grand, which gave the government a fantastic return on their money. But most did it for no financial consid-eration at all. Only because they believed. And Jason Harper under-stood the power of belief as much as Adolph Hitler or Kim Jong-pak or anyone else. But he was able to actually achieve what they set out to do. He did what everyone knew had to be done. The only tragedy were the millions from the upper quadrant who got caught up in the mania. Thankfully, the economy had weathered the storm. And it did a lot to correct the intractable worker-management income imbalance, as it pushed up wages for the rank-and-file who enjoyed higher demand with their diminished supply. It all further enhanced the popularity of the Pragmatist Party and its leadership, most particularly Chairman Harper.

———

Roy never understood what Mark was talking about when he said things like "bits" and "bytes" and "source code," but he listened anyway. His friend was agitated and worked up, so he did his best to follow along, which he did when he finally arrived at the conclusion. "Roy, the bottom line is that this guy who everyone loves so much, Chairman Harper, has exterminated millions of people, including my daughter." Saying those words out loud, "exterminated" and "daughter," caused him to choke up, so he paused with a clench fist pressed against his pursed lips. His eyes closed tight to dam the tears. Mark whimpered, "He killed her, Roy. He killed her."

With those words, Roy was transported in an instant back to the triage tent in Korea. One of his own had just taken a bad hit. There was a casualty in his platoon. The unlikely aroma of gun smoke and green tea returned. He bolted straight at attention, just as he did when a commanding officer entered the room. He had not felt this way in years. He was alive. Young again. Significant. "How sure are you about that, Mark?" his voice both lowered and slowed, as he inquired.

"One hundred percent, Roy. Look, it's all right here." Mark handed him a rough draft of the document titled "Judas Project." Roy skimmed it, focusing on certain passages and diagrams as he flipped through the pages before reaching his own conclusion.

"You know, Mark," he began, seeming far away this time. "Momma always told me I was going to do something great. She always told me that I was going help lots of folks. Make a difference. And, you know what, Mark? I always believed her. I always believed Momma. And here I am now, eighty-three years old and I haven't done it yet."

"Roy, what are you talking about?" Mark interjected, confused about where this was going.

"Now, hold on, hear me out. Listen to your elders," he waved. "I've always believed that about myself. I used to think that my purpose was saving the world from bad guys, but then I came to realize that the only thing I was doing was following orders. And all those people on the other side? They were doing the same, Mark. And you know what? The only people it helped, the only people I ever helped, are the people giving those orders. The politicians. The government. They tried to control me, and they did. They lied to me, so they could take what they wanted. Take, take, take. And what did they ever give me in return? Nothing. The only orders we should have ever followed—you, me, and those five hundred people I killed—are the orders from the Big Guy upstairs," he said, pointing upward.

A long silence followed. Mark was determined to obey Roy's order allowing him to talk. To get it off his chest. The old man had a fire in him he had not detected before. An energy, a determination, a resolve. Roy then declared, "I'm going to liberate Jason Harper."

"What?!" Mark recoiled. That word "liberate" chilled him to his core. "You've got to be kidding, Roy. You're only kidding, right?"

Roy fixed his gaze from below the brim of his Korea II hat directly into Mark's eyes. It was clear that he was not kidding.

"I'm going to right a wrong. I'm going to snipe his ass and put an end to this nonsense. I'm going to sacrifice one to save millions."

"But Roy, this is crazy, you're..."

"That's enough!" Roy interrupted. "I told you I take orders from no man. That includes you. I love you like you my own son, Mark. But what he did to Maggie was wrong."

Mark tried attempted to douse the flames. "Roy, come on. Het's be honest here. I can hardly admit this to myself, but Maggie was not going to be around much longer. She was suffering and sick. Terminally ill. At least now we have her memory and can interact with her."

"You listen to me," Roy said, leaning in with his face just inches from Mark. "And I mean this with no disrespect because I don't know a damned thing about computers and bits and bytes and all that stuff you're always talking about. But I do know this: It's not real. None of it. You wouldn't know the difference, though. You've never taken a life, you've never pulled the trigger. You've never seen a soul rise up and leave this Earth. You don't know what I know, because you can't know. You've lived a cushy, sheltered life in that comfortable little cubicle of yours. And that's great. Good for you. You never got your hands dirty because you didn't have to; the government didn't make you."

"Roy, stop, please." Mark held his hands outstretched, palms out and upright. "I get it. I realize that I can't know those things, but I do know this: a quarter of the country has been wiped out, something like one hundred and three million." Mark paused to think carefully and rationally about how to continue, determined to settle the passions now overflowing in his friend. "Those lives are gone. There's nothing we can do to bring them back. There's nothing we can do to bring Maggie back. We can only focus on here and now, on Ben and Angela and you and me. On the future. We have to keep moving forward, Roy, we have to keep doing our best. They stopped the CHD program. It's over. Killing someone is not going to save any lives."

"Come on, Mark. You're a smart guy. You know as well as me that they're going to restart that program any day now. People are clamoring for it. They're whipped up into a frenzy over this thing like wild dogs fighting over a can of Alpo in the middle of the gas chamber. Chairman Harper is nothing more than a salesman. He can't resist supplying the demand, giving people what they want. I'm going to give them what they need. I'm going to save them from themselves. I'm finally going to make Momma proud. I'm going to do something great."

Mark would tell the interrogators that he did not believe Roy, it was only bluster and bravado. That was mostly true, but it was the look in his eyes which left some doubt. Only during the lie detector test did Mark reveal what he had actually been thinking that night: Roy was an old man losing his once firm grip on reality who was also physically incapable of doing what he had threatened to do. On both counts he had been wrong about his friend, Roy Baker.

37

The ribbon cutting ceremony had been advertised for months. It was three states over, but drivable in a day. Roy had grown weary of the commercials, just as he had with anything to do with the government. But now, as his ancient Army-issued footlocker creaked and groaned as it opened, he felt himself enveloped by the musty aroma—and by peace. His purpose had revealed itself, the path was clear through the milky cataracts. Looking back on the trajectory of his life, he realized that everything he had done was only another step to this point. The end was in sight. The last few steps had arrived. He understood his purpose.

His fatigues fit, just as they had before. Tinged with mold, they felt cool against his wrinkled skin. He ran his hand across his chest and felt his name badge. *BAKER.* The dog tags gleamed through their patina from the bottom of the box. Reaching down, he retrieved them by the chain, studying them in his hands with nostalgic admiration. One by one, the other items were rediscovered: the commando knife, the camouflage face paint, the canteen, the binoculars, the shovel, the tripod, the gloves. The only thing he would not be trusting were Liberator's bullets. They had long since exceeded their ten-year shelf life. There were plenty to do the job, but he was sure they had spoiled by now. It was too bad, he would tell himself, because he relished the poetry in using government-issued ammunition for the job. The box of fresh, live rounds was the most difficult item on the list to procure. He had to sign in three places before they would allow him to walk out with the .50 caliber rounds. He wondered if this would be the paper trail leading back to his old Sears Craftsmen.

Although he knew he would not eat them, he went ahead and bought some freeze-dried meals anyway. A good soldier always shows up prepared. It would only be three days, he reminded himself, and he would frequently fast for seventy-two hours at a time in Korea. Going without food meant not having to relieve himself, which is critical when posting-up in the sniper's nest. But going without food also calmed his nerves and heightened his senses. For Roy, fasting was a spiritual experience. He could hear God speak when he lied still for days at a time, preparing his soul to liberate another.

––––––

This mountain was composed of garbage, not granite. To the security team, he was just one of the few remaining Quadrant 3 shantytown non-factors scouring the slopes for something useful, something of value. A bottle of soap with half-a-squirt remaining. An aluminum can which could be recycled. Some copper wire, which was as good as gold. The only thing setting him apart was the size of his backpack. It was much larger than most. But it would only indicate that he was one of the more successful scavengers. The event was still almost four days away, and the priority for the White House advance team was mostly focused on having a good time while it worked through its checklist. The hillside had been secured. Roy moved in and out of the binocular view finder. Just another non-factor. It was also unusual to be wearing a green t-shirt with matching pants and black combat boots. He probably shoplifted them from an Army surplus store. It didn't matter. He was not causing any trouble—just one of the hundreds of parasites who spend their days sucking every last drop of the remaining blood. The mountain would be going away soon, launched into a low orbit along with all the other trash.

From the corner of his eye, Roy continued to monitor the security tent as he pretended to sift and scrutinize the scraps. When he was sure he was not being watched, he slipped behind a mound that jutted out, blocking him from sight. He then dropped his backpack to his feet and promptly emptied its contents, first slipping on the fatigues, then painting his face. Next, he sat down and began to assemble the rifle. The barrel reattached with a satisfying click. And the scope twisted into place in one motion. He crammed in a full magazine of ammunition and ripped the bolt back. A bullet entered the chamber. Double checking the safety, he confirmed it was in the locked position. Roy then retrieved his entrenching tool, a miniature shovel, really, a collapsible spade. They called it an "E-Tool" when he was in the service. Everything was repacked, except for the gun and the shovel, which he laid down with care before evacuated his bladder one last time.

It was one of the very first things he learned in bootcamp, the Army Crawl. With his rifle resting in the valleys of his elbows and the E-Tool clipped to his belt, Roy lay prone and wriggled his way to the spot he selected approximately fifty yards away. These few minutes would be the most dangerous part of his set-up. There could be someone rummaging through piles of trash higher up the mountain who would spot him. Even if they did, he reasoned, they would likely shrug it off. People did all sorts of odd things on the junk piles. The schizos yelled at themselves; the winos puked on themselves; and the vagrants pissed on themselves. This would be no different. A crazy old man who finally lost what remained of his sanity and started crawling around on the ground believing he was a cat or a snake or something. When he arrived at the backside of the mound, he peeked over the crest to confirm that this was the place. From here, he had a clear view of the front of the 2BIRDS. He knew from the television that this is where they always assembled the podium. They would place the lectern directly in front of this very spot.

Roy stopped. As he continued to lie flat, face first, he reached around to his belt and unclipped the spade. He would spend the next hour digging. Each time he cleared some more, he burrowed deeper. Dig, burrow, dig, burrow. From the backside, it appeared as if his legs became shorter until his boots finally entered the cavity and his entire body disappeared from site. He had perfected this technique long ago, and he was surprised by how much easier it had been to dig into trash compared to the hard, compacted topsoil covering Mount Paektu. The main difference with the mountain of garbage was that the den never held its form. Instead, everything collapsed around him. He became engulfed in refuse, a part of it. He noted the irony, which only intensified his resolve.

As he lay prone, hidden from view, he pushed the last few boxes and bottles away to form a tiny window. He slowly pushed his rifle through the opening. From the outside, the camouflaged barrel would blend in with its surroundings. Just another piece of steel rebar slathered in mold and slime and filth. He twisted the dials on the scope, and the scene came into view. The distance readout told him he was 5,284 feet away—six feet short of a mile. The .50 caliber would have no problem from this range, but it was going to be difficult to judge the wind. For the first time, Roy became concerned about his preparedness. Had he been away from the front lines for too long? Would he be rusty? Would he flat-out miss the target? He quickly chased those thoughts from his mind. This was not the time, he told himself, he must remain focused. He had a job to do. Orders to follow. Lives to save. A destiny to fulfill.

———

The sniper's nest was fully operational just before nightfall. Roy watched as the flood lights clicked on, fully illuminating the stage. He fell asleep as the team from the local events company hustled to place row after row of rented folding chairs in the VIP area. Roy began dreaming of Korea. He was a young man again. He was in control. Only this time, he was taking orders from the source. God told him to do it. His voice was clear and decisive. He had heard it before while half-asleep, deep into enemy territory with his gun locked and loaded. But he never listened. Instead, he followed the orders of his commanding officer. A man. Only a man. Not God. He would never make that mistake again. God was telling him what to do now. He was revealing to him the consequences of not doing this. Millions more will be killed. *They will march to their graves if you don't do something about it, Roy!* Taking one more life—separating one last soul—will save millions of others. It's a chance for redemption. Millions is so much more than five hundred, or in this case, five hundred and one. With one squeeze of the trigger, the ledger can be brought into balance, the debts paid. Wrongs made right. It's not too late. You can be good again. Forgiven. Just one more squeeze.

With nothing else to do, Roy visited with the Creator for the next three days. His voice had become rhythmic, an incoming tide lapping the wooden pylons of a fishing pier. *You can be good again, Roy, forgiven.* Through the scope, he could see the seats begin to fill with well-appointed dignitaries and their spouses. Circling the cordoned VIP section, for what appeared to be miles in all directions, the gates corralling the general admission standing room only section were gorged. A sea of purple. Roy became curious about the placards some of the people were carrying, so he placed the crosshairs on them in an attempt to read their messages. One woman finally stopped swinging her arm, so he could make out the words, "Immortality for All!" Another was written in oversized block lettering across three lines, "End the Moratorium!" A peace symbol was drawn inside the first "o." It occurred to him that the networks never showed the protestors on television.

Roy heard the helicopter before he saw it. The unmistakable "whoop, whoop, whoop" was followed by rumbling as it maneuvered above. He worried for a moment that the rotor wash may blow the trash off of him. The concern was short-lived as he watched the chopper trail away, making a loop over the crowd. The Apache gunship had been added to the ribbon cutting ceremonies in recent years as a deterrent to anyone with any big ideas, as well as a vantage point to spot hecklers and protestors. One by one, they would call down to security on the ground and the handmade signs would be confiscated and destroyed on the spot, as the trouble makers were led out making room for another, more well behaved purple-cladded reveler. The whirlybird continued to fly the same pattern, occasionally hovering in place for a few minutes, before continuing. Roy noted the flight path.

One after another, they appeared at the lectern in order of importance. Roy did not recognize any of them, but assumed they must have been the mayor, the senator, and the governor. He could not hear what they were saying. He was too far away. At this distance, it was just a series of noises. Then everything changed. It started slowly as the crowd realized what was happening. Jason Harper was striding across the podium waving to everyone. The thunder carried the energy of twenty football stadiums, all cheering the game-winning touchdown at the same time. That's what Roy had estimated the size of the crowd to be anyway, about twenty stadiums. Whatever the number, it was overwhelming. He wondered how many of them had seen a human head explode.

He paced and smiled and bowed before finally signaling it was time to stop clapping, which seemed to go on for an hour. Roy's watch said it had only been eleven minutes. He would have to wait until he found his place behind the microphone. He would be at his most static at that point. Roy knew all about stasis. He learned about it during Korea II. You had to anticipate when the target would slow down and stop—stasis. You never pulled the trigger when he was gathering wood or taking a drink. You did the moment he got off his feet for a break, or laid down the chopsticks. Jason Harper was about to become static. A sitting duck.

The crosshairs revealed a familiar wiry and fit thirties-something man of a medium build. Two shocks of gray covered the area from his temples to his ears. He beamed and gestured with enthusiasm. Roy could hear the crowd roar in proportion to the size of his movements. Now, if the target would just hold still. With his index finger, he clicked the safety to the unlocked position. *Red means dead.* The rifle was live. The crosshairs remained steady, while the head bobbed and wiggled. Roy again worried about the wind. It was the one thing that he hadn't been certain about. The purple American flags affixed to the towers holding the stadium flood lights appeared to be blowing down and to the right. They were of little help. From this distance, the bullet ought to have enough force to remain true. Maybe compensate just a bit, aiming ever so slightly up and to the left.

Again, the crowd roared its adoration. Jason Harper appeared to laugh. Then, he gripped either side of the lectern and drew a breath. Stasis. Roy exhaled at the same time he squeezed the trigger. Bam! From his scope, he could see the left shoulder disappear behind a crimson cloud. The sniper inhaled and exhaled once more before pulling the trigger again. Bam! His target turn and ran toward the 2BIRDS immediately behind him. His security team followed. Bam! He went down, clutching his right leg, which was now turned the wrong direction and dangling at the knee. The entrance door opened and closed and locked. The Chairmen disappeared to safety.

The cameras embedded inside the 2BIRDS would reveal what happened next. Jason Harper inspected his wounds in bewilderment. As soon as he realized the extent of his injuries, he began to flail and thrash. Outside, two members of his security team peered through the porthole while pounding on the door, screaming at him to unlock it. They could see he was in shock. He could not tolerate the sight of blood, especially his own. He stumbled over to the main control panel and fell onto the buttons. The next few frames would be the source of unending controversy. *Had he meant to do it? Or, was he blinded with pain and overcome with panic?* Depending on the camera and its vantage point, each provides a different answer. One shows him leaning over as he appears to punch in a specific sequence. Another depicts a wild, wounded animal terrified and grasping at the panel in a desperate attempt to hold himself upright as his leg dangled. The next frames capture the unbearable pain registering on his wincing face. He appears to be unaware, until the last moment, that his body has risen before accelerating upward and out of sight. Slowly then suddenly.

The gunship pivoted. Someone on board saw the flashes of light and smoke on the hillside. Roy scrambled to clear away the trash, expanding the opening so he could crawl out. The air was chilled and seasoned with gunpowder. He struggled to his feet. His eighty-three-year-old frame, which had been laying prone for three days, was not cooperating. As he lifted himself up, his knees buckled, and his back seized. He got himself on two feet and attempted to run, but all he could muster was a fast limp-walk. The Apache closed in from behind. Roy looked for cover and spotted a gulley just ahead. He would be safe there. He felt the reverberation of the engines as they sped closer. Bent at the waist, he leaned forward, digging hard, pushing himself, remembering boot camp. He had always imagined what it would feel like to be torn apart by hot led, but he was surprised by the stillness of it, the warmth—and the peace. He had done something big—something great—he had saved millions. It was his last thought before the tracer round split his head into three jagged, uneven parts.

38

The battering ram pulverized the Sapin's front door with a single swing. Mark had finally fallen asleep after tossing for hours. He shot up when he heard the noise followed by the shouting. By instinct, he ran toward Ben's room, but found him in the hallway. Father and son, both in boxer shorts, were blinded by the flashlights beaming into their eyes. Mark pulled the boy behind his body. A moment later, he found himself laying under a pile of grown men. The lights, the fists, the insults, the yelling combined into a single terrifying wide-awake nightmare. He screamed in protest as the handcuffs ratcheted down with angry intent on his wrists. His mind raced.

"Mark Sapin," the voice boomed from the darkness. "You are under arrest for treason against the United States of America."

A light switch flipped on and Ben was joined by his mother at the banister. They watched in horror as four of the twelve commandoes rushed their captive out through the unhinged front door and into the crispness of early dawn. The remaining eight ransacked the home, stuffing anything catching their interest into oversized black bags marked "Evidence" with a yellow sans serif embroidery. One called out, "I found his computer!" Angela screamed obscenities and pleading repeatedly, "Why are you doing this?!" She then began hurling paperback books at them which she grabbed from the shelf. A man scrambled up the stairs to restrain her, putting his hand over her mouth. Ben punched and kicked at him. The man wrapped him up, too. The three of them watched the frenzied search below. Ben was careful to not reveal his focus, but he never let it leave the corner of his vision. The wooden plank, his father's hiding spot, was going undetected by the goon squad. Ben found himself running out of air, so stomped his heel into the man's foot until he adjusted his grip allowing him to suck in a breath as if he had just swum the length of the pool underwater. With full sacks hoisted over their shoulders, the team hustled out. Angela remained defiant, immobilized with rage, violated. "Why are you doing this?!" she shouted once more as she chased them out. The last man to leave, the one who had been restraining her and her son, called back "Turn on your television, ma'am!" before disappearing.

The tires squealed as Ben escorted his mother into the living room. He felt her unsteadiness as his right arm gripped her waist. She fell into the couch as he reached for the remote. He powered on the television and saw his father looking back at him. It was the same photo that was on his ID badge from work. Then, a new photograph flashed on the screen. He immediately recognized it as a younger version of Uncle Roy. The words were impossible to comprehend: "assassination; treason; aiding and abetting." The view went next to a scene from a few hours earlier, the banner scrolling at the bottom identified it as a 2BIRDS ribbon cutting ceremony. It showed the crowd scramble and trample and panic as Chairman Harper grasped at what remained of his left shoulder. He ran toward the entrance of the 2BIRDS when his lower leg bent the wrong direction. Dragging it behind him, he shut the door as two of his armed guards pounded on the porthole glass. The camera then cut to an Apache helicopter lighting up the side of a garbage mountain with a massive burst of tracer rounds fired from both of its rotary machine guns. The commentator made a brief appearance before another photograph filled the screen. It was Dad.

He was gazing down the barrel of a rifle he appeared to be straining to lift. His eyes were crazy and wild, unlike any expression he had ever seen his father make before. Roy stood behind him, steadying the weapon. That's when the commentator made another dramatic announcement, "Ladies and gentlemen, I have some breaking news to share: Mark Sapin has been taken into custody. I repeat, Mark Sapin is now in custody."

———

The shroud was finally lifted, and the fluorescent light burned his eyes. His handcuffs were removed. Mark counted sixteen people in the room. He guessed it was no more than two hundred square feet. They all snarled at him. No one said a word until a woman made her way to the front of the table and placed a cup of coffee before Mark. "I know you like it with cream and two sugars," she said in an unexpected chipper and breezy tone.

"Thank you," Mark replied by reflex.

"Mr. Sapin, do you understand why you are here?"

Mark nearly leaped out of his skin to exclaim once again that he had absolutely no idea.

The woman then placed a laptop on the table and turned up the volume. The blood drained from Mark's face as he watched the broadcast. He was in complete shock. *He did it—Roy had actually done it.* Hanging his head, the room spun as he attempted to gather his thoughts before speaking. "I'm guessing you want to talk to me about my neighbor."

"No, Mr. Sapin," she reached into a folder to retrieve the black-and-white photo, which she placed on the table. "We want to talk about you."

Mark studied the image. He could not believe it was him. He remembered that night, but not that expression. It seemed so foreign. That face is not one he makes. He considered it may have been a deepfake, that he was being framed. "I didn't do it," he whispered.

"We know," she whispered back. "But helping a man pull the trigger makes you every bit as guilty as pulling the trigger yourself."

His mind went blank. Shock. The spinning room accelerated. He searched for a friendly face. They all sneered. Then he remembered. "I want a lawyer. I'm not talking anymore without a lawyer." As if he were a stand-up comic who just nailed the punch line, the room erupted in laughter.

"I'm sorry, Mr. Sapin. It sounds like you must not follow politics. The Prags canceled Miranda rights for high crimes against the government last year. You will be required to speak for yourself. And we're not going anywhere until you do."

Mark gulped hard, but his throat did not move. He thought to ask a question. "Where am I?"

The woman caught the glance of a man standing at the other side of the room and thought momentarily about whether to answer. She was the one who would be asking the questions, but it presented an opportunity to establish rapport. You catch more bees with honey. Also, he was not going anywhere. He had nothing to gain by knowing where he was being held. It would likely set him at ease, loosen him up. "You are in the interrogation room at your local police station. You were here four months ago to pay a parking ticket, Mr. Sapin. Law enforcement learned from the JFK assassination that you should never move the suspect. If they had kept the perp in place back in 1963, what's his name, Oswald, Lee Harvey Oswald, in local custody he would not have been shot himself. There are millions of people who want you dead now. Do you understand, Mr. Sapin?"

Mark leaned forward, dropped his head into his hands, closed his eyes, and began rocking. Digging into his scalp with his fingernails, he begged to wake up from this nightmare.

———

Angela straightened her living room in defiance. So much of its contents were gone, but she was determined to return to normalcy as soon as possible. The hole where her door had been was allowing the chilled air to overcome the normally warm space. Ben tacked up a blanket to cover it. She turned on the heater, started the fireplace, and grabbed a broom. The two said nothing as they worked. Books were returned to the shelves, the rug pulled straight, and lamps flipped upright. The horrors that lie ahead were unimaginable. All they could do was focus on the here and now, the task at hand. One of the neighborhood kids, a friend of Ben's, pulled the blanket back and poked his head through the opening. "Are you coming to school, Ben?" he called out before announcing, "You're late." The only thing Ben could manage to say was, "No, not today." The kid did not inquire any further, instead he walked on to class alone as he tried to piece together the ghost-white expressions at the Sapin's. He did not watch the news.

When he was sure it was safe, Ben scurried over to the wooden plank. His mother was in the shower and he was out of sight from the window and the door opening. His heart pounded in his ears as he raced to lift the black box. Just as quickly, he lowered the plank back into place and ran his empty hand over it to ensure it was flush, just as he watched his father do. He then scampered up to his bedroom and settled in at his desk. The box was locked, but it was flimsy. He was sure he could open it, but he needed tools. He stashed it under his bed and bounded down the stairs and out to the garage. The garage door was wide open, so he pressed the button to close it. Then he headed to his dad's red Sears Craftsman toolbox, reaching instinctively for the top shelf where he always hid a carton of Winterfresh gum. It was gone. He opened one drawer after another, first finding a hammer, then a pry bar, and a screwdriver. Before he began the pounding, he listened for the shower. It was still running. On the second swing, he split it open. The thumb drive glided into the USB port and its files appeared on the screen. Ben downloaded Judas_Project.doc first. Then, he renamed it BSapin_english39.doc, which was the same nomenclature he was required to use for his homework before changing the security settings to "Public—anyone can view," and uploading it to his school server. He did the same thing with the CHD source code, renaming that one BSapin_math46.cpp.

Confident that everything was now backed up in the cloud and hidden away from view, he leaned into his monitor and opened the file called Judas_Project.doc. His father began by introducing himself: "My name is Mark Sapin. I'm a data analyst. I'm not a programmer, but I can read source code. I'm married to Angela Sapin and we have two children, a twelve-year-old, Ben, and a seven-year-old, who is now deceased, Margaret Angela Sapin. We called her Maggie. We live in…"

Ben continued to read the document, skipping and scanning much of the background his father had provided. Until he landed on it: "The person who wrote the code referred to himself as Judas Iscariot." This was followed by a long explanation of who that person had been in history. "He identified Jesus Christ to his captors by referring to him as 'Rabbi,' which is how they knew who to arrest. Judas was known as a traitor and died a violent death. Whoever was writing the code was very careful to not reveal himself. Everyone knows that Jason Harper does not write code, nor can he read it. Judas was crying out for help, but he had to conceal his message. So, he used binary—zeros and ones—to communicate. And it was brilliant, because for someone who didn't know the difference, it just appeared as more numbers on the screen. But for somebody like me, or anyone that can read code, it was an obvious anomaly. I could see it immediately because it's nothing but dead code. In other words, it's code that is inactive and serves no purpose in running the software."

Ben then consulted the chart below and matched it up with the screen-shot image affixed above. It was filled with eight-digit sequences of zeros and ones. The first one, "01001000," was listed next to an "H." After it, "01000101," came before an "E." Then, it was "01001100," which translated to "L." Finally, there was "01010000," or "P." Together, they spelled the word "HELP."

Ben then skipped ahead to learn what his father had translated from the sea of binary. "HELP," the paragraph begins, "RABBI HARPER MUST BE STOPPED. HE IS LYING. HE HAS NOT SOLVED THE

CONCIOUSNESS QUESTION. THIS CHD SOFTWARE IS A DEEP-FAKE CONCIOUSNESS IMITATION. IT IS VIRTUAL REALITY ONLY AND NOTHING ELSE. HE IS KILLING MILLIONS. SEE ECSTACY PROTOCAL STARTING ON LINE 893129135541. HELP."

The document continued, as Mark wrote: "He referred to Jason Harper as 'Rabbi Harper,' of course, because he was trying to identify the guilty party without alerting the guilty party of what he was doing. He calls himself Judas because he understands the implications for what he is doing. He is blaming the man that so many refer to as 'the Messiah,' and who believe he is the reincarnation of Jesus or the brother of. The programmer knows that no one will believe that 'the Chosen One,' Chairman Harper, will have been solely responsible for the murder of millions. Including my daughter, Maggie Angela Sapin."

Under the section labeled "Ecstasy Protocol 893129135541" Ben read on.

"Do you ever wonder why all of the recently digitized say the same thing? 'I'm in ecstasy.' It's right here," the screenshot lists the code with its translation. "It was another attempt by Judas Iscariot to cause people to question the software. But Chairman Harper would not release the source code. And now you can see for yourself why." In all caps, Mark wrote, "IT DOES NOT WORK."

Over the next few more pages, more anomalies are documented. "And what about that other saying, 'I wish I would have done it sooner?' That can be found right here in this spot." The text is followed by another screenshot complete with arrows and additional diagrams of interpretation.

Ben was leveled by emotion. His sister was dead. Maggie was gone. They were left only with her memories, a hollow interactive digital replication. It was not her. Only an airbrushed approximation of her likeness, no different from the soulless ReadyMed robots which had continually streamed in and out of the house. And his father, his dad, was taken, too. As devastated as Ben was now, he was relieved to finally know the truth. He had always suspected as much. That word "ecstasy" had always bothered him, too. He did not know what it meant, but he was sure Maggie didn't either.

Two lives were lost, three including Uncle Roy, but it paled in comparison to the millions who would be saved. But none of this would matter—all of it, everything would be wasted—unless everyone could somehow learn the truth.

39

More than anything else, Mark looked forward to his trips to the bathroom. The windowless conference room was all he had known for nearly a week. At least he guessed it was a week, it could have been more, but not likely much less. The days and the nights all blended together. People came in and out of the room at all hours, never turning out the lights, or even so much as dimming them. When he would nod off, he was awakened with an abrupt shake, and usually some yelling. Mark had read enough spy novels and other who-done-it mysteries to understand. They were doing all that they could to extract a confession. There was sleep deprivation, food deprivation, sensory overload, disorientation, good cops and bad cops. The only thing Mark had any control over at all was deciding when he needed to use the restroom. He was cautious in his management of the privilege.

It was not the bathroom itself that mattered. It was the control, the self-determination. It was the only bit remaining. Aside from the few minutes he would get to himself in the stall—two guards on either side of the thin steel walls—it was the walk down the hallway he thought about most. The only fragment of hope was found through the twin plates of bulletproof glass looking out to the courtyard. Halfway between the men's room and the interrogation room was Mark's only connection to reality. He measured them again in his mind, imagining they each equaled two of his size eleven-and-a-half shoes placed end to end, about two-feet by two-feet square. They were heavily tinted, so the day always appeared as night, and vice versa. That was intentional, and he knew it. But they looked out to a single leafless tree. That tree—and its inhabitants—were his last chance.

The interrogators refused to answer his questions about Angela and Ben. And when he asked, they would double down on the cruelty and mind games. He learned to stop. But he did not, and would not, tell them about Maggie. About their agreement. The two birds. A red one and a blue one. A cardinal and a blue jay. The bathroom break was another chance to scan the tree through the window. Was she there? As his strength faded—it had been taken from him with intent—the guards had to provide assistance for his trip to the restroom which required twenty-seven steps from door to door. He counted and measured everything. It was the only thing left. That, and the tree.

On occasion, the guards would show some mercy, allowing him to watch the tree for a moment or two longer than it would have taken to drag him past. Through the window, Mark would first count the birds, then identify them. "Eight birds, eight birds. All of them black, black birds, eight black birds." He was careful to share this only with himself, but the guards overheard his mumbling and would report back to the senior officer that the captive was losing his mind, perhaps hallucinating, talking to himself about birds. His food rations increased, and a few catnaps were allowed. It was important to keep him alive and free from psychosis. Those orders came down from President Cribb himself, along with a reminder: "Do not move him. Remember what happened to Lee Harvey Oswald."

"I'm going to run through this one last time," the line of questioning began. Mark knew it would not be the last time. He had answered this for them at least a dozen times before, each of them was to be "one last time." The interrogators, Mark counted seven around the table, plus two more behind the cameras, took turns speaking. Another one of them—he had long since stopped looking up to make eye contact, instead he kept a steady gaze on the backside of his interlocked fingers

—started in again. "Tell us about your last communication with Roy Baker."

"One day, he was no longer there. He never mentioned anything about it." Mark told them that he stopped by on his walk home from the train station, just as he always did. There were two beer bottles on the bannister enclosing his front porch. One of those bottles was empty. This time, Mark revealed that it made sense to him now, in hindsight. Roy had always referred to empty bottles of beer as "dead soldiers." He believed that Roy had a premonition. He knew he was going to die. Under the bottles, there was a handwritten note. It said only, "Gone fishing." That was their last communication. Mark said again that he did not drink the other beer. When pressed by the interrogators, he answered the same as before: "I don't know, I just don't really like beer. I only drank it because Roy thought I did."

––––––

The minivan loaded with PTA moms stopped by the Sapin house just after dinner, as it always did in the days following Mark's arrest. Angela was grateful for the support, although she suspected a few of them—the purple flag wavers—were only there to keep an eye on her, to ensure she did not flee the country. Whatever the case, standing on the steps of the police department headquarters downtown for a few hours each evening holding a candle seemed to help. She felt like she was doing something. It wasn't much, but it was something. As she walked out the front door, she called up to her son, Ben, "I love you, Benny. Be good. I'll be home soon, okay?" Angela then hoisted her purse over her shoulder without noticing it was a few ounces lighter. Her keys were missing. Ben strained to listen over the printer laboring on his desk for confirmation of her departure.

With a hole punch, Ben was meticulous as he transferred the contents of the printer tray to the three-ring binder. Tiny discs of discarded paper covered his floor. He wondered what his mom would say. He then scooped up his slingshot, the carton of BBs, and scampered down the stairs with the binder cradled to his chest. Darkness was approaching much faster than he had expected. He would have to get to work right away. The stolen key slipped into the ignition, and Ben waited impatiently as the motor in the driver's chair inched forward. Remembering the garage door calamity, he drew a deep breath to steady his nerves before reaching over to switch the family car from "autopilot" to "manual control" before sliding the shifter to "R."

If Angela had turned around, she would have seen her twelve-year-old son driving past, craning his neck to see over the wheel. Ben wished there had been more than just a few dozen people showing up to support his dad, but he did not dwell on the thought. He reminded himself to stay focused. He had work to do. The downtown streets were mostly empty as they almost always were this time of the evening, especially on a weekday. Most people were at home planted in front of the television with a full belly. Ben was strategic and intentional, this would be his ultimate "diabolical plan," and it required two things: empty streets and a tuned-in local audience. He now had both.

He stopped the car, lowered the window, and extended the slingshot just as he had at Ridgecrest. *Plink! Plink! Plink!* The camera bot, which had been in sleep mode on the sidewalk, turned and began rolling forward toward the vehicle. Ben tromped on the gas pedal, squealing the tires as he sped away. The robot continued to follow. On the next block, Ben did the same thing. *Plink! Plink!* Another camera bot powered up and began pursuing the family car. Again and again, he fired, and they followed. He guessed he had twenty camera bots now trailing him in an unwieldy pack, one by one, their tiny red dots went on indicating they were now streaming to a live audience. Ben continued the sequence: gun the engine, squeal the tires, then tromp on the brakes and skid to a halt. Allowing the camera bots to catch up before leaving them behind again in the review mirror, the only thing visible in the darkness was a swarm of red dots appearing to lurch forward and back. But never stopping. They continued in pursuit.

Everywhere around the city, regular programming was interrupted. "This is KCZX-TV News providing you with exclusive, live footage. Our camera bot is bringing this remarkable scene to you as it unfolds from downtown where a vehicle continues to speed, reaching up to eighty miles per hour, before stopping violently. We advise everyone to say away from downtown at this time. And be sure to say tuned to KCZX-TV News as we keep you updated on this development."

The chief of police saw the scene unfold on the television screen in his office. A sergeant holding a recently poured cup of coffee poked his head through the door to mention the phone calls coming from downtown. "Do you want us to check it out, boss?" He rubbed his temples for a moment and sighed before answering. "No, I need everyone here." The police department, just like all the others, was a only a shadow of what it once was. After most of Quadrant 3 had been digitized, nearly all the criminal activity disappeared along with it and so, too, did the cops. Supply and demand. Many of the chief's officers opted for the Prag's retraining program. Headquarters was a ghost town now, and he had long since lost his patience for the federal goons down the hall who continued to harass one of his neighbors.

Mark should have been considered innocent until proven guilty, not the other way around. The chief lived in a Craftsman, too. Just like the Sapins. He never knew them, never met them, nor Roy for that matter. He suspected that Mark probably had something to do with the assassination. He saw the black-and-white photo just like everyone else. But he did not agree with the new laws. Miranda Rights had been established for a reason. As much as he hated criminals and crime, he could not stand to see someone wrongly convicted. It happened too often, especially to people like him. People with dark skin. His brother had spent twelve years in prison before he was uploaded. The chief resented the feds who had taken over his police department. This was his town, and these were his people. Mark Sapin was probably guilty, but he was also his neighbor. That used to mean something.

––––––

Ben thought back to the day his dad dragged out his old video game system. It was an Atari 2600 given to Mark by his grandfather. He was so excited to show it to his kids. Angela rolled her eyes as he untangled the wires before plugging in the cartridge. There was no respawning or going on forever in those games. No endless life. When you died it flashed the words "Game Over." That was it, the end. There were no cheat codes to speed you forward or take you back. No returning to the same spot time and again to master whatever it was that killed you in the first place. You actually died. And you were dead. Gone. From the building rooftops above, he imagined that he now resembled his dad's favorite game, Pac-Man. He was weaving through the streets with the ghosts—Blinky, Pinky, Inky, and Clyde—on his tail in hot pursuit. Only in this case, Pac-Man was teasing them. Stopping to let the ghosts catch up before speeding away again.

The family car again skidded to a halt on Center Street in the exact spot Ben had planned. It was empty and lined with glowing lamp posts. They provided plenty of light. Everyone would be able to see. He tugged the seat belt tight as he gripped the wheel with his sweat-soaked palms. The frenetic collection of red-dotted robots grew closer in the review mirror. Ben waited until they caught up before stomping on the gas pedal. The citywide viewing audience leaned in. This was it. The car sped toward the "T" intersection. A dead end. It was going much too fast to make the turn. The KCZX-TV News anchor chimed in, "It looks like this may be a suicide, folks." Ben's head whiplashed into the seat as the car raced forward. Just before it went headlong into the cinderblock wall, he put all of his weight on the brake pedal, slamming it to the floor and yanking the steering wheel hard to the left. The vehicle slammed into the wall broadside, flipped, and rolled twice onto the sidewalk before coming to a rest on the passenger side. The camera bots raced each other on their way to the wreckage as they remained focused on the smoldering vehicle. The audience watched as the wreckage continued to rock back and forth before it finally settled. Pushing and elbowing, one by one, the robots muscled their way for shots of the driver who lay crumpled face down in the twisted metal. On the screen, viewers could see his rib cage under his bloodied t-shirt expand and contract. *He's alive!* They all leaned in.

Ben turned himself over, careful to avoid the shattered glass. He then looked up through the driver's side window, which now doubled as a sunroof, to see a dozen red dots staring back at him. The viewers at home gasped in delight. *It's a kid!*

The twelve-year-old boy pushed himself up, wiped his sweat and blood matted to a shock of hair away from his eyebrows as the gaggle of camera bots backed away to form a semicircle around the smashed-up car. Ben climbed out of the window standing with the underside of his car as the backdrop. The spotlights embedded in the robots were blinding. He paused for a moment to gain his composure before starting to speak. "My name is Ben Sapin. My dad is Mark Sapin." The viewing audience was stunned. "My dad has been wrongly accused in the assassination," he stumbled over that word "assassination" before trying again. "The assassination of Chairman Harper. He didn't do it. He had nothing to do with it. My Uncle Roy did it." He then paused before reconsider if he should go ahead and say it before he actually did. "And I'm glad he did because Chairman Harper killed my baby sister. Her name was Maggie. Margaret Angela Sapin. My dad called her Peanut. She was just seven years old and the best little sister a guy like me could ever ask for. She was digitized—uploaded to the 2BIRDS. She was killed. Chairman Harper killed her, just like he killed those one hundred and three million other people, too. He's the bad guy. Not my dad. Not my Uncle Roy. Jason lied to us. There is no CHD. There is no immortality. He tricked us, all of us."

Ben then waved the three-ring binder in front of the camera bots. "It's all right here," he said as he turned to the first page. "This is called the Judas Project. My dad wrote it. Mark Sapin. He wrote this. You can find the document by going to my shared folder at the Harper Elementary 813 online portal. It's a Word file called 'BSapin_english39.doc.' If you want to see the CHD source code for yourself, then download 'BSapin_math46.cpp.' I'm going to read out loud what my dad wrote right now: 'My name is Mark Sapin. I'm a data analyst. I'm not a programmer, but I can read source code. I'm married to Angela Sapin and we have two children, a twelve-year-old, Ben, and a seven-year-old, who is now deceased, Margaret Angela Sapin. We called her Maggie. We live in...'"

The chief of police remained glued to the broadcast, just like everyone else around town. He had heard enough, and it only confirmed his suspicions. After thirty-eight years in law enforcement, you develop a sense for when someone was lying. And also, for when they are not. He had sat behind the mirror during many of the Mark Sapin interrogation sessions and he never once spotted a liar. And he sure as hell had never seen a child, Ben, do something like that for his father. He had heard from others that Roy Baker was a good man. An eccentric, for sure, but a good man. The Korea II veterans who had served with him on Mount Paektu had spoken to the network correspondents on his behalf. The chief also learned from his auntie that they were distant relatives, he and Roy. If they had been friends, which they should have been because they were neighbors separated by only a few miles, they would have probably called one another "cousin."

The pieces were not fitting together as they had been presented. His mind, and a few others, had been changed by a twelve-year-old boy.

40

Mark was near defeat. He knew that much. So did the woman who had been leading the interrogation, the good cop. But that approach was no longer working. She was about to turn bad. It was after his latest trip to the restroom which had become more frequent, and more difficult for the guards who complained that they had to tear him from the windows. Mark sat down and rocked back and forth as he muttered the same nonsense the team first noted two days earlier. "Six birds, six birds, six birds—one blue, one blue, one blue!" He became excited then crestfallen before continuing. "Two black, one brown, one speckled, one yellow and brown. Six birds, one blue, twenty-seven steps."

The woman leaned in with both hands on the table. Just inches away from his face, she ordered Mark to look into her eyes. In an instant her demeanor shifted, her voice lowered. "Listen, Mr. Sapin, we've screwed around here long enough." The change in her tone snapped Mark out of his trance. He lifted his oily, stubbled face to meet her gaze. "We both know you did it. Either you finally take responsibility for your actions, or I'm going to have those damned windows covered." Complete exhaustion had arrived long ago. This was defeat. There was no fight left. Nothing in the tank. He could not remember the last time he slept. The questions never ended. The always on lights burned his eyes. The around the clock noise was maddening. It could all be over if he lied. If he told them he had done it. By now, he was not sure that he hadn't. He was not sure of anything, whether it was day or night. How long he had been there. What happened to his wife and his son. He stopped drinking the once-a-day protein shakes, or whatever they were, two days ago, around the same time he started talking to himself. If he just admitted it, then this nightmare would be over. They would surely send him to the electric chair, or maybe they would make an example of him at a public hanging. Whatever it was, at least the pain would finally cease. He would join Maggie again wherever she was. If she was. And Roy, too.

Mark was forming the sentence in his mind, preparing himself to say "Yes, I did it" when he was struck with a wave of renewed energy. His spine stiffened. He clenched his jaw and his fists as he snarled at the woman in defiance before drawing a breath from below his empty belly and declaring with conviction once again, "I had nothing to do with it." The woman sprang to her feet, wheeled around and called out to the hallway, making sure Mark could see her when she said it. "Cover up the windows!" His newfound strength drained in an instant as his head dropped into his arms crisscrossed and folded on the table. Against his will he heaved and sobbed as he called out, "No!" Sweat and tears arrived at every pore. His hair was matted. His beard misshapen. His eyes bugged out and red with tiny throbbing veins tangled up in every direction. He was descending into madness, his fingers loosening and slipping from the reality he once gripped with strength and confidence. He had been logical and thoughtful and rational. He did not realize, until now, that those things could be taken. They could be stolen. No different from a car or an expensive watch. It was theft. The woman, the interrogator, was stealing. And nothing could be done to stop her.

———

Millions of mourners arrived in Colorado Springs to pay their last respects to Chairman Harper. The networks replayed the assassination on a continuous loop, and it was taking a toll on the nation's collective psyche. The police chief only half-listened to the funeral broadcast. He was distracted by the crowd gathering outside. Until now, it had been only a small collection of candle-wielding, slow-moving middle-aged women. This group was animated and agitated. He could not tell for sure, but they seemed to be angry and yelling something in his direction. Some arrived in small groups, others alone. A few hoisted signs and waved flags. Objects flew. Hollering could be heard. Not the words, but the energy. He walked to the front door.

As he scanned the mob from left to right, he watched it grow in both size and intensity, a hurricane gathering kinetic energy over the ocean. If it made landfall, it would do serious damage. He heard the chant start up again. *Free Mark Sapin! Free Mark Sapin! Free Mark Sapin!* That's when he stood atop the edge of the brick flower bed, the highest point above the steps in front of his building, and began waving his arms to get them to quiet down. "Listen up, everybody. I know you are tired of this. It's been a lot of strain on our city. I'm tired of it, too." Those words only further incited. "Hold on now! Hold on!" the chief again appealed for calm and quiet before deciding on the fly to change his approach. "Now, you've heard from me. But I'd like to hear from you." Everyone yelled out at once, many of them gesturing with fists, some of them with baseball bats and sticks. Many in the crowd had prepared for tear gas with homemade masks. Resisting his instincts, which told him to head back inside, he instead stood his ground. These were his people. He knew them, and they him. "I'm going to need for you to talk one at a time. This is going to be just like when we were back in school, okay? Please raise your hand and I will call on you." An elderly woman in the front row lifted her hand, which was attached to the elbow holding her purse. "Yes, ma'am, you first. Would you like some help up?"

The chief spotted two men, armed guards, from the interrogation team who had exited the front door and stood behind him. He turned and gave them a long, disapproving look up and down.

"My name is Gloria and I live in the shantytown, what's left of it, anyway. That man, Chairman Harper," the woman began, her voice stronger than her age. "He did the work of the devil." The crowd roared its approval. "He took away my son and his family. My grand-children, everything. He murdered them all. He tricked us!" The electricity intensified. She waited for it to cool. "I watched little Ben—God bless his soul—as he raced around downtown. We all watched. Which is why we all know the only person who has told us the truth is Mark Sapin. He should be set free." The crowd called out its approval.

One by one, the chief of police assisted them as they climbed up and down from the brick flower bed, so they could offer their testimony about how their families had been destroyed by the CHD program.

"I've lived in the shantytown all my life. I know a lot of y'all. I'm Jackie...

"They call me Big John, I'm also from the shantytown..."

"Hi, my name is Casey, and I'm a proud SOB from Quadrant 3!" the man said as he flashed the three-fingered salute on both hands before pumping them in the air. The crowd had been whipped into a frenzy—angry and frothing, wounded and cornered. It was ready to pounce. And the chief knew it. He could smell it. That's when he stepped back up to the top of the flower bed.

"Look, everybody. We all want to keep this peaceful. I know you're angry. And, to be honest with you, so am I." The two federal officers guarding the door exchanged quizzical reactions to his statement. "I'm ready for all of this to end and for our city to return to normal. None of us asked for this. This isn't our problem. I know a lot of you have a bone to pick, and I don't blame you. But I am begging you to work with me here, to handle this peacefully."

Angela arrived at the front steps of the police department headquarters minutes before Ben. She had been picked up by her friend with the minivan. Ben saw the growing crowd on his phone and rode his bike. They came upon a scene which was equal parts inspiring and terrifying. People were rallying for Dad. They all understood now that their loved ones were gone, murdered. They were unable to bring them back, but they were angry and wanted to do something. They wanted to right a wrong. They wanted to take action. The only action they could now take was to free Mark Sapin.

Through the glass doors, the police chief could see the entire collection of federal goons, all of them gawking back at him. He returned to address them. The woman in charge, the good cop turned bad, stepped up front. She began by chastising him, something about "control your people." That's when he finally lost his patience with her. He had earned his stripes, dammit, and he was not about to let some paper pusher the Prag's sent to his city tell him what to do. "Let me tell you something," he growled back, leaning forward and jabbing his fore-finger into the purple flag pinned to her lapel. "I'm the only thing standing between you and that mob out there. They are ready to tear you apart limb from limb. I know my people, because they are my people. They just found out that your boss murdered their families. They're not about to listen to a bunch of purple flag wavers."

The woman bristled, and with the same icy ruthlessness Mark had just experienced when she took away his windows, her eyes narrowed and her lips pursed before she barked, "Stand down, Chief! This is my jurisdiction. I'm in charge now." She then waved the armed guards out into the crowd. "Secure the perimeter! One man spaced every forty meters!" The feds waded out into the writhing and boiling human ocean which cussed and taunted them as they passed. Camera bots, all the same ones from the night before, videoed the frenzy. Their red lights on. The local broadcast showed the undulating crowd which prompted more to join. Soon there was a flood of people engulfing not just the front steps, but completely encircling the police department headquarters—a toxic stew made up of bloodthirsty vigilantes and curious onlookers. The chief again exited the front door to see the crowd pouring in from the street in all directions. He turned to glare his contempt at the woman before trotting back to his office. With a click, his microphone powered on and his voice reverberated throughout the building. After following the usual protocol, including announcing his identity—everyone immediately recognized his distinct baritone—he began his final instructions. "I order everyone to stand down. Stand down. Remove all of your firearms and weapons and stow them away in your lockers, now. Meet me at the front door in three minutes for your evacuation orders. There will be no firing on anyone. That's an order. And it applies to everyone."

The police chief addressed his staff, which had assembled at the entryway as requested. He told them to stay put until he said otherwise. "My priority here is to keep you safe, to make sure you go home to your families tonight," he explained. "This crowd here is ready to rip us to shreds. I can talk to them. They will listen to me. I need for you to do the same. I need for you to listen to me." The police department employees nodded their heads in agreement. He noted their fear. The crowd was becoming emboldened. Rocks were flying.

Again, the police chief climbed to the top of the flower bed. This time his voice was not heard. The animus had magnified. The roar was deafening. He immediately stepped back down and reentered the doors. "Everybody follow me! Do as I do!" he shouted above the deafening crowd. "Hold your hands up high above your head! Make sure they see that you don't have any weapons!" One by one, he placed his hand on their backs, ushering them out to the top of the steps. For the first time, they understood their precariousness. "Go! Go! Go!" he shouted, until the woman, the good cop turned bad, cut to the front of the line. "No," he stated, flat and firm, with his outstretched hand. "Not you. You've got jurisdiction. You stay here." Her face dropped in disbelief before pivoting and retreating down the hallway.

A disorientation had struck Ben as if he had been bobbing at sea with a shifting horizon. Animated bodies were bumping into him. He was bouncing. He gripped a handful of the back of his mother's sweater just as she instructed him to do. She pushed her way through, inching toward the minivan. In all directions, people wailed in distress. Their loved ones were dead. Killed. The mob circled the armed guards, pacing and snarling and stalking, directing every ounce of their rage and hatred toward them. The guards swiveled their heads as they repeatedly commanded, "Step back!" They communicated further by waving their assault weapons. That's when someone was pushed—or they pounced—and a single gunshot reverberated through the plaza. It was immediately followed by screams and then the unmistakable burst of machine gun fire. The aggregated rage climaxed as a frenzied bedlam. A lifetime of resentment fueled the punishing blows. The armed guards did not stand a chance. They were swallowed whole by the wild pack. The lucky ones were killed instantly by their own weapons which had been turned against them with astonishing ease. Then, all at once, the crowd took the form of a surging tidal wave crashing against the building, pushing its way through the front door and spilling over into the hallway.

Inside the interrogation room, Mark had been in and out of conscious-ness when he heard the shots. Then he saw the door burst open and a swarm of people enter. They were shouting and cheering. Two men, each wearing backward-turned baseball caps, gripped Mark under his atrophied arms. Their faces were hidden away from the tear gas that never came. One wore a bandana tied off in a triangle. The other donned a painter's mask, a tattered and frayed respirator. They said nothing as they hoisted him in unison, draping his half-asleep fore-arms over their shoulders. Mark's legs were useless. He was weak and had difficulty holding his head in place. He struggled to comprehend why the crowd filling the hallway erupted in cheers as they dragged him through. People everywhere smiled and strained to touch him. They cried in delirium calling out "Thank you!" before the chant was again coordinated. *Free Mark Sapin! Free Mark Sapin! Free Mark Sapin!*

They arrived at the front door, and Mark was startled by the natural light. It was blinding and stark. The workers had abandoned the 2BIRDS when they caught wind of the gathering crowd. They were all here now. There was no trash floating overhead. No shade. Only the blistering sun. Although he did not walk, Mark could feel himself descending the stairs. Floating. Draped from behind the two men carrying him out of the building, he could only see the backs of their heads. On his left, he recognized the front side of the reversed hat. It was dull and faded and grease-stained, more of a light pink than the proud crimson it had once been. The logo centered on the crown was a familiar mascot—fierce and determined—the head, a profile, of a cardinal.

Mark's coherence began to return. He then glanced to his right, as both men tightened their grip on his wrists in tandem and continued speeding through the fracas. The cap belonging to the other man was of a cheap, plastic mesh variety, a "trucker hat." Above its ancient and tattered royal blue brim was framed another team mascot—a blue jay.

Mark watched as the two backward-facing hats continued to bounce side by side in front of him. Sun rays beamed down from above. They were embraced by the warm and cleansing light. Mark's face spasmed and contorted before he surrendered to a full-body exorcism of regret and pain and guilt. Uncontrolled sobbing and heaving took hold. The light amplified.

The crowd parted, outlining an undulating path to the minivan. A woman waving her arms beckoned them forward. The two men, without a sound, laid Mark on his back in the middle of the floorboard between the seats. Angela and Ben jumped in behind. The door was immediately closed shut. Mark stained to lift his head. He wanted to see his rescuers. Against the ocean of bodies moving past, he spotted one of them. A ray of sunlight illuminated his silhouette. He was radiant and still, watching, seeing—beholding—from outside the glass. His face remained shielded by the bandana, but Mark could see the eyes. *Windows to the soul.* They were innocent and inquisitive and loving and brave.

She was there.

AUTHOR'S NOTE

Writing is a process of discovery. It's a journey. Many describe it as a solitary act. Not me. I always feel the presence of the reader—you—as I put one foot in front of the other. Thank you for walking along with me. As the book you just read was my first attempt at fiction, I would like to take a minute to introduce myself and to talk a bit about the story behind the story.

I live in a place Oprah Winfrey once deemed "America's Happiest City," San Luis Obispo, California. There, together with my wife, Sheryl, we publish a local magazine. If you live in a town of any size, then you surely have a magazine there, too, so you probably have an idea of what I am talking about. We set out to make ours different when we launched that first issue coming out of the wake of the Great Recession. It was a restart for us. Our previous business went down in a blaze of glory and we were two—maybe three—days away from moving into my father-in-law's mother-in-law unit in his backyard along with our three very young kids. To know me, and my story, you first have to understand this: *SLO LIFE Magazine* saved my bacon, all of our bacons, for lack of a better way to put it.

We hustled. Sheryl taught herself Adobe InDesign and was able to assemble a prototype, which is a three-ring binder showing our vision for the publication. I then hit the streets. Pounded the pavement where I heard one "No" after another. Once in a while, a prospective advertiser would nibble, "Let's see how you do in your first year—come back next year." Of course, this presented an obvious chicken and egg problem: There can't be a second year unless there's a first. Someone has to advertise in this thing and advertise now, or my family of five is going to be moving in with Grandpa Marvin.

I drove all around California's Central Coast listening to Tony Robbins yell at me about how great and powerful I was, except I did not feel great nor powerful. Until that is, someone finally said, "Yes." It was difficult to hold back the tears in that moment, but I did, at least until I made it back to my truck. It's been said that there is no better time to make a second sale than immediately following the first—in addition to the Tony Robbins CD's, I was also listening to what Zig Ziglar had to say. He was a sales guru, and he talked about momentum, and how it is possible to get on a roll, a win streak. He said something like "prospects want to buy from winners," or something along those lines.

Zig was right. I got hot, *en fuego,* as I like to say, and people started writing checks. Enough checks to pay for that first print run. We even managed to squeeze a tiny profit out of the gate, but we did it mostly by not spending any of the money because we needed it for diapers and to turn the water back on (I'm not kidding). Still, I promised the advertisers that the magazine would be delivered to "every single home in town." It was the one part of the business that I really had not thought through very well. When I did the math on mailing the magazine to everyone, I could see that it would put us deep in the red. But, just like Mark Sapin said in the book, "There is always a way." Since we live in a college town, I suspected that Cal Poly may hold the answer. So, after recruiting a dozen or of its students, we canvassed the entire city, dropping the new magazine off on everyone's doorstep. It took a week, and I wore out a pair of running shoes in the process, but we did it. And it cost a fraction of what it would to send it through the mail, which is how we do it now.

One by one, the people of San Luis Obispo tripped over the new start-up magazine sitting on their doormat. On the cover was a close-up of an equally close friend, my only friend, Lief McKay. We were new to town, which makes the idea of starting the local magazine all the more absurd. Lief was the first person, the only person I had met up to that point. We bumped into one another during the early part of the new school year as we stood outside of the kindergarten classroom waiting for our kids to be released. For those unfamiliar with the scene, and I mean this with no disrespect, but "kindergarten pickup" is dominated by moms who treat it, at least it was true at Bishop's Peak Elementary, as if it were Happy Hour. And to them, it was often their only shot at talking with someone their age. So, they would huddle together in excitement for their daily social ritual, while us dads were left to fend for ourselves. That's when I met Lief, the only other dad around that day.

After introducing himself with a "G'day, mate," and a handshake that caused me to wince in pain, I was intrigued by his accent. The question I asked changed my life forever: "Tell me, where are you from?"

When it came time to write the articles for our first issue of *SLO LIFE Magazine*, I immediately thought of Lief. Yes, he was, and is, a fascinating fellow, but again, he was the only one I knew who would actually do it. And by "it," I mean volunteer to be on the cover of that inaugural issue. Remember, all I had at the time was a binder, a prototype. There was a lot of trust involved in allowing for the plastering of one's face on a wholly unknown publication. And strategically, I knew his trust in me would be amplified after a beer or two. So, I suggested that we meet at Laguna Grill. In a quiet booth away from the bar, I clicked on my voice recorder and started asking some lame questions about the rugby team. At the time, he was the captain of the SLO Rugby Club and I told him I envisioned a cover article recounting the history of the team. As we sat there and nursed our IPA's, I could see that he was almost as bored as I was. Then, I had a hunch.

I said, "Lief, I know you have already told me the story, but I want to get it on tape for background. If you wouldn't mind, can you tell me again as if you and I were meeting for the first time, Where are you from?" At some point, the voice recorder seemed to disappear as I became lost in the tale he told. There was an against-all-odds love story, an incident involving the accidental merging of his moped onto to our local freeway, Highway 101, growing up in rural Australia, his gone-too-soon father, who was a potter, and his artist wife, and their two young children. By most accounts, Lief is an ordinary guy. But, and this is a big "but," he's an extraordinary character. It was a revelation.

The cover story was not about the SLO Rugby Club, because outside of a handful of people, no one cared about the SLO Rugby Club. What people care about are other people. People care about Lief. The magazine was successful because I got out of the way and let the characters tell their own story in their own voice. From the very beginning, all of our cover features are presented as first-person question and answers. And they all begin in the same way: It's me sitting down, powering up the voice recorder, and asking that same question: "Where are you from?" Then, I just shut up and let them talk. The more I can keep my mouth closed, the better the interview. I would like to think I have some unique skill in this area, or maybe it's just a trustworthy face, or something like that, but the truth, as I have learned, is that people want to be heard. It's one of our most innate desires as human beings. That's why those interviews would sometimes go for as long as three hours, as I learned their entire life story.

My challenge, and it was significant, was to listen to the tape afterward and glean the nuggets, the diamonds, which I would use to write the article. Since I was hell-bent on preserving their voice, it was a mission of addition by subtraction. Most of what they said would be cut. The magic would be found in choosing what to keep. Over the years, I developed an ear for the "hooks," in other words, what I knew our readers would most want to know. What made for a good story. And what didn't. As I sat there and listened, I could begin to see the printed page, the final product, in my mind. I did not realize it at the time, but I was learning to write fiction.

Adults like to ask kids, "So, what do you want to be when you grow up?" I had experimented with all the usuals: firefighter, astronaut, quarterback, archaeologist, but there was one that I mostly kept to myself: novelist. It just never sounded that cool, or tough—not like "football player," anyway. But, to this day, I have always had a strong recurring vision. I first remembered it when I was with my mom and my sisters during one of our many visits to the library. The vision goes something like this: It's me, sitting at my desk on the second floor of an old farmhouse, clanking away on my latest novel, occasionally looking up from my keyboard to take in a sweeping view of a rolling, tree-pocked landscape. I did not realize it until recently, but that is exactly the experience I had while writing this book. The vision had become a reality. But allow me back up for a moment.

My wife and I have always talked about planting deep roots on some acreage. We talked about having a "family compound," a place where our kids and, eventually, their kids, and their kids' kids, could call home. It always felt like a long way off and probably an impracticality, especially here on the Central Coast of California. In some ways, she and I developed the same psychology found in the older generations, the people who lived through the Great Depression. They would save every nickel and dime and button and safety pin in preparation for the next crash. Well, sure enough, the next crash did arrive, and it was called the Great Recession. Warren Buffett, the legendary investor, has famously said something like, "You can tell who has been skinny dipping when the tide goes out." Well, the tide went out, and we were caught buck naked. It was beyond painful. When you are on a first-name basis with the repo man—yes, his name really was "Bubba," it said so on his shirt patch—you learn very quickly that you never, ever want to go back to that place again. Ever. The only way to prevent it is to stockpile some cash.

I had heard someone say, "If you save just twenty-seven dollars a day, after a year you'll have $10,000." I found out how many business days there were in a year which was 261. So, when I divided $10,000 by 261, it came out to thirty-eight dollars and some change. Without fail, on my way home from work, I would stop at the ATM to withdraw forty bucks. Then, I would go to our bedroom closet and remove the floor-board at the back and retrieve the fireproof black box. Incidentally, this ritual inspired the hiding spot for Mark Sapin's thumb drive in the book. The whole thing felt adventurous, clandestine, which is why I kept after it. Sure enough, by the end of that first year, we had $10,000 tucked away beneath the floor. And best of all, it was hidden away from Bubba. The next year, the business did a little better, and I upped the withdrawal amount to $60 per day, then $80. It forced us to budget the groceries money closely and Sheryl was gracious and forgiving when our debit card would not process for her as she stood with a full cart and three hungry kids at the check-out stand. But we both agree now that the little bit of indignity, which felt so acute at the time, worked out for the best in the long run.

We continued to rent the little house on Catalina Drive for ten years. Each day, no matter how busy, I stopped by that ATM just up the street. It did not take long for the black box to overflow with Andrew Jacksons. Then, I had to get a bigger safe and bolt it to the floor, which really upped the intrigue. My kids would huddle with me as I spun the clicking dial, right-left-right. Before long, they got into the act, asking me to also deposit their allowance. At some point, we had accumulated quite a haul, and I realized how crazy it was to keep that much cash on hand (for the record, I no longer keep any cash—we move it around electronically like normal people). While it had been giving us a tremendous peace of mind at one point, it was now conjuring all sorts of wild thoughts, many of which could serve as plots for perfectly serviceable spy novellas. We thought about taking it to the bank, but wondered how we would safely transport that many twenty-dollar bills, now totaling somewhere in the low six figures. And even if we could, would they be obligated to file some type of report with the FBI? Would we have to worry about our own government coming after us in addition to the Russian spies who were already hiding in our backyard? I'm telling you, paranoia.

One day, my wife and I had to kill some time between picking up and dropping off kids, so we went for a drive. The previous day, someone we knew, who was in the market to buy a home, gushed about a "magical property" in a place called See Canyon. The only problem, they said, was that it was just raw land. They told us they would have bought it if it had a house on it, any house. We were also finally dipping our once-bitten-twice-shy toes back into the real estate market, and had been contemplating making an offer on our rental house, which we had grown to love.

We had been to the canyon once or twice before. It's famous for its quaint apple orchards, which swell with U-pick tourists and nostalgic locals each fall. So, we drove out there to have a look around. After slipping though under a canopy of oaks, we found the gravel road with a "Land for Sale" sign. We crossed the bridge and then stepped out as the heavens opened up and we could hear angels sing. Well, it was not quite like that, but we immediately understood the repeated use of the adjective, "magical."

That pile of cash sure came in handy. And so did YouTube. I spent the next two-and-a-half years working two jobs: magazine publisher and construction worker. I hired a mason—all cash—and he and I built the concrete foundation. I then taught myself to read the plans, and I framed the house myself. Grandpa Marvin was there to lend a hand. He damned near lost one of his legs in the process. I hired out some of the specialty trades, but only after negotiating hard. "How much would you charge me to do XYX? Now, what if I were to pay in cash? And I mean cash-cash. Cash on the barrelhead cash. No receipt necessary." At the end of each day, my hands throbbed, and I was dead tired counting out musty blood-, sweat-, and tear-stained twenty-dollar bills for everyone on the job site. Best of all, I was also able to do quite a lot of barter. "Say, how about you do our architectural renderings, or our bathroom tile, or our pantry shelves, and instead of me paying you, I'll give you free advertising space in *SLO LIFE Magazine*?" It worked like a charm, and I will always be grateful to those who agreed to such onerous terms, even though we'll probably be running their ads for this lifetime and the next. I believe that many of those contractors were not taken by the deal I had offered, but, instead, they were caught up in my story: a hammer-wielding writer who watched far too many how-to videos on the Internet. They saw me in the same way I saw Lief —a character.

It took a village. I would frame the walls on the ground, for example, then invite family and friends to do a barn raising. It was all marketing. I learned that if you called it "barn raising," instead of "free labor" you could get a lot more help. It just sounds so much more romantic to say it that way. By the way, this experience was inspired Mark Sapin's fascination with how his old Craftsman-style home was originally built. His conversation with Roy Baker felt personal to me, and I got a little choked up when Roy set out a beer for him the next day after Mark helped him install the screen door. There were so many instances during my homebuilding experience when the same thing happened to me. It was "neighbors helping neighbors," as Mark relayed. And it is true that "many hands make light work," just as Gramoo and Roy both claimed. In case you were wondering, my grandmother, whom we call Ammu, which rhymes with Gramoo, serves as the real-life inspiration for that character. She's ninety-eight now and just as full of life and curiosity as ever. She loves it when my sister, Katie, sneaks her out of the "old folks home" and brings her over to her house on Sweet Court to binge watch whatever is trending on Netflix. I've heard the dramas based on British royalty are her favorite. For those shows, my sister makes both of them tea and they snack on finger foods, just like the monarchs. Before Ammu moved out of her house on the ranch which was surrounded by gnarled, ancient walnut trees, and into the retirement community, she gave me all of her books that I once curled up to read in her den. They sit on the bookshelf next to my desk and keep me company now as I write. I spent many hours in Ammu and Grandpa's den, just like Ben did with his grandparents.

For much of the two-and-a-half years I was moonlighting in construction, I would need an extra set of hands. Often, I found myself more college students, or a friend who wanted to show their kid "what hard work was all about." The dad would usually tap out before the kid, but I appreciated the company just the same. Occasionally, I solved my labor shortage by logging on to Craigslist. The talent was varied to say the least. Beggars can't be choosers. I was offering rock-bottom wages. But again, it was cash. One day, I received a lengthy email to one of my job postings from a guy named Craig. It struck me as funny that someone named Craig was contacting me from Craiglist, but he seemed to have the right qualifications. And his long and grammatically correct reply stood in start contrast to the other curt and punctuation-less responses. He wrote about how he had worked at his family's business—Dollhouse Construction, his last name was Doll—since he was a kid. I was sold. So, Craig from Craigslist showed up and the first thing I asked him to help me with was sheeting the roof. Now, if you do not know anything about construction, let me tell you that this is a dangerous part of the process. You're crawling around on the roof rafters, again, my office is two-stories tall, and lugging around four-by-eight sheets of plywood. If the wind catches just right, those things will double as a sail. You can go flying forty or fifty feet without a problem.

I climbed on top of the roof and asked Craig from Craigslist to hand up the plywood, one piece at a time. Straining and grunting, I set them in a holder I had framed-up earlier, but it did not feel very secure. Sure enough, it snapped, and a half-dozen of those sheets became airborne. I called down, "Duck!" and everything went silent under a billowing cloud of dust. My heart stopped with the realization that I may be culpable for an innocent man's death. Then, I inched toward the edge to get a view of the ground. Below me, I saw Craig from Craiglist curled up in the fetal position, eyes clenched shut, cradling his head with both arms. I was relieved to not see any blood. "Hey, man, are you all right?" I inquired. He told me he was, but he groaned for good measure before dusting himself off and asking if we could switch positions. This time, he would be on the roof while I handed up the lumber. It was a great idea because I'm not crazy about heights. Craig from Craiglist turned out to be the perfect sidekick because he also knew Bubba and loved getting paid in twenties. He was always my go-to, and still is, when I need an extra pair of hands. Another character added to the collection.

Still, most of the time, I was working solo. I loved the quiet, the solitude. The fresh air. Since I am so often sitting at my desk, it was a welcome change to use my hands to do something other than type, or nudge a mouse around. But it also allowed my mind to wander. I spent quite a lot of that time conceptualizing article ideas for the magazine. A year or two prior, news surfaced that the iconic Morro Bay smokestacks were going to be taken offline. According to the reporting, everyone was up-in-arms in the 1950s when they constructed the three

450-foot towers next to Morro Rock, now everyone was equally upset about the idea of removing. This NIMBY phenomenon, as you probably guessed, informed my writing in the book about the mountains of garbage—no one wanted to see them come, then everyone eventually accepted them, before finally embracing them. The same was true here on the Central Coast. It was clear that most of the people around now had grown up with them as a backdrop, and they wanted them to stay. But the question remained: What do you do with them?

I began brainstorming ideas. What about a rotating restaurant like the one they used to have at the Space Needle in Seattle? Someone mentioned converting it to a climbing gym. I thought that was a decent idea. Then, for some odd reason, I imaged it growing in height from 450 feet to 62 miles, tall enough to poke into outer space. That was when I first conceptualized 2BIRDS. Since space is a vacuum, it's conceivable that it could become something akin to a giant cosmic straw. The creative floodgates opened and, as I continued sawing and hammering, I came up with many unusual scenarios. What could you do with such a thing?

My wife, Sheryl, and I have a standing Friday morning meeting. It would be more accurate to call it "a walking meeting," because that's what we do, we walk and talk. Since we are partners in every sense of the word, it gives us a chance to check in with one another, as well as to solve any problems going on with the business or lingering issues with our family. "I can't figure out how to get Donovan to do his homework," or "Who are we going to put on the cover?" are common themes. Those walking-talking meetings are incredibly productive, even when they are not. Sheryl is the family spark plug, and she tends to run a little hot. Over the years, I have learned how to release some of her steam when she begins simmering to a boil. Sometimes she lets me have it. I can always tell when she's mad because she starts stomping ahead, leaving divots in her wake. We have also had some knock-down, drag-outs, yelling at each other on the trail. It's all positive, though, because any and all hard feelings or bad vibes are vented, released into the ether, never to be seen again. I always think of it in the same way many of us think about earthquakes here in California:

lots of little shakes are great because they relieve the built-up tension brewing at the fault lines and reduce the odds of The Big One. Mostly we walk the Bob Jones Trail, which connects San Luis Obispo to Avila Beach. But on this particular day, we were on the Johnson Ranch Loop Trail. It was near the end of our walk when she floated a question she had never asked me before: "Have you ever thought about writing fiction?"

Without hesitation, I told her the idea I had for 2BIRDS. I was animated and excited. When I finally took a breath, she turned to me and said, "You need to drop everything you are doing and go write that book." I was two-thirds of the way through another non-fiction book, a sequel to *Great Hunger*, which was essentially a career guide inspired by my sixteen-year-old daughter, who is a junior in high school and starting to ask the question, "What am I going to do with my life?" The fascinating part of that book, *Great Hunger*, as I can see now in retrospect, was that I wrote it as much for myself as I did for her. I can understand that my first instinct, to become a novelist, was spot-on. It was what I am made to do. In case you were wondering, *Great Hunger* has nothing to do with the Irish potato famine. Instead, it's based on the world's last known hunter-gatherers, the Kalahari Bushmen, who talk about finding meaning in their work. To para-phrase: "little hunger" is the food for the belly and the roof overhead—the basic necessities—while "great hunger" is the search for something larger than oneself, which you can find only by serving some higher purpose. That thing is found in a state of flow where you lose all sense of time and space. That happened to me when I wrote 2BRIDS.

It may also be useful to share with you that I studied Political Science at UC Santa Cruz, home of the fightin' Banana Slugs. There, I dove deep into the classical writings on politics and the economy. I was particularly intrigued by the English scholar Thomas Malthus. Among other things, he wrote an essay in 1798 called *The Principle of Population*. In a nutshell, he was quite gloom and doom, arguing that the population was growing exponentially, while the food supply was only increasing in a straight line. Essentially, his argument was that humankind would soon run out of food because there were too many mouths to feed. Obviously, most of the world made it through the next couple of centuries with plenty to eat, but that paper left a lasting impression on me. I think about it to this day when I am stuck in traffic, or gobbled up by a crowd at a concert or at the fair. In theory, at least, Malthus had a point. It was simple math, which is why Alex Cribb repeatedly used that line in the book: "It's simple math."

Additionally, I have been perplexed by the hyper-partisanship that has gripped America in recent decades. It always puzzles me just how worked up people get over their hard-baked ideologies and how quick they are to dehumanize anyone who does not agree with their particular point of view. For years, I have thought to myself that there had to be a better way than the two-party system because, in my humble opinion, too many people are simply joining a tribe where they are being played by their leaders, not to mention the many media outlets which have sprouted up to cash in on the exploitation of those impassioned differences. "Wedge politics" drive me crazy. That's how I came up with the Pragmatist Party and their slogan, "Follow the truth wherever it leads." It seemed like a good idea, but it also leaves plenty of room for mischief, particularly when you start asking the obvious question: What is the truth? Then, it gets really interesting when you throw in an all-powerful leader. Enter: Jason Harper.

My thinking on Jason evolved significantly while I was writing. Originally, I had him pegged as a fairly typical, and somewhat one-dimensional psychopath, but as I sat down to tell his story, I found myself being much more nuanced in his treatment. I actually like Jason quite a lot and found myself mourning his death. I'm interested in knowing your thoughts, as well. You can email me at hello@TomFranciskovich.com. In so many ways, I found myself rooting for him. Just like so many of his contemporaries, I wanted him to succeed. I wanted him to get the CLIMA prize money. I wanted him to do good. And, in his mind, I believe that he did believe he was doing good. Lots of good. And, truth be told, I debated with myself quite a lot concerning the Acid Theory in Chapter 4. If you remember, Jason's childhood friend, Ryan Mendoza, was interviewed about how he witnessed Jason consuming a massive dose of LSD at the Hilliard

House, which is what many had attributed his creativity to, but he also has a spiritual awakening of sorts. He is reunited with the souls of his deceased grandparents and comes away from the experience having directly experienced an afterlife. That belief, more than anything else, made what Jason did with CHD understandable. He believed that people who did it were going to be in a better place, certainly much better than the shantytowns. It was a matter of belief —a matter of faith.

An exploration of faith, as you know, turned out to be the predominant theme of 2BIRDS. That surprised me because I did not set out to write a book about faith. It just came out as I was feeding my own great hunger. I did not outline this book before writing it. I just sat down and the preceding pages flowed through my fingertips. Toward the end, as I was looking to wrap it up and bring it in for a landing, I scribbled on some three-by-five cards, but that was the extent of my planning. In the world of writing, and you may already be familiar with these terms, there are "plotters" and "pantsers." The plotters are the ones who write the extensive outlines complete with the Roman numerals and letters, while the pantsers, just as the name implies, fly by the seat of their pants. For the most part, I am a pantser. Every once in a while, I will poke my head up to make some notes to ensure I am not straying too far off course. Pantsing has always served me well, however, because it allows me to visit places I had no idea existed, such as with the very complicated Mr. Harper.

The same is true with Mark Sapin. He ended up being a lot more inter-esting, at least to me, than I first envisioned him. And I have to be honest, his character did not come easily. I admitted this to Sheryl one day, while I was deep into writing the manuscript. She thought it may be because I had too much in common with Mark. Writing the scene where he his talking to Maggie as she laid in bed toward the end of her life was agonizing. I just wanted the torture to end. As a dad to a daughter myself, it all felt too close to home. Dads and daughters have a unique bond and the protection instinct is strong. It was emotionally challenging to get my head in that space, to wear his shoes. Because I didn't want to. But without that scene, the rest of the story doesn't work. There would have been no emotional connection. It had to be done.

One other thing that surprised me as I was writing was just how many references to other books I ended up making. As I mentioned, libraries and books have always played a major role in my life, as I am sure they have with you, which is why you are with me now reading these words. As you know, it's difficult to explain to non-readers just how powerful the written word can be and how long they can reverberate. It really is true that a good book can change your life. At least that is what my mom used to say to me. There was a line in the book, *The Pursuit of Happyness* (sip), where the main character talked about the library being a "dangerous place" because of all the things you could learn. (Curiously, that line was conspicuously absent in the movie starring Will Smith and his son.) That always stuck with me—"dangerous place." I'm also continually drilling this idea into my kids. It's the same basic marketing principle at work when we talked earlier about "barn raising" versus "free labor." For most, it's no contest: "dangerous place" is much more intriguing than "library." The mind automatically conjures an image for the library. For too many people it's some combination of boring, old, and quiet. Now, calling it a "dangerous place," on the other hand, unlocks the imagination allowing it to gallop free and wild. I also like to say, at least to my kids, that "readers are leaders." I always credit my mom for teaching me the fundamentals of marketing. When were kids, hungry and asking for a snack, she made us "surprise plates," while other moms made their kids "apple slices with peanut butter and a slice of cheese." Do you see the difference? They were the same thing, but surprise plates won every time.

There were some other things that happened during my long walk. First, I had intended for 2BIRDS to be a one-off standalone novel. But after I finished writing, I realized that it deserved a sequel which I am working on now. (It's on track and scheduled to publish this summer, 2020.) Also, I did not expect Mark and Angela's son, Ben, to emerge as a central character like he did. But I bonded with him, and I hope the same happened for you. He's a special kid, and you'll be hearing more from him soon. And I don't know about you, but this story felt very cinematic to me. I will admit that I would love to see it on the big screen, so I'm going to take a shot at adapting it into a screenplay. Why not? I just finished writing my first novel, so why not write my first screenplay, too? If you would like to receive updates on my progress on the sequel and the screenplay, as well as all things 2BIRDS, it would be an honor to continue walking together, forging a new path. Please be sure to subscribe to my website, which can be found at TomFranciskovich.com and drop me a line to say, "Hello."

With gratitude,

Tom Franciskovich

hello@TomFranciskovich.com

p.s. Novelists these days are successful, or they are not, based on the quality and quantity of their online reviews. If you enjoyed reading 2BIRDS as much as I did writing it, then I humbly invite you to share your recommendation with rest of the world by leaving an honest review wherever you purchased your copy. And please don't forget to tell your social media friends, too!